WILDSIDE

**The Best in Today's Fiction . . .
for Today's Readers**

WILDSIDE

STEVEN GOULD

TOR

A TOM DOHERTY ASSOCIATES BOOK
NEW YORK

This is a work of fiction. All the characters and events portrayed in this book are either products of the author's imagination or are used fictitiously.

WILDSIDE

Copyright © 1996 by Steven Gould

A Tor Book
Published by Tom Doherty Associates, LLC
175 Fifth Avenue
New York, NY 10010

www.tor.com

Tor® is a registered trademark of Tom Doherty Associates, LLC.

ISBN: 0-765-34246-4

First Tor Teen edition: November 2003

Printed in the United States of America

0 9 8 7 6 5 4 3 2 1

For Rory

John Jackson and Rusty Allen for flying info. Martha Wells, Rory Harper, Geary Rachel, Tom Knowles, and Laura J. Mixon for helpful abuse and critique. Beth Meacham for saintly patience and finishing touches. And, again, Bob Stahl for asking that first question.

Prologue

Masha,

   Sorry, I'm dead.

   Less than two kilometers from gate. Compound fracture left tibia and fibula. Like extra knee. Damn old brittle bones. Bleeding stopped but smell attracting company.

   Tried to straighten break—passed out. Woken by wild dog sniffing leg. Ran when I shouted. Don't want to pass out again.

   Have .45 and extra clip. Killed one dog. Others on it before it finished dying.

   Will save last bullet.

Built tiny fire with deadwood and grass in reach. Out of water. Will put note in canteen. Should protect.

   Great pain. Pitiful fire but makes me feel better.

Dogs left when sabertooth came—back after I killed it. Small smilodon, immature, I guess. Canines less than four inches. Seen bigger stalking bison. Dogs like it. Dogs may get to like me if I keep killing things.

Time to put note in canteen.

   Dogs left again.

   Dire wolves.

Part 1

Preparations

One

"They're Extinct."

Clara drove a motorcycle. Rick's junker was down for the count and his mom wouldn't let him use her car. Marie, despite her pilot's license, didn't drive, and Joey, the idiot, had his license suspended for DWI. So I drove. I didn't even want to go, but there you have it, Charlie to the rescue, one more time.

That week Dad was flying the DFW-DC-Boston route, so Mom said I could take the big Lincoln Town Car. I dressed like a chauffeur, in a black suit and billed hat.

Rick was sitting on the porch steps when I pulled up. He was wearing a tux, a plastic florist's box in his big hands. I jumped out of the car and held the rear door open. He laughed, but stopped almost immediately with a nervous look over his shoulder.

"Come off it," he said. "I'll ride in front."

"Nope."

He shrugged. "Okay. Let's get out of here, before my mom starts up again." He folded himself into the backseat. The Town Car was huge, but Rick, though thin, was over six feet four. With him in it, the seat looked only adequate instead of luxurious.

When we were moving I asked, "You want to talk about it?"

He met my eyes for a moment in the rearview mirror, then looked away. "No," he said. "I don't."

I dropped him at Clara's, so he could do the P.P.P.O., the pre-prom-parental-ordeal, and drove on.

I had to go up to the house to get Joey. His father let me in. "Nice outfit, Charlie."

"Thank you, Mr. Maloney. Where's Joey?"

Someone said, "Ow!" from the back of the house. Mr. Maloney pointed over his shoulder with his thumb. "They're in the kitchen, but be warned, it's not a pretty sight."

Tiny Mrs. Maloney, standing on a step stool, was pinning a white rose boutonniere on Joey's tux jacket while Joey's older sister, Lisa, was putting on the silver-and-ebony cuff links. "Why didn't you do this before you put on the jacket, you idiot?"

Joey wiggled. "Well, excuuuuuuuuse me. I don't wear a tux every day, you know." He saw me. "Ah, thank God. Help me Charlie Ben Kenobi, you're my only hope."

"Hold still!" said his mother.

Mr. Maloney went to the refrigerator. "You want a beer, Charlie?" Mrs. Maloney started to say something, but clamped her mouth shut.

"No thanks, Mr. Maloney. I'm driving."

Mr. Maloney blinked. "Ah, good point." He looked at Joey. "Very good point."

Joey blushed.

Mr. Maloney took a beer for himself, then, with the refrigerator still open, said, "Coke? Sugared, I'm afraid. Er, we don't have any diet Coke."

It was my turn to blush. "No thanks, Mr. Maloney. Gives me zits." Not to mention adding to my already hefty waistline.

Joey's torturers released him and we fled. Good-natured injunctions about "having a good time" floated after us. In the car, Joey said, "Sorry about Dad. He means well."

"It's okay."

Marie lived only two blocks from Joey. "I'll wait," I said. He nodded, swallowing nervously. Marie's father knew about Joey's DWI incident. I got out and leaned against the car, visible from the house, proof to Marie's father that Joey wasn't driving.

They didn't stay inside long, but Marie's father escorted them to the car and shook my hand. "Hello, Charles." He always called me Charles. He and Marie left Vietnam in '75 and his English, though quite good, never lost the accent.

"Hello, Mr. Nguyen. How are you?"

"I am fine, Charles. I've let Joseph know that if you weren't driving, he would not be taking Marie to the prom. I depend on you to bring her home safely." He paused. "To bring all of them home safely."

"Daddy!" Marie exhaled sharply. She looked gorgeous. She was wearing something low-cut and tight in white, with a black silk shawl. In flat shoes she was my height, exactly, but tonight she was taller. "Show some tact."

Joey stared at the ground.

I held the back door open and winked at Marie. "Certainly, Mr. Nguyen. You can count on me."

On the way to Clara's, Joey ragged me, his voice pitched in a nasal whine, "Certainly, Mr. Nguyen. You can count on me."

"Shut up, Joey," Marie said. "It's not Charlie's fault, now is it?"

I looked into Marie's eyes in the rearview mirror. She looked back, worried.

" 's okay," I said.

Joey shrugged and looked out the window for a moment, then said, "Sorry, Charlie. And thanks for driving us."

Marie kissed him and I felt knives in my gut. "You're welcome."

At Clara's house we had to go in for pictures. I held my hat to my chest and wore sunglasses and my black leather flying gloves.

Clara, tall and blonde, was wearing a strapless black gown with ruffles, and her mother kept tugging it up even though it really didn't seem to be slipping. "Mom, enough all ready!" She usually wore unisex clothes—men's shirts, jeans.

"Leave her be, Margaret," said Mr. Prentice. "How can I take the picture if you're in the way?"

We stood still and faced the lightning in groups and pairs. Then

I took a shot of the two couples with Mr. and Mrs. Prentice.

In the car Clara said, "What took you so long, Charlie? I thought I'd die!"

I was surprised and pleased when Joey said, "My fault. Trouble with the tux." He didn't mention Mr. Nguyen.

Next stop was the Texan, perhaps the best restaurant in town. I dropped them and went home to wait for their call. They'd offered to treat me, collectively, as payment, but I'd said I'd take payment another way.

I also didn't want to see Joey and Marie together any more than I could help it.

I'd eaten earlier though I wouldn't have minded something more. Mom and I were on a diet together and it seemed my stomach never stopped rumbling.

I spent the time reviewing the FAA Instrument Flight Rules. Mom was watching another nature documentary on TV, so I read in my room, as far from the refrigerator as possible. The phone call came after an hour and forty minutes.

"We just asked for the check," Marie said.

"What did you have?"

"Lobster. Heart-of-palm salad. Raspberry mousse for dessert."

"Aaaaaggghh. Okay, okay. I'll be there in ten minutes."

"You should've been here, Charlie. It wasn't as fun without you."

"Um. See you in a few."

In the living room, Mom was looking at the screen with the perpetually surprised and intent expression with which she watched all things. "I'm going now—I'll be back late, so don't wait up."

She put down her notepad on a stack of wildlife journals and walked across to me. "Drive carefully. Mrs. Paige tells me that prom night is a time of increased consumption of alcoholic beverages by underage drivers." She reached out and adjusted my tie. "Don't let one of them crash into you."

"Okay, Mom." I kissed her on the cheek. "Don't fry your brains on too much TV."

She laughed, then sobered. "After this, it's a *Nova* on extinctions."

"Oh, goody."

I picked the guys up two at a time, so I could walk around, open the door, and hand them out in front of the Hilton, where the prom was. Marie protested, but I said, "Let's do it right." Most of the kids had driven themselves and were walking in from the parking lot, so both couples had a decent audience when I did the act.

Joey made a big show of tipping me with a twenty, but I'd promised ahead of time to give it back later. Marie squeezed my hand as I helped her out. Nobody seemed to recognize me, which was good, I guess.

This time I parked the car and waited in the lobby. The tuxedos and gowns drifted by, like some musical. There was a chair in the corner, screened by a potted palm. I settled there, my FAA regs for company, but I didn't read. Instead I watched them flow by, like I watched them in the hallways at school. In-groups and out-groups, nervous singles, girls in stag groups, and popular jocks with beautiful girls. Most of them tried to act older, to fit the clothes. Some of them tried being pompous. A few of them were even natural, acting no differently than they did in jeans.

But, as usual, I watched from outside.

The music drifted from the ballroom, a slow number. I thought of Joey's arms around Marie and I got up, went into the hotel restaurant, and had a second supper.

Someone shared their flask of whiskey with Joey during the prom and he was a little loud, a little clumsy. He wasn't obnoxious, though—he just smiled a lot. Marie, Rick, and I consulted and decided coffee was in order. Besides, none of them wanted to go home yet. What was the point in being home before midnight?

I had my own agenda.

"Come on," I said. "We'll get coffee from Jack-In-the-Box and go out to my place."

"Your place?" said Clara. "What about your mom?"

I shook my head. "Not my parents'. My place."

Only Marie knew what I was talking about. We'd done touch-and-go practice landings on the grass strip there, but we'd never stopped. "He means the ranch—the ranch his uncle left him."

"Where is it?" asked Rick.

"West," I said. "Over by the Brazos. Twenty minutes."

Joey spoke. "We could go dancing instead. Over to Parrot's."

All four of them were in the back. Clara, plastered to Rick's side, said, "My feet hurt enough. I'm not used to heels. What's out there?"

I tried to control my breathing, to keep my voice calm, to make it seem as if I didn't care. "A house. A barn. A hangar. An airstrip. A lot of trees."

"Anybody live there?"

"Me," I said. "After graduation."

"Whoa. Really? Your parents are okay about that?"

"Pretty much. My dad would like to hangar his plane there, that's why we put in the hangar. Better than Easterwood, cause it would save the hangar fees, but he's not willing unless somebody lives out there. Too much chance of vandalism."

"So, like he'll pay you instead? Since it's your land?"

"Ha. He'll continue to let me fly the plane. That's payment enough."

We reached Crack-In-the-Jack and I ordered four coffees and one hot tea to go. "Try not to spill it, guys. Or I'll hear about it."

I paused at the end of the driveway. "So, my place?"

"Sounds boring," said Joey.

Rick shrugged. Clara whispered something in Rick's ear, and he crossed his legs, then said, "Let's do it."

Marie looked from me to Joey. "Sure. I've wanted to see what the place looks like from the ground."

Joey looked stubborn and I said, "Come on, Joey. I've got a surprise for you out there. I've got a surprise for all of you."

He relented. "Oh? Sure, why not. If there's a surprise."

"Let's just say it'll be worth your while."

* * *

Joey threw up halfway there, but gave us enough warning that Marie got the electric window open. He got it all outside, thank God.

"I don't feel so good," he said.

Marie was frosty. "Imagine my surprise."

I handed him my tea, untasted. "Here—rinse your mouth out with this."

There was a combination padlock on the gate. I closed it behind us—there weren't any cattle on the place, but I didn't want anybody to wander in. We drove on a gravel road through the live oaks, down a hill, then came to the cluster of house, barn, and hangar. I stopped the car before the barn in the light from a mercury vapor light mounted on the barn that lit the grass and dirt patch between the buildings. I killed the car and we piled out.

"How you feel, Joey?" Marie asked.

"Okay. Thirsty."

I unlocked the house and turned on the living room light. Then went into the kitchen and bathroom, before returning to the living room with a big plastic glass.

"It'll taste a little funny. It's well water. Here's some aspirin, too."

He took three aspirin and drained most of the glass.

Clara and Rick were on the couch. They stopped necking when I spoke to Joey. "Nice place," said Clara. "Was this your uncle's stuff?"

It was old furniture, not quite old enough to be antique, but old enough to be "vintage." Some of the chairs were patched. It was neat and uncluttered, like Uncle Max left it. I tried to keep it that way. "Yeah. I like it."

"Did I see a second floor?" she asked.

"Yeah. There's three bedrooms up there, but it gets really hot. Uncle Max's room is on this floor, at the back."

I couldn't stand to wait anymore. The tension was building, had been building, for over a week. The evening had made it worse. "What are you doing this summer, Clara?" I asked. My voice was ragged and anxious. All four looked at me, surprised.

Clara tilted her head to one side and looked at me with narrowed eyes. "Uh, I was going to work part-time at the stables, to pay for the feed and board on Impossible, and I was going to get at least one other job. We don't all have scholarships." She glanced sideways at Marie as she said this.

Marie shrugged. "Scholarship isn't going to help *that* much. I've got a job interview with Dillard's the week after graduation."

"Rick?" Some of the tension was still there, and I took a deep breath. Then, more calmly, I continued, "What about you? This summer, I mean."

The corners of his mouth tightened. "Dad wants me to spend it in Dallas working for his company. I don't want to, but if I don't find a job here that pays well enough, I'll have to." More reluctantly he said, "Child support payments stopped last February, when I turned eighteen. Even with your coaching in calculus, Charlie, I didn't qualify for any of the scholarships I applied for."

I turned to Joey. Before I asked the question he said, "I'm going to join the army."

"What?" Marie was as surprised as any of us. "What do you mean?"

"You know. Go down to the recruiting office at Northgate, walk in, sign up. That's what. Do you think I'm going to get to college any other way with my grades? I've got four sisters and a little brother; Dad was laid off six months ago, so all we've got is the money from Mom's secretarial work. Lisa is talking about dropping out of A&M so she can get *another* job. No way I'm going to make it on my own." He sipped from the last of his water, his eyes on the floor. "To be honest, I'm not sure I want to go to college. Sure didn't do Dad any good."

Marie shrugged helplessly and put her arm around Joey's waist. He kept his eyes down, but leaned into her.

The silence was like a still pond and I dropped my pebble with great care. "Payback time," I said.

Joey looked up. "Huh?"

"You guys owe me for tonight, right? For driving you around."

Marie said, "Sure." Joey nodded, his eyes narrowing, wondering what the cost would be. Rick just said, "For other things, too." Clara's reaction was more like Joey's.

"Here's the deal. I've got a secret. It's not illegal. It's not immoral. Some might say it's not even possible. But it's a secret and I want it kept that way. You promise not to tell anyone what I'm about to show you. Not your friends, your brothers, your sisters, your parents, your priest." I looked at Joey when I said priest. "That's the payment I want. To give me your word and keep it."

"I haven't been to confession in four years, Charlie. And if it's not immoral, why should it matter?"

"Just promise."

Marie said, "Okay, Charlie." She looked a little hurt. She was my best friend, and she didn't know what I was talking about. Well, I didn't tell her everything since she started going out with Joey.

Joey looked relieved. The cost, it seemed, was acceptable to him. "Sure, Charlie. It's a deal."

Rick said, "I promise."

Clara licked her lips. "Well, if what you said about it not being illegal or immoral is true, then I promise as well. If it turns out that you're lying about that, then all deals are off."

I gritted my teeth together. "Of course."

There was a set of barrister bookshelves next to the door. I lifted the glass door on one shelf and pulled a book from it. The place was marked with a reddish brown feather. "Look at this." I put the book down on the coffee table, open, facing the couch. Marie and Joey came over and looked down. Clara and Rick leaned forward.

Joey said, "Mourning doves, aren't they?" Joey and his father hunted.

Clara read from the caption. *"Ectopistes migratorius,* Male and Female Passenger Pigeon, see Pigeons—Columbidae, order Columbiformes."

Marie said, "Passenger pigeons? They're extinct. Wiped out by hunting in the late 1800s, right?"

"That's right," I said. "Though technically, the last one died in captivity in 1914. Her name was Martha. Bring the book. Follow me."

I led them back outside, to the barn. It was set partially back into the hill. The first story was mortared fieldstone with wood siding on the hayloft above. I unlocked the padlock and swung open one side of the large double door, found the light switch, and pulled the door shut behind us.

The barn was square, about thirty feet by thirty feet, with a hard dirt floor. There were five stalls on the right-hand side and an ancient gasoline tractor parked on the left along with various attachments: a plow, a disker, a small utility trailer, and an old rotary hay mower. At the back left-hand corner, a worktable stood with all of Uncle Max's tools hung in neat rows on the wall above. A table saw beside the bench stood under a canvas tarp.

I glanced at the back of the barn, where several hay bales were stacked nearly to the ceiling and felt a sharp stab of grief. I looked away quickly and led the guys to the back corner stall. The pigeons started cooing when I opened the door.

There were sixteen cages, handmade of chicken wire with wood framing. They were stacked four by four, one bird per cage.

Marie and Rick looked at the book, then back at the cages. Then back at the book again. Clara grabbed the book from them and flipped to the textual description. She read, "Grayish blue above, reddish fawn below, resembling Old World turtledoves, but larger, thirty-two to forty-three centimeters in length, with a longer pointed tail and a greater wingspread. Males have a pinkish body and a blue-gray head."

Halfway through the description, Joey backed out of the stall and began looking around. He climbed up the ladder to the loft, but all he found was hay. By the time he lifted the tarp on the table saw and looked beneath it, the other three had emerged from the pigeon stall.

"What are you looking for?" asked Marie.

Joey was frowning, his lips pursed. "A time machine," he said.

All four of them looked at me. They seemed a little afraid.

"Wait a minute," said Rick. "These don't have to be passenger pigeons. Didn't the description say they were similar to turtledoves in coloration?"

"These are much bigger," said Marie.

"Back breeding. Selecting for size. Breeding for larger and larger turtledoves. Is that what was done, Charlie?"

"No."

Marie took a stab at it. "Then what about cloning? Didn't you say that the last passenger pigeon died in 1914? They had refrigeration, then. Did they freeze some tissue and did somebody clone these, using doves or pigeons as host mothers?"

I shook my head.

Finally Joey just asked, "What are they, Charlie? What are those birds in the corner?"

"They're passenger pigeons."

He digested that. They all did. Finally he said, "So, where's the time machine?"

"There isn't one."

Clara almost shouted. "Then *how did you get them?*"

I folded my arms. "I'm not going to tell you. Not yet, anyway."

Rick smiled, then, and the others looked at him, puzzled. "So, what are you going to tell us, Charlie?" I could see that some of the possibilities were occurring to him.

"How'd you like enough money for college, without working for your dad in Dallas this summer? All of you. How'd you like enough money for college at any school in the country? Full board and tuition without any jobs on the side?" I paused, a bubble of hysterical laughter breaking out. "Hell. If it works out, enough money for the rest of your lives."

Two

"It's Loaded So Be Careful."

Graduation was an ordeal. Marie's valedictory speech was okay—I'd helped her with it—but the last thing I wanted to do was listen to the Reverend Bates and the president of the school board as they tried to simultaneously prepare us for the future and immerse us in our past "happy days" at Bryan High.

It was so far from my experience that I was beginning to know how Joey felt after the prom.

Luckily I brought a book.

Dad surprised me by swapping shifts with another pilot so he could be there. That morning, for graduation, my parents gave me a leather flight bag, a Blackhawk headset with liquid cushion pads on the earphones, and an AVS flight computer.

I'd been using Dad's headset and flight computer unless he was Pilot-In-Command, then I wore a cheap crew headset that hurt the ears after twenty minutes.

There was mingling, after, and my hand was shaken by kids who never even noticed me while we were in school. Mom stood and talked with Mr. and Mrs. Prentice and Mr. Nguyen, watching everything with wide eyes. At least she left the notepad at home . . . this time. I saw Dad hang up the pay phone in the hall and come back into the auditorium.

Joey was tugging at his collar and wanting to go, but his parents were having a great time. "I'd just as soon never see this place again," he told me just before Dad came up.

"I know what you mean," I said.

"Congratulations, Joey," said Dad, shaking Joey's hand. "What are your plans?"

"Thanks, Captain Newell. For the summer, I'm going to work in, uh, wildlife management." He shot a look at me.

I'll kill you, I mouthed.

Dad nodded amiably, then turned to me. "I took the standby spot to get free for this and my number just came up. A pilot failed his physical and I have to replace him on the DFW—KC—O'Hare run tonight. You want to fly me up?" He spread his hands. "Only if you want to. If you've got plans or a party or something, I can take the commuter."

I was surprised. I had over 360 hours, but I didn't think Dad trusted my flying. In fact, when I'd gotten my Instrument Flight Rules ticket two months before, he'd acted more surprised than pleased.

"What's the weather?" I asked cautiously.

"Marginal VFR here—ceiling at fourteen hundred. It's socked in at Dallas—nine-hundred-foot ceiling. No cells." No thunderstorms, he meant. "Supposed to get better, not worse."

"Okay." I paused. "Uh, we should get going. The Mooney's empty."

"You didn't fill it last time?" Irritation.

"She was still hot. You can get more in her if you fill her cold." He shrugged. "True, but you could've waited for her to cool down."

I looked down. You could get water condensation in the tanks if you left it empty. "Sorry," I mumbled.

Mom drove us home and we changed and Dad packed an overnight. I drove us in my truck, a used and battered Mazda, to Easterwood and left it. I'd be coming back. Dad filed an IFR flight plan into DFW while I got the Mooney fueled and did the preflight.

Then Dad came over to the plane and did it all over again.

The flight was tense. I fumbled my response to the Fort Worth Traffic Control Center and received Dad's standard lecture on keeping radio communications short and to the point, there's a lot of people up in the air gotta use the same frequency, don't you know? Then I had thirteen-knot crosswind component on the landing and bounced the plane, something I haven't done in months, not even for the IFR examiner who'd made me pretty nervous.

I offered to pick Dad up when he was done with the next series of flights but he said, "No. That's okay. I'll take the commuter down."

On the way back everything went right. I handled my clearance, ground control, tower, and departure communications with brevity and clarity, my radio navigation brought me right into the landing pattern for Easterwood, and the landing was smooth as silk, one faint "chirp" from the tires as they spun up to speed.

Of course Dad wasn't there to see it.

I put the plane in the hangar, cleaned the bugs off, and went home.

The Monday after graduation, Joey, Rick, and I drove down to Houston in my pickup and shipped four male passenger pigeons to four different addresses. We used a freight company that routinely handled live animals. I paid cash for the freight and I lied about my name, address, and phone number.

One week later, we drove back to Houston, bought twenty dollars in quarters from a bank, and made a few calls. The first phone booth we used was at the Galleria, the huge mall on the west loop. Rick stayed with the truck; Joey and I took the quarters in.

It was a weekday morning, the mall just open. On the ice rink on the bottom level, a girl was doing axels while her instructor counted aloud. We found a phone in a quiet alcove and I dialed the first number, then put in four dollars as directed by the computerized voice.

The phone rang twice and was answered, "National Zoo."

"Dr. David Elsner, please."

"Who shall I say is calling?"

"The Lazarus Company."

She put me on hold and then a man's voice said, "This is David Elsner." He sounded wary.

"Did the pigeon arrive all right?"

"Who is this?"

"I'm the one who sent you the pigeon. The *Passenger pigeon*. You know, *Ectopistes migratorius?*"

"All right. Yes, the pigeon seems to be fine." His voice lowered and became very intense. *"Where did you get it?"*

"Well—that's my secret. I'm pleased that he arrived okay." I paused. "Pity that they're extinct—they're such pretty birds."

His voice got louder. "Where did you get it? Don't you know it's illegal to traffic in endangered species?"

I winced and gritted my teeth. "Passenger pigeons are not on the endangered species list, Dr. Elsner. I'm not doing anything illegal."

"Well, they *will* be if they survive as a species! Are there any others?"

"I was just coming to that."

"Ah."

"I have four females for sale."

"We'll take th—uh, how much?"

"Twenty-five thousand dollars each."

"What! A hundred thousand dollars?"

"Yes."

"That's outrageous!"

I paused. Was it? I'd thought about it a lot, but I didn't have anything to compare it to. In fact, I thought it was cheap, considering. "You're absolutely right, Dr. Elsner. It's outrageous. You should go to another supplier."

"What? What other supplier?"

The computer voice asked for more money. I shoved quarters in.

"I'm sorry, Dr. Elsner. I didn't quite hear that."

"What other supplier?"

"Of extinct species? Well, there's uh . . . gee, I don't know of any other suppliers."

His voice was grim. "I see. You know, if you're capturing these in the wild, you *are* endangering the species. The population has to be tiny."

"I'm pleased to tell you that this is not the case."

"What's not the case? That you aren't taking them from the wild? Or that the population isn't tiny?"

He was digging as hard as he could.

"Sorry. I take it you're not interested in purchasing the birds?"

"Uh—I have to talk to the acquisition board. Can you give me two weeks?"

"There are other zoos. I'll give you until the day after tomorrow. I'll call you at the same time. Good-bye."

"No, wait a—"

I hung up.

We moved to a different pay phone on Westheimer, just inside a supermarket, and called the Nature Conservancy. The conversation was similar to the first one, a mix of desperation and hostility. "We buy land—habitats—not animals!"

"So, you're not interested?"

"I didn't say that."

I gave them the same two days.

From a phone on West Gray I called the San Diego Zoo. They definitely wanted the females and they had authorization to proceed. I looked around to make sure the guys were out of earshot. "Here's our bank account. Electronically transfer the hundred thousand within the next two days and we'll ship the birds to you."

"What? No contract? No paperwork? How do we know you have them?"

"I already delivered my evidence of good faith. Remember? It eats pigeon feed and shits."

"How about half before delivery, half after?"

"There are other zoos."

They agreed that there were other zoos. They also agreed to my terms.

The next phone was on the Northwest Freeway, on our way back out of town.

"Sierra Club."

"I'd like to speak with Mr. Saunderson."

"May I have your name?"

"The Lazarus Company."

"Uh, your name please?"

"John Smith."

"One moment please."

I listened to classical music as she put me on hold. My watch read 3:02. I started the stopwatch function. At forty-five seconds I hung up.

"Another phone," I said. "Somewhere else."

We drove away from the freeway and stopped at a 7-Eleven.

"Sierra Club."

"This is John Smith of the Lazarus Company, again. Your phone system hung up on me. I need to talk to Mr. Saunderson." I started the stopwatch again. The hold music stretched on and on. I hung up.

Rick looked at me, his eyebrows raised. Joey looked annoyed. "How are we going to sell them the pigeons if you keep hanging up on them?"

"I could be wrong, but I think they're trying to trace the call."

Rick said, "On what grounds? Don't they have to get the police involved to do that? We didn't do anything illegal." He stood beside me at the phone. Joey was leaning against the hood of my truck.

"I don't know. I don't like it, though." I got back into the truck. "We'll give it one more try. If he isn't on the line in under a minute, I say we blow off the Sierra Club."

Joey and Rick climbed in the other side, Joey straddling the stick shift, Rick with his knees pulled up to fit in the seat.

Joey said, "Blow off a hundred thousand dollars?"

"Which would you prefer? Losing the hundred thousand or three hundred thousand?"

He didn't answer.

"Sierra Club."

"I want to talk to Mr. Saunderson right now."

"He's very busy. Can't you wait a minute?"

"No."

"Perhaps you could call back later."

"Perhaps you could connect me now or Mr. Saunderson will never hear from me again. I'm pretty sure that's not what he wants. You have fifteen seconds." I held the watch next to the mouthpiece and started the stopwatch. It chirped loudly into the phone.

There was no music this time. Another voice came onto the phone. "This is James Saunderson."

"One hundred thousand dollars for four female passenger pigeons. Are you interested?"

"Uh, that's a lot of money."

"Four females of an extinct species is quite a lot of bird. You have two days to think it over."

"How do I know—"

"Two days." I hung up.

We drove back to Bryan.

After dropping Rick and Joey off, I drove out University to the mostly empty strip mall across from the Hilton. In one corner, next to a pool hall, the strip's only other tenant was a small office. The sign on the door said, *Luis Cervantes, Attorney*.

I pushed in through a mirrored glass door. Sylvia, Luis's paralegal, was typing on a computer.

"Hello, Charlie. He's next door."

"Business is that good?"

She shrugged. "We were busy this morning. It's enough."

"Thanks."

I went next door to the pool hall. The tables were crowded together and, when it's busy, you can hardly take a shot without hitting other players. It was early, though, and there were only a few people in the place. Luis was in the corner, playing eight ball against himself.

"Hey, Charlie, grab a cue. Or would you rather go flying?" Luis was a small man, my height, but where I'm big boned and over-weight, he's trim and perfectly proportioned. If you don't have any-thing to scale against, he doesn't look short at all. He makes me feel even fatter than usual.

I said, "Thunderstorm coming in."

He grinned. "Good IFR weather."

"For idiots."

Luis was working on his Instrument rating. I met him in instru-ment ground school and, later, flew with him as a safety pilot when he flew "under the hood" to simulate instrument conditions.

I took a cue from the wall and leaned on it while he sank all the balls.

"So, what's happening?"

"Incoming money."

He raised his eyebrows. "What?"

"A wire transfer into the account."

He banked the six ball into the side pocket, then set up on the seven. "How much?"

"One hundred K."

The cue scraped across the felt and the cue ball hopped sideways. He swore and rubbed at the blue mark on the green. "One hundred thousand? Who from?"

"The San Diego Zoo."

He scratched at his head. "I didn't believe it. I'm still not sure I do. You sold them pigeons?"

"Yeah."

"And you didn't steal these birds, right? Or illegally import them?"

"Right. Really. But they're still going to want to know where I got them and I can't tell them. So that's why we set up the Austin account, right?"

He took another shot. "Right. How much do we transfer to the private account and how much do you want to hold back for taxes?"

"We're going to declare a loss the first year. Expenses."

"Expenses? Expenses?" He put the cue down on the table and leaned forward, his hands on the felt. "How much money are you expecting in?"

"Well, I expect either one, two, three, or four hundred K. I hope we're talking four hundred—it's not that unlikely. That's within the month, but it's really start-up money. We won't see the real money until next year."

"Real money? Four hundred K isn't real money? What kind of expenses are you talking?"

"Better you shouldn't know."

He got a pained look on his face. "Come on. No bullshit. You're sure this isn't illegal? You've got to tell me. I'm your lawyer, but I won't be if you're not straight with me. What sort of expenses?"

I took a deep breath and licked my lips. "Building materials. Aircraft. Fuel. Advanced flight instruction for five people. Radio and weather equipment." I didn't mention the weapons.

"Weather-monitoring equipment?"

"Yeah."

"Weather-monitoring equipment." He shook his head. "I don't believe this. Look—just shoot pool. We'll talk about this if the money comes in."

"When."

"Huh?"

"*When* the money comes in."

He got a pained expression on his face. "Rack 'em."

The Five moved me the next day, descending on my parents' house to help me box stuff. I didn't know what else to call us—Lazarus Company was a fictional front for dealing with the zoos, the Austin account was in the "Lazarus Company" name, and the corporation was called, "Wildside Investments." Maybe later we'd be the Wild-siders.

The probationary period on Joey's DWI conviction was over and his dad let him use his full-size pickup. I left the bed and dresser, but took my desk, computer, and bookshelves.

Mom was strangely quiet as we packed the two vehicles. When we were ready to leave she gave me a small cooler with sandwiches and sodas, for us to eat out at the ranch. There were tears in her eyes.

"Mom. I'm coming home for supper, remember?"

She shook her head. "I know. That's not the point. Never mind. You can bring your laundry home if you want."

"There's a washer and dryer on the ranch—it'd be silly."

"You'll wash something in hot and ruin it."

"I won't wash *anything* in hot. Don't worry. See you at supper." I kissed her on the cheek. She started crying in earnest. I was glad the others were outside, by the trucks.

We drove out, Marie with me, Rick and Clara with Joey.

"Your mom is sad about you moving out, isn't she?" Marie asked, in the truck.

"Yeah," I said. "It's a pain."

She just looked at me and didn't say anything. I remembered that she'd barely known her mother and felt stupid.

I moved my stuff into Uncle Max's room. Mom mothballed his stuff to the attic a couple of years ago, after he'd been missing for five years already, so the closet and dresser were empty. It felt weird putting my things in there.

Then we gathered on the front porch to eat Mom's sandwiches.

"What now, Boss?" said Joey. He pulled an insulated bag from behind the seat of his dad's pickup. "Anybody want a beer?"

Marie glared at him.

Rick said, "I'll take one."

Clara had one as well.

"Charlie? You want a Bud?"

"No, thank you."

Joey popped his top and drank a large swallow. "Well, Boss, what now?"

"We wait."

"What for?"

I started to answer, but the phone rang inside. I went and picked it up. It was Luis.

"All right—when."

"What do you mean?"

"It was 'when.' The bank called half an hour ago—the transfer is in. My associate in Austin transferred it and I put ninety thousand in the working account." The public account was opened originally by Richard Madigan, an Austin lawyer who went to law school with Luis. He knew about Luis, but he didn't know about us. He received two percent for his trouble. Luis received eight percent.

Something felt odd in my stomach and the bite of sandwich in my mouth seemed dry. "Good."

"Is that all you can say? Good?"

"Very good."

I heard his hair brush the phone as he shook his head. "Keep good receipts, dammit."

"I will. Thanks, Luis."

I hung up the phone, then took a small notebook out of my shirt pocket. From the third page, I dialed a nonlocal number. A voice answered, "Texas Institute of Aviation. Jack speaking."

"Mr. Reed? This is Charles Newell. I've got those three students I told you about."

"For the combined IFR, starting Monday?"

"Yeah."

"And payment?"

"They'll have a cashier's check when they arrive."

"For the whole amount?"

"Yes."

"Certainly—that would be fine. Give me their names?"

I gave him Joey's, Rick's, and Clara's full names. He gave me registration information, and we said good-bye.

Out on the porch, Joey had started on his second beer. "Well, Boss. You were going to tell us what we're waiting for?"

"Don't call me that. And we're not waiting anymore."

He put his beer down. Clara, Rick, and Marie stopped eating.

"We've got the first money. I've enrolled Rick, Clara, and Joey in flight school at the Texas Institute of Aviation at Brenham. It starts Monday and runs six days a week for the next three months. When you're done, you'll have an IFR ticket."

They all started talking at once.

"Whoa! Who goes first?"

Marie, with uncharacteristic vigor, said, "How come they get the flight training? I'm almost there now."

"Exactly—you get different training. Don't sweat it—you'll also get an IFR ticket out of it, trust me."

Joey was scowling. "Don't we have any say in this? You just enroll us? What if we don't want to learn to fly?"

I was stunned. The thought had never occurred to me. How could they not want to fly? It was like not wanting to breathe. "Uh, well, what do you want? Wouldn't you like to fly? The instruction and flight time cost over eight grand for each of you. Lots of people would jump at it."

Joey blinked. "For eight grand I could go to college."

"It's peanuts, Joey. You'll get lots more if you do it my way. But I need the pilots. I thought you liked the idea of flying."

He shrugged.

Clara broke in. "Well *I'd* like to do it. I've always wanted to learn to fly. Two things, though. What's an IFR ticket, and who's gonna take care of Impossible and pay for his stable and feed?"

Marie told her. "IFR stands for Instrument Flight Rules—it means you can fly in limited visibility, on instruments."

I nodded. "Also, as of Monday, we're all on salary. Five hundred a week to start—will that cover Impossible?"

"It sure will!"

"What about you, Rick?"

He was smiling. "I'm with Clara."

I turned back to Joey. "Well, Joey?"

"Why?"

I didn't say anything.

"Why the flying? What's it for?Sure, I'd love to learn to fly. I've been crazy about planes for years—you've seen my radio control models—but why do you want to pay for it? What are we going to do that requires five pilots? Start an airline?"

I looked down at the porch and said, "I can't tell you. Not yet."

"Can't or won't?"

I looked him in the eye. "Won't."

"What if we won't do it? What if we wash out of flight school? Why should you spend the money if it isn't going to do what you want?"

I shook my head. "The money isn't important. It's nothing. Not compared to the secret." I raised my hands, palms up. "I don't blame you for being pissed off. I don't blame you for feeling not trusted. But in a way, it's not *my* secret. It's not mine to share."

Marie scooted over by Joey and took his hand. "So when, Charlie? Aren't you going to have to share it anyway, eventually?"

I thought about Uncle Max. What would he want? What I planned to do would probably not please him, regardless of whom I told.

"Okay. You're right. I'll show you. Wait here."

I went into the house, unlocked Uncle Max's gun cabinet, and took out the thirty-ought-six with the five-shot clip and the Mossberg twenty-gauge pump shotgun. I double-checked that they were loaded, and took an army surplus shoulder bag holding a pair of binoculars and more ammo.

When I walked back on the porch with the two weapons, Joey's eyes got wide. Everybody was watching me very carefully.

"Here," I said. I handed Joey the thirty-ought-six. "It's loaded so be careful. Anybody else hunt?"

Rick and Marie shook their heads, but Clara said, "I shoot skeet with a gun just like that."

I gave her the Mossberg. "It's also loaded. Follow me."

I walked toward the barn.

Three

"So, You Think He Went Through and Got Munched?"

I unlocked the padlock and swung the door open. When they'd trooped in, I shut it behind us. The afternoon sun shone through cracks between boards, pushing long rays of light across the suddenly dark place and making floating motes of dust glitter like stars. I flipped the light switch on, then closed the padlock on an inside hasp, locking the door from within.

Joey rolled his eyes and let out his breath. Marie watched me carefully, her face still. Clara and Rick raised their eyebrows at each other.

"Help me move this hay," I said, moving to the back wall and pulling down a bale from the top row. I had to stand on tiptoe to snag the wire and caught it as it fell.

"All of it?" asked Clara. She leaned the shotgun into the corner, carefully. Joey copied her.

"Just this center section," I said, pointing. We stacked it to the side, in front of the empty stalls, passing it bucket brigade fashion. When we'd pulled the top two rows off, they could see the door-frame. Things went faster, then, and we soon uncovered the entire thing.

It was a double door set firmly into the back wall, with a heavy wooden frame mortared into the fieldstone. The door wasn't as old as the barn and was mounted with large chromed hinges and rein-forcing straps. The door was closed with a three-foot-long, four-by-four drop bar set into steel brackets. In addition, there was a padlock hasp, very large, mounted to the door with round-head bolts. A large security padlock, the kind with a barrel cylinder, secured the hasp.

"Jesus," said Joey. "You'd think it was Fort Knox."

I smiled. "Interesting choice of words." I lifted the bar and set it to the side. "Get the guns. There's another door on the other side of this, but I don't know if anything's gotten past it."

"Anything? What sort of 'anything'?" asked Clara. She wiped her hands on her jeans before picking up the shotgun.

"Animals. It could be anything. Wolves. Wild dogs. American lion." I gritted my teeth. "Mammoths."

"What are you talking about?" Joey said.

"Passenger pigeons." I unlocked the padlock but left it in place. "Joey and Clara, stand about ten feet back from the door. Marie, get that big flashlight from the workbench and stand behind them. Rick, get the other side of the door."

Joey moved to his spot, but kept shifting back and forth. "This is ridiculous. What are we doing this for?"

I snarled at him. "You want to know, don't you? I didn't want to show you this yet, but you insisted! Or should we just go back and finish lunch?" I was sweating more than shifting the hay should account for, and my stomach didn't like the thought of food at all.

Joey shrugged. "Okay, already. But when this turns out to be some gag . . ."

He and Clara stood next to each other, guns at the ready, pointed high. Marie flicked the flashlight on and shined it on the door. I took the padlock off the hasp and said, "Safeties off?"

Clara said, "Yes."

Joey said, "Oops. Now it is."

I looked across at Rick.

Rick said, "Fast or slow?"

"Slow."

The hinges screeched and I made a mental note to oil them. We kept pushing until the doors stopped against the inner wall. I peered into darkness. That it was dark was a good sign. It meant the far door, at least, was closed. Marie's light showed a packed dirt floor and rocky walls and ceiling. There were timbers bracing the ceiling. About a hundred feet down the tunnel, a thin vertical line of light could be seen.

There didn't seem to be anything in the tunnel. "May I have the shotgun, please?"

Clara hesitated, frowning. I said, "Doesn't matter. If you're more comfortable with it, by all means."

"I'd rather keep it," she said.

I wondered if she was more worried about what was in the tunnel or about me with a shotgun? I smiled at her. It occurred to me that I gained everything by involving her, by involving them all. "You and Marie check out the tunnel all the way to the far door, please. Especially the floor."

"The floor?" asked Marie?

"Snakes," I said.

Marie stepped backward involuntarily and Joey started to laugh. "Get stuffed," she said to him, and walked forward again. "Come on, Clara." They walked six feet in front of us, searching the floor with occasional sweeps of the ceiling and walls. We stopped two yards from the door.

"No snakes," said Marie.

This door was just like the last one, a double steel-banded door, set in a timber frame that was mortared into fieldstone. There was a hinged drop bar on this side, with a wire loop that threaded through a hole in the door so the bar could be lifted from outside as well. Rick pointed at that and said, "How come this door doesn't lock?"

I looked at him for a moment, then said, "You don't want to be locked out on the other side of *this* door."

He blinked and licked his lips. "Well, if I'm picturing this right, this door should open onto the other side of that small hill your barn backs up against. If that's the case, we'll be facing nothing more dangerous than your airstrip."

I put my hand on the catch. "Safeties off?"

"Yes," said Clara. Joey nodded.

I pulled against the door. It hadn't been opened in a while and it took effort to pull the two sides open. We blinked in the bright sunlight.

When we'd gone into the barn, it had been overcast. The sky outside *this* door was so blue it hurt the eyes.

I held my hand out for the shotgun. This time Clara didn't protest, clicking the safety on before handing it to me. I eased out the door, checking both sides, and then looked up, to check above the door. It seemed clear.

"Come on out," I said.

We were standing on the side of a small hill in knee-high golden grass. Before us, the grass stretched level for a while, then dropped away into a valley where huge cottonwoods lined an unseen river. The wind blew gently and the grass shifted like the surface of water. A large flock of birds flew to the south in a sky so cloud free that it seemed as if someone had dropped a giant porcelain bowl over this place, a bowl so big that its edges were hidden behind the hills and the trees.

I pushed the door shut behind us and used the wire to raise the bar so it dropped back into its brackets.

Marie was the first to speak. "Where's the airstrip? There's the Brazos, but I don't remember those trees. And where are those cotton fields that we line up on to land at your strip?"

Rick said, "There aren't any telephone poles. You have a major power line south of your place. I don't see the towers. I don't see any cattle. The place to the east of you runs cattle, right?"

Joey pointed. "Look, those black spots on that hill over there. Those are cattle."

I took the binoculars out of the bag and handed them to Joey. "Look again."

While he held the field glasses to his face, I scanned our perimeter again.

"I don't believe it!"

"What, Joey?" Marie said.

He handed the binoculars to her. "Tell me I'm seeing things," he said.

Marie looked through the binoculars at the opposite hill. "Buffalo?"

"Let me see that!" Clara said. Marie reluctantly gave up the binoculars.

Clara stared. "They *are* buffalo. Big buffalo." She swung the glasses slowly across the herd. "Uh, they're upset about something—they're starting to move."

We could all see the dust that rose up from the moving black dots. Rick took his turn with the binoculars. "They're coming this way."

The edge of the herd grew closer, the forerunners dropping out of sight for a moment in the shallow valley before us. We could hear them now, a surprising sound, low and deep, hundreds of hooves pounding the ground. On the far hill, more dark dots kept coming over the ridge, and dust rose above them like smoke. We'd seen only a part of the herd before.

I said, "Technically, they're bison. Back up. We'll watch from the doorway."

They moved back with me, without question, because the sound was now a pounding that we could feel with our feet. I kept my eyes on our rear, especially the hillside above the door. It could be I was overcautious, but I didn't care.

Uncle Max hadn't been cautious enough.

We reached the doorway. Marie opened it and we backed in, keeping our eyes on the valley below. Three, four, six buffalo came into sight, then a steady stream, following the rising hill into the meadow that corresponded to my airstrip on the other side. About a hundred yards in front of us, they swerved to our left, to the low point of the ridge, to run into the next valley.

Marie said something to Joey, but he shook his head, unable to hear her over the wave of noise. She shouted, "They're huge!"

They were taller at the head than any of us, with the possible exception of Rick. At the shoulder, they towered far above us. I yelled to be heard. "I believe these are woods bison. They're bigger than plains bison."

A cow, running with a half-grown calf, swung wider than the rest, coming closer to us. The calf was laboring, unable to keep to the pace of the adults. A bull swung wider still and came between us and the calf. It peered at us, turning its head left, then right. It shook its head and bellowed, its long beard flapping below its chin. Its short curved horns seemed longer and sharper than before.

I edged closer to Marie's ear and said, "Hold still. If he charges, we shut the door. Nobody shoots. Pass it on." Moving slowly, she told Joey, who told Clara and Rick.

Suddenly the bull spun away from us and charged to the left, bellowing. I saw something tawny streak through the grass, then rear up, screaming, clawed paws raised, lips drawn back from huge curved teeth. The bull charged forward and the cat jumped to the right, racing around the bull for the calf, but by now other bulls charged out of the black rolling mass, between the cow and the cat. With a higher-pitched bawling sound, the calf found hidden reserves of strength and ran back toward the herd, its mother beside it.

The cat turned aside and streaked away from the charging bulls, vanishing back into the grass.

Joey shut his mouth and shifted his grip on the thirty-ought-six. "We're going to need bigger guns," he shouted.

I shrugged, nonchalant. When he looked back at the bison, I carefully wiped my sweating hands off on my jeans and checked the safety on the shotgun again.

The herd took another five minutes to pass and, by the time they did, the dust was dimming the sun and making us breathe carefully through our noses. There were wolves following the stragglers. Big wolves trotting through the dust like ghosts in fog. I shut the door before they got near us, secured the bar, and we went back through the tunnel to the barn.

This time, nobody made fun of the way I locked the door in the back wall. Joey even gave the lock an extra tug. We stacked the hay back where it had been and locked up the barn. The sky was still overcast but not with dust—just ordinary clouds. Joey and Rick walked over the top of the hill, lining up on the barn, to satisfy themselves that there wasn't a herd of bison on the other side of it.

They were back in five minutes, quiet and thoughtful. Joey flopped down on the edge of the porch. Rick stood on the porch steps, his arms crossed.

"Well?" said Clara.

"It's not the same place," said Rick. "Just what it should be. The ranch next door and the other end of the runway. No buffalo. No wolves." He paused for a moment, then said, "No saber-tooths."

I took another sandwich from the cooler and didn't say anything.

"So that's the secret?" said Joey.

I nodded.

"What's happening, Charlie?" Marie asked.

"I'm eating lunch."

Clara raised her voice, "You know what she means! Is it a time machine? What's that stuff on the other side? Did we just go back in time? Those were ice age mammals, weren't they?"

I put the sandwich down. "that's what I first thought, too, but I don't think so."

Rick uncrossed his arms and sat down, leaning back against the porch post. "Why don't you start at the beginning, Charlie. We know about the door in the barn—we might as well know the rest."

I looked at each of them in turn, waiting. Joey looked as if he was angry about something he couldn't understand. Marie's eyes were wide and she kept moistening her lips as if they were dry. Rick's face was blank, as if his mind was a universe away. Clara looked downright excited.

I cleared my throat and began. "Okay. It starts when I was seven. My dad was still active duty air force and stationed at Patrick Air

Force Base in Florida. During the summer break, they shipped me out here to spend a month with Uncle Max and Aunt Jo.

"Well, Uncle Max took me hunting with him. I use the term loosely—he'd take a rifle and a pistol and we'd go through the tunnel and walk. He never shot anything, though once he fired in the air to turn away this hairy elephant."

"Mammoth?" said Clara.

"I don't know. I was only seven. Mammoth or mastodon, I'm not sure. Had a wonderful time, though. Until I went back to school." The corners of my mouth turned down and I frowned. "I tried to tell my classmates about the stuff I saw and they said I lied. The teachers weren't too hard on me—they suggested I had an 'over-active' imagination. No one believed me and eventually, I came to doubt it myself.

"The next time we came here was when my Aunt Jo died, when I was nine. We were living in Atlanta—Dad had left the air force and was working for the airlines then—and we flew into Houston and drove up. We stayed in town, in a hotel, and the services and reception were at the Methodist Church, so we never got out here. I thought about the door during the funeral, but the memory was like memories of pretend games you play when you're a kid and it was all tangled up with memories of Aunt Jo alive.

"Uncle Max visited us a few times after that, but we never talked about the door. Seven years ago, he disappeared."

"Disappeared? I thought he was dead," said Marie.

"He probably is."

Joey said, "So you think he went through and got munched?"

I lowered my head and stared at Joey over the tops of my glasses. Marie hit him on the arm. "What a thing to say!"

"When did you discover the door again, Charlie?" Rick asked.

"When Dad was transferred to DFW, Mom didn't want to live in the metroplex—she and Uncle Max are from here, so Dad decided to commute. Mom came back several times to try and find out what happened to Max and to make sure the place was okay. He left a will naming her executor and a power of attorney in her name. The power of attorney was in effect, but the will didn't go into effect until he was finally declared dead three months ago. That's when I inherited formally."

"What about the rest of your mom's family?"

"There isn't any. Their parents died before Dad and Mom were married. My dad's side of the family goes on and on, but it was always just Uncle Max on Mom's side." I blinked. "Maybe that's why Mom took my moving so hard. I'm her only blood kin."

"And the door?" Joey said, impatient.

"I'm getting to it. We knew all along that the farm came to me in the will, so I was 'allowed' to do most of the upkeep on the place. Mow the place with the tractor, rake, cut up the dead trees, paint. Fix the fences. I was standing in the barn one day, and the memory of going hunting with Uncle Max came back, very strong.

"The hay was stacked like it is now—but it was older hay, years old and dry, and it kept cracking and falling to the floor. Every week or so I'd rake up the pieces and put them in the compost heap, but one day I decided that it would make more sense to get rid of all the hay, once and for all.

"As you might imagine, I found the door then. The locking brackets were empty and I found the bar just inside the door. I figure Uncle Max expected to be gone long enough that he didn't want someone finding the door, so he restacked the hay behind him before closing the doors."

I paused to take a breath and Rick said, "Didn't they look for him? I mean, the county sheriff's department? Didn't they come out here and search? Why didn't they find the door?"

"Apparently they spent most of their efforts interviewing his neighbors, his friends, and places like his bank. By the time they started asking around, he'd been missing about a month—that is, they found a month-old bank record of a small cash withdrawal that was done in person at a teller and the utility bills had been paid by checks dated from that same week. One theory was that he had an accident away from the house so they had dogs out in the woods all around and down by the river. Another theory was that he was fishing the river and he fell in."

Joey shook his head. "The sheriff's department couldn't find its ass with both hands." Joey's DWI arrest had been by a county deputy, so the statement didn't make much sense—they'd found *him* after all.

I continued. "Anyway, I stuck my head out the far door and confirmed that it wasn't just a tunnel through the hill. I thought about telling my parents about it, and I thought about telling the police, but I didn't."

Marie asked, "Why not, Charlie?"

"Because Uncle Max had already been gone for five years. And he'd kept it a secret for as long as I'd known him. And it was mine. Or it was going to be. I wanted to know what it was before I handed it over to anybody else."

"How the hell did you catch those pigeons with buffalo stampeding all over the place? I wouldn't think any pigeons would land," Rick said.

"To be honest, you don't see something like that very often. It was a freak. I'm glad it happened because it showed you how different the other side can be, but it took me a week of walking around the other side before I saw any buffalo. Lots of tracks, but no buffalo, no sabertooths. Did see some wild dogs, maybe some wolves. And passenger pigeons. So many they darkened the sky and their shit made the ground white."

"Well I wouldn't have told anybody," said Joey. "The government would be all over your ass." He looked a little sheepish. "I hate to say it, but I understand why you didn't want to tell us."

"You guys were right," I said. "I had to tell you sometime. I'm going to be even more honest with you—what I want to do is dangerous. If we don't trust each other—if you don't trust me—it won't work. Worse, it could get some or all of us killed."

They were quiet for a moment, staring at me. I wondered if what I'd said was too melodramatic, but after that buffalo stampede, I doubted it would be taken that way. Clara asked the next question.

"What is it, Charlie, that you want to do? That you want *us* to do?"

"Well, to know that, you have to know what the other side is."

"Do you know?" Rick asked. "It's driving me crazy. We wiped out most of the buffalo and we wiped out the passenger pigeons. Did we wipe out the sabertooths? Anyway, does the tunnel go back in time?"

I shook my head. "No. I'm pretty sure it doesn't—if we were to go back through the tunnel in another six hours, do you know what we'd see?"

"Well," said Marie, "it would be dark."

"Yes. And if it weren't cloudy you could look up and see the positions of the planets and the moon and the stars. No satellites, though."

"So?" said Joey.

Clara turned to him, "It could tell you what year it was. The moon was closer to the earth in the past, the planets line up in particular patterns. Even the constellations change positions over a great enough time." She faced me. I'd never seen her like this; she was excited and, even better, she was excited about what *I* had to say. I smiled in spite of myself. "What would we see, Charlie?"

I paused. "Exactly the same sky you're used to. The moon would be the same size and it would be in the same phase. The constellations would be where you expected them to be and they'd be the shape you're used to. The planets would be in the same place."

"So it's the same time," Clara said, beating me to it. "It's not the past or the future."

"So what is it?" asked Marie.

They waited for me and I drew it out for a moment. I wasn't used to this much attention. It felt good.

"It's the same time, but it's a different earth." I paused. "It's probably a different universe."

"Different but parallel," said Joey.

Rick looked at Joey with new respect. "Whoa, Einstein. Pretty quick there."

Joey flushed. "I've seen *Star Trek*. What else accounts for the same landscape, the same biology?"

"Well, not completely the same," Clara said. "We don't exactly have bison roaming the streets of College Station."

"So why are there bison there? Why are there passenger pigeons?" Rick said.

It was Clara who said, "Because there aren't any men, er, humans. At least not in this area, perhaps not in this hemisphere." She turned to me. "Am I right?"

I nodded. "Let me put it this way—I haven't seen any sign of humans and when I took a portable radio far enough away from the tunnel to avoid leakage, I don't get any radio broadcasts. Not FM, not AM, not shortwave. I've checked several times during day and night. If there are humans on the other side, they don't broadcast and they haven't made it into this area."

"And that's why there are all these extinct species, right?" Clara leaned forward, still excited. I looked into her eyes for a moment and smiled.

"That's certainly what I think," I said.

"So what's the plan, Charlie," Joey said, leaning back. "Are we going to sell more extinct species? Mastodons for sale, mammoths for rent? Anybody for a saber-toothed tiger? They make excellent pets—warn the mailman, though."

I shook my head. "We're going to have a hard enough time keeping the secret with the pigeons we're selling now. If we continued to sell extinct species, someone would think what you did, Joey— that someone has a time machine. Don't you think the government would be interested in that? Want to win a war? Wipe out the country before it was ever formed. Eliminate the fathers of tyrants. Kill Hitler as a teenager."

"Yeah, yeah, yeah," said Joey. "We've all seen *Terminator*. We've all seen *Star Trek*. But it isn't a time machine, so they can't do that."

"Doesn't matter," I said. "Who's going to tell them? Who are they going to believe? Besides, there's plenty of reasons for them to want the secret. You want the best bomb shelter there ever was? You want a place to put all the radioactive waste there is without endangering humans? All the toxic waste? They'll want to do on a very large scale what I want to do on a small one."

"And what's that?" said Clara.

"If man hasn't been on this planet, or at least in this hemisphere, then he hasn't drilled out the oil that's there, he hasn't lumbered all the forests, and he hasn't mined out all the minerals."

"You want us to drill for oil?" asked Clara.

I shook my head. "Uh, uh."

"Lumber?" asked Marie. "There's plenty of trees over there."

I shook my head again.

Rick said, "You don't need to fly anywhere to go for lumber or oil. There would be plenty in a Texas never visited by man. Which is it, Charlie?" He paused. "Gold or silver?"

I sketched a salute at Rick with one finger.

"Gold." I said.

Four

"We Want to Be Able to See any Predators."

Marie and I flew the Mooney to San Antonio the next day. We took four female pigeons with us, their cages strapped into the backseats. I let Marie get some simulated instrument time in, "under the hood," as I flew as safety pilot. This entailed her wearing a baseball cap with an aluminum screen that blocked her view out the windshield, but let her see the instruments.

We walked the pigeons half a mile to an air freight company that handled live cargo, and shipped them to the San Diego Zoo using the same fake return address. I hoped they'd arrive all right.

Then we walked over to the main passenger terminal and did the pay telephone thing again, calling the National Zoo, first.

"David Elsner here."

"Have you decided about the pigeons?"

"Which pigeons?"

"The *passenger* pigeons—what did you think I was asking about?"

"I wasn't sure it was you. We haven't gone public with their existence—for all I knew, you were calling about one of the zoo's carrier pigeons."

"Well, now you know. What did you decide?"

"We'll take them."

I gave him the account number. Like the San Diego Zoo he kicked a bit about the payment up front, but I remained firm. "You send the money, we'll send the pigeons."

"I'll see what I can do," he said.

I called the Nature Conservancy next. The woman there threw me a curve ball. "We'll give you a million dollars for all you have. Provided, of course, that they're the real thing."

I paused, seriously tempted.

Into the gap she asked, "How many do you have?"

I flinched. "I have four. One hundred thousand as previously indicated. You *already* know they're the real thing." *One million dollars?* "Perhaps we can discuss more pigeons after delivery of these."

She started to argue.

"Look. Right now I'm selling these four. I don't have to sell them to you. They could be sold elsewhere. Since you already have the male, that'd be a pity."

Quickly, she said, "Agreed. How do we pay you?"

I gave her the account number. She noted it down, then said, "We'll transfer 125,000."

"Why? The price is 100 K for the four."

"Twenty-five thousand more as a fee that you *will* talk to us later."

"I said *maybe* I'd sell you more pigeons."

"Just to talk. It doesn't obligate you to anything more than that." She paused and I heard her moisten her lips. "My father saw the last passenger pigeon in the Cincinnati Zoo when he was a young boy. You know, the human race doesn't often get a second chance like this."

"You don't know the half of it," I said, then hung up.

I leaned my head against the wall by the phone kiosk.

"What's wrong?" Marie asked.

"You want something to eat?"

"Give me a break. Aren't they paying the money?"

I started walking down the terminal, toward a concession area.

"Softer. Do you want the whole world to know? Yes, they're paying the money. They're doing their best to make me feel guilty, too."

"About the money?"

"About endangering a species."

She rolled her eyes. "But you're not. How many are there on the other side?"

I inhaled, long and deep, then exhaled slowly. "Millions. You're right. It makes me feel bad, though."

She nodded. "I know what you mean. It's hard to keep it secret. My father's bought the corporate internship story. He's pleased that I'll make more money than Dillard's will pay, but it's very hard not to tell him the truth."

I swallowed. "Don't."

She shook her head. "Of course not. But it's still hard and it must be harder for you, talking to those people who want to know so badly."

"Oh. Yeah, speaking of which—" I turned back from the concession stand and went to another phone kiosk.

Mr. Saunderson of the Sierra Club was ready to pay. I gave him the account number with some misgiving, remembering the trouble I'd had the first time I talked to him. Still, I gave it to him and got off quickly.

"What next?" Marie asked.

"Let's go see a man about a plane."

We flew north to a small municipal field at San Marcos. In the pilots' lounge at the fueling station we found a short, dumpy man with muttonchop sideburns and a baseball cap with fake military markings.

"Mr. Vail?" I asked.

"That's me. You Charlie Newell?"

"Yessir."

He pointed at the door. "Osprey's this way."

We followed him out and around the corner. There was a small yellow-and-white airplane. It was a fiber and foam composite sea-plane, with the engine mounted above and behind the two-seater cockpit. It had streamlined floats below the wings and they cleared the ground on extended landing gear.

"It's cute," said Marie.

The man looked at her and smiled indulgently. "It's a beaut, isn't it?"

I looked at it dubiously. "What's its cruise speed?"

"One-thirty. Top is one-forty. Stalls at sixty-three."

"Range?"

"Three hundred and fifty, at cruise, with reserves."

I winced inwardly. It was too small and too slow, but the price was right and it was a kit. It could be built on the other side, if we had to.

Vail pointed his finger in the air. "Shall we take a ride?"

"Uh. I'd like to see the inspection papers, if I could, and your license and logbook."

He looked insulted.

"No offense. My dad flies for the airlines. He'd kill me if I ever got in a plane without inspecting the paperwork. Besides—if I buy it, I'll be looking at this stuff first anyway, right?"

He shrugged and dug the paperwork out of the plane. It was in order, right down to the last engine service. His pilot log was okay. To ease things, I gave him my log and license to examine while I went over his.

He had half the hours that I did and didn't have his Instrument Flight rating. Humph.

We preflighted it together. The cockpit canopy hinged at the rear, latching at the very front of the plane. When I saw that, I almost backed out, but the latch was doubled. If it failed in flight, it would flip right back into the engine and prop. More and more, this seemed like a poor choice.

Twenty minutes later, I knew it was.

"What'd you think?" he asked, once we were back on the ground. "Honestly?"

He winced. "Don't like it, eh?"

"It's too small. Every time you change engine settings it dives or pitches up because the line of thrust is above the plane. If you reduced power abruptly while landing, you could pitch up and stall the airplane well above the ground. Not good. It's also too stiff and heavy in the ailerons. And it might land okay on water in still air, but I'd hate to see what it would do in a heavy chop. Sorry. It's too small for us."

He looked unhappy. "Well, now you know why I want to sell it."

I offered to pay him for his gas, but he shook his head. "Nah. Didn't use that much."

Marie and I left. "Was it really that bad?" she asked, once we were in the air flying back to Bryan.

"You could get used to the handling weirdness. But it doesn't have the range, it doesn't have the capacity, it doesn't have the landing gear for a rough field. The only thing it has going for it is its price. I thought we might be able to get it through the door, but that one-piece composite construction means we'd practically have to rebuild it if we took the wings off. It's just not right for our needs." I smiled. "You know what Rusty says about flying boats, don't you?" Rusty was one of the flight instructors at the Brazos flying club.

She nodded and we said in unison, "They're not really boats. And they're not really planes."

We made one more stop, at Easterwood, to top off the tanks, then flew on to the ranch. The rent on the T-hangar was up in two days and Dad wasn't going to renew it.

Marie handled the landing, floating the plane on the ground effect until the last possible mph of air speed was bled off, then set it gently down. It rolled to a stop quickly on the soft field. We hand pushed it backward into the hangar, cleaned the bugs off, and locked it up.

Joey met the truck from the lumberyard at the ranch gate and let them in, riding back to the barnyard on the running board. The rest of us were waiting by the open barn door.

"Got a bill of materials for Charles Newell," said the driver, climbing down with a clipboard in his hand.

"That's me," I said.

He handed me the clipboard. "If you'll check them off while we unload, it'll go more quickly." He looked up at the barn. "Great barn. You going to extend it?"

I looked up from the clipboard. "Something like that."

They used the truck's hoist and began unloading bundles of wood, plywood siding, roofing materials, bags of dry premixed concrete, and fasteners. Last off were five forty-foot-long steel I beams, for the roof expanse.

"All there," I said, and signed it off. Joey followed them back to the gate, to secure it, and we got busy.

While Joey, Clara, and Rick moved the hay, I started up the tractor and moved it out into the yard, pointing back at the barn. Then Marie and I made a sledge out of a one-inch sheet of plywood by hammering two four-by-fours lengthwise along its edges, then screwing two heavy eye bolts near the end of each four-by-four. We left the flat side down and hooked it to the back of the tractor with chain.

Clara and Joey took up the shotgun and rifle and checked the tunnel, then opened the far side.

"All clear," Joey shouted down the passageway.

I was very nervous. All three doors to the other side were open; the barn door and both sides of the tunnel. The air pressure was obviously lower on the other side, too—a brisk wind pulled pieces of hay down the floor of the tunnel.

Rick, Marie, and I began throwing lumber onto the sledge. When it was piled to the point of instability, I dragged it down the tunnel with the tractor, Rick riding atop the sledge and steadying the load. I slowed at the far doorway until Joey waved me ahead. He and Clara stood guard outside, facing different directions. I pulled the sledge off to the side, then Rick and I spilled the material off and dashed back for another load.

It took an hour to move everything. The steel I beams were too long for the sledge, so we dragged them two at a time, with more chain.

At the end of the hour, I was exhausted. If we'd been able to switch places, things would've been better, but I was the only other person with firearms experience, and nobody else had driven the tractor. This would have to change.

We closed up the tunnel, restacked the hay, then Clara and Joey swept away the tire and drag marks in the barnyard and barn interior.

Thirty minutes later, my dad and mom drove up to find the five of us in front of the hangar "waxing" the Mooney. Actually, we'd waxed it in the morning before the lumber arrived but we had cans of wax open and were buffing it with clean rags.

"Hi," I said as they got out of the car.

"What a nice surprise," said Mom. She picked up the can of wax and peered at the contents list, squinting at the fine print.

Dad walked up, then pointed to a section of the wing I was buffing. "Missed a spot."

"Ah." I rubbed a bit of dried wax from the crack between the wing and the flap. It was the kind of thing Dad did, always pointing out the defects, and, normally, it would bug the shit out of me.

This time, however, I'd put that wax there twenty minutes before for just that purpose. I guess I'd hoped to be able to "discover" it myself. Ah well.

"Are the bags in the trunk?" I asked, polishing the last spot.

"Yes." He handed me the car keys.

Joey cupped his hands and I tossed them to him. He and Rick went to the car while I opened the Mooney's baggage compartment.

"We fueled it at Easterwood, then topped it from cans when we got back here."

"We?" he asked.

"Marie and I did some cross-country IFR work yesterday."

He nodded, turning to Marie. "How'd it go?"

"Great."

"So, how's this summer program working out, that your mother told me about?" he said, turning back to me.

"Good, so far, though it doesn't really start until Monday."

"That's good." He started to preflight the plane.

Rick and Joey returned with their luggage and I stowed it, putting Dad's flight bag in the front.

Dad completed the exterior check, double-checked the door on the luggage compartment, and climbed in to get to the left-hand seat. The Mooney has one door on the right, so the pilot has to enter before the passenger in the right-hand seat. I helped Mom up to the wing step. She buckled in and I said, "Have a great vacation. Don't bring me back one of those T-shirts that says, 'My parents went to Colorado and all I got was this lousy T-shirt.' "

Mom blinked and, after a beat, laughed. "Time will tell."

Dad said, "We'll be back next Tuesday—be sure and mow the strip."

"Right. Fly safe." I backed away without closing the door. In this heat they'd taxi to the end of the runway with it open. Dad shouted out "Clear!" and we moved over by the car. He started up the power plant, moved the props to coarse, and started taxiing away.

He did his engine run-up at the end of the runway, then, after Mom shut the door, he put the throttle to the firewall, accelerated smoothly, and lifted off. As he started his climbing turn to the north, he wagged his wings.

I lifted my hand involuntarily to wave back, even though they wouldn't be able to see me. I turned away, angrily.

"Come on, guys. Let's get back to the other side."

The temperature on the wildside was in the upper sixties and dry, a welcome change from our side's eighty-nine degrees and ninety percent humidity. The wind was from the south and it waved the buffalo grass like water. There were a few dots of black to the east that might be buffalo, but nothing close.

The air was clean in a way that surprised the nose, the mouth, and the lungs. I mean, the ranch was out in the country, but I had neighbors with propane and diesel tractors, pickup trucks, irrigation pumps. There was a coal-fired power plant forty miles away. And those neighbors who grew cotton used insecticides and fertilizers.

There were no neighbors on this side. It seemed like a sin to run the tractor here—each puff of exhaust a profane act.

This time I stood guard, circling slowly on the hillside above the doorway, while Rick and Joey stacked the materials, using four-by-fours to keep them off the ground. Marie took a tape measure and a compass and started laying out the walls, directing Clara, who marked the corners with wooden stakes, then strung string three feet off the ground.

Rick and Joey finished organizing the supplies and joined me on the hillside.

"How do you feel?" I asked.

Joey shrugged tiredly without saying anything and Rick said, "I could use a break. How much sunlight do we have?"

I looked at my watch. "Five hours, though we don't want to push it. We want to be able to see any predators."

"So," said Joey, "what do you want to do first?"

I knew exactly what should be done first, but said instead, "You're the only one of us who's worked in construction. Why don't you supervise this job?"

"Oh, yeah?" He wiped sweat from his face.

"Keep in mind that we need to get the big stuff done by Sunday afternoon, the stuff that takes all of us. You guys start flight school on Monday and Marie and I will be working on the rest off and on."

He straightened. "Where are those plans?" He walked off toward Marie.

Rick waited until he was out of earshot and laughed softly. "He bitched and bitched about this work the whole time we were stacking stuff. You made him *want* to do it."

I smiled. "Look out. He'll work us hard."

What power in another universe? Use an extension cord. Want water? Run a hose.

Okay, so I had to send Rick into town to buy enough heavy duty extension cord and industrial water hose to reach, but it worked. I had my doubts. First time I drove the tractor into the tunnel, to see if it would fit, I'd expected it to stop working halfway down the tunnel.

After all, if it's a different universe, who says it has to have the same laws?

I think I've read too much science fiction.

We set the uprights in concrete, in holes at least four feet deep. I say "at least" because the ground closest to the door was higher than the farthest ground, and we had to dig the holes deeper to keep the roof line at the proper slant (high in front, low in back). We didn't worry about leveling the floor inside, but we did keep the walls horizontally square by digging an appropriate trench in the high ground.

The concrete was set by Saturday night, and Sunday morning we raised the I beams, using the tractor as the muscle for a pulley. We installed four-by-fours as roof joists and started covering them with one-inch sheets of plywood.

"Jesus," Joey asked, taking a break from boosting panels up to Rick. "Why'd you go with one-inch? We gonna be walking around up there?"

"Maybe," I said. "But it's a sure bet that even if we don't, *something* will. I'd just as soon not have one of those sabertooths come crashing in on me."

"Ah! Good point, that. Very good point. What are we going to do about the walls, then?"

"What do you mean?"

"Some predators dig."

"Uh. I hadn't thought about that. What do you suggest?"

"Uh, well, we can dig a trench, before we put the walls in, and pour a concrete foot."

"Ow. Take too long. Look, we have to berm it in back, to blend with the hillside around the door, right?" I pointed to where the walls would enclose the doorway so that it opened into our hangar.

"Yeah."

"Why don't we berm it all the way around? Except at the doors, of course. We can pour a concrete foot there."

Joey looked at the plans. "As long as we seal the walls with plastic before we pile the dirt, that should work. But that's a lot of dirt. Wouldn't it be easier to do it my way?"

I shook my head. "I'll rent one of those minibulldozers." I pointed out at the grass. "See that bump there, and that one? That's where the airstrip goes. Gotta smooth it out. There's also a buffalo wallow to fill."

"What's a buffalo wallow?"

"Well, it starts out as a puddle, then buffalo roll in it and it gets deeper. So, next time it rains, it collects more water and it becomes even more popular. Over and over, deeper and deeper." I pointed to where the edges of a depression could be seen about 150 feet away. "The one that's over there is six feet lower than the surrounding ground."

"Where does the dirt go?"

"It goes away with the buffalo, caked in their hides."

We went back to working on the roof. We saw wolves or maybe coyotes that afternoon. Though they came as close as two hundred yards, they seemed disinclined to come closer, especially after we resumed hammering.

We quit at five, all the plywood panels in place, the first row of tar paper tacked down, and the rest of the building materials moved under the roof. We had three more hours of good light, but Joey, Clara, and Rick had to be up early.

All of us were sore. We caravaned back into town and ate at Pepe's Tacos.

"Ask him," Clara said to Rick.

Rick exhaled sharply and put his burrito down, then looked at me.

"Ask me what?" I asked.

Rick exchanged glances with Joey, then said, "What would you think about a roommate?"

"At the ranch?"

"Yeah. You have those rooms upstairs and I'm really anxious to get out of my place. My mom is about to drive me crazy."

I bit my lip. I'd thought about asking Rick *and* Joey if they wanted to stay out there, but I didn't think they'd want to, so I hadn't asked.

He saw me hesitate. "You don't have to, of course. At the rate I'm being paid, I could afford a small apartment, but I'd rather save the money. Of course I'd pay *you* rent."

"Don't be silly. It makes sense, for the project. How about you, Joey?"

Joey looked surprised. "You mean it?"

"Why not? Don't you share a room with your little brother?"

"Yeah, the little twerp. But it's air-conditioned."

"Oh." I pushed a fragment of taco shell across the linoleum. "I think the project can come up with some window air conditioners."

Marie put her diet Coke down so hard it splashed out onto the tabletop. "It's not fair!"

"What isn't?" said Clara.

"It's not fair that you *guys* get to move out, and we don't."

I spread my hands. "You're welcome, too. All of you are."

She rolled her eyes. "Like my father is going to let me move in with three guys."

"Complain to him, not us. You're eighteen, aren't you?" I looked at Clara, who was frowning thoughtfully.

"It's not that easy, Charlie," Clara said. "You know things are different for girls."

It was Rick's turn to put his drink down hard. "You just screamed at me the other day for saying 'girls' instead of women. Is it different for women?"

"It is. It is if we ever want to deal with our families again. Besides, how would your mother react if she thought I'd moved in with you? It's bad enough that she hates me and doesn't want you to see me. What do you think she'd be like then?"

Rick raised his hands. "You're right. Guys moving in with guys is not the same things as guys moving in with girls, er, women."

I leaned forward. "Well, then, why don't you and Marie get an apartment together? There's that complex just this side of the west bypass that's a lot closer to the ranch than town. They have really low rent, don't they, cause they're so far from the university?" I scribbled some figures on a napkin. "I think we could budget the rent into the project without too much trouble."

Clara blinked. "That's closer to the stable, too."

Marie looked down at the table. "I'm not sure my father would let me. I mean, I'm all he has."

Joey scowled. "You can ask. Be sure and mention that it's with Clara. He likes *her*."

"I'll try," said Marie.

And Clara said, "Me, too."

Five

"Get Out of my Life!"

I taught Marie how to drive the tractor the next day, which was a challenge, since she doesn't drive a car. Some of the concepts from flying carried over, though, since the tractor's throttle was a lever you set and left alone, like an airplane's. She practiced by mowing the airstrip.

When she finished, it was noon and hot. We took a break for lunch, then filled up the tractor and took it through the tunnel to the wildside.

I rode shotgun, literally, perched beside Marie on the rear fender, as she mowed the area under and around our unwalled roof, cutting the grass back in a hundred-foot radius.

It was cooler on this side, though the sky was clear and the sun high. It seemed like it was always cooler. When we took a break, I mentioned it to her.

"Maybe they're right about global warming. I read somewhere that if you followed the geologic record of temperature change, our earth should be in a small ice age. Maybe this side is. It's also drier here—did you notice? When a lot of water gets tied up in glacier ice, things dry out."

"That would explain why the Brazos is so much smaller on this side."

"Oh, is it? We haven't been down there yet."

"I've explored that far. The floodplain is just as big, but the river itself looks more like the Little Brazos."

We mowed the grass for this side's landing strip next, making it extra wide. We spooked rabbits, birds, and some small deer from our path, then some thin-legged red wolves. The noise from the diesel tractor seemed to puzzle them, and I relaxed a bit, not quite as worried about being jumped by something.

After a while, it became clear that the wildside landing strip couldn't go in the exact same location as its tame counterpart. Besides the buffalo wallow and the bumps I'd discovered before, a gully cut through one part, hidden by the grass.

Fortunately, many of the obstacles that were on the tame side weren't on this one. We mowed two wide strips at ninety degrees to each other, so we wouldn't be as constrained in bad crosswinds. Zero one five/one nine five and one oh five/two ninety five.

This took most of the afternoon. Afterward, I walked over the ground. It was hard soil and very dry, and, if it drained well enough, we could use it year-round.

Against my better judgment, I asked Marie if she wanted to go see a movie, or something.

"No, Charlie." She looked troubled, and added gently, "Joey and the others will be back from school in an hour."

"Right. Don't know what I was thinking." We put the tractor back in the barn and I drove her into town.

And so the week went.

Dad and Mom arrived back, as planned, on Tuesday afternoon. Mom brought me a large geode, saying, "This is not a self-referential T-shirt." She showed me a book she'd bought herself: *The Effect of Ozone Layer Depletion on Transalpine Ecosystems.*

"Great. I like the geode." She seemed pleased, then I told them about Joey and Rick moving in. Dad was okay about it once I said they were paying rent, then rushed off to make a commuter flight to DFW.

Evenings, the Five gathered in town or the ranch and, with ritual-like regularity, recounted the deeds of the day. First the students, with a steadily growing excitement about flying that Marie and I could both remember and envy. Then Marie and I would talk about the progress we'd made on the hangar.

By Friday, we'd finished the walls and had assembled the doors, large sliding panels that hung on rails. When open, they'd stick out to each side of the building, opening nearly the entire front of the hangar.

That night, at Pepe's, we met again. Rick and Joey were mock-sulking. Clara had soloed that day, after ten hours' instruction. Marie gave her a high five, followed by a hug.

"So, lunkheads, what's taking *you* so long?" I asked. Before either of them answered, I added, "Ten hours is *really* soon. It took me twenty and Marie did it in seventeen."

Joey abandoned the sulk and said, "My instructor said early next week, probably."

"Mine, too," said Rick.

We toasted Clara and talked about the weekend—we planned to move Rick and Joey into my place. I'd picked up two window air conditioners from Sears the day before. Joey was going to install them.

Marie told us, then, that her father had said yes. She looked a little troubled.

"What's the matter—didn't you want him to?"

She looked down at the table. "He's thinking of returning to Vietnam—to look for family. He was grateful that I wouldn't be here alone."

"Well, great . . . I think," said Joey. "Are you okay?"

She shrugged and the corners of her mouth turned down suddenly. "I've gotta go to the bathroom." She stood abruptly and walked off, stiff-legged.

Without saying anything, Clara rose and followed her.

Joey looked baffled. "What was it?"

I was a little angry with him. *I* knew what was the matter—why didn't he? He was the one involved with her after all.

Rick said, "You've got a big family, Joey. Marie only has her father and it might not be that safe for him to go back to Vietnam. They might not let him leave again."

"Oh." Joey said, and looked back toward the bathroom, brow furrowed. My anger lessened somewhat.

We talked in a subdued fashion about moving the guys that weekend. After a while, Clara and Marie came back.

"We'll go look at the apartments tomorrow morning while you guys are packing," Clara announced. She pointed at Rick and said, "He hasn't packed anything yet."

"I have too! All my records and all my videotapes," said Rick.

". . . and no clothes and no books and no toiletries," added Clara.

Joey laughed. "Hell, my brother's been helping me pack. He can't wait. I tell him what's going and he puts it in boxes. He'll do anything to get his own room." He didn't look at Marie, but he sidled next to her and put his arm around her and pulled her close.

Marie didn't look at him either, but she put her hand on his leg.

Peace, of sorts. Inside, I bled.

Clara, Marie, and I checked out the apartments the next morning. They picked a two-bath, two-bedroom apartment with a tiny kitchen and a decent-sized living room. I used the business checkbook to pay the deposit and three months' rent. They arranged to move in the first of the month, in two weeks. The manager asked what "Wildside Investments" was.

"We're an autonomous collective," I said, and left.

From there we went to the ranch and swept and dusted Joey's and Rick's rooms. Clara dragged the mattresses downstairs and beat them with a broom.

"I didn't think they were so bad," I told her.

"Well I'm not sleeping on it unless this dust is dealt with," she said.

"But you're not . . ." I felt my ears go hot. "Oh."

She blushed, also. "You might as well know. It's going to be obvious once Rick is living with you."

I was having trouble talking. "Y-your business," I finally managed.

She smiled and slammed the broom into the mattress.

We were under instructions to come for Rick when he called— no sooner. We didn't move Joey—he arrived with his entire family. Joey and his dad were in the lead, with Joey's belongings in his father's pickup. The rest of the crowd followed in the station wagon and when they unloaded, it seemed like a clown car from a circus, an improbably large number of persons climbing forth to stand in the barnyard looking about.

There were so many of them that it only took one trip to carry Joey's stuff up to his room. He gave them a quick tour and I offered ice tea in the kitchen. I had to resort to mason jars when the glasses gave out, and Marie chased children away from the barn and hangar.

When they left, the silence was palpable. "Whew!" said Clara. "I can't imagine that much noise around all the time."

Joey blinked. "Huh? What are you talking about?"

Rick called then and we drove out to his place in my truck, Marie and Joey in back. He had most of the stuff stacked on the porch or already loaded in his junker, a '78 Camaro with broad swaths of primer brown streaked across it. I say junker but now that the project had paid for some mechanical work, it ran fine. Joey, Clara, and he used it to get to flight school every day.

"Let's go!" he said, lifting three boxes at once and heading for the truck.

"Whoa, Samson," said Joey. "We can help too."

"Well, do it then," Rick snapped.

"Your mom home?" asked Clara, frowning.

He shook his head, dumped the boxes in the truck, and went back for more. Marie took a stack of clothes on hangers that were draped over the porch rail and I grabbed his boxed stereo.

"I'm going to get a glass of water," Joey said, and started to open the front door.

"No!" shouted Rick. "Uh, I mean, we'll go by Pepe's and get something on the way, okay?" Rick's voice pitched high, and he was licking his lips.

"Joey," I said. "I think we better grab the stuff and get going."

"Why?" asked Marie.

" 'Cause I don't think Rick's mom knows he's moving out."

Clara dropped her box on the lawn. "You said you asked her!"

"I did," said Rick. "She said no. I left a note. She gets off work soon, guys. Can. We. Go?"

We loaded up so fast that I was afraid the neighbors would think we were robbing the place and call the cops.

The next day the Five went to the mall, crowding into Rick's junker. We'd been issued the paychecks on Wednesday, direct deposited to our personal accounts. Luis had a local accountant handling that, as well as withholding, social security, and insurance payments. We'd found an okay insurance plan through the Chamber of Commerce. Of course this meant Wildside Investments had to join the Chamber. I did *not* go to any of their lunches.

Anyway, what with flight school, work on the hangar, and moving the day before, none of us had had a chance to spend some "mad money."

I ended up with a few shirts picked out with Clara and Marie's help. They bought some jewelry and some house stuff for their apartment-to-be. Joey and Rick spent their time in the record store.

We did the food court thing and a movie, then went back to the ranch, where the two couples vanished upstairs. Two different stereos played different music through closed doors.

For a while I tried to work on my lists, things to be done, materials to be purchased. My imagination, though, was too concerned with what was going on up in Joey's room, so I grabbed my flight bag, pushed the Mooney out of the hangar, and went flying.

The wind was slightly from the south and east, so I did a left climbing turn on takeoff, glancing around for other traffic and following the dirt road from the gate. That's when I saw her.

I didn't realize it was a "her" at first. There was a vaguely familiar white Volkswagen Rabbit parked at the padlocked gate, just off the main road, and a figure was climbing over the gate. I throttled back and trimmed for level flight and took a closer look. Not only was it a "her," but a "her" I recognized.

I popped the landing gear down, engaged three-quarter flaps, and did an abbreviated landing checklist while completing a very tight rectangular pattern. I turned final in a thirty-degree bank, watching my airspeed to keep from stalling, chopped most of my throttle, engaged the last notch of flaps, and put it down, quicker than I would've thought possible, straight and smooth, slipping automatically to handle the crosswind.

I shut down, jumped out of the plane, and ran for the house. I figured I had five minutes before the woman finished the mile walk from the gate.

"Rick!" I shouted as I pounded up the stairs. His door was shut and I could hear music from both rooms. I pounded on the door. "Rick!"

After about ten long seconds the stereo was turned down, then the door opened a crack. Rick, apparently wearing no clothes, was standing with the door shielding most of his body. Behind him I could see the corner of his bed. Clara's bare foot stuck out from under a sheet. "What is it?" He sounded very annoyed.

"Your mother is walking up the road from the gate."

His eyes widened. "She's what? Here?"

"Yeah," I said. "I suggest you put on a tie."

"How do you know?" he said. Clara's foot disappeared and I heard the rustle of sheets.

"I went flying I saw her. I landed quick."

"Uh, I'll get dressed. Uh, do me a favor and hide Clara's motorcycle, okay? It'll be bad enough, but if she finds her here . . ."

"Okay." I didn't wait for him to finish.

Clara's motorcycle, a 550 dirt bike, was by the front porch, and luckily she'd left the steering unlocked—I held the clutch in and pushed it across to the hangar. It was heavy—I nearly dropped it as I turned the corner and strained for a moment to hold it up. Then it was balanced with the kickstand down and I went outside and shut the hangar doors. I could see Mrs. Bockrath, then, coming around the turn in the road, past the live oak trees that shield the house and barn from the road.

I went back to the Mooney and double-checked the switches and settings. Normally I'd roll it back into the hangar at this point, but I didn't want to open the doors.

My movement in the plane attracted Mrs. Bockworth and she came straight to the plane, arriving after I'd finished the checklist.

"Hello, Charlie," she said. Beads of sweat covered her forehead and made circles on her blouse under her arms. She was an attractive woman with heavy thighs and a lined forehead. She was a registered nurse and worked in geriatrics at St. Joseph's. Her hair was dark, without a touch of gray. I wondered if it was dyed.

I pretended to be surprised. "Mrs. Bockrath! Did you climb the gate? If we'd known you were coming, we would've unlocked it."

"Why do you lock it? Especially with y'all here?"

"Insurance. This airplane costs over a hundred thousand dollars. That's why the lock and the no trespassing signs."

She shrugged. "It didn't hurt me to walk—I don't get near enough exercise." She nodded at Rick's car. "I see Rick is here. Is he inside?"

The front screen door slammed and we both turned to see Rick on the porch. He was barefooted, in jeans and a T-shirt.

"Excuse me," she said, and walked across the yard to him. He held the door for her and they entered the house.

After looking at the sky for imminent disaster, I decided I could leave the plane alone. Imminent disaster was more likely to come from inside the house.

They were talking in the kitchen, but their voices stopped when the screen door shut behind me. I walked down the hallway and paused in the kitchen door. Rick was pouring her a glass of tea as she sat at the table. He looked up at me with desperate eyes.

"Don't mind me," I said. "Just passing through. Off to my room to hit the books."

Mrs. Bockrath looked up, a stiff smile on her face. I went on down the hall and into my room, shutting the door behind me. Normally, I'd turn on the A/C, but I left it off and stood against the door, listening, sweating.

"Thank you," she said, for the tea.

Rick didn't say anything. I imagined him shrugging.

"How can you stand this heat?"

Rick answered her, sounding defensive. "I've got A/C in my room. And the window unit in the living room will cool the kitchen if necessary."

"It's not like central air, though."

"It's fine," Rick said, his voice tight.

"I want you to come home," she said.

"No."

"I insist." She sounded like she was talking to a child, firm, taking no nonsense.

"Not relevant," Rick said.

"Don't you take that tone of voice with me, young man! I didn't carry you in my body for nine months, raise you for eighteen years, to have you behave that way with me! I'm your mother and you'll do as I say!" Her voice got louder and louder.

My heart was racing and I wanted to put my fingers in my ears, to shut her out. Poor Rick. I wouldn't want to hear that from *my* mother.

She went on. "I want you to go upstairs and start bringing your things down right now!"

I was surprised at how quiet Rick's voice was when he answered. "Time for you to leave, Mom. I'll drive you back to the gate."

"Did you hear what I said, young man!"

The dam broke and Rick shouted back. "Yes! I heard every stupid word."

The intake of air as Mrs. Bockrath gasped was audible. "Who do you think you're talking t—"

He cut her off, outshouting her. "Who do you think *you're* talking to? I'm not a child. I'm not your little boy anymore. I'm eighteen, and I'm not living with you, and there isn't a damn thing you can do about it." I heard her chair scrape back and her feet scuff as she stood, then Rick said in a softer voice, "I'm sorry Dad left you, Mom, but he did, and I can't be him. Get somebody else in your life." He paused. "Get a life."

She started crying. "It's that Prentice girl. You're living with her, aren't you?"

"No, Mom. Clara is living at home, though she's moving into an apartment soon."

"With you!"

"No. With Marie Nguyen."

"But you still see her!"

There was a creak from the stairway and Clara's voice said, "Yes, Mrs. Bockrath. He still sees me."

Mrs. Bockrath's tears turned back to rage. "What are you doing here?"

Clara, with more accuracy than good sense, said, "I was invited."

"You slut! How dare you try to sink your claws into my—"

"Mother, that's enough!" Rick was very loud. "Get out of this house!"

"Well, I never!"

"Now! Out! Out! Out!" He kept repeating it, louder and louder. I opened the door to see him backing her into the hallway, past Clara, to the front door. "OUT!" He didn't touch her, but his voice and expression kept her moving backward. "OUT!" He backed her through the screen door. "Get out of my life!" he finished, and slammed the door and locked it.

He turned, a horrible lost look on his face, and stood for a moment, his back to the door. Then, with an angry shrug, he walked woodenly up the stairs. Clara looked from me to his retreating back with wide eyes, then followed him up the stairs.

I unlocked the door and went through it—Rick's mother was walking stiffly across the yard. I didn't call to her, but instead got in my pickup, started it up, and drove up beside her.

She looked at me, through the passenger side window, as if she didn't know what or who I was. Twin streaks of water cut her cheeks. I leaned across and pushed the door open.

"I'll give you a ride to the gate."

She bit her lip, then climbed in. "His room was empty. I came home and it was empty, like he'd never been there."

I didn't know what to say.

She went on. "His father did the same thing. I came home and his things were gone, packed. It was the same."

She didn't say anything else until we got to the gate and I unlocked it for her, then waited until she started her car and drove away.

She thanked me, but her face was frozen and her eyes were dead.

Six

"He's Gonna Stall."

As soon as I got back to the house, I called my mom.

"What'ch doing?"

"Cataloging my journals. I'm thinking of putting some shelves in your room—is that okay?" She sounded anxious.

"It makes sense, Mom. They're overflowing the living room, after all. Make it into a library. It'd be nice to walk around the house without knocking a pile over." Then I told her the entire saga of Rick and his mother.

"That must have been very distressing," she said. "Did you know he hadn't told his mother that he was moving in?"

"Not when we arranged it. Besides, Mom, he's eighteen. He's already said he'd get an apartment rather than live at home. Better he should live here with me and Joey."

"I suppose," she said. "What'll I do if she calls me?"

"Why do you think I'm telling you this?"

"Oh. Your father handles this sort of thing much better than I. He doesn't seem to be as disturbed by irrational behavior. Perhaps it was all that time in the military. I wish he was home."

I didn't.

She sighed. "I suppose it will work out okay. Time will tell."

The next morning Marie and I hung the hangar doors, using the tractor and a pulley to lift them into place. Pulled shut, the interior of the hangar was cavelike, lit by a thin slit of light coming between the doors.

I pounded two four-foot lengths of two-inch pipe into the dirt until they were flush with the surface of the ground, then mounted drop bolts to the doors above them. With the bolts dropped into place, we could set our guns down for once and work inside without fear of cats and wolves.

The rental company delivered the Mini-Cat, the miniature bull-dozer, at noon. The driver went over the controls, fuel, and lubrication with us, then drove away. We secured the gate behind him and drove back to the house.

Marie didn't even wait for the pickup to roll to a stop before she was out and into the Mini-Cat.

"Hey!" I said, smiling. "You don't even drive!"

She fastened the safety belt and started it up. "I'm learning," she shouted over the engine.

After driving it around the yard until she got the hang of steering, she learned how to use the blade by cleaning up the dirt road that led out to the gate, filling holes and scraping bumps.

I spent the time rigging the wildside hangar with fluorescent shop lights, stringing extension cords along the rafters from a power strip near the tunnel door. I hoped we wouldn't blow a fuse. The barn was on a hefty 30-amp breaker because of Uncle Max's power tools, but I could see using more than that before we were done.

I switched on the power strip and the lights flickered before brightening to a steady light. The new lumber and the steel roof beams contrasted strangely with the grass-covered, uneven ground below.

Marie brought the Mini-Cat in and started to change all of that. Shortly after she started, we had to open the doors to let out exhaust fumes, so I stood guard outside the door with the shotgun. She piled the excess dirt outside, along the walls. Later, after covering the lower walls in heavy plastic, we pushed it against the walls and packed it down.

I hoped the torn up buffalo grass would take and decided to water the dirt banks regularly.

The promised electronic fund transfers (including the Nature Conservancy's extra twenty-five thousand) came in and, rather than make three different flights to different locations, Marie and I drove my pickup up to Waco and shipped pigeon brides off to their lovelorn future grooms.

I was nervous—it would be a lot of trouble for them, but I was afraid the "customers" might be watching all the shipping outfits in Texas that handled live freight. Because of this, I stopped short of the freight office and pulled into a coin-op car wash.

"What are you doing?" asked Marie.

"Cammo."

I reached for a bucket from the back of the truck. The pigeons were cooing and some fluttered in the cages as I scraped the bucket across the truck bed.

"I wondered what that was for," said Marie.

The bucket had four inches of mud in it with a gardening trowel sticking up. I crouched at the front and back of the truck and plastered the license plates, careful to leave bare spots and parts of numbers uncovered. I added more to the bumpers and to the fenders behind the wheels to make it look plausible. There'd been thunderstorms off and on all week.

When we unloaded the birds at the freight office, we both wore baseball caps and sunglasses. The clerk followed us out, after I paid, making small talk, but I just said "Thank you," got into the car, and drove away, as if he wasn't saying a thing. He stared after us in the rearview mirror until we turned the corner.

I took side roads out of town, washing the mud off with a gas station hose in Mexea.

"Am I crazy, or was he suspicious?"

Marie bought pop from the machine. "You're crazy—but he was acting weird. I'm glad we don't have to ship any more birds."

I watched the rearview mirror but it was clear all the way home.

* * *

One Wednesday, Marie and I bought a small plane, accent on "small."

It was a Rans Coyote S6, a homebuilt two-seater, practically an ultralight, with a little sixty-five-horsepower engine—no electronics, no radio, no nav except for a magnetic compass. The wings and fuselage were covered with dacron sailcloth and, empty, the plane only weighed 435 pounds. It didn't have the range we needed, but it was a good start since it cruised at 100 mph, climbed at a respectable thousand feet a minute, became airborne in less than 150 feet, and, most important, the wings *folded* back so it would just fit through the tunnel.

During the demo, the owner and builder, a local flight instructor I knew slightly, turned the engine off at five thousand feet, glided east to a freshly plowed field, and actually *gained* altitude over the next several minutes, circling slowly in the thermals. I drove into town and returned with a cashier's check for twelve thousand dollars.

Marie and I spent the afternoon getting tail dragger and type qualified, making several takeoff and landings apiece.

We weren't used to taxiing in a tail dragger. Since the third wheel is in the very back, the plane tilts up on the ground, making it impossible to see directly forward when all three wheels are on the ground. So you do serpentine S-turns as you taxi, to get some sense of what's ahead. Takeoff and landing were different, too, a tail dragger requiring more of a three-point landing.

At the end of the afternoon, though, we'd had the additional type sign-offs added to our logbooks and, because Marie didn't drive, she got to fly the plane back to my place, while I drove the truck home.

Also, that day, both Rick and Joey soloed, to the relief of Clara. "Thought they'd *never* do it," she said.

She was spritzed with ice tea for her comment.

The new plane, wings folded demurely and resting out of sight in the barn, was admired.

"We should take it out this weekend," said Joey.

"Oh?" I said. "You have your private license all ready? And you've been type certified for this aircraft?"

"Hey, I can fly a plane," said Joey. "Just did." He stuck his head in the cockpit. "Hey, somebody stole the steering yokes."

"They're control sticks," said Marie. "Another reason why you're not flying this plane until you get more hours in. Besides, we're building the control tower this weekend, remember?"

"Work, work, work. If it's not school it's build, build, build. Don't we ever get a break?"

I patted the side of the plane. "If we get the tower done, Marie and I can take turns flying with you guys on Sunday."

"All right!" Joey said.

"If."

Thursday morning, Marie and I flew the Coyote, running through basic and emergency procedures, drilling with simulated forced landings. After four hours of this, including a stop to refill—the plane only held eighteen gallons—we landed back at the grass strip, taxied into the barnyard, and shut down. While Marie topped off the tanks, I folded the wings back, then we started to push it through the tunnel.

"Damn! Hold it!" I'd been steering from behind, by lifting the tail end of the plane by the tail wheel assembly. Marie was pulling from the front. The prop had to be turned forty-five degrees to clear the top of the door, but the folded wings cleared both sides of the door just fine. However, the tail section was too wide.

Marie squeezed back past the plane and I set the tail down.

"What's the prob—oh. Shit."

Fortunately, the tail spar was not one piece. It took us an hour to take one half of the horizontal stabilizer off, which let us get the thing all the way into the wildside hangar. I could've pulled it off in less than fifteen minutes, but I wanted it to go back on *exactly* like it came off, so we labeled all the fasteners and Marie did a sketch. Working under the fluorescents, we reassembled and double-checked the tail assembly and unfolded the wings.

If the grass hadn't grown too fast on our wildside runways, we could just open the doors and go.

We peeked out into the wildside. A gentle breeze blew from the north and the sky had scattered cumulus about ten thousand feet.

"What do you say? Shall we take it up?" Marie had a wistful expression on her face.

I licked my lips, seriously tempted. If we were right about the wildside, no human had ever flown there. I'd been limited to the distance I could walk or drive the tractor.

"I don't think we should," I said.

She said, "Ah, come on, Charlie. What's all this for, if not that?" She took my arm. "Pretty please?"

I winced and pulled away from her. "Save it for Joey." Even I was appalled by the bitterness in my voice.

She frowned and turned away.

"I'm sorry," I said. "I didn't mean it."

"No, Charlie. I knew how you felt about me. I just didn't realize you still did."

She turned back toward me, but I couldn't face her. I reexamined the fasteners on the horizontal stabilizer. In a lighter tone, she asked, "So, why do you think it's a bad idea to go flying?"

I didn't say anything for a moment. "Who you going to file our flight plan with?"

"We go flying from the grass strip all the time without filing."

I smiled without humor. "Sure, on the tame side. If we go down in Brazos County, don't you think somebody's going to see us? Especially when we land in their pasture or parking lot? If we go down in Brazos County on the tame side, do you think something's going to eat us?"

"Oh."

"We need radios and somebody here who can come after us. Christ, I almost think we need another plane."

"Why?"

I walked to the crack between the hangar doors and peered through. "You want to drive my truck across the river? There aren't any bridges. I don't think it'd get past that stream at the end of the runway."

"So we don't go over the river. We stay right here, over the field. And only one of us flies it, so the other can come get them if they're forced down."

I thought about it.

"Okay, I want to get the wind sock from the other strip."

We went back to the other side and got the wind sock and guns. In addition, I hooked our makeshift sledge to the tractor and drove it through the tunnel.

"Why?" asked Marie.

"If I have to come get you, because you crashed, I don't want to carry you back. Also, I'm pretty sure," I said, patting my belly, "that you couldn't carry me back, but you *can* drive the tractor."

We had to do one more thing before I'd consider flying. We opened the hangar doors cautiously, Marie doing the pushing, while I stood by with the rifle. Then I took two old broom handles and some cardboard out across to the other side of the runway and pounded the broomsticks into the ground and, by poking holes in the cardboard, mounted the cardboard vertically.

Then I went back and handed the shotgun to Marie. She took it very carefully, respectfully, and, I think, fearfully.

"This is the safety. If this little red thing is sticking out, it's ready to fire. If it's in, it can't fire. You pump a shell into the chamber with that, just like the movies." She worked the action, pointing the barrel in the air. "That's right. That leaves three in the magazine." I nodded at the target. "Go to it."

"Do I have to?" She didn't look happy.

"Let's play it out. I crash out there in the tall grass and you get the tractor and come for me. On the way there, a sabertooth decides the noise from the tractor is more interesting than scary. Or, you get to the plane and I'm disabled and the wolves are pulling at my unconscious body. Or—you crash, are *not* unconscious, but before I can get to you, a sabertooth does?"

"Isn't this a little paranoid? Every predator we've encountered has avoided us."

I bit my lip. "I've thought about this a *lot*. Doesn't mean I'm right, but consider the consequences of being underprepared, rather than overprepared. If we walk a little wary, ready for trouble, the worse that can happen is what we expect." I used my most telling argument. "We don't know what happened to Uncle Max."

"Ah, I see your point." She pulled the gun to her shoulder, sighted, and pulled the trigger. The right fringe of the right target disintegrated and Marie jumped at the noise. She fired again, but flinched away in anticipation of the bang and the shot missed completely.

"There were guns at the border when we left Vietnam," she said, almost to herself. Then she aimed carefully and squeezed the trigger. The cardboard target on the right flopped to the ground, the pole cut in half. She shifted to the other target and put a burst into its top central portion.

She turned back to me. "Satisfied?"

"Yeah." I showed her how to reload. "Fire in the air first. Loud noises are scary. You might not have to hit anything."

I offered to flip a coin to see who would go first, but she shook her head. "You discovered it, Charlie. You should go first."

I wasn't going to argue. We preflighted the Coyote, strapping the thirty-ought-six in the right-hand seat. I put an extra clip in my pocket. Marie shut the doors, then took the shotgun up the hill at the back of the hangar, where she could climb up onto the roof. When she was on top, I climbed in, strapped in, squeezed the primer bulb, turned on the ignition, and hit the starter button.

I did the run-up and magneto check while taxiing. If there was anything in the high grass waiting to pounce, the noise of the little Rotax engine probably scared the shit out of it. I reached the downwind end of zero-one-five, used the flap handle between the seats to extend full flaps, and pushed the throttle all the way to the instrument panel. Even in the soft grass, the wheels came off the ground in under 150 feet. I kept the plane down in the ground effect until it reached seventy miles per hour, then climbed at a thousand feet a minute until I was fifteen hundred feet above the field.

I flew a basic rectangular traffic pattern, then, keeping clear of the Brazos and watching my wind drift so I stayed over the hangar.

We've marked our planet, so much, we humans. I didn't realize how much until I looked out over the wildside. No buildings, no roads, no telephone and power lines, no plowed or unplowed fields with nice straight lines. The hangar, below, looked alien, and even the Brazos, longtime aerial landmark, was different, smaller, with a slightly different path.

From fifteen hundred feet I could see for fifty miles. Strange to see so far without seeing a trace of human activity. Saw a dust cloud to the east, so large I thought it might be a grass fire, but it was buffalo. In the reeds lining the river, I saw something larger even than buffalo, with a long, mobile nose that tore at the tree branches. I was tempted to buzz it, to get a closer look, but we'd agreed to stay away from the river. I did one more circuit, then drifted down under minimum power and full flaps to land safely in the grass.

Marie met me in front of the hangar and traded places, taking the shotgun with her, instead of the rifle.

"There's a small group of mammoth in the river bottom," I told her, and described what they were doing and where, then I backed away and took up a perch on the roof.

She was up for thirty minutes and the only thing she said, after landing, was, "It makes me feel so *small*."

"Yeah."

We put the plane away in silence.

The control tower was really the "Richardson Prefab Deluxe Deer Blind," a thirty-foot bolt-together galvanized steel tower with a small shack at the top. "Comes complete with icebox, gun stand, lightning rod, and bench seats for four hunters." A truck dropped it off in bundles and boxes late Friday, and Marie and I moved it into the wildside hangar with the tractor.

It was designed to set up out in the woods, on unprepared, uneven ground. After some discussion with Joey, I decided to mount it at the back of the hangar, with two of its legs shortened and mounted on the roof, and its other two legs resting on the hill behind, four feet lower.

Joey cut and framed a square hole with a raised lip in the roof, then built a ladder inside, against the back wall, so the hole opened beneath the tower. While the rest of us were assembling the tower, he built a tar paper-covered hatch.

When we were done, we covered the outside framework of the tower with hardware cloth, heavy wire mesh with half-inch-square holes. This let us climb from inside the hangar to inside the control shack without exposing ourselves to predation.

"Think this stuff would really stop one of those sabertooths?" Clara asked.

"It'd slow 'em down," I said.

When we were done, late Saturday, we crowded into the top, opened all four upward-swinging panels that were the "windows," and watched the sun go down. Joey, last through the hatch in the middle of the floor, handed up a small cooler.

"Anybody want a beer?" he asked.

I looked at my watch—it was eight-thirty. "If you want to fly tomorrow morning, no beer after midnight."

"Good grief, don't be such a prick, Charlie. Didn't I bust my ass all day? Don't I deserve to relax now?"

I held up my hands. "Sure. Relax away. Just don't drink past midnight, okay?"

He shook his head. "I know the drill. They go over it in ground school several times and we've even been tested on it."

I thought, but didn't say, *and they told you about DWI in Driver's Ed*. "Sorry. I'll take one."

He blinked. "A beer? You?"

"Sure. We all worked hard today. The trapdoor is great."

"I'll take one," said Rick.

"Me, too," said Clara.

Joey looked at Marie and she said, "Oh, what the hell."

"Wow, two firsts." Joey handed out the cans.

"Where'd you get the beer, Joey?" asked Marie.

Texas drinking age was twenty-one. We were all still eighteen. Marie, in fact, had only just turned eighteen.

"Rick got it," Joey said. "He's so tall, nobody cards him."

I sipped slowly at the beer. I didn't like it. Neither, apparently, did Marie. When Joey reached for another, she said, "Here—I'm not going to finish this one."

Joey crunched the can he was holding into a compact clump and started to pitch it out of the tower.

"Don't! Uh, please." I held out my hand for it. "We don't leave trash around. That's what people do on the other side. This place is clean—let's keep it that way."

He shrugged and handed it to me.

"Besides, if we leave trash around—food trash—we'll attract scavengers. Let's keep the animals from associating this place—or us—with supper."

The sun went down and a million stars shone like diamonds. We closed up the tower and went back to the tame side.

Early Sunday morning I went over to the airport pilot's store and dropped a thousand dollars on a portable intercom station powered by a nine-volt battery, and two handheld aviation transceivers. On the way back I picked up Marie. Clara drove out on her motorcycle and was cooking breakfast for Rick when we got back.

I went over to the wildside and mounted the intercom box and the handheld radio between the seats, behind the flap handle. Later, I'd add an external antenna to improve range, but the two radios would handle anything we did today and the intercom set would let us plug in two command sets and talk normally over the noise of the Rotax engine.

Clara and Rick showed up, next, so I sent Clara up into the

control tower with one transceiver, and Rick and I preflighted the Coyote.

"You take the left-hand seat," I said. "I'll probably land it—the Cessnas you've been flying are a lot heavier, but you can take it off, if you promise to let go of the controls if I tell you to."

"Gee, I left my logbook in my room."

I shook my head. "I'm not an instructor—you can't log it as instruction time and you can't log it as solo time. And even if you could—we're not in Texas anymore, Toto."

We started it up and I showed him how to do S-turns as he taxied, to avoid buffalo and other obstacles. He got the hang of it after a few wild swings back and forth. Luckily, we didn't have to worry about other aircraft or running off the runways—we'd mowed them very wide.

At the end of the runway, he lingered over the checklist, spending a lot of time trying to get the feel of the stick. The Cessna he'd been taking instruction on had a steering wheel-like control yoke. We did the engine run-up, checked both magnetos, then set flaps and pushed the throttle all the way in.

In just the two days since we'd flown it, the grass had grown enough to add another fifty feet to the takeoff run. I watched Rick carefully, ready to shove the stick forward if he pulled it back far enough to stall the plane, but he got it right, letting just a little stick lift the nose and start us on up.

"Climb at seventy," I told him. "A little more back stick. Level off at fifteen hundred—you can take the engine back to 1800 rpm. That should give you about ninety miles per hour of indicated air-speed."

He left it a little late, leveling off initially at 1570, then yo-yoing between 1575 and 1450. "We're getting too far from the field. Leave it for a second and do a standard left one-eighty."

He complied, managing to trim it at fifteen hundred. Back over the field we did a spiral climb to five thousand, where I took him through low-speed stalls and standard left and right turns.

"It's quicker than the Cessna," Rick said. "To respond, I mean."

"It's a thousand pounds lighter."

I left him in control all the way to the base leg and took over at five hundred feet. He'd been training with a tricycle landing gear and I didn't want to confuse him with a different landing technique.

Clara was next. She really seemed to have a knack for flying, getting the feel of the controls almost immediately. Rick's turns, while competent, had been slightly uncoordinated, the stick moving before or after the rudder. Clara's turns were precise and when I told her to level off at fifteen hundred, she hit 1495 and smoothly edged up the last few feet. I saw why she soloed after only ten hours. We went through the same turns, climbs, and stalls before Joey's voice came on the radio. "Hey! There are people waiting, you know."

"Asshole," Clara said on the intercom.

"Hold your water, Joey," I transmitted. "You'll get your turn."

We stayed up another fifteen minutes. Clara took it all the way to final approach before I took over.

The tanks, two nine-gallon tanks in the wings, were down a third, so we topped off with a jerry can and I turned it over to Marie and Joey after describing what we'd done.

Joey started to climb into the left-hand seat but Marie hooked his collar and said, "Hold it, Hotshot."

"He turned, annoyed. "What? You want the left-hand seat?"

"Preflight, Joey. Preflight."

He looked at me. "Didn't you guys preflight?"

"Sure," I said. "So?"

"They're not going up in it," Marie said. "*We* are. And, even if things were perfect when it was checked over, it's been through two landings since then."

Joey grumbled, but involved himself in the preflight, looking at the oil level and draining gas into a jar to check for water. Clara and I climbed into the tower to join Rick.

"Joey taxis too fast in the Cessna, too," Rick was saying as I followed Clara up through the hatch. I stood up in time to see the Coyote turn too fast at the end of the runway and spin sideways

270 degrees. The tail wheel plowed a furrow in the grass.

I picked up the radio and transmitted, "Having a little trouble out there?"

Marie's voice came back. "Just practicing a few S-turns." Her voice was tight.

"Are those printed esses or cursive?" I said, but I kept my thumb off the transmit button.

The Coyote, at a more sedate pace, straightened, then accelerated down the field, lifting off sharply.

Too sharply.

"He's gonna stall," said Clara, but the nose dropped abruptly, before too much airspeed was lost, and the plane settled into a shallow climb to build up airspeed. When it turned, the bank was clean and sharp and I knew that Marie was at the controls.

We went down to meet them when they landed, thirty minutes later. Joey jumped out of the Coyote before it stopped rolling and walked past us, stiff-legged. Marie leaned out the engine fuel mixture, then, when it died, switched off the magnetos and went through the rest of the engine shutdown checklist.

I walked up to her door and swung it up.

She was crying.

I stood there frozen, helpless, then Clara pushed the rifle into my hands and shoved me aside. She unbuckled Marie's restraining harness, helped her out of the Coyote, and walked her past Rick and me, into the hangar.

I looked at Rick and he shook his head, a distant expression on his face.

"Shit," I said.

We refueled the plane and put the control locks in place. When we rolled it back into the hangar, Marie and Clara were sitting by the control tower ladder. Marie wasn't crying anymore, but the corners of her mouth turned down sharply.

I didn't know whether to be happy or sad. I wanted to fire Joey, to kick him off the project, but doubted very much that the secret would stay a secret if I did. Maybe they'd break up and I'd have my chance with Marie. Maybe I should give him a raise.

"You okay?" I asked Marie.

She shrugged.

"What happened?"

"I don't want to talk about it."

"Oh." I stood there awkwardly for a moment, then went through the tunnel to the tame side. I found Joey sitting in the kitchen drinking a beer.

He didn't look happy.

I tried again. "What happened?"

"I fucked up. I wanted to show Marie what a great pilot I am and I screwed up. Didn't taxi right, nearly stalled us on takeoff—she took over until we were at altitude—and she didn't say anything about it, just 'I have control' when she took the stick." He lifted the beer again and drank in large swallows. "I shouted at her—I've never shouted at her before. She didn't deserve that."

I leaned against the doorway, my arms crossed: "Well, *I* don't think so. It's not her fault that she does something better than you do. She's been at it longer, after all."

He looked down at the tabletop. "I know I was wrong—give me a break."

"Don't tell *me* She was crying when she got out of the Coyote."

He winced. "Oh, shit."

I stood aside for him as he got up and went out, heading for the front door. He left his beer can on the kitchen table. I hefted it—it was almost empty. I drained what was left into the sink and then stomped it repeatedly until it was flat—and then some.

Seven

"Do You Have the Mossberg Stainless Steel Twelve-gauge Pump with the Optional Pistol Grip?"

Luis Cervantes called me Monday morning. "Let's go flying."

"Okay."

It was our code phrase for "let's talk and not on the phone." I met him at Easterwood airport, in the pilots' lounge. He took coffee and I took tea in paper cups, dropped our money into the can, and walked outside to stand in the shade.

"There are inquiries," he said.

"Who is asking who?"

"The public account in Austin has had inquiries about the account ownership. They didn't find out—but Richard did arrange to be told if it happened."

I turned my head to watch a twin-engine plane do its takeoff run. "Who did the asking?"

"The San Diego Commercial Bank *and* the People's Bank of San Francisco."

I licked my lips. "The San Diego Zoo and the Sierra Club."

"Well, those are the banks their payments came from."

The plane rose off the pavement smoothly. The landing gear came up. "What's their next step?"

Luis was watching the plane also. "Um. They'll probably check the Austin city records to see who's doing business as 'The Lazarus Company.' "

"What will that show?"

"Nothing—we didn't file a D.B.A. So, they'll go back to the bank and try again, more subtly this time. The information is private, but you'd be amazed how easy it is to get. If you pose as an IRS agent, for instance, and phone in and say something like 'I need to send a copy of their paperwork to the company but all we have is their account number—could you give me that address?' "

"Will that work?" I asked, worried.

"Usually. But we arranged for extra care on this account. If the IRS calls, the bank will wait for a subpoena and identification before they release any information. Ditto any other inquiries, no matter who they pose as." He shrugged. "We used the bank most of the Texas legislature uses. They're used to spotting unauthorized inquiries—the press is after that stuff all the time."

"So they won't find out?"

Luis turned his attention to the passenger terminal on the other side of the airport. An American Eagle turboprop was whining up to speed. "They'll find out . . . eventually. But then it'll just point to him and he's a lawyer acting for a client. They'll have to involve the authorities and make some sort of claim at criminal activity to get the information out of him." The ground crew pulled the chocks away from the turboprop's wheels and it began to roll.

I said, "So, for a while, we're safe."

The plane reached the end of the taxiway and turned onto the active runway. Without stopping, the turbines increased to one hundred percent and it took off, climbing steeply, more steeply than any plane I'd ever flown.

"For a while," said Luis.

On Monday, Marie and I went to Triangle Sporting Goods, a store that sold guns and hunting supplies but also specialized in "home security" products. They have a giant plastic moose on the roof that the university fraternities are always stealing.

Business was slow—deer and duck season didn't start for months—but a man was browsing the fishing lures. We walked up to the gun counter.

"What can I do you for, today?" asked the clerk, a balding man with thick glasses whose Lacoste sports shirt covered a slight potbelly.

I took a list from my pocket. I'd prepared it after going through the gun magazines with Joey and Clara. "Do you have the Mossberg stainless steel twelve-gauge pump with the optional pistol grip?"

"Sure." He turned and took a pump shotgun from the shelf behind him. Instead of a stock it had a black plastic pistol grip. "Eighteen-inch barrel. Uses three-inch or two-and-three-quarter-inch shells, adjustable choke—"

"Okay," I said, before he got warmed up. "I'll take five."

"Five? Five shotguns?"

"To start with. You have them in stock?"

"Uh, yeah. We've got six in stock."

"Great. I also need vehicle mounting clips for the shotguns, the vertical kind. Like those used in police cars."

"Ah, the locking kind."

I thought about it. "Do they hold the gun securely when they're unlocked?" I didn't want to have to fumble for a key when a sabertooth charged.

"Yeah, but anybody can grab them out of the car, then. Kids."

"Ah. I understand." No kids where we were going—very few cars, though I intended one of the clips for my truck. "I'll need eight of the clips. I'll also need shoulder straps for the shotguns."

"Hold up, there. Let me start gathering this stuff together. How're you going to pay?"

"When we have the total, I'll go get a cashier's check—how's that?"

He blinked. "Fine. Just fine. What else do you need?"

I looked at the list. "Cap-Stun gas in the eight-ounce cans."

"You're not going hunting, are you? Not with this pepper Mace stuff."

I shook my head. "Home security. I'll take ten of those air horns and twenty replacement air cartridges."

"The boating horns?"

"Yeah." These were very loud compressed gas horns used on small power- and sailboats. They were loud enough to hurt—I hoped animals would think so.

He began piling the merchandise behind the counter, running a tape on the adding machine as he went along. For a moment I looked down at the 9-mm automatic handguns in the glass case, but you have to be over twenty-one in Texas to buy a handgun. To buy a shotgun or rifle you only had to be eighteen. I added ten pads of tear-off targets, five sets of hearing protectors, five sets of wrap-around shooting glasses, a wall mount gun rack with ammo drawers, a case of shells with bird shot, a case of three-inch shotgun shells with number three buckshot, and a case of shotgun shells with rifled slugs.

"I think that's it. What's the damage?"

"With tax, it comes to twenty-three-sixteen and sixty-three cents."

I wrote it down, went over to my bank, and came back with the check. I filled out the registration papers and we packed everything in the truck, stacking the ammo on the floor and the guns behind the seat. I didn't think it would be a good idea to leave them in the pickup bed in back with everything else.

We installed the wall rack on the back wall of the wildside hangar, hung the guns, and stored the ammo.

On Tuesday morning, Marie and I rode over to the Texas Institute of Aviation with the rest of the gang to start an Airframe & Power course, i.e., how to be an aircraft mechanic. While the three of them were flying, the two of us had classroom in the morning and lab in the afternoon. We'd be doing it for six weeks, three days a week, and we'd finish up about the time they finished their flight courses.

We also signed Marie up on a Monday, Wednesday, and Friday schedule so that she'd finish up her IFR and commercial ratings at the same time.

On the way home that afternoon, I said, "There's a skydiving class on Sunday. Four hours classroom and practice in the morning and two static line jumps in the afternoon."

"Why would anyone want to jump out of a perfectly good airplane?" said Rick. He was driving, Clara beside him. I was also in the front seat—Joey and Marie were fondling each other in the back.

"Well, suppose you ended up in a plane that decided to stop working? However, my reasons have more to do with runway preparation. There's a lot of flat land out there, but unless we walk over it, inspect it up close, we're gonna miss some of the holes and rocks and logs. If we jump people in, before we land, they can inspect and mark a runway."

"And if it's totally unsuitable for a runway?"

I shrugged. "We walk to where the terrain *is* suitable."

Joey leaned forward. "We're moving the girls on Saturday. Aren't we ever going to have a weekend off?"

"Probably not," I said. "Everybody in for Sunday? I have to reserve space in the class."

They all agreed, though Clara seemed less enthusiastic about it. "Whatever you do," she said, "don't tell my parents. The flying thing is freaking them out as it is. My mom'd have a cow."

"Um. Perhaps you shouldn't tell my father, either," said Marie.

Rick, with a wooden expression, said, "Well, you can tell my mom. I don't care if she has a cow."

Rick's mom called him every evening. Rick no longer answered the phone at the ranch, either screening it with the answering machine or making us get it. As I was tired of lying to his mother, I also screened calls. Joey didn't care, though. Even if Rick was sitting right in front of him, Joey cheerfully told her, "Rick's not in, Mrs. Bockrath, can I take a message?"

My mom received a call from Mrs. Bockrath, as well. She reported the conversation to me.

"I was very distressed when Charlie moved out, too. It's hard to let go, isn't it?"

"He's too young!"

"This culture doesn't handle teens very well, does it? Young or not, he's legally an adult. What do you expect me to do?"

I'd spent an anxious week worrying about what my father would think, but last week, when I'd had supper with my parents, Mom told Dad about it. He'd shaken his head and said, "Woman has a screw loose. Keep the gate locked." Sometimes Dad is okay.

Anyway, Clara said, "No need to tell your mother *anything*. She's called my mother several times and said *horrible* things about me. Last time my mother hung up on her."

Rick's wooden expression became a grimace, and his hands tightened on the steering wheel. "Let's not talk about her, okay?" Clara glanced sideways at him. "Sorry."

I set up a target range on the wildside, using bales of hay for the targets and the hill by the hangar as a backstop, but it was Clara who taught everyone how to shoot.

"Look," she said. "Without the stock it's not really designed to fire like a rifle. You don't hold it up to your cheek and sight down the barrel. Instead, hold it like this." She held her right hand, gripping the pistol grip, to her side just below the ribs. Her left hand was on the pump, supporting the barrel. "Be consistent. Pivot at the waist to adjust your aim right and left. Raise and lower your left hand, uh, that is your non-trigger hand, to raise or lower your aim."

We all put our ear protectors on and then she turned abruptly to fire, not at the target before her, but the one on the end. Then she shot at each target in turn, as fast as she could work the pump.

Five shots and five targets. We were shooting at thirty feet and with bird shot and the targets were large enough that the grouping was visible. She was slightly high and slightly to the left of dead center, but it was the same on each target.

She turned back to us. "Not too bad. I'm used to a twenty-gauge." She looked at the sun—it was after seven. "We got another half hour. Let's make some noise."

We set up group target practice for twice a week, after that, with individuals practicing whenever they wanted.

Whenever we were carrying the shotguns for protection, we loaded them with buckshot and rifled slugs, alternating every shell. We were also carrying the Cap-Stun gas, the air horns, and extra ammo hung on a nylon harness.

"Charlie's Rangers," Joey said.

"Give me a break," I said. "More like a street gang." But I wasn't unhappy with the thought.

Money drained out of the account at an alarming rate. Sure, there was still more than three hundred thousand dollars, but the insurance payments and the withholding and Luis's cut and the bookkeeper's fees and the instruction fees and our weekly salaries steadily pulled the balance down.

And I bought things.

I bought a ground station for Wildside Base, several thousand dollars' worth of radios and antennas. One transceiver for voice traffic, one transmitter to broadcast a continuous AM homing signal (Morse "W" for wildside), and a transmitter for ATIS. ATIS stands for Automatic Terminal Information Service, a continuous loop broadcast of local weather and airport procedures.

Normally a human would record this info every half hour or so onto a tape loop, but we were not exactly overstaffed. My next purchase was a PC-based automated weather station which took input from externally mounted sensors and logged it *and* used a voice board to transmit the information on the ATIS transmitter, using a clear but mechanical tenor voice. It sounded something like the voices used by the phone company's directory information. "Time One Zero Four Five. Temperature Seven Five. Wind One Two Knots at Three Zero Five. Barometric Pressure Two Nine Point Three. Precipitation Zero." Pause. "Time One Zero Four Six. Temp—" You get the idea.

By the time I finished mounting antennas, rain gauge, wind vane, and anemometer on the roof of our control tower, it looked more like some scientific outpost than a deer blind. I ended up mounting the wind sock on the front edge of the hangar roof, to keep it from fouling on the antennas.

More money—I had another phone line run to the house with an extension to the barn. The phone company charged me twelve hundred dollars to run the extra line from the road. When they were done, we ran phone line through the tunnel and put extensions in the hangar and control tower.

Had an electrician run a 220 line from the meter at the house to a new breaker box in the barn. When he was done, Joey and Marie replaced the extension cord with fixed wiring, replacing the power strips with permanent outlets. More money.

Bought a voice-activated recorder for the tower to record incoming transmissions when there wasn't anyone to hear them. More money.

Had a security firm install an electric eye across the dirt road on the inside of the gate. If anybody drove or walked across it, it set off a buzzer in the house, barn, and (after we wired it) the wildside hangar. More money.

Bought a small tank-trailer, four feet around and six and a half feet long which held six hundred gallons of aviation gasoline. The company that serviced Easterwood and Coulter field agreed to come by and fill it as needed. If we lowered it four inches by letting air out of its tires, we could pull it through the tunnel with the tractor.

Bought parachutes (parasails, actually), bought four more portable aviation transceivers, bought wilderness survival kits, bought a thousand-dollar celestial sextant. More money.

The account dropped below three hundred thousand.

Joey jumped but admitted later that he didn't particularly like it. Marie jumped without hesitation, landing with a huge grin on her face. Clara wanted to go again, right *now*. Rick froze in the doorway.

"You don't have to," I shouted into his ear over the noise of the engine and the wind in our faces. "Nobody will blame you for good sense." Then, with a twinge of guilt, I added, "Your mother would probably prefer it."

That did it. His clenched hands released the doorframe and he thrust himself convulsively out into the void.

I'd been so worried about who would jump and who wouldn't that I hadn't realized how terrified *I* was. I had to close my eyes to jump and didn't open them until after the chute opened.

At that point it was fine. After all, it was just another aircraft, right? Steerable, with *excellent* stalling characteristics. I turned into the wind and ended up bringing the chute down twenty feet away from Clara, flaring as much as I could and falling in the fashion we'd practiced all morning. It was a halfhearted effort, though. My downward speed was almost nil.

The second jump was better all around. Knowing what was going to happen eliminated most of Rick's fear. Joey still didn't like it, but expected he could do it. Marie and Clara wanted more free fall, and I was able to keep my eyes open.

We signed up for tandem free fall sessions the following Sunday, weather permitting.

The fourth week of my A&P course, I took delivery on a two-year-old Maule M-7-235 Super Rocket. Contrary to its name, it wasn't a rocket, but an airplane—a STOL single-engine tail dragger that, with the optional jump seat in the baggage area, could seat five. This particular plane had been used by a West Texas rancher and flown off of dirt strips on his ranch. It cost us eighty thousand and had minimum IFR avionics.

Once insurance had been arranged, we used it to commute to T.I.A. for classes, all five of us jammed in, Marie stuck in the jump seat because she was lightest and Rick in the right-hand seat because he was longest.

On days of the week when I wasn't along, Marie was Pilot-In-Command and the others took turns in the right-hand seat. We also received a significant reduction in the T.I.A. course fees by providing the Maule as a teaching aircraft. Marie, Joey, Rick, and Clara took some of their instruction and solo practice time in it, once they'd been type certified.

"It makes you lazy," said Clara. "I go back to the Cessna Skylane and my rudder work suffers."

In most planes, a turn is executed by banking with the control yoke while giving an appropriate amount of right or left rudder with the rudder pedals. On the Maule, the ailerons were spring linked to the rudder servo tab, making normal balanced turns possible even if one's feet were completely off the rudder pedals.

Of course you still had to use rudder for slipping sideways on crosswind landings, or spin recovery, and other maneuvers. Still, the Maule was a pleasant and forgiving plane to fly as well as being tough as nails.

We also did the periodic maintenance in our A&P lab, having it signed off by our instructor, who was not only A&P certified, but also an Aircraft Inspector, the next level up.

Later, we went back to driving, while the Maule sat in the A&P hangar and, under our instructor's guidance, Marie and I removed and refastened the wings, did rivet work, and completely overhauled the engine, even though it wasn't due for another two hundred hours. We also added Maule Air's optional auxiliary fuel tanks in the outer wing to extend the range.

By the time we finished the course, I was confident of our ability to do scheduled maintenance ourselves, and, most importantly, get the Maule through the tunnel *and* flying on the other side.

It was easy to arrange the surprise—after all, I had three more days a week out of class. We were flying the Maule home from T.I.A., having completed written and practical exams. We were done, carrying certificates, licenses, and in general, good feelings.

Marie had the jump seat in back, while Clara and I sat in the middle. Joey and Rick were at the controls, with Rick calling the shots.

Scary. It was the first time that we'd flown with them when neither Marie nor I were within reach of the controls.

They did fine. If they flew by the numbers more than by feel, they at least *knew* the numbers. This pitch attitude at this power setting results in this rate of climb. An approach speed of 1.3 times full-flap-stall speed results from this power setting and this pitch attitude. V sub x, best angle of climb, is achieved at this airspeed. V sub y, best rate of climb, is achieved at that airspeed.

Joey put the Maule down on the grass at a slightly higher speed than I would've, but I didn't feel in danger, and the grass stopped the plane without undue wear on the breaks.

"Pretty good," I said, when they finished the engine shutdown.

Marie hit my arm from behind. "Pretty good? It was great! You guys are good pilots and don't let anybody tell you differently!"

Everybody piled out. Unlike the Mooney, the Maule had plenty of doors—pilots' doors port and starboard and a double door starboard rear that let large loads be stowed.

"Well," Joey asked, "how do we celebrate?"

It was the first time we talked about it. By common consent we'd avoided the subject since it was possible that one of us could fail our exams at first attempt.

However, I'd talked privately to their instructors and they'd been confident.

"Why don't we get out of the sun and *then* decide," I said.

I held back and entered the house last.

"What's this?" said Marie, the first one in.

There were four large boxes, wrapped, with each of their names writ large upon. They looked from them to me as I came in the door, curious.

Joey said, "*That's* why you went back into the house this morning!"

"I'm just glad none of you failed. I would've had to dash in here ahead of you and hide them." I grinned. "Congratulations, guys." They still looked at me. "Go on! Open 'em."

There was a great rending of paper. I stepped into the kitchen and pulled the bottle of champagne from the refrigerator and the glasses from the cabinet.

"Utterly cool!" said Clara.

The boxes held flight jackets, G-1 navy goatskin, with lamb fur collar made by Cooper, the company that makes them for the navy. The guys' last names were embroidered on the left breast, and on the back was embroidered a sabertooth's head in profile, mouth open, snarling and the words WILDSIDE INVESTMENTS below.

I opened the champagne and the cork ricocheted off the ceiling. Clara caught foam in one of the glasses. I poured for all.

"Don't you get a jacket, Charlie?" asked Rick.

I put down the now-empty bottle and opened the closet. Another flight jacket with NEWELL on the front hung there. Even though it was too warm for it, I put it on, like the others, and took my glass from Clara.

"What do we toast?" said Rick.

"Finishing flight school!" said Joey. "The end of all that work."

I shook my head. "I'll toast the end of flight school," I said. "And I'll toast new pilots and techs. But it's not the end of 'all that work.' " I raised my glass. "To the beginning."

Part 2

Explorations

Eight

"There Are Wolves."

"**P**arking brake," Clara said.

"On." I said.

"Flaps at three-quarter."

I clicked the flap handle three notches. "Check."

"Elevator trim four degrees up."

I dialed it in. "Check."

"Calibrate altimeter to 370 feet."

I twisted the adjustment knob. "Check."

"Dial heading to one-eight-four."

I twirled the knob until the gyro-driven heading indicator matched the magnetic compass. "Check."

"Set fuel to fullest tank."

They were all topped off, but we'd used a bit taxiing to the end of the runway, so I switched over to the unused left tank. "Check."

"Set propeller control to full increase."

I pushed the prop control knob all the way in.

"Mixture to rich."

I pushed that knob all the way into the dash. "Check."

"Carburetor heat to cold."

I tapped the switch—it was already set. "Check."

Clara had a good voice for the checklist. I never had trouble understanding her as I sometimes did with Joey or Rick.

"Check engine temp."

The needle was clear of the cold peg, warmed up by taxiing. The outside air temperature was fifty degrees and, even if the engine was warm, we weren't. The flight jackets were more than decorative. "Temperature good." You didn't want to do the engine check until the oil was warm enough to move.

"Throttle to 2800 rpm."

I pressed the throttle release and edged the knob forward until we had 2800 rpm. The Maule strained against the parking brakes. "Check."

"Magnetos."

My hand was already moving. You don't want to run high rpm while sitting still any longer than you had to. I clicked the magneto switch to "Left" then "Right." At each position, the tachometer dropped about 50 rpm. When I returned the switch to the "Both" position, the engine returned to 2800. "Check."

"Engine instruments."

We both looked at the oil pressure, cylinder head temperature, and manifold pressure gauges. "Nominal," I said.

"Set idle."

I pulled the throttle back out. The engine vibration lessened and the tach settled back on 600 rpm.

"Set ADF to two-one-six."

I dialed the frequency into the Automatic Direction Finder. The needle swung to thirty degrees, the relative bearing of the control tower and homing beacon from our position at the end of the runway. "Check."

"Check clocks."

I twisted in my seat. Mounted on the ceiling, between and behind the front seats, were two Sony eight-millimeter video cameras. One was focused on the instruments and the other was pointed through the windshield, focused on infinity. The LCD readouts on the side of the cameras were both within two seconds of the plane's dashboard clock and my watch. "Check."

"Cameras on."

I hit the "Record" buttons, starting them roughly at the same time. "Check."

"Seat locked and restraining harness fastened."

We both checked our seats to make sure they were firmly locked to the adjustment rail. Nothing worse than sliding backward from the controls on takeoff. Not only could you find yourself unable to reach the rudder pedals, but you could pull the yoke back and stall. I yanked on my shoulder and belt straps. "Check."

"Clearance."

"Do it," I said.

She thumbed her transmit button. "Wildside Base, this is Maule one seven baker ready for takeoff."

Joey had the tower. "No critters on or near the runway. Wind is five knots at one-nine-three. You are cleared."

Clara took up the checklist again. "Doors locked."

"Check."

"And checked," she said, twisting back from her door. "Time is eight-one-five." She wrote it in the log. "We are ready."

I released the brakes and pushed the throttle smoothly forward, listening for any hesitation in the motor while I could still stop us on the ground. The prop bit air and pulled us slowly forward, bumping over the grass and shaking the plane. At twenty knots the tail wheel lifted off the ground and we gained speed at a higher rate. The ride became less bumpy as the weight of the plane was taken by the wings. I kept a little right aileron and some left rudder to counteract the slight crosswind and, when the plane came up on the ground effect, I held it there, ten feet off the ground, and pulled in the flaps while I waited for the airspeed to build up to V sub y, best rate of climb.

When we'd achieved it, eighty-five knots, I pulled the yoke back. The ground dropped sharply away and I began a climbing turn to the left, until we were headed due north. We climbed to thirty-five hundred feet and held it there, adjusting our heading until we were tracking due north, even if our nose was pointed four degrees left of north. Our ADF needle pointed at 176, but, since it didn't change, we knew our ground track was actually due north, into the unknown. I set the autopilot and took my hands off the controls.

I'd flown north from the ranch—more times than I could count—but all my landmarks were gone. No Highway 6, no town of Hearne, and no cotton fields. And the invisible landmarks, the VOR and VORTAC radio beacons, the outer, middle, and inner VHF Marker Beacons, were gone, too. There was just one Nondirectional Beacon out there, the one at Wildside Base, where there were dozens in range on the tame side.

Instead, brown buffalo grass and primary growth forest covered the land. Rivers and streams, normally dependable landmarks, could not be counted on. In the absence of man-made dams and dikes, the riverbeds wandered over different ground. Also, the flat expanses of silver, brown, and green formed by man-made lakes and ponds weren't there. We thought we identified the Navasota River, but we couldn't be sure.

There were dams, though, which surprised me, making me wonder if the wildside *did* have man. The binoculars showed me mud, log, and brush embankments and, in one revelatory moment, small brown animals that dove into the water.

Beavers.

Also more buffalo, antelope, deer, and birds. I don't know if we had the image of a bird of prey or if the noise from the motor scared them, but birds, if airborne, would head for the ground, and, if feeding in the open, would head for trees and brush. Once, a large eagle, perhaps a golden, rose from below and flew toward us, as if to challenge us, but we were moving too fast and he was left far behind before he even neared our altitude.

We pushed on, checking and correcting wind drift as we went along, keeping our heading constant, our ground track due north.

We spoke about the things we saw, speculating about the identity of the geographic features below and the animals, partially for ourselves, but mostly for the cameras, since the intercom was patched into their audio input jacks.

At an hour and forty minutes, roughly two hundred miles, we turned west for fifteen minutes, then headed south, parallel to our northern course and over different territory. We were back at Wildside Base by twelve-forty and I put the Maule down as softly as possible.

I didn't think my bladder could take a hard landing without something giving way.

Clara left me to do the engine shutdown, running for the tunnel and the bathrooms on the other side. Me, I stood on the ground, the Maule screening me from the tower, and relieved myself in the grass, before climbing back in and shutting down properly.

As soon as the Maule was refueled and the video cameras reloaded, Marie and Joey were taking it out, fifteen degrees west of north for the same distance. And the next day it would be Rick and I in the morning and Marie and Clara in the afternoon, again and again, at least two flights a day, weather permitting, until we'd seen all of the land north of us within a radius of two hundred miles.

"Better take a jar with you," I told Joey.

We were socked in on Friday by cold drizzle that was half-fog, half-rain. The temperature dropped to forty-five on the wildside and I wondered, if this was early August, what would January be like?

Weather on the tame side was ninety-seven degrees, clear, and humid. Today, the air pressure on the tame side was higher than on the wildside, so there was a draft of warm air coming through the tunnel, but, since all of us were in the hangar, we kept the barn side of the tunnel shut tight, so the draft wasn't enough to counteract the cold. We wore our jackets zipped up.

We were seated on folding chairs at one end of a makeshift table—a sheet of plywood supported by sawhorses. At the other end of the table, two small color TVs played flight tapes back. On the table at our end were US Geologic Survey and Aviation maps of East Texas.

"Look," said Rick, punching numbers on a calculator. "The time/speed calculations put the plane right *here*." He put his finger down on the map and then pointed at the TVs. Both videotapes were in pause mode. On the left-hand screen was a river winding through trees, framed by the out-of-focus nose and spinner of the Maule. The right-hand screen showed the instruments, most importantly, the heading, airspeed, and ADF indicators.

Marie took the calculator from Rick. "Look, either the geography is radically different or you've made a mistake. Let's see, 1.2 hours at one-four-zero knots gives us 168 nautical miles, minus a head-wind component of, oh, two knots, or 2.6 nautical miles. One-six-five-point-four." She looked at Rick's scribbling. "That's right. Did you get the angle right?"

Rick glared at her, but pushed the parallel rulers across at her. She replicated the ADF angle on the compass rose and marched it across to the location of Wildside Base. "That's right, too."

"Thanks ever so much," said Rick.

"*But* you used the wrong scale. You used statute miles instead of nautical miles."

"What? I couldn't have."

She showed him, measuring out a distance two more inches along the bearing line. "See? That makes it the Trinity River . . . I think. It *is* on the wrong side of the valley."

"It's the Trinity," said Joey, looking at the Aviation map. He ran the tape slightly forward, to the other side of the valley. "See this ridge?" He pointed at the map. "It's got the same shape as the one on the north side of the valley. You're looking at Rochester Park. Welcome to Dallas."

Joey complained about the pilot/copilot arrangement we'd set up. Since Marie had more than twice the flight time than Clara, Rick, and Joey had, she and I were pilots in command on all the exploration flights. This meant that Marie and I were flying every day, but that each of the others didn't fly every third day.

"Your time will come," I told him. "More hours."

"Yeah, sure."

They rotated, so that Marie and I flew with them all, one after another. Rick, despite his calculation blunder with Marie, was good with navigation, though a little clumsy at the controls. Joey became a good seat-of-the-pants pilot, steady and smooth in his control handling. Clara was the best, though, showing progress far beyond her experience.

We had another fight over the first refueling base. "Look," I said, "we all have equal experience jumping, right?" They nodded. "We need two pilots and two jumpers. One of the pilots needs to be Marie or me."

"If you say so," said Joey.

"I do. So, it boils down to who wants to jump?"

Everybody raised their hand but Rick.

"Okay," I said. "That simplifies things. I'll jump and Marie is Pilot-In-Command. Clara and Joey, decide which of you jumps. The one who doesn't fights it out with Rick for second pilot."

"What?" I flinched away from four angry voices. Nobody was happy with that. After heated argument we decided that a coin toss was a more acceptable way to decide the matter.

Marie and I flipped a coin first, to decide who would be pilot in command. She lost, which is to say—she would be pilot. Then Clara, Joey, and I matched coins to decide who would jump. Clara came up with tails to my and Joey's heads.

"Shit!" she said.

Last, she and Rick tossed for the remaining pilot seat. Rick lost and got stuck with the tower.

"Figures," he said.

The flight was cold and noisy.

We left at dawn, as soon as we could tell the weather was okay. The double rear doors on the right had been removed for our jump operations. Joey and I had the backseats and spent our time shifting about, trying to get comfortable despite the cold air blasting in and all the gear strapped to us.

Besides the primary and emergency parachutes, we had our shotguns suspended from our belts and secured to our right thighs with

Velcro straps. We were also carrying survival kits, handheld radio, air horns, and Cap-Stun gas, as well as orange smoke pots and flares.

Marie's voice in our intercom headsets said, "There it is."

I leaned forward, looking over her shoulder.

We were flying at twelve hundred feet, mostly to avoid freezing, our airspeed reduced to one hundred knots by the drag of the open doors. We were 170 miles due north of Wildside Base, east of where Dallas would be on the tame side. Our target was a meadow floored with grass, wildflowers, and a few low bushes in the middle of a shallow valley. A stream at the bottom of a deep gully hugged one side of the valley, well away from the meadow. Unlike other possible sites, the chances of flooding seemed remote and the low sides of the valley were far enough away that wind shear effects were minimal.

Clara acted as jumpmaster. "Get ready to drop the pot."

Marie reduced thrust and dropped down to four hundred feet above ground level. I took an orange smoke pot and waited. When we were over the edge of the meadow, I pulled the pin and dropped it through the door. It hit just off center and the orange smoke drifted up the valley, giving us a rough indication of the wind direction and speed below. Marie banked the plane in a standard turn.

"Two minutes," said Clara. "Prepare for the equipment drop."

I shifted around to reach the luggage area behind me. There was a large duffel bag with a small cargo chute. I unclipped its restraining strap and edged it closer to the door. A static line from the chute was already snapped to the frame of my seat. I waited.

Marie's circle was precise, bringing us directly over the valley again. She straightened on her former course.

Clara held up her hand. "Wait until we're more upwind . . . now." She dropped her hand and I pushed the duffel out the door. There was a jerk felt through the seat as the static line came up short and I saw the multicolored chute blossom.

Marie pushed the throttle in to climb for our jump. Joey and I took off our headsets. My eyes were still following the cargo chute while I reached for my helmet and goggles.

Marie suddenly said, "Shit!" and the plane's nose lifted sharply. I twisted forward in time to see birds, hundreds of them, rising up in front of us from the low ridge we were crossing, spooked, perhaps, by the plane. One hit the left wing and another hit the frame of the windshield. Marie was trying to climb above them but the stupid things didn't know which way to fly. She seemed almost clear when one hit the propeller and feathers and blood sprayed the windshield.

I waited, frozen, to see if the propeller was all right. Marie was clear of the birds now, climbing at a thousand feet a minute and swearing under her breath. One thousand feet. Two thousand feet. Three thousand.

I let out my breath. "Whew. For a moment there I thought—"

Then the propeller came apart and the plane shuddered, unbalanced torque forces on the engine shaking us like we were in a blender.

"Kill it! Kill it!" I said, but Marie was already running through the SLIM list, switches, leaning out the mixture, ignition, and master, as she shoved the yoke forward to keep airspeed up. The shuddering died and, when the propeller slowed to windmill, we could see that most of one side of the prop was gone, jagged metal showing where it had broken. I glanced at the altitude—thirty-two hundred feet. Marie banked the plane back toward the valley in a shallow turn, trying to save as much altitude as possible.

With the engine off I could hear Clara transmitting. "Mayday. Mayday. Rick do you read? We have a broken propeller. We're trying for the Royce City target, bearing due north, one-seven-zero miles."

My hands itched to be on the controls, to be doing something.

"We're jumping," I shouted at Marie, trying to be heard through her headset.

Joey turned wide, frightened eyes on me. "What? You coward!"

I shook my head. "The less weight in the plane the better. We're deadweight, right now. They'll have a longer glide, better landing, if we get out." I moved back to shout in his ear alone. "And we'll be able to render aid if they crash."

Marie looked over her shoulder. "He's right, Joey!"

"*You* take my chute," Joey said, reaching for the connector.

"There's no time, goddammit! Go!" She turned back to the controls.

Clara was still repeating our location and situation over the radio. We might be too low for Rick to hear us.

I flipped off my seat belt and released Joey's too. He looked down, surprised, and started to fumble for his static line. "No time," I said, then grabbed his harness and threw myself sideways, off the seat and out the door. Joey dragged across the doorway, but I didn't let go.

The ground seemed frighteningly close, but hard to see because we didn't have our goggles on. I saw Joey reach for his D ring and miss. I grabbed it and yanked—his chute deployed and he jerked up, and away, pulling out of my grasp. I found my D ring and pulled. The wind and noise went away and I was floating, drifting on the wind, about fifteen hundred feet above the ground.

I spilled air to the right, twisting so my back was to the wind and I was facing the valley. The Maule was gliding down, steep, to keep airspeed. Marie didn't have the altitude to turn into the wind on landing so she was going to have to do a downwind landing. I hoped the landing gear would take the extra speed. I hoped there weren't hidden ditches and rocks.

I saw the flaps deploy and then she was pulling up, just clearing the trees, then flaring out and floating above the ground. There was lots of meadow left when she touched down and I saw the wings wag as one of the forward landing gear bounced into and out of some depression, then through some bushes, then the plane slowed and she was braking to a halt, unhurt, undamaged.

Above me I heard Joey half yell, half sob inarticulate relief, and I nodded agreement.

I turned the chute slightly. Joey was well above me, I found, once the canopy didn't block my view, and it looked like he was steering just right, spilling as little air as possible to stretch his glide out. I concentrated on doing the same thing, hoping to make the meadow.

Didn't.

I crashed into the trees on the wrong side of the stream, plunging down between, through, and off of branches. I ended up fifteen feet off the ground, bruised and scratched, but otherwise unhurt. The last thing I'd seen before entering the trees was Joey drifting overhead, well clear, and heading for the meadow.

For a moment I just hung there, completely limp, swinging slightly. Songbirds, perhaps stilled by the noise of my passage through the tree, started up again, bright fragments of music against a verdant green backdrop.

Then I heard a rustling in the underbrush and turned my head.

There was this bear.

It came out of the underbrush from behind me, curious, I think, about all the commotion. I heard it grunting softly to itself as it padded along on all fours. I twisted in the harness to see.

Well, at least I wasn't on the ground with it, I thought, but safely above it. I reached for the air horn and, without pulling it out of the harness, pushed the plunger.

A noise like ten thousand balloons being rubbed blared out and the bear dropped back on its haunches, surprised. I tried it again, wincing at the noise. The bear turned its head and looked at me, then came forward again.

Stupid horn.

When the bear was directly beneath me, I found myself surprised at how close it was. I hadn't realized how big the thing was.

And then it stood on its hind legs and reached up and its claws brushed the soles of my boots.

I curled, drawing my feet up and hauled myself even higher on the shrouds. The shotgun strapped to my side poked me in the ribs. I considered using it. Instead, I reached for the pepper Mace, flipped up the safety shield, and pointed it at the bear's face. It reached up again, coming higher this time, and I sprayed right into its eyes and snout.

It fell over backward rubbing at its snout and roaring, then, shaking its head, it ran into the brush, slammed into a tree, bounced off, and continued into the brush, its roars accompanying the sound of breaking branches and rustling leaves.

I was glad it ran *away* from the meadow.

There was the obnoxious noise of an air horn from the direction of the stream. I tapped mine in answer. Then hung on to the shrouds with my right hand and released the harness with my right. The disconnected straps hung down and I hand-over-handed down them until my feet dangled less than six feet from the ground, then I dropped and rolled.

I was brushing myself off when I heard movement in the underbrush. I pulled the shotgun free and jacked a round into chamber, but kept it pointed in the air.

Clara and Joey came through the underbrush together, shotguns held high, like mine.

"Hi."

"You okay?" asked Clara.

"Sure. How's Marie? How's the plane?"

"They're fine—well, except for the propeller, I guess. Where's your chute?"

I pointed up.

"Ah," said Joey. "That was a good idea, honking to let us know where your were, but why didn't you use your radio?"

"Uh, I didn't think about the radio. I had a visitor." I showed them the tracks and told them what I'd done to the bear.

Joey looked around nervously. "We really need more firepower," he said.

"What we need is to get out of these woods, so we can see what's coming."

"What about the chute?" asked Clara.

I looked up. It didn't look torn, but the shrouds were tangled in the branches. "Later."

Joey used his handheld radio to tell Marie that they'd found me intact, then they led me back to the clearing, showing me the rocks they'd used to ford the stream. Marie waved when we broke cover.

"Did you hear from Rick?" I asked Clara as we walked across the meadow.

"Maybe. I thought I heard something, but I'm not positive. We were awful low on the horizon."

Marie hugged me when we reached the Maule, surprising me. Felt good. "Nice flying," I said.

"Amen," said Clara.

Marie shrugged. "Scary stuff. It was easier, though, when you guys bailed out."

"The weight?" I asked, doubtful. The weight shouldn't have been that significant—I really wanted to be able to render first aid if they'd cracked up.

"The responsibility. I still had to worry about Clara, but at least I didn't have to worry about you two."

"Well, so much for preparing the landing field *before* you land. How's the plane?"

Marie shrugged. "Don't know about the engine—we shut it down pretty quick. I checked out the landing gear—it's fine. They make these Maules tough."

I started shedding equipment, stacking it inside the Maule. "Clara, why don't you see if you hear anything on the radio. Joey, stand guard. Marie and I are going to take the prop off."

"Why?" Joey asked. "We don't have a replacement."

"True, but we don't dare run the engine to see if it's okay, until I pull the unbalanced prop off."

"Ah."

I took the tools out from under the copilot's seat and we went to work. It takes a lot of work with just hand tools. It wasn't like pulling a simple fixed pitch prop. We had to take off the entire head of the Hartzell constant speed propeller. At least we could replace the blade, instead of the entire assembly, *if* the engine was okay.

An hour later, I had the propeller assembly sitting on the ground,

I started up the engine and tested it briefly. I left the cowling off—with no propeller, cooling was a major problem. It ran smoothly, even with a brief stint at 2000 rpm.

I shut down the engine and the radio came alive.

"Coyote three five zulu to Maule one seven baker."

I pulled headphones on. "Rick? What the hell are you doing off the ground? Over."

"Jesus! Are you guys all right? What the hell happened?"

"Bird hit the prop. Everybody is fine, though. What are you doing in the air? If you crash, what the hell is going to happen to us?"

"Don't worry. I made arrangements. I'm fifty miles north of the base at ten thousand feet. It's the only way I could reach you on this dinky hand radio. I can come ahead and fly you out one at a time, but only if we use the fuel from the Maule for the trip back."

"Don't—we can fly the Maule out, but we need a new blade. You'll probably have to get it from Houston. Hang on." I read him the part number off the prop and told him where to find the phone number for a parts dealer with Hartzell spares. "And what kind of arrangements did you make?"

"Tell you later. This stupid plane doesn't have a heater and I'm about to freeze. One way or another, I'll contact you at 10:00 A.M., tomorrow. Can you guys last the night?"

"We'll manage."

"Three five zulu out."

"One seven baker out."

We recoverd the cargo duffel from the edge of the meadow and unpacked it, removing a chain saw, an ax, a machete, a shovel, and two dozen four-foot wire-stakes with fluorescent orange streamers on one end. We cleared the flattest part of the meadow, chopping out the brush to below ground level, filling in the worst holes, and marking a thousand-foot runway with the stakes. At the midpoint, to one side, we set up a wind sock.

Near evening, Joey went down to the far end of the meadow, his shotgun loaded with bird shot, and killed a wild turkey. I backed him, "loaded for bear," as the expression goes. The turkey, though wary, didn't know to be scared of us at thirty feet. His loss, our supper.

We collected enough firewood for the night—with the chain saw that wasn't particularly difficult—and built a fire near the plane. Joey cooked the turkey on a spit over coals. I was surprised when he pulled beer out of the cooler we'd brought the lunch in. I looked at him.

"Hey. By the time we were going to eat lunch, the plane was going to be on the ground, and I wasn't going to be jumping again, much less flying. Why shouldn't I have brought the beer?"

The turkey was good. We ate most of it and burned the bones and scraps to discourage scavengers. We split the night into four two-hour watches. When Marie woke me for my turn, she said, "There are wolves, those long-legged red ones. They don't like the fire, much, but they were getting used to it."

" 'Were'?"

She shrugged, obviously pleased with herself. "I waited until they were downwind and gave them a dose of the Cap-Stun. Even from thirty feet they did *not* like it." She wrapped herself in a Mylar space blanket near the fire and pillowed her head on her flight jacket.

I heard wolves howling from far away as I fed the fire, but nothing bothered us the rest of the night.

Joey and I took the machete and the chain saw and retrieved my parachute the next morning. I brought it back to the meadow and folded and packed it on the grass with Clara's help. Joey offered to kill something for lunch, but I said, "Let's see what Rick says at ten, first."

We gathered at the plane, at ten before, anxious and curious. Rick came on the air at five minutes till.

"Coyote three five zulu to Maule one seven baker."

"We're here, Rick. What's the news?"

"I'm en route. I'm carrying your prop blade and three jerry cans of gas strapped into the right-hand seat."

"Who'd you file your flight plan with?"

"Your lawyer."

"Luis? You told Luis?"

"No. I gave him a sealed envelope. If we don't call him by ten tomorrow morning, he's going to open it. Good enough?"

"What if bad weather moves in? What if we're okay, but can't get there in time?"

"Uh. I didn't think about that. Do you want me to head back and change the instructions?"

I looked at the sky. It was clear as a bell. "What was the barometer reading when you left?"

"Uh," he paused, obviously looking at the numbers he'd recorded on takeoff. "Three-zero-point-three-five."

"Can you still get the ATIS now? I mean, see what it says now."

"Will do. Give me a few minutes."

We listened to static while he switched over to the other frequency. In forty-five seconds he was back.

"Three-zero-point-four-zero. You copy?"

"I copy. Come on ahead—looks like the weather might hold."

The Coyote didn't have any electronic navigation equipment. Without the ability to at least get a bearing on Wildside Base, he wouldn't find us. But find us he did, flying north until he crossed the Trinity, then following it west until he reached the junction of the east fork of the Trinity. It was only thirty miles then, and we set off an orange smoke pot ten minutes later to guide him in the last bit. He touched down easily in the tall grass and rolled to a quick stop.

Clara hugged him after he'd shut down the engine. He held her tightly for a moment, then said, "Nice place you have here."

Marie and I replaced the propeller while Joey and Rick refueled the Coyote from plastic cans. The assembly ran slightly rough until I added a counterweight to one side, then it smoothed out.

Clara decided to fly back in the Coyote with Rick. For a moment,

I thought about my senior pilot/junior pilot rule, then I shrugged and said, "Okay. We'll give you a forty-five-minute start—that should get us all back about the same time."

The Coyote lifted off easily, the bumpy grass almost lofting it into the air. We put out our fire, packed up the equipment, and followed three-quarters of an hour later.

We passed them in the air. The Maule landed at twelve-thirty and the Coyote came down ten minutes later. We were laughing when we came out of the barn, the giddy laughter of disaster survivors, but Marie, who was in front, stopped abruptly. I looked up.

Luis Cervantes was standing on the porch.

N ine

"Faced with Jail, It's Really No Choice, Right?"

"You're all right, then," he said. He was holding an envelope in his hand. His face was frozen.

I nodded. Our adventure suddenly seemed foolish—childish. "Luis, you know Marie. This is Clara and Joey and, I guess you've met Rick."

Rick shook his head.

"No. I wasn't there when the envelope was delivered. Sylvia took it," said Luis.

"Ah. Let's get out of this heat."

I shut the barn and locked it. On my way across to the house I started to sweat and took off my flight jacket and carried it the rest of the way.

In the living room we hung our coats on the rack by the door and stood around for a moment, awkward. "Drink? There's tea."

Luis looked like he was going to explode, but Rick said, "Tea for me," echoed immediately by Clara and Marie. Joey said, "I'll take a beer."

Luis sat suddenly and shook his head. "What the hell—beer."

Clara helped me. They didn't talk until we were back in the room handing out drinks.

"What's going on, Charlie?" Luis asked, after one pull on his beer. He tapped the envelope on the side of the beer can. "What's this about?"

I licked my lips. "We ran into some mechanical trouble," I began. "Rick had to bring us a part, but, in case he ran into—any troub—er, problems, he wanted someone to know enough to come get us. He didn't have any problems, though."

"What kind of problems?"

"Mechanical. Weather." Animal.

"Why didn't you just call?"

"Uh, no phone."

"Where were you?"

Silence. I could say, "Up near Dallas," but it would be a lie and I hadn't lied to him yet and I didn't want to. Finally I said, "I'd rather not say."

He stood, walked across to the coat rack and ran a finger across the snarling sabertooth head on the back of my jacket. "You're wearing coats in August." He turned and faced us. "The barn is locked like a bank vault but the house was unlocked. You turned in receipts to the bookkeeper that include shotguns and tear gas, airplanes, long-range fuel tanks, and aviation gas at six hundred gallons a pop. On top of all this, you left sealed instructions for me to open in the event you failed to contact me by tomorrow morning. What the hell is going on, Charlie? Isn't it about time you told me what this is all about?"

I became aware of a chill in my right hand and looked down to see my glass of iced tea, untouched and beaded with condensation. I stared at it for a moment, then drank deeply from it, looking over the edge of the glass at the guys. They were watching me, their faces still.

I finished the rest of the tea, then said, "You'll need a jacket."

I showered quickly and changed before we took him through the tunnel. He hung back—the passage was dark and the steadily increasing chill as we neared the hangar was daunting. The others followed behind us.

"How deep does this cave go?" he asked.

I laughed. "You'll see. We'll have light in a minute."

There was light from the edges of the hangar doors, but until I hit the switch for the fluorescents, the interior was a jumble of shadows. Luis blinked at the light, looking from the Maule parked facing the door to the Coyote, parked off to the side, its wings folded. He became aware of the chill and pulled on the coat he'd been carrying under one arm, an old fleece-lined denim that used to belong to Uncle Max.

"Uh—who wants to get the tower?" I asked.

"I will," said Marie. She went to the back wall and put on the webbing harness with the Cap-Stun gas, air horn, and ammo. Then she took her shotgun from the rack and checked the load. The others followed suit and Luis's eyes opened wide as he saw the guns. Marie put her gun on safety, slung it over her shoulder by its strap, and climbed up the ladder to the trapdoor in the roof.

Joey said, "We'll get the door." He and Rick pushed the doors wide while Clara stood by, gun at the ready. Light flooded in and Luis stepped forward. I said, "Hang on a second," and put on my harness and grabbed my shotgun.

"Okay."

There was a small group of bison, perhaps four bulls and six cows, grazing at the end of the runway. A flock of cattle egrets, white against the blue sky, arose from the grass, startled by the movement of the doors.

"Why is it so cold?"

It wasn't that cold—about sixty-five—but compared to the tame side it was chilly. "That's the way it is, here," I said. "We think this is a mini-ice age."

"Here?"

"Here. Where do you think you are, Luis? Look at the end of the runway."

He'd glanced at the bison when we came out, but they were at least a hundred yards away. He hadn't registered them as anything but cattle.

"Those are buffalo." He said it almost accusingly, as if we'd put them there on purpose.

"Bison, actually."

The cattle egrets started to settle, but Rick and Joey started walking toward the bison. Luis flinched as Rick touched off his air horn and the flock of egrets exploded up again. The bison closed together in a defensive formation, bulls in front of the cows. Joey touched off his air horn, a long blast of sound, then Rick echoed him. The bison moved off the runway and out of sight behind the hill.

I turned around and looked up at Marie, in the tower. "How's the weather?" I shouted.

"Barometer's dropping, wind's out of the east," she called back.

"See anything?"

She scanned the horizon with binoculars. There were some high, scattered clouds above. "Nothing, really."

Luis watched this exchange, then said, "Where are we? How did we get here?"

"Don't you remember? The wardrobe with the coats?"

He looked confused.

"Sorry. The tunnel. The tunnel in the back of the barn, remember?"

He nodded, slowly.

"Good. Let's go flying—want to show you some more."

We took the Maule up, after preflight. The propeller vibration seemed normal, but I was concerned. I pointed out the Brazos River and the Little Brazos and the Navasota River. "That's where Easterwood is." I pointed at an empty stretch of grass and shrub. "On the other side, that is."

It slowly sank in. "Where are the people?"

"There aren't any on this side. None that we know of. Try the radio. Try all the frequencies. You'll find Marie on 121.6 and you'll find our ATIS on 124 and you'll find our AM beacon at 216."

He clicked through the comm frequencies, then the ADF; finally, he started clicking through the VOR frequencies. He found our stuff, but nothing else. "You sure this radio works?"

I nodded. "In the hangar you can pick up stuff that leaks through the tunnel—Easterwood tower. But you can't get it up here."

I found a larger herd of buffalo, some antelope that bounded along the ground, and then, in a meadow near the Brazos, two mammoths tearing at the grass with their tusks scraping the ground. I circled slowly, five hundred feet above ground level, and let him get a good look. All the time I talked, telling him about Uncle Max and how I'd discovered the tunnel in the back of the barn.

The sky to the north darkened and Marie reported that the wind had shifted to the north and was increasing. I landed and we put the plane away, closing the doors on the hangar as the norther hit.

Large drops of water pelted the hangar doors and Marie dropped down through the roof from the tower and closed the trapdoor. Her hair was tangled and water spotted her jacket.

"Wind's gusting to fifty," she said. "Hope the tower doesn't go."

The six of us walked back through the tunnel and out of the barn. The sun beat down like a hammer and the humid, hot air stuck in the throat. The weather was nothing like the other side.

"So, Luis, are you satisfied that we're not running drugs out of Mexico?"

He pulled his jacket off. "Drugs would explain a lot. Like everything I just saw—you put LSD in my iced tea?"

I stared at him, then realized he was kidding. We entered the house and hung our coats.

"How did you do it? The tunnel, that is?"

I saw Marie about to answer him, and quickly said, "I don't think you should know. I think, as our lawyer, you should be in a position to say, 'I don't know how they do it.' " I changed the subject, before the others could ask me what on earth I was talking about. "I own the ranch free and clear. The taxes are paid up and there are no liens against it. There don't seem to be any humans on the other side—hell, it doesn't even seem to be the same planet, much less the same country. The doorway is on my land. What's our legal position? Who owns the other side, Luis?"

He stared at me and his mouth dropped. Finally, he said, "Well—

you do. Right up to the point that the feds find out about it."

He stared for another long beat, then said, "So don't let them find out."

On the wildside, a high pressure zone and lower temperatures followed the norther through, leaving us with clear, untroubled skies. We resumed operations the next day, two flights a day to the Royce City airstrip.

The first trip up, Joey and I climbed a solitary pine next to the new strip and topped off its thin upper trunk, then mounted an AM radio beacon with a south-facing solar panel to charge its batteries. It broadcast Morse "R" for Royce. At the south end of the runway we mounted a wind sock.

Every trip after that, the Maule carried fifteen five-gallon plastic containers of aviation gas strapped securely into a cargo space made larger by the removal of the rear seats. We could've carried more, but landing on a rough field with 450 pounds of highly flammable cargo right behind your seat was nervous-making enough without approaching the weight limits.

At the end of the week we had 525 gallons of avgas stored under a tarp in the shade of the pines. We took three days and replaced the double rear door with a sliding one, suitable for opening in flight. We were ready for the next step.

The next base, Comanche, was 150 miles north west of Wildside Base, roughly 150 miles from the Royce City base. This time we actually did it as planned. Since I got to jump last time, I was pilot this trip with Rick as copilot. Clara and Marie went in first, by chute, and leveled a spot or two, cut down a small tree, and dragged a log away. The Maule came in smoothly, with no mishaps from birds.

I was still glad we were now carrying an entire spare prop assembly.

We took a week and a half to stockpile fuel at Comanche since we lost three days to fog and rain. We used the opportunity to have more avgas and plastic jerry cans delivered.

I also took a bunch of wildlife video, making Rick trudge through wet grass mud so that he could watch my back. In the rain I was able to get relatively close to bison, antelope, and even a group of red wolves. There were some weird ground birds as well, which turned out to be Atwater's prairie chicken, an endangered species on our side.

Now that Luis was in on the secret, he came over on the weekend and flew a fuel run as my copilot. This pissed off Joey, since it was his rotation *and* Luis didn't have his IFR ticket yet.

I took Joey aside. "Look, Luis is our buffer against the feds. If— no, make that *when* they come looking for us, he's got to keep them off us. Don't you think it's important to keep him happy?"

He didn't like it, but he took it. When we got back that evening, he was drinking beer on the porch. I counted cans. "Rick help you with that six-pack?"

He ignored me and popped the top of another beer. There were five empties lined up neatly on the edge of the porch.

"Where is Rick?" Rick was running the tower when we landed the plane. As soon as he'd finished helping us fuel the Maule and roll it into the hangar, he'd gone back to the tame side. Luis and I'd dawdled over closing the doors, watching a large flock of white cranes fly overhead, then followed about twenty minutes later.

"He drove Marie and Clara back to their place." The sentence, when it came, was angry.

"Without you?" I asked, genuinely surprised. The four of them did nearly everything together.

"Yeah. Without me. So?"

I shook my head. "Nothing. You and Marie have the first flight tomorrow—don't drink much more."

"Give it a rest, Chuckie," he said.

I shrugged and walked Luis to his car.

"Is he going to be all right?" Luis asked.

"Of course," I said.

"Right. Thanks for the flying time—it's different."

"You're welcome."

After he left, I walked back to the barn and used the phone there to call Clara and Marie's apartment.

"What's with Joey?" I asked when Clara answered the phone.

"He started drinking after you left. Marie and I finished mowing the tame strip and found him on the porch. She asked him to stop with three beers. He said nobody tells him when to stop drinking, not even her. It went downhill from there."

"Oh," I said. "What's Marie doing now?"

"She's scrubbing the kitchen floor."

"Well, that's not too bad."

"Oh, yeah?" said Clara. "She just cleaned it yesterday."

"Oh."

"That all you ever say, Charlie? 'Oh'?"

"Well, uh, oh. Talk to you later."

Joey brought his beer in and turned on the TV. I wondered why he had to drink so much. I wanted him to stop. "I'm going into town to see what's playing at the dollar house. You want to go?"

He just shook his head.

I felt obliged to carry through, relieved, in fact, to be away from him. I grabbed my keys, then paused at the front door, my hand on the knob. I heard him open another beer can. I considered reminding him about Federal Aviation Regulations but knew he wouldn't listen. I settled for slamming the door.

When I got back, three hours later, he was slumped over on the couch, asleep, and a pyramid of empty beer cans on the end table reflected blue light from the TV.

I turned the set off, threw away the cans, and covered Joey with a blanket.

I got up at seven the next morning. Joey wasn't on the couch anymore and the blanket was lying on the stairs. He must've woken in the night and gone to his room. His door was shut, but Rick's wasn't. Rick's bed was empty and, though a mess, didn't seem to have been slept in recently.

This was confirmed when he drove up fifteen minutes later with Clara and Marie. "What's for breakfast, Charlie?"

They looked at me expectantly and I said, "Omelets, I guess. It's the only thing I know how to make."

I cooked while Rick did yesterday's dishes. The girls were dubious at first, but finished the omelets after tasting. "Never had apricot preserves in an omelet before," Clara said.

That week we were running fuel direct to Scurry, three hundred miles from Wildside Base, striking out for Colorado. This was well within the range of the Maule but meant running only one trip a day, so we usually didn't start until nine or so. Still, the day was getting on. "Who wants to wake Sleeping Beauty," I said.

Marie grimaced, then said, "I'll do it."

She came back in five minutes. "He looks *terrible*."

"Is he coming?"

"Yeah, he's in the shower. What's happening with the weather?" She kept glancing at the ceiling and rocking on her heels.

I'd gone over to the wildside to check the weather before they got there. "It's okay. Partly cloudy. High clouds—maybe seven thousand."

Marie nodded, then turned abruptly. "I'm going to go start preflight." She walked out, followed by Clara.

Joey came down ten minutes later, walking slowly down the staircase and holding on to the rail.

Rick and I watched him from the foot of the stairs. "You want breakfast?" I asked.

He shook his head slowly and tightened his mouth into a thin line. When he reached the bottom of the stairs, he staggered and I put out a hand to steady him. His breath hit me like a hammer, rich in exhaled alcohol.

"Christ, Joey. You're in no shape to fly."

"Bullshit," he said.

"Rick, you're up. Take this flight."

"Hey!" said Joey. "You're doing it again. First Luis, now Rick!"

"You're still drunk, Joey. I told you to take it easy last night. I put ten empty beer cans away. Are you trying to kill yourself?"

"None of your business," said Joey.

I turned away. "Rick, go on."

Joey tried to grab Rick's arm as Rick left, but he missed and sat down hard on the bottom step.

"Jesus, Joey, you know what the FAR says."

"The FAA isn't even on the wildside," he said weakly.

"So? The regs are like that to keep things safe. You want to kill yourself and take one of us with you? Marie?"

He put his head down in his hands and said, "Fuck you."

I left him and went over to the wildside. Marie was standing guard while Clara and Rick loaded the plane with plastic jerry cans. After the load had been secured and triple-checked, Marie and Rick climbed in and started up.

Clara came up into the tower with me and watched them take off. "Joey's really being an asshole, isn't he?"

I licked my lips. "Yeah, I guess so." I stared after the Maule until it vanished, a shrinking dot blocked by the horizon. "Why does she stay with him?"

"Marie? Love, I guess. She and Joey have problems, but boy do they love each other. I wish Rick and I had half the passion." Her voice became quiet at the end of that sentence and when I looked at her she blushed. "I'll go get the tractor. It's my turn to mow the strip."

Before she left, though, the front gate alarm went off, a long buzz that indicated a car passing in front of the beam.

"Who could that be?" I said. My dad was flying that week and Luis, though he now had the combination to the front gate, knew to call before coming out.

"I'll check," said Clara.

She came back with the tractor through the tunnel, from the barn, and parked it outside the hangar. She used her radio to call up to me. "It was Joey. He took Rick's car. And now I don't have anybody to ride shotgun while I mow the strip."

I switched on the voice-activated recorder and went down to ride shotgun while she mowed. I also kept my handheld radio tuned to our traffic frequency and an earplug in my ear, but its range wasn't anywhere near that of the base station in the tower. As we drove up and down the strip I cursed Joey's name under my breath. I hoped nothing happened to Rick and Clara, especially while I couldn't hear them.

When I checked the recorder afterward, there'd been nothing received. Marie checked in on their return leg a half hour later with no problems.

She was not happy when I told her about Joey. Rick was furious. "I didn't give him permission to drive my car!"

"Where were the keys?"

"Uh, on the kitchen table. That's where they were after breakfast."

They landed an hour later.

"Any word?" Marie asked after they'd finished servicing the plane and putting it in the hangar.

I shook my head.

"I'll make some phone calls," she said.

We adjourned to the ranch house. Marie tried Joey's parents, keeping her voice untroubled. He wasn't there. She tried some of Joey's friends from the wrestling team—most of them weren't home, either at work or gone away for the summer. The few that were home hadn't seen him. She asked everyone she did reach to have Joey call if they saw him.

"What now?" asked Clara.

I started to say, "I don't—"

Marie said, "We go look for him, of course."

"We do?" Clara said.

Marie turned a hurt look on Clara. "Wouldn't you? What if it were Rick out there?"

"Depends," Clara said. "Rick's an adult. If he chose to leave, I'd respect that choice and wait for him to call or return."

"Are you saying Joey's not an adult?" Marie looked close to tears.

"Do you think he's acting like one?" Clara replied.

Marie looked down at the floor.

"It's my car," said Rick. "I want to find it before he wrecks it. I'm not sure the insurance covers the car when I'm not driving."

Clara put her arm around Marie's shoulders. "It'll be okay. Honest. I'll use my motorcycle to look if Charlie will drop me at the apartment so I can get it."

I shook my head and took my keys out of my pocket. "Somebody should stay here in case he comes back or calls." I handed the keys to Rick. "Take my truck—I'll wait here and man the phone."

"Thanks, Charlie," Marie said. They left.

While I was working in the tower or helping Clara mow the lawn, I'd kept my imagination under control, but now, alone in the empty house, I was sure that Joey was out there telling everyone he knew about this tunnel into another world.

I turned on the TV, switching to the news, and was shocked to see a news story on passenger pigeons.

"Spokesmen for the San Diego Zoo, the National News, The Nature Conservancy, and the Sierra Club announced today that they are in possession of four male and sixteen female passenger pigeons. This bird, which was believed to be extinct since the last-known specimen, Martha, died in the Cincinnati Zoo in 1914, was slaughtered by the millions during the latter half of the nineteenth century."

The screen switched from the news anchor to a group of four men standing in a cluster before microphones. A man adjusted his glasses as he read from a statement. "The birds are definitely passenger pigeons. Genetic material obtained from preserved passenger pigeons at the Smithsonian Institution contains over 99.999 percent of the same gene sequences. Interestingly enough, the differences between our individual live specimens indicates that they are not closely related, but are from a wide and diverse gene pool of this species." He paused and looked up at the cameras. "The four male birds were donated anonymously. The sixteen females were sold to us by the same party, also anonymously.

"We haven't the faintest idea where these birds came from and we very much want to find out. I'll take questions now."

The phone rang.

I stared at it, irritated by the interruption, then remembered Joey. I turned down the volume on the TV and picked up the receiver.

It was the police.

"Thank God there wasn't anybody else involved," said Luis, "or we'd be facing liability claims out the wazoo."

Rick, Clara, Marie, and I were in Luis's office. Rick was pacing back and forth, unable to sit still. Marie was perched on the edge of her seat. Clara sat back in her chair and I leaned against the wall, my arms folded.

Joey was in the hospital for observation. He had stitches in his left arm and a slight concussion. If not for the bump on his head, he'd be in jail. Technically, he was under arrest right where he was.

"This is a second offense DWI and Joey's over eighteen now. He won't get any breaks from the court. The *only* thing going for him is that it was a single-car accident—that he hurt only himself."

"What about my car?" said Rick, angrily. "What about my insurance rates?" Rick's car was totaled when Joey ran off the Highway 6 east bypass into a ditch, rolling the car three times before it slammed into the concrete frame of a drainage tunnel running under the road.

Flying lessons must've been good for him. Drunk as he was, he was wearing his seat belt.

"We'll take care of your car," I said. "I'm sorry about it, but it's just a 'thing.' It's replaceable." I turned back to Luis. "What can we do about Joey?"

Luis spread his hands. "Depends. If Joey will go immediately into an alcohol treatment program and AA, he may get off with losing his license, community service, and probation. Otherwise, he's probably looking at six months in jail."

"Well, he's got to," Marie said. "Faced with jail, it's really no choice, right?"

"Hopefully," said Luis. "His father is a little hard to deal with. He wants to fight it, which is just plain stupid. Joey's blood alcohol level was .21 over an hour after the accident. There were empty and full beer cans in the front seat. Not only would Joey be sure to do jail time, it wouldn't do him any good. He's obviously got a problem." He looked at me, his eyes narrowed.

"Yes. He has a problem," I said. "I was wrong the other day when I said he'd be all right. And it's our problem, too."

Luis nodded, satisfied. "Luckily, Joey's parents can't afford legal help to try and fight it, so they're stuck with me or a court-appointed public defender. Besides—thanks to Charlie's call, I got there first and Joey named me as his attorney before his father could go to work on him."

"Is that going to be a problem? What if his dad talks him into somebody else?"

"Won't happen. I had a long talk with his mother. She understands *exactly* what will happen if they try to fight it. She's far more concerned about Joey than the family reputation."

"What did you mean it's *our* problem, Charlie?" asked Clara.

"It's our problem because—" I looked at Marie . . . at her haunted eyes. "Well, because Joey's one of us."

I didn't say, *because if he talks about the tunnel, we lose it.*

But I wanted to.

Ten

"You Walk Quiet, but Your Face—Well Your Face *Stomps* around like an Elephant."

We shut down operations for two days, while the crisis sorted itself out. Well, to be perfectly honest, while Luis brilliantly managed the situation.

Once Joey was released from the hospital, he was taken to the county jail, in Bryan, and processed. At Luis's suggestion, we let him sit there for six hours before Wildside Investments went bail. Luis and I drove him from there to his parents' house.

"Why did we come here?" he asked. "Why aren't we going to the ranch?"

Luis said, "We have to talk about your legal position."

All of Joey's family were inside, including his father, who looked more nervous and upset than I'd ever seen him. Marie was there, too, with Mr. Santos from the Greenbriar Substance Abuse Center. Mr. Santos was an "interventionist," and his job was helping families convince a substance-abusing member to get into treatment.

It was painful.

Luis presented the legal consequences of not going into treatment. I presented the job-related consequences. "You keep drinking and you'll never fly again. The FAA could pull your ticket right now." Mr. Santos presented the physiological consequences of alcohol abuse. Then Joey's family and Marie presented him with examples of his drinking—acts that had hurt them that were direct consequences of his alcohol abuse.

I hadn't realized there were so many. Apparently, in school, with his wrestling team buddies, he'd been more prone to drink than he had while in flight training or working with us. There were two minor auto wrecks that hadn't been reported, the family paying for the damages directly. He'd been fired from the previous summer's construction job for drinking-related insubordination.

Joey got more and more still, his eyes reddened, and he seemed on the verge of tears.

His father was inarticulate, talking about Joey's behavior in a strange manner, essentially trying to justify it. Mr. Santos interrupted him. "Your father is not quite ready to deal with his own drinking problem, Joey. I'm afraid he feels that he can't talk about your alcohol abuse without accusing himself."

Mr. Maloney started to say something, but his wife put her hand on his arm and he subsided. Finally he said, "You're our kid and we love you. We want what's best for you."

At the end of this, Mr. Santos presented Joey with the treatment option.

"You do this, and you'll still have a job," I said. "Our insurance company will cover most of the costs. Wildside Investments will cover the rest."

He didn't really argue at all. "When?" was all he said, his voice quiet, hoarse, his eyes red.

Marie brought a suitcase out from the hallway that she'd packed at the ranch that morning. Mr. Santos said, "Now. They're ready for you at the center. You'll go through two days of detox and four to six weeks of the program."

"What about the legal stuff? The DWI charges?"

Luis spoke up. "I obtained a two-month postponement of the initial hearing this morning, contingent on your entering treatment."

Before Joey drove away with his father and Mr. Santos, I managed one moment with him alone.

"We need you, Joey. We need you alive and sober, but we need you." I dropped my voice slightly. "If the tunnel is still ours, you'll have your place back—and a full share of the profits . . . and work." He started to cry, and I finished lamely, "So come back."

Rick and I left in dawn's pregray, when we could just make out the end of the runway. Three and a half hours later we landed on the border between Texas and New Mexico, or where that border would be on the tame side. Here, it was a meaningless and invisible line dividing identical sections of high plain.

The *Llano Estacado*, the staked plain, was what Coronado named this part of the country. Buffalo grass stood so high, and stretched so far, that there were no landmarks. His expedition resorted to pounding staves into the ground to mark their path and to give identifiable features to this sea of grass.

Our fifth and latest fuel dump was in the middle of a recent prairie fire burn, a black scar of soot and stubble shot through with the tiny green sprouts of returning life. It stretched several miles, fanning out in a pointed oval shape from the original lightning strike. The surrounding grass was still chest high and, though a landing would've been possible, taking off in it would've been very difficult. The fuel store was in the very middle of the burn and we didn't have to worry about predators approaching under cover.

This fuel dump was the first site that required refueling to reach and return. The Maule, at its most economical cruising speed of 160 mph, has a range of 930 miles. This was in still air, of course, and didn't count winds, head or tail. We were 450 miles from Wildside Base, just a bit too far to do it round trip on onboard fuel. We were also out of range on our VHF aviation radios, so we'd purchased a shortwave base station for the tower and a powerful portable shortwave for the plane.

The sky was immense. Well, okay, the sky is always immense, but there were no hills, or trees, or buildings to obstruct it. There was just the grass and the sky. It made me feel tiny, stuck to a surface that looked down into an immense depth as if the airplane flew us *up* to this place and if we weren't careful, we'd fall off into the sky.

We hurried the off-loading—there was a danger of not having enough daylight if we dawdled. Sweating, and a little out of breath, I used the shortwave to check with base before flying back.

"We're at Stateline, Clara, and unloaded. Can you read us?"

"Loud and clear, which is a miracle, considering."

"Considering what?"

"A front just blew through here with a lot of thunder and lightning. The barometer began dropping about an hour after you left. I tried to reach you on the VHF, but you were out of range. The barometer is *still* dropping and we have gusts to forty-five knots."

"Which way is it headed?"

"The wind is all over the map just now, but it seemed to move in from the east."

"Oh." I looked around the horizon. The wind was slightly from the south and there wasn't a cloud in the sky. "I guess we'll fly back to Scurry. If it's still clear there, we'll try for Comanche. Then we'll refuel and check in with you."

"Okay. You run into any IFR conditions, you do a 180 and go back to the last clear base."

"In your ear."

She laughed. "I didn't quite hear that, Charlie."

"I said, 'Will do, dear.' You want to talk to Rick?"

Her voice changed. "Uh, not necessary. Check in when you can."

"Uh, right. Out."

"Out," she said.

I turned to Rick. "What's that about?"

He shrugged. "Um. Nothing, really." He looked down at his feet.

"Nothing?" I started the walk around, checking the leading edge of the wings, then the prop. "Didn't sound like 'nothing.' "

Rick popped the catches on the engine compartment and began a visual inspection. "We had a fight."

I was surprised. Joey and Marie fought. Rick and Clara were more easygoing. They had arguments but they were usually humorous—exchanges of one-liners and wisecracks. "What about?"

He left the engine cover open for me to double-check and ducked under the plane to check the air pressure in the main landing gear tires. He mumbled something that I didn't hear.

The engine seemed fine. No loose wires, no unexplained oil, no broken mechanical linkages. I secured the cover and joined him in looking over the tail section. "What did you say the fight was about?"

He frowned.

"If you don't want to talk about it, that's cool. I didn't mean to pry." I flicked a dead bug off the leading edge of the tail. "I guess I do need to know if it will affect the project though."

He stood up after checking the air pressure in the tail wheel, an odd look on his face. "I guess I do want to talk about it. Let's get airborne first."

We bumped across the stubble, raising a cloud of black dust before the weight came off the wheels. We turned to the southeast, set the ADF for the next fuel depot beacon, and climbed to altitude.

Rick trimmed the plane at fifty-five hundred feet and switched on the autopilot. Even after the plane was flying smooth and steady, he looked over the instruments and at the horizon, frowning.

I waited.

After a while he began talking.

"The last week, since Joey went into the treatment center, Clara stayed home with Marie. To keep her company—to comfort her. I stuck this out the first two nights but I got bored, so two nights ago I went out. By myself."

"So Clara got mad about this?"

"Hell, no. She practically pushed me out the door. I went and hung out on Northgate."

Northgate was a line of bars and restaurants on the north side of the university campus.

"What happened, did you go back to their place too late?" A terrible thought came to me. "Or did you go back to their place *drunk?*"

He shook his head. "No. The problem was that I didn't go back at all."

I blinked. "Uh, you didn't come back to the ranch that night, either."

"That's right."

"Jesus, Rick. What are you trying to do?"

He winced. "I'm not trying to do anything. It just happened."

My mind raced, trying to figure out what this meant to the mission. Joey was a bad enough security risk without Rick sleeping around.

"Was it a one-night thing?" I asked.

He glared at me. "Give me *some* credit."

"Well, actually I was hoping it *was* just a one-night thing."

"Well it wasn't. It was an old relationship."

"Anybody I know?"

"Maybe. Chris Valencia, last year's graduating class."

I was flipping mentally through the girls of last year's senior class when it hit me. "Christopher Valencia? Chris is a boy!"

"Hey, he's older than me. Wouldn't you call that a man?"

I was stunned silent.

Rick shrugged. "Surprise." He glanced sideways at me, a wary look on his face—like a dog who expects to be kicked.

"I didn't know," I finally said.

"You weren't supposed to. Except for a few gay friends, only Clara knew. But that gets really old, Charlie. You helped me in school. You brought me into the project. You're my friend and you should know—whatever the result."

"What result? Did you think I'd fire you?"

He shrugged. "Don't know. I hope not, but we've never talked about it. It's hard to tell about anybody until they're confronted with it. I've seen too many people come out and lose their friends and family."

I felt my ears get hot and was thankful for the headset. My thoughts were confused. I'd made up my mind on this issue long before, but I'd never been confronted with it—not personally. "I guess I'll have to think about it. But you're crazy if you think I'd kick you off the project. Or push you out of my life."

He blinked and looked away, then nodded to himself.

"Does your mom know?"

He shook his head.

"What about you and Clara?" I asked.

"I don't know."

I was silent for a moment. "Uh, what do you mean? Give me a clue."

"I love her. She's understood things about me and made me feel good about them. But I felt more alive with Chris than I have in a year. I tried to tell myself that I was more bisexual than gay—that it was the person that mattered. I know people like that. Mostly hetero with the occasional gay fling. I told myself that I could be as excited about a woman as I could be about a man."

The corners of his mouth pulled down. "I was lying to myself."

I didn't know what to say, so I said nothing.

The front was visible, a wall on the far horizon, when we passed Scurry, so rather than risk traveling on to Comanche, we landed. We spent the time until the storm hit screwing tie-down stakes two feet into the soil and securing the plane as best we could. We even had time to refuel, so we did, figuring any extra weight in the plane would make it more stable. When the first fat drops hit the wing, we climbed back inside.

The rain made so much noise that conversation was difficult. There was so much lightning that I questioned the wisdom of staying in the plane, but decided, on the whole, that I'd rather be out of the rain. The wind wasn't as bad as I feared. We were partially sheltered by a low hummock.

After two hours the weather settled to a soft, steady rain. This lasted until after sunset, and we were stuck there for the night.

Fortunately, there was room to stretch out in the rear of the plane since the rear seats had been removed for cargo space. Rick and I took turns, one sitting guard while the other slept.

In the morning we had high scattered overcast and Clara reported clear skies over Wildside Base. Our field was damp, but not too soft to take off. We checked the plane out, recovered the mooring stakes, and lifted off.

It was eleven-thirty when we touched down at Wildside Base. Marie was in the tower and she came down to help us service the aircraft and push it into the hangar.

"Where's Clara?" Rick asked, his voice casual. He looked around.

Marie gave him a dark look. "She just left."

"Oh. Isn't it her turn to do maintenance?" He sounded relieved.

"Give her a break, Rick." Marie looked angry. "She spent all night in the tower, listening on the shortwave in case *you* needed anything." She turned away, clenching her jaw.

I put my hand on her shoulder. "How are *you?* Did you get enough rest?"

She shrugged and her face relaxed a bit. "I've been better. They won't let Joey have visitors until next weekend." She looked up. There were shadows under her eyes and I could tell her thoughts were far away, with Joey.

We closed the hangar doors and went through to the tame side.

Rick paused in the sunlight, basking for a moment in warm sunshine. He paused by his rent-a-car and looked it over. "Mind if I grab the first shower?" he asked.

"Go for it."

I went in and fixed myself some eggs and toast. Marie sat at the table and accepted some tea, but she just held the cup between her hands and stared out the kitchen window.

Rick showered quickly, put on clean clothes, and stuck his head in the kitchen door.

"You want some eggs?" I asked.

"I'll grab something in town—do we need anything, while I'm there?"

I opened the fridge. "Get some milk. And some more Diet Pepsi." I looked at him. "Guess you aren't going to Clara's?"

His smile died. "Not yet. I'll talk to her later."

I started to speak, then stopped myself. After a moment I said, "Be careful. Watch security. Okay?"

He rolled his eyes. "Of course!" He left.

Marie shook her head and pushed the tea away from her. I sat down and took a bite of my sandwich, but it tasted dry and flat.

"Shit," I said.

Marie said, "Yeah."

I found Clara at the stables, riding her horse, Impossible, over training jumps. They had one set of bleachers, faded and weather-beaten, and I climbed to the top seat and watched.

She saw me when she was finished, after she'd dismounted to open the gate of the arena. There were shadows under her eyes and she looked like she wasn't enjoying herself. I walked with her back to the barn and Impossible's stall.

"Rick told me about Christopher," I said.

She blinked and leaned into Impossible. "Oh." Impossible nickered. He was an old quarter horse, brown with a white sock. The hairs on his face were flecked with gray.

"Are you okay?" I kicked the side of the stall. "Shit. Of course you're not okay. Sorry. That was stupid."

She smiled briefly. "I know what you meant, Charlie. I'm bearing up."

She tied Impossible's halter rope in the corner and unsaddled him. "Hang this in the tack room, will you? The rack has my name on it."

I took the blanket and saddle, backed out of the stall, and looked down the aisle. I stuck my head back in the stall to ask her which direction. She had both arms around the horse's neck and was crying. I backed out of the stall quietly and, with only a little backtracking, found the tack room at the far end of the barn.

I made a lot of noise coming back into the stall. She wasn't crying anymore and she was briskly brushing Impossible's coat. She looked at me with reddened eyes.

"It's okay, Charlie. You don't have to scuff your feet quite so much. I'm presentable."

"Huh?"

"Charlie—you never scuff your feet. You walk around like a mouse. Even when you were overweight."

"Uh . . ."

"Oh, shut your mouth. Something will fly into it. There's another brush on the rail."

I picked up the brush and started working the other side of the horse. After a minute I handed a bandanna across Impossible's back, "You have horsehair on your cheeks." While she wiped her face I said, "I'm worried about things."

"Things? Who's a thing?"

"Okay. I'm worried about you. I'm worried about Rick. I'm worried about the project."

"Don't worry about *me*, Charlie. I'm not telling anybody about the project. I don't know about Rick, though." She gave me the bandanna back.

"Oh, Jesus, Clara. It's not just the project. I know you don't particularly like me, but I do care if you're happy or not."

She dropped down into a crouch, looking at me from under the belly of the horse. "What makes you think I don't like you?"

I shrugged. "You know you wouldn't have hung out with me unless Rick wanted to. You even complained about it."

She looked down at the bedding. "Um. That was before the project." She blinked. "In my callow youth."

"That was three months ago."

"We all have to grow up sometime."

I bit my lip. "Do you really think I've lost weight?"

She opened her eyes wider. "Don't you weigh yourself?"

"Uh—I've been busy." I didn't want to say that scales terrified and depressed me. "My clothes have been fitting different, but the last time I weighed myself, I was the same. I haven't had to trim the aircraft any differently."

"Well, that doesn't surprise me—you've turned a lot of flab into muscle. Your shirts are still the same size, but it's because of your shoulders and chest. You need to get some different pants, though— look at the way they're bunched up under your belt. At least put a few darts in the back."

Maybe I was slimmer. I glanced back at Clara. She was staring at something a million miles away and the corners of her mouth were drawn down.

"What do you want, Clara?"

"I want *Rick!*" She stood abruptly and I could here her sniffing. I handed my bandanna back and she took it. I heard her blow her nose heavily. "Sorry," she said. She walked to Impossible's head and started to hand me back my bandanna. "Uh, I'll wash it, first." She tucked it in her back pocket, then took Impossible's bridle off. After a minute, she said, "You meant, what do I want that I can have?"

"Yeah."

"I don't know." She led me out of the stall and closed it, absentmindedly stroking Impossible's neck over the gate before she turned away. She dropped the bridle off in the tack room and we walked outside into the hot August sun. "We're quite a pair, aren't we, Charlie?"

"What do you mean?"

"Unrequited, incorporated. Me with Rick. You with Marie."

I swallowed. "I wasn't aware it was that obvious."

She laughed. "You walk quiet, but your face—well your face *stomps* around like an elephant. Besides—I live with Marie, after all. It's not like we don't talk."

My ears turned red. "Oh."

She hugged me suddenly. "It's okay. And I *do* like you, Charlie. You're okay. More than okay. And if I ever thought different, you can be sure it was stupidity on my part."

It was my turn to blink away tears.

We had good weather the next two weeks, and were able to start a new depot on high plains of New Mexico near the Colorado and

Oklahoma borders. There was a small town in that location on the tame side, so we named the base after it—Moses. We were very close to our destination, now, a short hop to the northwest from the new base, but risks were about to increase exponentially.

Since Marie or I were Pilot-In-Command on every flight, Clara didn't have to fly with Rick, which she preferred. They were talking, but Clara kept him at arm's length—strictly project business—unless he was willing to return to their old relationship. Marie was still mad at Rick for hurting Clara, so she flew with Clara while I flew with Rick.

A couple of nights a week, Rick slept away from the ranch. I didn't have to ask if he spent the time at Clara's.

Marie's disposition improved greatly when she was able to visit Joey on weekends. He'd been shaken and clung to her like a drowning man. I had mixed feelings. I'd been hoping they'd break up, that I'd have my chance, but it was good to see her smile again.

Clara spent all her spare time at the stables, with Impossible.

I purchased oxygen sets for the Maule. The next series of flights would clear ten thousand feet—God help us—over the Rocky Mountains. We spent a day doing test flights over Wildside Base, flying clear up to the Maule's operational ceiling of twenty thousand feet, to test engine performance and the oxygen rigs. I hoped to keep below fifteen thousand feet over the actual mountains—the danger from icing would be bad enough as it was.

Rick and I took the first foray into the mountains. Our destination was only forty-five minutes flying time from the base at Moses, but we played it safe, a simple high-altitude flyover of Cripple Creek, Colorado, videotapes running. Rick took three rolls of 35-mm stills, as well. The weather was clear and the mission went as planned.

We were running out of time, though. There was snow on most of the peaks and glaciers in some of the high valleys. If we didn't finish in the next month, we were stuck until next spring.

All our flyovers were two-day trips. Spend the day getting into Moses, then refuel and stay the night. Wake up rested for the mountain flight, turn around after the flyover, and head straight back. If the flyover was short and the winds were right, we didn't need to refuel until Wildside Base. If we were in danger of running into our reserves, we'd stop at Scurry or Comanche to refuel.

At Cripple Creek, our potential landing sites were few. The best one looked like it would take substantial ground prep and I didn't know about parachuting in at that altitude. There were also a few flattish spots above the timberline, but they were spotted with snow. However, a glacier valley five miles downstream had a tilted meadow that looked flat enough. If we landed going uphill, it would compensate for the higher than normal ground speed necessary at that altitude.

Twice, Rick and I were caught by weather and had to return to Comanche after running into advancing weather. Once, Marie and Clara were socked in at Moses for two nights. Rick spent the time in Bryan and I lived by the shortwave, camped in the tower, dashing back to the house for food and drink, then returning to eat by the radio.

When they were within an hour of home, I turned the tower back over to Rick, showered, and slept for ten hours.

Despite perfectly clear skies, we didn't fly the next day.

Eleven

"We've Lost the Tunnel."

Joey was released from the treatment center on a Friday and went to his first AA meeting that night. "Actually, it's not my first. We had them every day in the center. I even ran some—it's part of the program. Gotta work the program—keep my support systems intact." He grinned but it wasn't the old Joey. This was someone who was both less *and* more sure of himself.

The old Joey presented a confident face to the world—very aggressive. I'd long known that it was a mask, a pretense that covered someone who was very unsure of himself. This new Joey was very tenuous and overtly insecure—haunted, almost—but you found under this something stronger, a desperate determination to win an inner fight.

We had a dinner for him on Saturday, early, before the AA meeting in downtown Bryan.

"Thank God they've got nonsmoking meetings. In the center it was so bad that I thought if alcoholism doesn't get me, lung cancer probably will."

He didn't want to fly, yet. The overnight missions would keep him away from AA meetings and, for the time being, he wanted to go every night. So he volunteered to do all the base maintenance and to take shifts on the tower.

"All right with me if you want to mow all the strips. Great, in fact," I said. "You can do some of the wildlife video, too. But you still need to get a couple of hours in every week, to get your reflexes back in shape and keep them there. Right?"

He nodded slowly. "I guess. I'll want a check pilot the first time or two."

"Just say the word. I have a feeling that Marie would be more than happy to 'check you out.' "

"Already did," Marie said, "last night. And he's performing beautifully." Then she had the grace to blush slightly, but Joey turned bright red.

I laughed and was surprised when it didn't hurt. Not too much, anyway.

Rick and I were returning from a low-level photo recon of our proposed Cripple Creek landing site. We'd been battling head-winds all the way back so we landed at Scurry for fuel.

After tanking up, I got on the shortwave to Wildside Base. Clara had the tower and answered immediately.

"Weather's clear here. How's it there, Charlie?"

"We got some scattered cumulus and the headwinds have been crummy, but we're okay. Should be in about four. What's going on there?"

"Joey and Marie just went to get the tractor. She's going to mow the Wildside strip while Joey rides shotgun, so it should be nice and smooth when you—"

She stopped transmitting.

"Sorry, Clara, you took your hand off the mike key. What was that?"

No answer. I checked the radio carefully. Power, antennas, frequency setting, digital self-diagnostics. Ten minutes went by with no further communication.

"What do you think happened?" The worry on Rick's face matched the feeling churning my guts.

I took a deep breath. "Either they're transmitting and we're unable to receive them, or they're not transmitting. If they're not transmitting, it's because they have technical problems or they have other problems."

"Other problems? What do you mean, other problems?"

In my head I pictured federal agents swarming over the hangar and tower, Rick, Clara, and Marie standing handcuffed, under guard. "Maybe Joey fell off the tractor and broke his arm. Maybe there was a power outage. Who knows? Let's get going—we know the weather is clear there and if we get above five thousand feet, we should be able to check the AM beacon."

"Right."

He tried to rush the preflight and I irritated him by being twice as careful. Still, ten minutes later we were in the air and wasting fuel by flying five knots below rated top speed instead of our optimum cruise speed. Still, with headwind, this only took our actual ground speed up to normal cruise. We took a bearing on the solar-powered AM beacon at Comanche, then switched over to 216, the AM beacon at Wildside Base. Nothing. When we reached five thousand feet there was still nothing.

"The oxygen sets are over half-full," I said, and kept climbing. We pushed it all the way to twenty thousand feet and there was still no trace of the Wildside Base beacon—Morse W.

"Shit. You're in control, Rick. Get us down to ten thousand feet and head for Comanche." With the Wildside beacon out, we would have to navigate in by dead reckoning. I pulled the chart out and began taking bearings on the Comanche, Scurry, and Royce City beacons. Over the next hour I calculated our wind drift. By the time we passed over Comanche I was able to say, "Steer one-oh-six magnetic. When we're one-eight-five off of the Royce City beacon, we'll be on the Brazos River and we follow it south to base."

"You want control back?"

I shook my head. "Nope." I started scanning through the frequencies, looking for anything. I'd swing back to the Wildside tower frequency every few minutes and try to raise Clara, but there was still nothing.

I kept my growing unease from Rick. Giving him control kept him busy, kept him from worrying too much. What did *I* do, though?

We hit the Brazos on schedule. Ten minutes later I heard Clara's voice on radio. "Come in Maule one seven baker. This is Wildside Base transmitting on a handheld radio, do you read?"

"Roger that, Clara. We read you. We're ten minutes up river. What's wrong. Is the power out?"

There was a burst of static and I thought we'd lost her again, when she said, "Well, you could say that. We've definitely lost power."

"What else, Clara? What else is wrong? Over."

"We've lost the tunnel."

Things looked normal enough as we landed. Marie, Joey, and Clara stood outside the hangar as we pulled up. Clara held the handheld radio while Joey and Marie stood by, armed. Clara's lips were tight, Marie was looking at Joey, worried, and Joey was scanning the perimeter, but the corners of his mouth were pulled down and he seemed on the edge of tears.

We shut down the Maule and joined them.

The lights were off in the hangar. One of the doors was opened two feet and the dark within was cut by a path stretching diagonally across the floor. Each of us had a flashlight on our harnesses. I took mine out and stepped inside. The others followed.

"Shut the doors," I said.

"What about the Maule?"

"Leave it for now."

Rick pushed the door shut and it was dark, then splotches of light lit the floor and walls as we turned the flashlights on.

The door was still there, and the tunnel itself. The tractor was parked in the tunnel and I had to squeeze around it. Beyond it, I found half the rotary hay mower.

Half.

It was still attached to the tractor. One side of it had plowed into the wall of the tunnel and was about six inches into the dirt wall, but the rear of it was gone, a straight edge of fused metal, like it had been cut with a very fine cutting torch. Beyond it, the tunnel continued for another eight feet or so, but ended in a rough rock and dirt surface.

"When it happened," Joey's voice said, "it was like a huge electrical spark and the edge of the metal glowed in the dark for several minutes." His voice was quavering. "I'm sorry, Charlie. I should've been more careful."

Marie's voice came from behind the tractor. "It wasn't Joey's fault. We were necking. I should've left him alone while he was driving. I stuck my tongue in his ear and he swerved. That's when the tractor hit the wall."

Rick started to squeeze past the tractor and I said, "Hold it. Let's get the tractor out of here—maybe turn it around and shine the headlights down here."

They backed up and I climbed up into the driver's seat. The tractor started right up and I backed it, first, until the attachment was away from the wall. Dirt and pebbles slid down to the tunnel floor. I pointed my flashlight at the gash in the wall and something dimly metallic reflected the light back.

"Watch your eyes," I said, and turned on the headlights. The four of them turned their heads and retreated up the tunnel. The fumes from the tractor stank in the confined space. I turned it quickly, in the hangar, and disconnected what was left of the mowing attachment as quickly as I could before turning the headlights back down the tunnel and turning off the ignition. I left the headlights on, though.

Rick asked, "Are you sure you want to do that? It's not like we can jump-start it with your truck if we run the battery down."

"Worse comes to worst," I replied, "we'll just use one of the batteries from the Maule to start it. Now let's see what we've got here."

I walked down the tunnel, the others close behind. Tall thin shadows preceded us, thrown by the tractor's headlights.

"Christ, I hope we're not stuck over here," Rick said, putting a voice to the unspoken thought in my head. "How much food do we have, anyway?"

Clara said, "We've got the survival rations in the Maule—call it two weeks or so. But we can hunt if we have to. Plenty of game."

I stopped by the gash, the others moved on down to the end of the tunnel. "Maybe we can dig through," Joey said. "Ah, what am I saying. We dig through this and we'll end up on the other side of this hill—not back on the tame side."

I knelt and shown my flashlight into the shallow hole scraped in the tunnel wall. A piece of metal, rectangular, about four inches long, with smooth edges, stuck out of the gash, pointing back up the tunnel, toward the wildside. It was a dull silver, like cast aluminum or tin except for a spot on its end where a streak of burgundy discolored the metal, the color of the mowing attachment's paint.

From the dead end of the tunnel I heard Rick say, "Christ, Joey, you really did it this time!"

Clara said, "Don't be any more of an asshole than you have to, Rick. Do you think anybody wants to be stuck over here with you?"

"Don't you?" he snapped. "Isn't this just want you'd want? Me to yourself and Christopher in a completely different universe?"

I flinched, but didn't look up. I heard Clara turn and walk back up the tunnel.

Rick said, "Hit a nerve, there, I see."

"Rick, shut up," I said, without looking up. I gingerly put my finger to the end of the metal. It moved easily, pivoting in a horizontal plane until it was perpendicular to the tunnel.

Rick said, "Stick it in your ear, Char—"

I looked up. They were gone. Where the rock and dirt face had been was the old tunnel, the door into the barn, into the tame side, lay just beyond. The lights on the tunnel ceiling, the ones Joey had installed, were lit on that half of the tunnel, but they were still out on the wildside. In the immediate foreground was the back half of the hay mower.

"Clara!" I shouted.

She didn't answer. I reached for the air horn on my harness and gave a blast, then yelled her name again.

She came running, her shotgun pointed at the ceiling, then slowed, her steps. "Oh. You got it back. Where are the others?"

Her face was a strange mixture of relief and resignation, overlaid with the tracks of tears.

"I don't know," I said.

"What do you mean, you don't know?"

"I don't. I pushed this lever back into place and the tunnel came back, but they were gone when I looked up."

"Maybe they're in the barn?" she said.

"There wasn't time for them to go to the barn. One second they were there—the next they weren't." She looked unconvinced. I snapped, "Well, then, go look, dammit!"

She flinched.

I dropped my voice back down. "Sorry. Maybe we better check the barn, anyway. Go ahead."

She looked down at the ground and blinked heavily, then nodded and started down the tunnel. She paused just short of where the back portion of the mowing attachment lay and pushed the barrel of her shotgun over that invisible line. Nothing happened. She took a breath and plunged on, skipping forward, then letting her momentum carry her into a run.

I let out my breath. I was glad she'd thought to check—I hadn't.

Clara reached the other end and opened the barn door. I heard her call their names. "Marie? Joey? Rick?" She turned back toward me and said, "No sign of them. Where are they?" This last question ended in a plaintive wail that cut me to the core.

Did I kill them? Did I exile them to some other universe?

"Come on back," I called. "I'm going to try shutting it off again."

She ran back, hesitating slightly before crossing the line. "How are you going to do it? Drive the tractor into the wall again."

"No. I'm just going to move this lever again." I bent down to do just that, then stopped. "Uh, maybe you better go wait on the that side," I said, pointing back toward the barn.

"Why?"

"Well, what if it doesn't work? I mean, what if it does shut the tunnel down, but then I can't get it back, after? At least right now, we have a way back home. If you wait on that side, you'll be all right, no matter what happens."

Her eyes widened. "Forget it, Charlie. Throw the switch."

I stood. "Really, Clara. I really think you should wait—"

"No! Now do it!" She swung her shotgun down. Instead of pointing at the ceiling it now pointed at the ground between us.

"Okay, okay." I bent back to the lever. This time, I watched the tunnel, not the switch. The pocket of dirt and stone that was the end of the tunnel flicked into place like a TV changing channels. There was just the tiniest flicker.

There was a sudden short scream from in front of us, and I jerked.

The tunnel to the barn was gone again and Rick and Marie stood before us, blinking in the light of the tractor's headlights. It was Rick who'd yelled.

Joey wasn't with them.

Clara and Marie asked the question at exactly the same time: "Where's Joey?"

Then Rick said, "He was standing right there." He pointed to a spot on this side of the 'line,' next to Clara.

"You mean he was standing next to us?" I said.

"No, no!" Marie shook her head violently. "He was examining the other dead end."

"What dead end?" said Clara.

I elaborated on her question. "What did you see when the tunnel went away? I mean, where were you?"

"We were right here," Marie said, pointing at the dirt beneath her. "Only the other side"—she pointed back toward us—"was also a dead end, sort of like this one, and we only had the light from our flashlights."

"There was no way out," said Rick. "It was like we were in a pocket in the earth."

"Joey went over to the other dead end, to look at it closely. He was quicker than we were—we would probably be with him if the tunnel hadn't come back."

I motioned them forward. "Come on over on this side, and we'll try it again."

They walked over the line. "Try *what* again, Charlie?" asked Rick.

"I can turn it on and off. There's some sort of switch—that's what Joey hit with the tractor. See?"

When they were far enough over the line I pushed the lever. The tunnel came back and, at the same time, there was a tremendous spark followed by the smell of ozone. Joey was facing us and falling backwards. Something hit the floor with a thunk. It was the back half of Joey's flashlight. The front half was missing.

"What the hell was that?" shouted Joey. He was sitting on the floor, blinking. Behind him was the second half of the tunnel with the door into the barn at the end.

Marie ran forward and crouched by his side. "Are you okay? Christ! What happened to your shoe?"

The tip of Joey's shoe was cut cleanly off. You could see his sock-covered toes inside. He stuck his hand in the hole and gingerly felt his toes. "Nothing, uh, missing." He was clearly shaken. "Nothing important, that is."

Marie helped him stand.

"So, we have the tunnel back?" Joey asked.

"Yeah," I said. "You uncovered a switch with the tractor. A way to turn the gate on and off."

"Gate?" said Rick. "Of course. It's a gate."

"So what was that cave we were trapped in?" Marie said. She tapped Joey on the chest, "And how did *you* get out of it?"

"I walked. When you guys disappeared, *that* side of the tunnel appeared." He pointed at the barn. "I stepped over the line but you guys plainly weren't there so I was turning around to look at the dead end again when 'poof'!" He pointed down at his foot.

Rick said, "The amazing gate-amatic. It slices, it dices! It makes julienne fries!"

Clara glared at Rick, but Joey laughed.

Marie didn't think it was very funny either. "Would you be making jokes if it had sliced Joey in two?"

Rick was unrepentant. "If you had rotors, would you be a helicopter? It didn't slice him and we're not trapped. Lighten up!"

I interrupted. "I know what that cave was."

"You do?" asked Clara.

"Look, you have these two dead end tunnels, in two different universes, right?" Nods. "When the gate is on, it connects the two tunnels—all but the last ten feet or so of each one." I held up my two index fingers and put them together, then slid one slightly past the other so the first joint of each finger overlapped. "Well, the gate *also* connects the two dead end pieces of the tunnels, forming a closed pocket. When you guys were in the pocket, Joey walked through the gate to the dead end side of the tame side's tunnel. When I switched the gate off, he was on the tame side and you guys were still on the wildside."

Joey shook his head. "I'm confused."

"You and me both," I said. "Let's see what we have here."

We dug into the wall that night, around the switch. The lever swiveled on a tapered metal arm that led back toward the barn, toward the line—the terminus between our world and the wildside.

I scraped the dirt away carefully, using a spoon, afraid to hit other controls or fragile machinery. The arm thickened as it neared the terminus, a gentle curve anchored to something hidden by the dirt. I dug on and in one spoonful the dirt went from a fine, sandy soil that flaked away easily to something glassy hard and fixed.

The lights showed me something that didn't look any different from the dirt around it but it didn't budge and the spoon skittered across it like it was greased. I pushed harder, and then harder, but the dirt under the spoon didn't move. Instead, the handle of the spoon bent.

We tried going around the smooth section, first above it, then below, then, finally, deep into the side, but the barrier went farther than the foot I was willing to dig into the wall or the two feet up or down.

Rick did an exploratory hole on the other side and, though there wasn't any switch, he ran into the glassy smooth immobile dirt. "Is it made out of this stuff? I'm dying to hit it with a hammer."

"No!" said Marie and Clara at precisely the same time.

"I'm inclined to agree," I said. "Whatever is here, let's not break it, okay?"

We packed dirt back into the excavation, mixing in a little water to stick it in place. The switch I left exposed, studying it carefully—top, sides, and bottom.

There were no helpful messages on it like, "Made In Japan" or "Created by benevolent aliens with a sense of humor." There were no clues from its manufacture. The pivot point was recessed and I couldn't see what sort of mechanism was within. There were no bolts or nuts or rivets or screws or clasps or staples or even zippers. Just a lever with two positions.

I found myself getting angry at Joey for discovering it.

Sure, the gate was a mystery before, but I could treat it like some freak of nature—something mystical. Now I had to worry who made it (Uncle Max?), who put it there, and whether or not they'd ever come back.

We didn't fly the next day.

"Ready," called Joey, from the tunnel.

Rick, Marie, and I stood back from the gasoline-powered generator. I would've preferred something cleaner, but we already had the six-hundred-gallon tank-trailer of aviation gas which we kept on the wildside and the generator could run on that. We'd just finished installing the generator in the hangar with intake vents to the outside and a tall exhaust chimney through the roof.

We walked back to join Joey and Marie at the gateway. At my request, they'd rewired the broken power line, using heavy-duty electrical sockets on each side of the gate and a short, heavy-duty cable with plugs on each end to bridge the gap. They did the same for the phone line and the wire to the ranch gate alarm, and made up a dozen spare cables, with appropriate connectors. Joey had also rewired the lights in the tunnel so the power for each half was on a separate circuit.

I switched my watch to stopwatch mode and nodded. Joey reached down and grabbed the short power plug and said, "Three, two, one—" and pulled it from its socket in the same instant that I pushed the button on my watch.

The fluorescent lights on the wildside half of the tunnel flickered out and I heard the starter motor on the generator kick in, followed by the deeper *thrum* of the gasoline motor firing and running up to speed. The fluorescents came back on and I stopped the timer.

"One-point-one-four seconds," I said.

Joey grinned. "Shall I reconnect?"

"Sure."

He put the plug back in. The lights didn't flicker, but the generator dropped back to an idle as its current load dropped, then, after thirty seconds of uninterrupted external voltage, it shut itself down.

I looked around. We stood in a quarter circle around Joey, who knelt on the floor by the junction box. All of us were in the wildside half of the tunnel, careful to avoid the invisible line where the gate was.

The gate switch that Joey had uncovered with the tractor was on the other side of the tunnel, currently covered by a piece of plywood leaning against the wall. I stepped over to it and moved it aside.

"Let's try it for real," I said.

Marie said, "Are you sure that's such a good idea?"

The others looked nervous.

"If I'm out there five hundred miles from base and the gate is shut down, I want to know that the radio and beacons will still be working. Why don't you guys wait over there, though, just to be on the safe side?"

Rick promptly walked six feet over the line and turned around. Marie, Joey, and Clara didn't move.

"Aren't you coming?" Rick asked them. "What if the gate doesn't come back? For all we know, it wasn't meant to be turned on and off so much. Something might burn out."

Clara said, "And leave Charlie over here by himself?"

Joey shrugged. "Can't do that."

Rick said, "What about your family? Your friends?"

Joey said, "Except for you, most of my real friends are on this side of the line, Rick. What's more, there's no beer over here. No alcohol."

Marie just took Joey's hand and didn't say anything.

Clara added, "I'm waiting here."

Rick shook his head angrily then stared over his shoulder for a moment at the barn. "I'm gonna hate myself if the damn gate doesn't come back on." He shoved his hands into his pockets and walked back over the line.

I looked down at the wall switch, but my eyes weren't working right and I was having trouble seeing it. When I said, "Ready?" it didn't sound like my voice at all. There was a lump in my throat and I was having trouble talking.

"Ready, Charlie," said Marie.

I moved the switch, then flinched as a fat electrical spark jumped from the power cable and the lights went out. I realized I'd forgotten to start the stopwatch and counted, "One thousand and one, one thou—" Then the generator kicked in and the lights came on.

I looked at the group, at the Wildsiders, at . . . my fiends. "Thank you," I said.

Marie and Joey smiled and Clara said, "For what?"

I shook my head. "Just thanks."

Rick was eyeing the switch. I turned back to it and pushed the lever back into place. The tunnel reappeared and his sigh of relief was audible even over the distant purr of the generator. When we replaced the cords, the generator shut down on schedule.

I stood, replaced the plywood over the switch, and said to Joey, "We should build a cabinet around the generator, to cut down on some of the noise." As the two of us walked back into the hangar I said, "You still have your radio-controlled airplane models?"

"Well, I left them with my brother. Why?"

"Let me bounce an idea or two off you."

* * *

The next day, the prospector arrived, a gasoline-powered mechanical gold panner. Marie and Clara were flying supplies into Moses, preparatory to our attempt to land at Cripple Creek.

Joey, Rick, and I dumped five buckets of dirt, two buckets of sand, and two buckets of gravel into the stock tank. Then we added one pound of iron filings and two cups of assorted washers, nuts, and bolts and stirred the whole mess with a shovel while topping the tank off with water.

The mechanical panner consisted of a thirty-foot-four-inch hose, a powerful water pump, and a series of shaker trays with smaller and smaller gratings. It was about the size of a washing machine.

I started it up and Joey shoved it down into the stock tank. Brown water spilled across the trays, which were shaking away. The lighter gravel, sand, and dirt flowed over the edges of the trays. The heavier iron bolts, nuts, and washers settled in the coarse trays, sorted by size along with a few heavier pieces of quartz gravel. The last tray, the fine one, collected the iron filings.

When we were done, when we'd sucked the tank dry and spilled water all over the garden, the pasture, and part of the driveway, we air-dried the filings and weighed them—fifteen and a half ounces. Pretty good recovery rate. If it worked that way for gold, we'd be in good shape.

We carefully disassembled the mechanical prospector and prepped it for flight. Clara and Marie got in before noon the next day and we refueled the plane, loaded the prospector, and Joey and I took it out, sleeping that night in Surrey. We rose the next morning with the dawn, flew on to Moses, and got back to Wildside Base before sunset.

Clara said, "Pushing it a little close, aren't you, Charlie? It's not like you have a radar-vectored guidance system to bring you in at night."

I looked down at my feet, then looked up. "There was frost on the ground at Surrey in the morning. When we got to Moses it was still there by midmorning." I looked at them all. "We don't have time to waste. Get a good night's sleep—we're going tomorrow."

Twelve

"How Are We Supposed to Climb *That?*"

Rick volunteered to stay behind.

"You know how I feel about parachuting. If you hit pay-dirt, you're going to be gone at least a week, right? Maybe longer?"

Joey didn't want to go that long without an AA meeting, but he wanted even less to be left behind. "Still don't trust myself, really," he said. "I'll have a hard time falling off the wagon if I'm seven hundred miles from the nearest beer, though."

I don't think anybody slept well. I spent half the night going over contingency plans with Rick and Luis.

"Okay, case one—you don't hear from us for three days straight."

Luis looked at the sheet before him. "We buy a Maule, hire an A&P, and rebuild it in the wildside hangar. The A&P never sees the outside of the hangar and he's blindfolded on the way out to the farm. If necessary, we seal the tunnel after we have him working on the reassembly and worry about him after we rescue you. How do you seal the tunnel?"

"Rick will take care of it if we have to do it. What Maule?" I asked.

Rick said, "There's one for sale in Houston, and two for sale up in Dallas. Whichever one we can get hold of fastest."

"Okay, case two—feds grab Luis."

Rick said, "When I don't hear from him on our two-hour schedule, I seal the tunnel, with me on the wildside."

"They move on the ranch?"

Rick said, "I seal the tunnel and wait on the wildside."

Luis added, "When *I* don't hear from *him* on the two-hour schedule, I start issuing press releases, subpoenas, and injunctions as well as bring in the Houston firm."

"You *suspect* they're moving on the ranch."

"I seal the tunnel and wait," said Rick.

"We haven't covered everything, I just know it," I said. "So keep your eyes open and use your initiative. But don't give up the tunnel unless you have to, to rescue us, and don't leave the farm while we're away. If you have to, have Christopher bring you groceries, but, don't break security. Okay, Rick?"

"Maybe I should just go with you guys. Maybe the waiting isn't such a prime post, after all."

"You've made your bed," I said. "Lie in it."

Rick grinned. "I will—but not alone."

We flew out the next morning, Marie and Joey at the controls. Clara sat sideways in her seat and looked back at the tower until distance swallowed it. When we'd climbed into the plane, Rick said, "Be careful, you guys. I don't want to have to come after you." He'd avoided eye contact with Clara, shutting the hangar door as soon as we cranked up the Maule's engine. He waved from the tower as we lifted off and then he shrank to insignificance, a tiny spot in the window of a tiny tower.

Clara finally turned in her seat, away from the base, and sank into herself, slumping in the seat and staring vacantly at the back of Marie's head. Her mouth was a straight line that turned down at the ends.

For a moment, I considered trying to talk to her, but to be heard we would've had to use headsets and the intercom, which would hardly have been private. Instead I made myself a nest of sleeping bags and caught up on my sleep.

The Maule was heavily loaded with food and survival gear, extra ammo, and spare airplane parts. We underfueled to compensate for the load, stopping instead at each of the fuel stations between the Brazos and the Colorado border and filling our tanks half-full.

We landed at Moses in midafternoon, pitched camp, and collected dried buffalo patties for our fire. The grassy plain spread around us in undulating waves. We cleared the grass around the plane for a hundred-foot radius, using the gasoline-powered Weedeater to chop the dry, brown stuff down. On the high plains of northern New Mexico, it wasn't as high or as heavy as it was back on the Llano Estacado, but we wanted to keep the predators back just the same.

I took the first watch, feeding the fire. Joey and Marie were sleeping in the tent and Clara was sleeping in the plane. I sat with my back to the fire—close enough to feel the warmth—far enough away to avoid catching on fire—and watched the darkness beyond my shadow. Occasionally I'd tilt my head back and watch the sparks from the fire climb toward the stars. Every ten minutes, my watch would beep, and I'd walk around the perimeter, then return to the fire, add more buffalo chips, and return to my seat.

I had no trouble keeping awake. I'd slept on the flight and my mind was on tomorrow. There were a thousand things that could go wrong and I was trying to think of each of them—and all the proper responses to each disaster, each complication, each injury, each mechanical failure. I was trying to think of everything.

And if this wasn't enough to keep me awake, I was uncomfortably aware of Marie and Joey in the tent. They were being relatively quiet but they *weren't* sleeping. I moved as far from them as I could and still watch things—the two hours went slowly.

Clara was awake when I opened the door to the Maule. "Everything okay?" she asked. She was staring at the cabin ceiling, her feet tucked under the rear seat and her body curled to fit around the cargo.

"All quiet," I said. And it was. Joey and Marie were finally asleep—I could tell—Joey snored. I grabbed a sleeping bag and a ground cloth and spread them underneath the plane.

She snaked out of her sleeping bag and grabbed at her back. "Ouch. That seat strut is a real pain." She sat in the door of the plane to pull on her boots. "Stay on watch long enough for me to pee?"

"A full bladder will keep you awake."

She poked me in the chest. "A full bladder will make me go off and leave you guys unguarded if I have to pee while on duty."

"Well, since you put it that way."

She took her shotgun around to the other side of the plane. When she came back, after a minute, she eyed my bed beneath the plane. "Leave room on the ground cloth—I'm not scrunching up again when my shift is over." She dumped her sleeping bag down beside mine, and said, "Sir, I relieve you."

I bowed. "You have the watch."

"Sleep tight."

"Don't let the saberteeth bite."

I fell asleep mentally dismantling and reassembling the landing gear near my head. Later I heard Clara wake Joey for his watch, then heard her sit heavily on the ground cloth beside me to take off her boots.

" 'severything all right?"

She took off her jacket and rolled it, lambskin lining out, to use as a pillow. "Everything's fine, Charlie. Go back to sleep."

I rolled over, away from her, and listened to her slip into the bag, zip it up, and lie back. After a minute I felt her back against mine. She was wearing long underwear, pants, a flannel shirt, and a winter sleeping bag. I was wearing much the same, and we were facing opposite directions. Still, I went from being half-asleep to wide-awake and very aware of her body.

An interminable amount of time later, she began to snore lightly, a regular buzz—whoosh that made me smile. For some reason this inelegant noise finally relaxed me enough to drowse, then sleep.

I dreamed of flight and my plane's engine was quiet, only making noise when it flew on its back, and then, only when it exhaled.

"Well, what do you think?"

It was a half hour after dawn. There was frost on the Maule but it was clearing rapidly as the sun rose. The barometer was steady, precisely where it'd been the night before. What little wind there was came from the east and the sky had few altocumulus clouds. I wrote down the barometer reading in the log and answered Marie's question.

"I think it's go. We need the sun a bit higher, maybe. Let's wait until we have all the frost off the wings. We'll have shadows in the canyons if we get there before midmorning."

We packed the plane carefully. Before we left, we used the shortwave to check with Rick. "Weather's good," he said. "Nothing heading your way from down here."

The first pass was above the ridgeline, dropping orange smoke pots out the window as close to the center of the valley as we could. I had my suspicions about the approach path. There were two canyons at right angles to our glide path that had high potential for crosswinds. We tried to drop three pots apiece where they intersected the Cripple Creek valley.

Try is the operative word—the ride was bumpy even above the ridgeline. The pots were only vaguely in the center, but they were close enough to see what the wind was doing.

"There," said Marie from the pilot's seat. "There's a pretty hefty crosswind at canyon number two. What do you make that—ten knots?" She was referring to the angle of the smoke stream. We'd tested the pots at Wildside Base, when we could read the wind speed from our weather station, and we'd worked out approximate wind velocities based on how the smoke rose.

"More like twelve, I'd say," I shouted, moving my oxygen face mask aside for a second. "We'll have to check it when we're down. Looks pretty calm, though, every place else." The pots drifted a little upstream in the valley proper, away from the cross canyons.

We circled for fifteen—minutes, watching the smoke while it lasted to make sure the still air wasn't a momentary fluke. "It's not going to get any better—let's do it."

Clara and I had won the toss. We were perched in the back with the duffels, dressed to kill—or at least dressed not to be eaten, frozen, or asphyxiated. Besides our usual chute and equipment harness we wore insulated overalls over our other clothes and each had a small oxygen bottle slung under our safety chute. I double-checked the whole mess, then slid the back door open. Frigid air blasted in, finding exposed flesh and biting it.

Clara lowered her goggles and wrestled the cargo pack to the edge. Joey shouted, "Now!" and pumped his arm down. Clara shoved the pack out.

The static line popped the chute open and popped the tab on a yellow-green smoke pot attached to the pack. We circled to watch it drift down. "Hmm. Drop us a little more east. We've got some crosswind up here as well."

The cargo pack landed in trees on the face of the west ridge. I couldn't tell how far up it was, but the ridge towered nine hundred feet above the stream below. It was going to be interesting getting it down.

"Are you sure?" asked Marie, her head turned to look at the chute caught in the trees.

"*We* can steer our chutes," I said. "The cargo pack couldn't."

Marie widened her spiral and brought us back a half mile east of the last drop sight and five thousand feet higher. Clara and I double-checked each other's gear to make sure that our chutes wouldn't tangle in any of our other equipment.

"Set altimeter!" shouted Joey.

Clara and I bowed our heads over the altimeter actuators on our chutes and put our thumbs to the set dials.

"Set to nine-er, fi-uhv, zee-ro, zee-ro."

We dialed in ninety-five hundred and locked the dials. Then I checked Clara's while she checked mine. I raised my hand, forefinger circled to thumb in an "OK" sign to Joey. No more talk for

Clara or me—we'd secured the oxygen masks for the jump, four straps around the back of the head, under the helmet, and then the helmet chin strap on top.

We swung into the doorway, side by side, ready. The wind pulled at us, hungry. Finally Joey pumped his arm and said, "Go!"

Eternity opened its mouth and swallowed us whole.

Clara went first followed "One-one-thousand, two-one-thousand" by me. We were not using static lines. This was a HALO drop (High Altitude-Low Opening) to avoid the crosswinds above the ridges and, hopefully, get us into the right valley.

She assumed the position, legs spread, arms up, but instead of leaning against a wall or a police car, she was leaning against a wall of air sixty feet below me and maybe the same distance off to my right. I saw her swivel her head, then drop a shoulder to slide sideways. I followed, half-watching her, half-watching the ground for—there it was. The yellow-green smoke from the cargo chute's pot was a smudge on the green, gray, and brown landscape below.

We had thirty seconds to get into position before our chutes would open automatically. I was also counting in my head, a monotonous "one-one-thousand, two-one-thousand." If I reached thirty-four without the chute opening, I was going to do it manually. I was also glancing at the altimeter. It was whirling around, a thousand feet every six seconds. I'd used a grease pencil to mark the target altitude. Again, if I passed it, I was going to manually open the chute.

Clara was gliding for the ridge opposite the smoke smudge. The valley was widest there, a flat meadow long enough to land the Maule once we dropped a couple of trees at each end. I tilted at an even more extreme angle and closed both the vertical and horizontal distance between us. She didn't see me until I caught the sleeve of her coverall. I couldn't read her face around her oxygen mask and goggles, but she took my hand in hers and we dropped on for five more seconds, still counting, still watching the altimeter.

Her actuator went off first and she was pulled from my grasp as her chute blossomed above. For a brief instant I thought my actuator had malfunctioned and my hand was tightening on the D ring when my opening chute yanked me upright and slowed my downward plunge by over a hundred miles per hour.

I couldn't see Clara—my own chute blocked my view above. The ground below was sliding briskly toward the east, which meant I was blowing west. I turned my parasail east and spilled air to slide into the wind, trading altitude for horizontal position. The east ridge was directly below me and, by now, about five hundred feet lower. I hauled hard on my right-hand brake loop and went into a spiral that dropped me rapidly. When I was much closer to the ridge I let go and steered west, crossing the ridge about fifty feet above the rocks.

I suddenly dropped thirty feet and cursed myself for an idiot. I shouldn't have gotten so close to the ridge. Where the east wind flowed over the top of the ridge there was a downdraft at the trailing edge—basic aerodynamics. I sank rapidly toward a rock outcropping that projected over the Cripple Creek valley. If I landed, I would have to climb down into the valley, but, worse, it was more likely that I would land, my chute would partially collapse, and then the wind would catch it and drag me off the cliff with only a moderate chance of slowing my fall before I struck some rock outcropping below. I steered to the clearer side of the outcropping, pulled my knees to my chest, and prayed.

The heel of my left boot grazed rock and then I was over, past the ridge, with nine hundred feet of air under my feet again.

I did the rest in a spiral, coming out well clear of the trees and then dropping gently into the meadow. My shotgun was out and I was scanning all around when Clara dropped onto the ground fifty yards away.

She let her chute collapse onto the grass and pulled out her shotgun. The wind in the bottom of the valley was light. She popped her chute harness and walked out of it.

I did the same. I was sweating. The temperature was in the high forties and we were dressed for the weather over a mile higher. I took my eyes off the surrounding grass and looked up. The Maule came down the valley below the ridgeline, keeping well to the middle. I dropped my helmet, took off the oxygen mask, and pulled my handheld VHF out of its holster. "You all right, Clara?"

She was still scanning our perimeter and her oxygen mask still covered her face, but she held up her free hand signaling "OK."

"You hear me, Marie?" I said, into the radio.

"Loud and clear, Charlie. You guys okay?"

"We're fine. No problems." I was turning as I said this. "Well, maybe one." I looked over the thick stand of pines that lined the creek on the west side of the meadow.

"What's that?"

"The cargo chute is halfway up the west ridge." The chute had alternating white and international orange panels and stood out clearly against yellow and red leaves where it hung in a stand of aspens. "It doesn't look like too bad of a climb, but it's going to take a couple of hours, at least, to retrieve it. Then we have to clear the field. Looks like you won't be able to land until tomorrow."

"You want us to hold station? In case you need help?" The Maule pulled back up above the ridgeline before banking back.

I thought about it. The Maule could probably circle the area for four more hours and still fly safely back to Moses. "No. Return to Moses now. Come back at eleven hundred tomorrow. If we're ready and conditions warrant, you'll land then. Hell, let's be real optimistic. Pack the mechanical prospector."

"The VHF certainly won't reach to Moses, Charlie. You sure you don't want me to check on you this afternoon?"

I looked over at Clara, who'd removed her oxygen mask and helmet and moved close enough to listen. "What do you think?"

"Every time we take off and land in the backcountry, it's additional risk. I don't think it balances."

I pushed the transmit button down. "Negative. Tomorrow morning—now stop wasting fuel."

"Be careful."

"You too. Don't break the plane, okay? It's the only one in the neighborhood."

"Don't break yourself. You're the only one of *you* in the neighborhood. Maule out."

"Cripple Creek out."

I holstered the radio and took up my shotgun. "See any wildlife?"

Clara gestured downstream. "I saw something big move into the trees right after we first landed, but it had antlers. Big deer or elk, maybe."

I looked but didn't see anything. The air was unbelievably crisp, laced with the smell of pine. The grass around us was less than a foot high, spotted with late daisies. The distant buzzing of the Maule was gone, cut off finally, by distance, and I could hear the creek in the distance. I took a deep breath with my eyes closed. Then I opened them and took the safety off my shotgun. "I'll stand watch while you strip off some layers."

"I'll just bet you would," she said. She set her shotgun down and removed her oxygen set, her equipment harness, and the insulated coverall. "Well, *that's* better." She stood watch while I did the same, then we repacked our chutes.

"You know," I said, "if we don't get the cargo pack by nightfall, it could be pretty chilly."

She smiled. "We can put the coveralls back on and huddle for warmth. Worse comes to worst, we can unpack the chutes and wrap ourselves in them. But I do want my sleeping bag, so let's go get it."

We walked cautiously through the pines.

"Well, damn," said Clara. "How are we supposed to climb *that?*"

The creek hugged the ridge face, a rock-strewn bed perhaps thirty feet across. We could cross it any number of ways, walking easily from boulder to boulder. In the spring it would probably be a different matter, with spring melt raising the water level substantially. It was several thousand years of spring torrents, though, that had created our problem. The water had undercut the face of the hill, cutting into the rock. Instead of the steep rocky hill I saw above the trees when I was still in the meadow, the lower part of the hill was a rock face, its very lowest part overhanging the base twenty to thirty feet above the ground. Looking upstream and down, the problem seemed equally severe.

"Next time, remind me *not* to put the climbing rope in the cargo pack."

"Upstream or down?" asked Clara.

We could see quite a way upstream and the overhang was clearly visible in that direction. Downstream, the creek wrapped around the hillside and we couldn't see as far. I pointed my shotgun that way.

The overhang was, if anything, worse in that direction, jutting out the entire width of the creek. However, this also solved our problem. A huge blue spruce on the east side of the stream grew up past the overhang, its trunk only a few feet from the cliff above. Unlike the other pines around us, it had low, easily reached branches.

Clara went up and checked it out. "This will do it, Charlie," she called from above. "There's a ledge and a couple of ways up." I joined her.

Above the overhang, the cliff was rough and easily climbed. Then it changed quickly to the steep hillside I'd been expecting, rocky, with lots of stunted pines and scrub to hold on to. I soon tired of the pine sap on my hands, but I didn't worry about my grip *slipping*.

It took us forty-five minutes to reach the stand of aspens where the cargo pack lay. It took another half hour to untangle the cargo chute and stuff it into the cargo pack. The cargo pack itself was a heavily padded duffel five feet long and two and a half feet in diameter. It weighed two hundred pounds and it had not been my intention to have to carry it anywhere. The idea was to have it land near the site and be able to unpack it, carrying its individual contents to where they were needed.

"Look on the bright side, Charlie. This time we have the rope."

"There's that."

We rested for a while, at the edge of the aspens, drinking water from our canteens and scenery from the world. The opposite ridge face had fewer trees and more rock. Something moved and I looked closer. "Bighorn sheep."

Clara had a small set of binoculars in her kit. We watched them jump from boulder to boulder where a missed landing would mean a fall to the death. I remembered my close brush with the ridge top and shivered.

"I almost landed on top of the ridge by accident," I said.

"I *thought* you were a little low, but couldn't really tell. Your canopy blocked my view. How much did you miss it by?"

"I dragged a heel."

She stared at me. "This is too dangerous. You could've hung up on the cliff or fallen."

"I know. Believe me, I know. Hopefully, we won't have to do any more parachuting, though."

We dragged the cargo duffel straight down the hill, Clara working from below while I belayed it from above with the rope, working in stages. Gravity is our friend, at least in this case. I was very glad I didn't have to take it *up* the hill. It only took an hour to work it down the hill.

When we reached the overhang we had to move it sideways, to reach a point where the stream wasn't directly below. We lowered it to the ground on a doubled rope, then pulled the rope back up and looped it around a convenient tree and rappelled down ourselves.

We were on the wrong side of the creek. Directly below the chute's landing place, the overhang wasn't as severe. I'm sure it overhung the creek during the spring melt, but in late summer we'd ended up on a rocky spit on the west side of the creek.

Above the streambed, the overhang had a raised shelf where some harder stone had resisted the cutting action of the water. The softer stone above formed a deeper pocket, a cave almost.

"Look." I pointed. "If we put a fire in the doorway, that would make a great camping site. Also a place to store equipment."

She looked skeptical. "If something doesn't already live there."

We checked it out cautiously. The only thing in the pocket was driftwood, carried there by the spring melt. I put on my television announcer voice. "This modest efficiency apartment features fresh air, good security, and it comes prestocked with firewood. This offer void where prohibited. Tax, title, and license not included."

Clara poked the firewood, looking for snakes and scorpions. "Okay," she said grudgingly. "It looks good."

We unpacked the ax, chain saw, and shovel and hauled them and the rope across the stream and into the meadow.

We took care of the trees at the sound end of the meadow first, two pines about thirty feet apart and growing over fifty feet into the air. They were right in the approach path and the perfect height to take both wings right off the Maule.

We cut an angled notch a little over halfway through the trunk on the side away from the meadow, then a straight cut from the other side. When it started to go, I yanked the chain saw out and backed away quickly. When the tree struck the ground it was almost gradual, with branches striking first and breaking with a rolling cracking sound, then the trunk proper struck and I felt almost lifted off the ground when the shock wave hit my feet. Then I was blinking in the cloud of dust and vegetable debris that blew out from under it.

I'd never dropped a tree that large. I felt simultaneously pleased with myself and guilty. And then we did it again. And twice more at the other end of the meadow.

"Seems a shame," I said. "All this wood, unused."

"Well," Clara said, "we can always use it for firewood. Nice thing about pine is that it burns green."

"Now *that* is a great idea."

The rest of the field prep involved cutting some bushes out flush with the ground and hauling the larger rocks over to the edge of the meadow. Then we took wire stakes with orange wind streamers on the ends and lined the runway.

It was only five o'clock when we finished, but the western ridge cut the sunlight off and we retreated to the cave and started stacking firewood for the night.

"What do you want for supper?" Clara asked.

"What's the choice?" I joined her at the duffel. "Lessee—freeze-dried stroganoff, freeze-dried chicken curry, or freeze-dried shoes."

She looked down. "Shoes? Oh, the beef stew. I didn't think it was that bad. Marie just didn't use enough water last night. She burned herself picking up the pot and spilled some of the water—then didn't want to take the time to boil more."

"I didn't know that. Where was I?"

"Talking to base on the radio."

"Base?" I blinked. "And how are you, Mr. Base? Did you remember to close your doors? Are your antennas okay? How do you feel without two planes in your belly."

She looked away from me. "Well, we had beef stew last night, anyway, so that eliminates that. Leaves the curry or the stroganoff."

I felt ashamed of myself. "Sorry. You don't make fun of how I feel about Marie." I picked up the aluminum pot and the Katydn water filter. "You choose—I'll go get the water."

She looked up at me, her eyes red. "You don't have any preference?"

"Well, maybe the curry."

She smiled. "Then we'll have the stroganoff."

I laughed and took the pot and filter down to the stream. The water unit was a pump with a combination ceramic, activated charcoal, and silver filter that would take out bacteria and parasites. It was an expensive one, but we'd chosen them because it was the one used by the Red Cross in disaster relief work. I squatted on a rock jutting out into the stream and flipped the intake hose over the next rock and into the running water. Something exploded out of the water and nearly yanked the water filter out of my hand.

My shout brought Clara up, shotgun at the ready.

"What was that?"

I was standing back from the stream's edge, the filter and kettle held up, like they'd protect me. My entire front was soaked.

The end of the water filter's hose was twisted and, upon closer inspection, proved to be bitten almost in half.

"Uh, I think it was a fish. Makes sense, I guess. It's not like anybody's fishing these waters. Well, the bears and the eagles, but no humans."

Clara got a strange look on her face. "Uh, this is Colorado. My father goes fly-fishing. There must be *huge* trout in these waters. Isn't there a fly in the survival kits?"

"Yeah. A spoon lure, a fly, and some bare hooks."

"There's a willow tree downstream." Clara said.

"So?"

"So, we don't have to have freeze-dried shoes for supper."

In ten minutes we were back with several willow branches, one of which she trimmed down to a supple wand about eight feet long. She tied the fishing line to the thick end and then again to the thin end, leaving another twenty feet to fish with. She tied the fly off and said, "Get back—I'm just as likely to hook you or me as a fish. This is almost the perfect time of day—though it's late in the year for this."

I took my shotgun and backed off.

She flicked the wand sideways once, then twice, and the line floated in the air, making a shape like a cursive S. The fly settled on the water near the other side of the stream. Clara pulled it with tugs and jerks, working it across as the current carried it downstream.

When it was downstream almost the entire length of the line, it vanished into the water and Clara jerked the pole back.

A fountain of water and fish exploded out of the stream. The pole folded nearly in half and I realized why Clara had tied it to the base as well as the tip. She stepped rapidly back from the bank and the fish splashed down again. The line straightened and Clara ran along the shore, letting the fish run ahead of her. Suddenly the fish jumped again and she yanked hard on the line. The line parted with a musical note, but not before the fish had been pulled sideways. It landed hard on the rounded stones of the near shore and began flopping.

"Oh, no you don't!" shouted Clara, and she ran down the rocky shore and reached it right before it flopped back into the water. She flipped it several feet back from the stream.

It wasn't until I saw her next to the trout that I realized how *big* the fish was. It was as long as my arm and my entire hand would've fit in its mouth, but with those teeth, I wasn't about to try.

"Wow. So, is it a salmon?"

Clara shook her head. "No. It's a trout. A brown trout, I think. Certainly not a rainbow trout—those are saltwater fish that were introduced into these waters by man." She picked up a round rock and whacked it in the head. I winced and the fish stopped flopping. "You know how to clean a fish, Charlie?"

"Yes."

"Good. 'Cause I've never done it before."

I looked at her in disbelief.

"Honest. The only other fish I caught, my dad cleaned." She picked up the fish with a couple of fingers hooked in a gill slit. "My dad would die to catch a trout this big. It's gotta weigh at least five pounds."

We walked back to the campsite. "It's your fish," I said, "so you have to clean it . . . but I'll show you how."

We wove a broiling basket from the remaining green willow branches and baked fillets over the coals. We ate a good portion of it, but it would've taken two more people to finish it off. Clara experimented with the fire to try and smoke the rest of it, but eventually ended up with more char than fish. She incinerated her mistakes.

"Charlie," Clara said after we ate, "I want to wash."

I held up one of the disposable wipe-n-wash packets.

She shook her head and pulled out all the aluminum cookware—a small kettle, a liter-and-a-half sauce pan and a liter sauce pan. We used a cooking pot to dip water from the stream for washing. Neither of us were too anxious to dip our hands into that stream, especially in the dark. She arranged rocks to support the pots over the coals and set out a small bar of soap and a bandanna to use as a washcloth.

"You've got the watch," she said. She pointed away from the fire, toward the open side of the cave and the stream. "Watch *that* way."

"Huh?"

She began unbuttoning her shirt:

"Oh." I picked up my shotgun and sat on the far side of the fire, my back to the heat and the cave. My eyes probed the dusk and I listened for creatures among the pines, but what I heard was the stream and the fire and the closer sounds of Clara undressing, then splashing water and hands rubbing across soapy skin.

My imagination supplied visual details and my body ached. I thought about Marie and checked my watch. It was over in five minutes. The air was cold and she probably didn't want to expose wet skin for long.

"It's okay, Charlie—you can look now."

I stood, deliberately casual, and turned. She was sitting, her legs tucked into her sleeping bag, and wearing her spare flannel shirt. Her shotgun lay across her lap, but she was toweling at her hair with a T-shirt.

"I wish Rick were here," she said.

I couldn't think of anything to say to that, so I just shrugged and added some wood to the fire. There was some water left so I bathed my upper torso, getting rid of the worst of the sweat from the day's work. My spare clothes were in the Maule, so I had to make do with my outer shirt, rinsing my smelly undershirt and spreading it near the fire to dry or not before morning.

The fire was just under the overhang and the smoke blackened the rock above. I wondered how long the smoke stains would last— human marks in this unmarked place. The trees we'd cut down bothered me, but forest fires and beavers probably produced the same result naturally. I consoled myself that even if I spent a lifetime, I couldn't begin to touch this wilderness in the way humans had back on the tame side.

Not unless you spend that lifetime letting other humans into this place. Like Clara, but for different reasons, my thoughts turned back to Rick and his lover, Christopher. There was a security nightmare I didn't even want to touch. Should we bring Chris into the secret? Rick hadn't asked us to, but how much longer could Rick maintain the relationship with that big a secret between them? And if I brought Chris in, how would Clara react? And would Chris be willing to keep such a secret? What friendships did he have that required complete candidness?

When I first found the gate, the secret had given me a sense of power. *I know something you don't know.* But the longer I held it, the thornier and heavier the secret became. And I didn't dare drop it, did I?

"What are you thinking about, Charlie?"

I looked up, startled. Clara was brushing her hair now. I'd been staring at the fire, crouched beside my spread T-shirt.

"I wish Rick were here," I said.

She frowned. "I just said that, but I didn't mean it."

"What did you mean, then?" I asked.

She looked away, out into the darkness, staring at nothing. After a moment she said, "I guess I meant I wish Rick still loved me." She half laughed, half sobbed, "I don't think that's what *you* meant, though." Her eyes glistened wet in the firelight.

"No." I hesitated afraid of hurting her more. "I wish Rick were here so I knew he wasn't talking about the gate to Chris."

"Rick wouldn't do that," Clara blurted out. "He'd talk to you first."

"How can you be sure?" I asked. I couldn't help myself—I said, "I mean, look what he did to you."

"What do you mean?"

Jesus, she was going to make me spell it out. "Well . . . Chris and . . . all that."

The corners of her mouth turned down. "He called first."

"What?"

"He called me first, and told me. From the bar. He didn't ask me—he told me. But he told me before he did it." The tears started in earnest, streaming down her cheeks. "He won't tell Chris about the wildside without talking to you first."

I found my bandanna, unused, in the pocket of my folded coverall and took it to her. She didn't see me hold it out, so I sat on the edge of her sleeping bag and wiped her face. She leaned against me, still upright, rigid, but leaning. I put my arm around her and she said, "Are you still watching the perimeter?"

I hadn't been. If something had come out of the dark in the past five minutes, we probably would've died, but I said, "Yes, Clara. I'm watching." I lifted the shotgun from her lap and put it beside me.

She let go then. The rigidity went away and the sobs came. I sat there, her head on my shoulder, stroking her back and staring into the dark. She fell asleep, later, sliding down into the bag. I pulled it to her chin and fed the fire until she woke by herself, near dawn.

She complained about my not waking her for her share of the night watches, but I didn't stay awake long enough to hear it.

Thirteen

"I Say Push It."

Marie landed the Maule into a fifteen-knot headwind, letting it slow to nearly thirty-five knots ground speed before touching down in the meadow. The brown grass quickly killed the rest of her speed, using less than two-thirds the length of our runway. She turned the plane and taxied back to where Clara and I waited, midway, near the cave and cache.

"Well, that wasn't too bad," Marie said, dropping to the ground. "Though you don't get nearly as much sleep when you have to split the watch two ways instead of four."

"Can't argue with that," I said. Clara let me sleep until Joey raised us on the radio, but I was still blinking in the morning light. "What's happening with Rick?"

Marie said, "Things are fine, apparently. We talked to him right before we took off. He's bored."

Joey looked around. "Well, is there any gold?"

I smiled. "Show him, Clara."

She held out a small Ziploc plastic bag and let it dangle. Its contents flashed in the sun. "I got this with the plastic gold pan this morning—in about twenty minutes right by our campsite while Charlie slept."

Joey hefted it. "Half an ounce, maybe?"

"Maybe."

"What was gold going for when we left?"

I'd been following the prices ever since we started the project. "The New York price was $392.50 a troy ounce."

"Oh," said Joey. "We'll have to get a lot more."

"We will," I said.

Even disassembled, it took all four of us to move the mechanical prospector to the stream's edge. We finished assembling it by one. "Who wants to get wet?" I asked.

"I'll start," said Joey. He put on the chest-high fishing waders we'd brought to work the water without freezing. While he did that, I fired up the gasoline engine and made sure the prospector was pumping water.

Joe picked up the six-foot length of PVC pipe clamped to the free end of the three-inch intake hose. "Where should I start?" he asked, shouting to be heard over the motor.

I pointed at the near bank. It was the inside bank of a curve in the stream, where slow water would drop gold dust.

Joey dragged the pipe over and thrust it down into the shallow water. The pump strained and there was a gush of clear water over the shaker trays, followed immediately by dark brown silty water laden with gravel. The water ran out of the discharge spout, splashed onto the rocks at the stream's edge, and then into the water. The silt immediately clouded the clear crystal water and moved downstream in a widening plume.

I shut the motor off.

Everyone looked at me, surprised.

"We need to move the prospector."

"Why?" asked Marie.

"We're dumping silt into the creek."

"Yeah. So?" said Joey.

Clara understood. "The trout, Joey. Remember the trout I told you about?"

"I don't understand. Every time it rains here, the runoff washes dirt into the stream—far more in minutes than we could do in days," Marie said.

"I don't know about that. We're going to be concentrating a lot of dirt on a little stretch of stream. Maybe it won't affect the fish at all. But we've got enough hose to go twice across this stream—let's just move this back far enough that the discharge runs through this gravel and rock before it hits the stream. To let the worst of it settle out."

Joey grumbled, but they helped me drag the prospector back twenty feet. Before we turned the motor back on, we examined the shaker trays. All of the rocks we were able to toss aside immediately, but there was a small nugget of gold about the size of a kernel of corn in the next tray and there was gold dust collecting in the fine pan, a thin scattering of tiny flakes.

"Hot damn!" said Joey, and plunged back into the water.

We rotated—one of us working the hose along the bed, another working the shaker pans, discarding the rocks and gravel that wouldn't wash out on their own. The other two rested and stood guard, though we hadn't seen much in the way of wildlife—and the motor probably scared away the rest. Every twenty minutes or so, we'd shut down the motor, remove the accumulated dust, and swap places.

We worked the deposit until four o'clock. When we'd finished drying and weighing our take that evening, we had thirty-three and a half troy ounces triple-bagged in heavy-duty Ziploc freezer bags.

"Not too bad," said Joey. "Not too bad."

We weren't able to reach Rick on the shortwave during the day, but after sunset, when we switched to our nighttime frequency, we were able to reach him with interference. He was glad to hear about the gold but mostly just glad the mountain landing had gone safely.

We had fish again for supper. Joey and Marie zipped their sleeping bags together at the back of the cave. Clara and I left ours where they were, near the fire, head to head with a small gap. After eating we sat there, Joey and Marie on Clara's bag, Clara and I on mine.

"How long are we going to push it?" Clara asked.

I shrugged. "Let's stick to the plan."

"The 'plan'? I thought the plan was 'let's play it by ear,' " Clara said.

"Weather permitting," I said. "That's the killer, isn't it?"

"Literally," said Marie.

We couldn't fly out of here in bad weather. Not only could adverse winds take us into the mountains, but at this altitude the chance of icing up the wings was high. The problem was, if we had bad weather, did we try and get out ahead of it or wait it out? It was close enough to winter that a snowstorm might stick us here until spring—which meant death. If we tried to leave just before the bad weather reached us, there was the danger it would catch us in the air. If we left now, we wouldn't be able to touch the gold deposits again until late spring, by which time we might not control the gate anymore.

"Who checked the barometer last?"

"I did," said Joey. "It rose two millibars. High pressure. I'd say tomorrow will be fine."

"Let's see what it says in the morning," I said.

"What does that mean?" asked Clara.

"We'll play it by ear."

The next afternoon, Clara was in the water, thigh deep, working a pocket on the inside of the bend, where the slower waters tended to drop gold out. The bend was up against low cedars, bushy and thick, on the side of the stream up against the cliff. On the other side, Joey was working the trays, discarding smaller rocks that weren't automatically washed over the side. Marie and I were seated on the bank, me facing Clara and Marie watching the trees behind Joey.

The mountain lion dropped off the cliff face almost directly above Clara, landing in the cedars and springing out right at her back.

I shouted and brought the shotgun up, but Clara didn't hear me over the prospector's gasoline engine and she was in my line of fire. Then, miraculously, Clara slipped and stumbled, bending down to steady herself on a rock. The front claws and teeth of the lion missed her neck and shoulders but the torso and back legs of the cat slammed into her side and they both went over, into the deeper water of midstream.

I was running sideways, then, upstream, trying to get an angle on the lion. The lion exploded out of the water, roaring, standing on its back legs and trying to get its footing. Clara's waders filled with water and she was having trouble keeping her head out of the water. The lion lunged toward her and I fired my first round, buckshot.

It was low, into the water, but a pellet or two ricocheted off the surface of the water and hit the cat and it twisted in mid-lunge, snarling.

Clara's head went completely underwater.

I chambered as fast as I could and took more time with the next shot—rifled slug. Red blossomed on the lion's shoulder and it snarled again, a scream like tearing metal.

Clara's hands were clawing at the surface of the stream and her face broke the surface again, to take a deep breath, then she sank again, just as the mountain lion's claws cut the air next to her face.

I fired again, buckshot again, and more red spotted the ribs of the lion, but it was still moving fast. Then Marie fired, behind me, a charge of buckshot that knocked the lion off-balance, to splash sideways. It came up again and lunged, at *us,* putting most of the stream's width behind it in two splashing leaps.

I fired again and Marie's shot, like a close echo, followed. One rifled slug hit its chest and the other its neck. The cat dropped into the shallows and didn't move.

I dropped the gun and plunged into the water, but halfway across the stream, Clara stood, shoulder deep in the water, coughing but clearly on her feet. I helped her across the stream and up onto the bank, unhooking the suspenders on the waders in the shallows to dump the collected water. Both of us were shivering hard.

Joey, who'd shut the mechanical prospector down at the first shot, ran back to camp for sleeping bags.

Clara sat in the sun and coughed more water out of her lungs. I took off my shoes and socks.

The mountain lion lay in the shallow, its muzzle underwater; bright red streams of blood flowed across the rocks with the current. After a few more minutes, when it was clear it wasn't breathing, I grabbed it by the scruff of its neck and dragged it up onto the dry rocks of the bank.

Clara, still shivering violently, said, "Th-th-thanks, Cha-Ch-Charlie."

My teeth were chattering, too. "A-are you o-ka-ka-kay?"

She blinked and said, "My b-back hurts."

I walked behind her. A spreading stain of blood darkened the light gray flannel shirt she was wearing halfway down her back, next to her spine. "Hold still," I said.

I found a tear near the stain and ripped an opening about eight inches long. One deep cut, about an inch and a half long, was seeping blood. Next to it, with a regular spacing, were two shallow scratches.

"It got a claw into you." I took my bandanna out and pressed it against the cut.

"Ow!" Clara jerked.

"Hold still. You're bleeding like a stuck pig. Not arterial, though, just a bad cut."

She twisted her head to see, but of course couldn't. "How bad?"

Joey arrived then, with the sleeping bags. We went back to camp, Marie walking with Clara to hold the pressure pad on her back while Clara held a sleeping bag draped around her. I wrapped a sleeping bag around myself, but I carried my gun, too. Joey walked point.

Back at camp, Joey and I turned our backs while Marie helped Clara undress and climb into a dry sleeping bag. I was warming up—only my pants were wet—so I fetched the medical kit from the plane.

Clara was lying facedown in the bag while Marie reached in to hold the pressure pad.

"Are you warming up, Clara?" I asked.

"Sure."

"We need to look at your back."

She flinched. "Okay. Got some aspirin?"

"Aspirin, acetaminophen, ibuprofen, or codeine."

"Uh, ibuprofen, I guess."

"Would you get it, Joey? And some water?"

"Sure."

I pulled the sleeping bag gently back. "You can let go, Marie."

Marie pulled her hand back. "The bandanna's stuck," she said.

"Leave it—we'll wash it off." I took a bottle of distilled water and squirted it under the edge of the bandanna, slowly working the bandanna free. Marie held a towel below the cut to catch the water and blood. The bandanna came free and I tossed it aside. The wound was seeping slightly, but the bleeding was greatly reduced.

When he saw the wound, Joey said, "Jesus, Joseph, and Mary! That's going to need stitches."

"Yeah. I'm afraid so. We'll need to leave soon. I think the stitches have to be in place within eighteen hours—otherwise it calls for reopening."

Joey said, "What about one of us flying her out and coming back?"

"What if the weather changes while you're gone?" I said. "We'd be snowed in and you couldn't get to us. Besides, after what happened to Clara, do you really want to try and do more mining with no guards?"

"Oh."

"Don't we have a suturing pack in the kit, Charlie?" Clara asked.

I swallowed. "Yeah. We do. A small surgical pack, but it's a last resort thing—like bleeding arteries, sucking chest wounds, the really gross stuff. We don't even have local anesthetics!"

Clara raised up on her elbows, pulling the sleeping bag in to cover her breasts. "What's the worst that can happen if we suture it now and wait?"

"Infection. Septicemia," I said. "I don't have *any* idea what's on a mountain lion's claws."

"Don't we have antibiotics?" she countered.

I resisted. "Dammit, Clara. This isn't Bryan. If something goes wrong, we can't drive across town to St. Joseph's!"

"And if we evacuate now," she said, her voice rising, "odds are we won't be able to get back here before late spring." Her voice dropped. "If I come down with an infection, we'll evacuate, but let's not jump the gun." Her voice raised again. "Dammit, Charlie, I *won't* be the cause of our quitting before we're done!"

I sighed, then turned and rummaged in the medical kit. "Here. Take two of these codeine and start on this Augmentin. We'll sew you up when the codeine has taken hold.

"Now let me get out of these wet pants."

Forty minutes later, Clara pronounced herself "woozy."

"Who wants to do it?" I asked.

Joey turned green. "Not me."

I looked at Marie. "You sew, Marie."

She licked her lips. "Well, if I had my Singer here, I wouldn't hesitate, but—"

Clara interrupted. "You do it, Charlie. You're the Eagle Scout."

"Who told you that!"

"We helped you move, remember? Your uniform was in your hanging clothes. What's wrong with being an Eagle Scout? Embarrassed?"

I turned back to the medical kit and pulled out the surgical pack. "I hope these stiches *hurt*," I muttered.

Clara laughed.

They did. Marie held her hands and Joey tried to distract her with jokes. I thoroughly cleaned the wound with sterile saline, then snipped away the ragged skin with sterile scissors. Then I put in four stiches, individually knotted, of sterile nylon, tied with the needle and a hemostat, then a "mattress" stitch, going in one side, out the other, back in on that same side, and back out on the original side, tying the two ends together. Then four more stitches to the end.

I put a light dressing over it and said, "Don't sleep on your back."

"Or anybody else's," said Clara, and promptly blushed.

We didn't do any more mining that day.

For the rest of the week, Clara took it easy, sitting or standing guard while the rest of us did anything that required lifting. We were a lot more vigilant when on guard and even when working the suction hose.

Clara's incision was red and tender the next day, but it improved steadily thereafter. I kept her on the oral Augmentin and checked the wound three times a day, a cheap thrill for me.

The weather remained mostly clear for five days, during which we worked our way upstream with steadily increasing yields. The fifth day we took 175 pounds of gold out of a seventeen-foot-deep pocket where the gold had been collecting for centuries. Our take for the week was 5432 troy ounces.

Around the fire we checked the figures again and again.

"If the price is still the same—" said Joey.

"It could be down," said Clara.

"It could be *up*," said Marie.

Joey took a deep breath, then said, "It comes to $2,148,464.64."

"Even if the price is down, we might be able to get more," I pointed out. "Mineral collectors will pay better than weight value for good nuggets and we have some beauties."

The day was overcast and the barometer was down. There'd been a surprise snow shower at noon the day before, followed by clear skies and a sun bright enough to melt the snow from the floor of the canyon. Some of the snow lingered, though, on the heights, an ever-present warning.

"We should break three million in another couple of days," said Joey.

"No. Let's not get greedy. We leave in the morning, as soon as we have enough light."

"Weather permitting," added Marie.

"Yeah. Weather permitting."

* * *

We checked the barometer at every change of the watch. It, and the temperature, dropped steadily and, from what we could tell down in the canyon, the wind shifted to the north. For the first time in the mountains, we heard wolves howling, but the sound was far away.

None of us slept well. We were up when you could tell the sky from the ridges above, but in the bottom of the canyon it was still dark. There was frost on our equipment and the rocks at the edge of the stream were coated with ice.

We packed the plane by flashlight and moved the equipment we were leaving into the back of the cave, up on a ledge that would hopefully be above the worst of the spring runoff. The plane would fly out light, which was good, but if we ran into any ice, it might not be enough.

At nine, it began to snow, very lightly. The visibility was still over a mile and it looked clearer to the south.

"Go or not?" asked Marie.

I squeezed my eyes shut. The wrong decision would kill us either way. I looked back at the dark north. "It can only get worse. Let's go."

We'd been doing the preflight over and over all morning, waiting for the light. I fired up the engine and taxied to the north end of the meadow. This was taking off with a tailwind, which was contrary to practice, but down at the bottom of the canyon it was only a slight wind, and it let us take off downhill and away from the incoming storm.

We cleared the trees by thirty feet and I kept it low, in the canyon, until I had top airspeed. Then we climbed. It was very rough when we cleared the ridgeline, shaking us like a rattle, throwing us against our seat harnesses hard enough to bruise. I swore at the pain and concentrated on keeping the controls steady.

We cleared ten thousand feet and went on oxygen. I stopped climbing at twelve, staying a couple of hundred feet below the cloud base, and ran for the eastern slope of the Rockies, fifty miles to the east. If at all possible, I wanted to go over those mountains under the cloud base, able to see them. There was always the danger of going up into the clouds and, while in or above them, having the visibility drop to nothing down below. So when you come back down, you fly blind all the way into the ground.

On the wildside, there weren't any radar-guided approaches to nice, wide, well lit runways. There were, instead, lots of trees, rocks, mountains, and no help for seven hundred miles.

I ran out of ceiling before I got to the shoulder of Pikes Peak and had to make the decision. Did I go up, into no visibility conditions, and hope, when it was time to descend on the other side of the range, that the visibility was good enough to land at Moses? Or did I head south, paralleling the range, until I got to Royal Gorge and follow the Arkansas River to the west, under the clouds?

We had the fuel to reach Surrey, the next fuel depot after Moses, but only if we took a more or less direct flight.

I headed up, into the clouds. The signal from Moses and Surrey came in loud and clear and Marie was working the vectors on the chart, recalculating our position on a running basis.

"We're clear of the range," she said, finally. "Well clear."

I took the Maule down. I was confident that I had five thousand feet of clear airspace between the aircraft and the rolling plains below. We reached ten thousand feet without breaking through, went off oxygen and continued the descent. Finally, at six thousand feet, only a thousand feet above the high plains, we came out into light rain. The outside air temperature was thirty-four degrees F and if it dropped even a little, ice would start coating the aircraft. I piled on the horses, sacrificing fuel efficiency for speed. The farther south I got, the better—the warmer.

We neared Moses. "Do we push it?" I asked. "If we keep going, we might outrun the front. Even if we don't, and it catches us, the farther south we get before landing, the more chance we have of not getting snowed in for the winter."

Marie looked out into the mist. "I say push it."

Clara and Joey agreed, but it was my responsibility. We were out of the mountains, out of the worst of it. Did I want to push on because it was the right decision, the safe one, or because I was worried about what might be happening back at the base?

For whatever reason, I flew on.

The rain finally stopped fifty miles north of Surrey and the cloud cover broke into scattered cumulus, but the front behind us was visible from the ground, a darkening of the northern horizon. Clara, Joey, and Marie refueled in record time while I checked in with Rick on the shortwave.

"The weather at base is clear, scattered altocumulus about eight thousand, maybe, and the barometer is steady," he told me.

"We're coming on in," I said.

"Of course," Rick said.

I fought down an impulse to scream into the microphone, *There's no "of course" about it. Winter is breathing down our neck!* Instead I signed off.

"How are you holding up?" I asked Marie.

"Fine—now that we're out of that weather. You don't look so good though."

I winced. "Thank-you-so-very-much." Sleeping badly the night before and the tension of the flight over the mountains had wrung me out like a damp rag. "You want to take it on in with Clara or Joey? I could do it, but it would be stupid."

She nodded. "Sure. Who wants the right-hand seat?"

Clara said, "Let Joey—he needs the hours."

When we were airborne, I slumped down in the seat and closed my eyes. Turbulence rocked the plane and I momentarily leaned into Clara. I straightened, but she put her arm around me and pulled me back. My head nestled into the hollow of her neck and shoulder. I breathed in and smelled woodsmoke, soap, and skin. I exhaled and smiled, trying to stay awake, to stay in the moment.

She woke me four hours later, on final approach to Wildside Base.

It was raining on the tame side, midafternoon. After we put away the Maule and closed down the wildside, Joey and Marie disappeared into the bathroom. The tub in there was old and very large, plenty big for two, whatever they were doing. For some reason it reminded me of Clara's bath, our first night at Cripple Creek.

Clara didn't want to ride her motorcycle back to the apartment in the rain. I offered to take her, but Rick surprised me by saying, "I'll give her a ride." Their interactions before the trip had been minimal, strained, and ultrapolite. Rick looked far more relaxed, more comfortable in her presence than he had before the trip.

Clara looked wary, but said, "Okay."

I made eye contact with her. "It's no problem, either way, Clara. I have to go talk to Luis, anyway."

She touched my arm briefly. "You need a bath before you go see anyone. So do I, for that matter." She dropped her voice. "It's all right, Charlie."

They left.

I sat on the porch and waited for the bathroom. The temperature was in the low seventies and the sound of the rain on the roof almost put me to sleep. When Joey and Marie were done with the bathroom, they disappeared into his room and closed the door.

I showered and watched brown water sluice off of me. I thought of Rick then, clean and neat as he looked when they went out the door.

We were back safe. We'd pulled over two million dollars in gold out of the remote reaches of wilderness Colorado. And I was miserable.

In bed, I tossed and turned, my thoughts wandering from the coming financial problems of gold conversion and taxes to the interpersonal dramas of our little group.

Finally, I fell asleep and dreamed of a woman who was sometimes Marie and sometimes Clara, and a man who was sometimes Rick and sometimes Joey.

But never me.

I woke, mid-evening, and wandered out into the living room. Marie was watching television, some movie-of-the-week thing based on a "real life story." She muted it when she saw me.

"Where's Joey?" I asked.

"He went into town for an AA meeting. Or as he put it—to go dancing."

"Dancing?"

"The Texas Twelve-Step."

I looked blank.

She laughed. "It's an AA joke."

I jerked my head over at the window, looking for my truck. "Uh, how'd he get there?" Joey's license was revoked. My truck, though, was there.

Marie's smile dropped. "He got his sponsor to give him a ride. They met out at the gate." She frowned. "He was scared. He was afraid of what they might think since he hasn't been for a week. I told him to tell the truth."

"That he's been in an alternate universe?" My voice rose a bit.

Marie smiled again. "Of course not. Just that he's been camping and sober."

I exhaled and headed for the kitchen. "Want anything to eat?"

"Joey's bringing Pepe's. He's getting some for you, too."

I stopped in my tracks. My stomach rumbled. "Oh. When did he say he'd be back?"

She checked her watch. "The meeting's only an hour, and he left at six. Anytime now, probably."

"I guess I can stand that. After a week in the woods, Pepe's sounds awful good." I hesitated, then asked, "Any word from Rick or Clara?"

She shook her head and turned the volume back up on the TV. Suddenly I wasn't hungry anymore.

I went into the kitchen and called Luis at home.

"How are you?" he asked.

"Tired."

"And was your trip successful?"

"Yes."

"Perhaps we should get together?" Meaning: *I'm dying to hear the details, but don't want to talk on the phone.*

I laughed. "Later. Unless you want to come out right now. I'm going to be in bed by ten."

"Okay. Funny thing today."

"Oh?"

"Called my friend in Austin." His lawyer friend, the recipient of the electronic fund transfers.

"Yeah."

"He's not in. I keep getting his answering machine."

I scratched my head. "How long have you been trying?"

"Just since last night."

I thought for a moment, trying to remember what day of the week it was. "Isn't this Saturday?"

"I know. He could've gone someplace for the weekend. It's probably nothing."

"Probably nothing. I'll call you tomorrow."

"Right." He hung up.

Joey was still gone and Marie was zoning in front of the TV. I went outside. The rain had stopped and everything smelled green.

I walked over to the barn and through the tunnel to the wildside. The gold lay on the plywood table at the back of the hangar, all the plastic bags collected in two old army surplus duffel. It weighed a bit over four hundred pounds. Rick, Joey, and I had carried each bag from the plane.

I fetched the wheelbarrow from the barn and dragged one duffel off the table and into it. I trundled the gold through the tunnel, one bag at a time, and hid it under the front porch, behind the steps, then put the wheelbarrow back.

Joey arrived as I was locking up. I met him and together we carried the fast food back to the house. "How was your meeting?"

"Good. I was surprised. What were you doing at the barn?"

"I moved the gold." I told him where.

He frowned. "I will treat those steps with more respect. Why?"

"We need to convert it to cash—I'm transferring it to Luis tomorrow. We've got the education trusts and the legal fund to set up."

"That's a lot of money . . . never mind—we can trust Luis." Joey shook his head. "Trust is a hard thing to learn."

I stared at Joey and thought about his alcoholism, Rick's relationship outside the group, the whole fragile mess. "It sure is, Joey." I clapped him on the shoulder. "We'll try and learn it together."

Joey looked at the porch steps. "What about the legal fund? Are we really going to need it?"

I nodded. "Looks like it. We may have to shut down the gate."

"Who's going to stay behind and throw the switch?"

"Well," I said, "hopefully, nobody. That's what I want to talk to you about."

Fourteen

"Go, Go, Go!"

I t was vacation time. It was still August. We had two weeks before school started and we'd worked like dogs all summer long.

The gang deserved a break.

"Then why aren't you resting?" Clara asked Joey and me.

I bit my lip. I didn't know where Clara and Rick stood and I was afraid to ask either of them. Rick hadn't come home the night before. "Just want to get the safeguards in place. So they're available." I wiped sweaty palms on my jeans. "Uh, would you like to go to the auction with me?"

"What auction?"

"The surplus equipment auction at the university. I need some junk for the gate."

"I'm riding Impossible this afternoon. When is it?"

"Eleven. You should have plenty of time."

"Okay—I'll take my bike so I can go straight to the stables after."

I looked down at my feet. I'd been hoping she'd ride with me, in the truck.

Joey was at the kitchen table working on a solenoid-actuated plunger, wiring it into the control of an electronic timer. "You need anything from town?"

"Uh—get some more D-Cell NiCads. Four."

"Right. See you."

Clara and I made our solitary ways over to the University Physical Plant.

A swarm of people were there before us, most of them examining the university vehicles up for auction outside. Clara and I moved into a large warehouse where the rest of the offerings were being displayed. Out-of-date typewriters, word processors, office furniture, lab equipment, tools, and the like were arranged on shelves or tables or floor, tagged with the appropriate lot number.

I signed up for a bidder number and then Clara and I moved down the rows, marveling.

"What on earth is that?"

"Haven't the faintest idea."

"And that?"

"It's a centrifuge."

"Oh."

Off to one side I saw something. "I think I'm in love," I said.

She looked at me oddly, then glanced at the object of my desire. "You're weird, Charlie. Really weird. I have absolutely no idea what that is."

"Me neither, but I think I'm going to buy it."

"It" turned out to be a polarized ion source—a ten-foot-high amalgam of vacuum pumps, high-voltage standoffs, dials, plastic rods, insulators, and magnetic coils topped off with a glass sphere. It looked like something out of *Forbidden Planet*.

The auction catalog informed us it was being sold by the Texas A&M Cyclotron Institute, where it had been used as a particle source for accelerator experiments. But not anymore. It had a major crack in its primary vacuum chamber and half the power supplies were shorted.

"It's perfect," I said.

"It's terrible. It'll fill the tunnel," Clara said.

"Nah. It'll come apart. You'll see. It'll be great."

I hurried off to put in my bid. It was a paper auction and you had no idea what other bidders might pay. I asked one of the junk dealers what they thought it would go for as scrap, and tripled that amount.

Then we went outside to wait for noon, when they would tally the bids.

"So," I said after a spell of uncomfortable silence, "how did things go with Rick?" My throat was dry and I looked away from her when I asked the question.

She kicked at a piece of gravel on the asphalt parking lot. "I don't know."

I looked back at her. She had her hands shoved deep into her jeans pockets and was studying the ground. "What does that mean?" I asked. *Did he spend last night with you?* "Is he still seeing Chris?"

"Yeah. Chris is seeing someone else, too, though. Rick isn't too happy about it, but they apparently don't have an exclusive relationship. For a minute, last night, I thought he wanted us back the way we were. But what he really wanted was to talk. He said that's what he missed about me—someone he could really talk to." She laughed. "Great sex aside, Christopher apparently isn't a very good listener."

"Oh."

"He still loves me. He just isn't *interested* in me."

I expected to see her cry, then, but her eyes were dry. She looked at her watch and said, "Noon. Let's go see if you bought Frankenstein's laboratory."

She didn't say anything else, but as we walked across the parking lot, she linked her arm with mine.

It took two trips in my truck to get the components of the polarized ion source out to the ranch. Between trips I rendezvoused with Luis at the airport and transferred the gold to the backseat floor of his BMW.

"I've got an armored car set to carry it to the dealer in Dallas. He'll send the gem quality nuggets out to some of the professional shows and give us straight bullion prices on the dust."

We finished shifting the gold and Luis shut the doors.

He was frowning when he turned back to me. "Richard still hasn't shown up. I reached his paralegal. She doesn't have any idea where he is. He didn't mention any trip to her. She's going to the police."

"So, this is it?"

"Probably."

"Is everything done?"

He frowned. "Yeah." He took a cellular phone from his shirt pocket. "I'm making the calls every hour. They don't hear from me in the ten-minute grace period and the lawyers in Houston get *the* call."

"You don't have to do this, Luis."

He shrugged. "We'll see. I take this client privilege thing pretty seriously. You haven't done anything illegal—I'm not letting them walk all over me."

"I've called you our wall before. I didn't realize how right I was. I appreciate what you're doing."

He got embarrassed. "Well, you've put enough money in my pocket that I can finally afford to get my IFR ticket and maybe buy a plane. I haven't really had to do much to earn it, yet, but I'll do my part."

Back at the ranch, after my second trip, I left Joey to concentrate on the timer and the solenoid while I "dressed" the gate.

I didn't think I had much time, so I didn't get fancy. I concentrated on the sides of the tunnel, building a parallel stack of power supplies, magnetic coils, and diffusion pumps. When I was done, the tunnel was narrower by a foot and a half and looked liked something out of a "Nova" episode. I braced it with angle iron and drilled a hole for the hangar cable yoke in one of the cabinets. The contraption straddled the terminus—the line between the worlds where we'd cut the mower and Joey's flashlight in half.

Clara came back to the ranch, even though we were officially off duty, and helped me touch it up. "It looks very businesslike from this side," she said. She walked around to the wildside of the tunnel.

"But only until you see the back. All these cables just hang off here. The vacuum tubes don't connect to anything."

I bent down and disconnected the hangar cable yoke—power, phone, alarm—and pulled the cable clear of the terminus. The lights on the wild half of the tunnel went out and then, as the generator fired up, flickered back on.

"Why'd you do that?"

I took her arm and led her up the tunnel, on the wildside, away from the terminus and my contraption. "You'll see." The switch was still covered with a plywood panel, to keep us from accidentally tripping it. I slid it to the side. "Close your eyes or look away from the gate," I said.

"You're going to shut it down?"

"Just for a moment. You want to wait on the other side?"

She looked amused. "No, Charlie." She crossed her arms and turned away from the gate.

I looked the same direction and threw the switch.

Even with the fluorescent lights on, the flash of light was tremendous, throwing our shadows stark and dark up the tunnel. There was also a sharp burst of white noise and I flinched. I looked back in time to see the back third of my contraption—cables, cabinets, vacuum lines, coils, and coolant lines—fall to the floor of the tunnel with a clatter.

"Hope that didn't happen on the other side, too," Clara said.

"Me, too." I stood and turned my head. "Ow."

"What is it?"

I touched the skin at the back of my neck. "Sunburn." I explored further. The back side of the tips of my ears and the side of my right wrist were also pink. "How about you?"

Clara's hair, though short at graduation, hadn't been cut in three months and it protected her ears and neck. Her arms had been crossed in front of her, shielded by her body. "I'm fine."

Working together, Clara and I carefully moved the fallen debris into the cul-de-sac at the end of the tunnel. There were hot metal edges to be avoided and molten rubber. The smell of ozone and melted plastic was strong. Then we moved back to the switch and activated the gate again.

The tame side of the tunnel flicked back into place and I released a breath I hadn't realized I'd been holding. I walked down and examined my contraption. The angle iron bracing was holding fine, but the backs of the cabinets looked like illustrations from *Popular Mechanics*—cutaway sections to show the interior arrangements of gadgets. The smell of ozone and melted plastic was doubled and I worried about the toxicity.

I sent Clara down to open the door into the hangar and I opened the door into the barn. There was always a pressure differential and the resulting breeze cleared out the tunnel quickly.

"What now?" asked Clara.

"We need a sign."

"From the Lord?"

"Ha. Ha." I picked up the half sheet of plywood that covered the switch and walked it back to the barn. There was a collection of paint cans, but they were ancient and we had to open five before we found some that was still liquid. It was dark red.

When we were finished, the sign said:

EXTREME DANGER!
DO NOT CROSS TERMINUS WHEN
GATE IS INACTIVE.
LOSS OF LIFE OR LIMB EXTREMELY LIKELY!

Then Clara waited on the tame side with the sign as I turned the gate off. I watched my watch closely for thirty seconds, then turned it back on. She was standing well back from the terminus, one hand to her throat, tense. When she saw me she smiled and relaxed.

I walked over beside her. "How'd the sign look?" I asked. I looked behind me but of course I didn't see it. The sign was leaning up against the cul-de-sac at the end of the tame side tunnel and to see it, the gate would have to be off.

"Good. Imposing. It made *me* afraid to walk across the line." She looked down. "I was also afraid the gate wouldn't come back." She looked back up. "What now?"

"More shopping."

We spent just over two thousand dollars at Sam's Club on canned and dry goods, vitamins, and over-the-counter pharmaceuticals. We had to stack stuff above the sides of the truck and use rope to hold it down, but we got it all in one trip. By folding the side mirrors on the truck flat against the sides, we were able to ease the whole load between the two halves of the "contraption" and straight into the hangar.

Joey, with a break for his daily AA meeting, continued working on the timer. When Clara and I finished stacking supplies in the hangar, Joey and Marie joined us, carrying two cardboard boxes of electronics equipment.

"It works. I've tested it fifty times, varying the times from ten seconds to three hours. I set it up before I went to my meeting, came back, and, bingo, on the button, it tripped. We can only try it for real, now."

"Good enough. What do you want me to do?"

"You run the wire—I'll put in the frame."

Clara and I cut a three-inch-deep groove in the tunnel wall, first down from the switch to the floor of the tunnel, then along the base of the wall out to the hangar. We ran a six-conductor wire along it, then filled it in, plastering it with mud. Then we sprinkled loose dirt over the wet mud, until the groove was completely hidden, indistinguishable from the other side of the tunnel.

Joey, meanwhile, set a plate into the dirt wall, next to the switch, pounding it back into the dirt to anchor it. On this he mounted the double-coil solenoid, connecting the actuator to the gate switch with a flexible rubber coupling and a hose clamp. He hooked the solenoid wires to a battery, to test it.

"Okay," he said, holding up a green wire. "We've wired the ground to the negative terminal. I now touch the retraction wire to the positive terminal—"

There was a loud "click" from the solenoid and the gate flickered, revealing the cul-de-sac and the electromechanical refuse from my contraption.

Joey released the wire. The gate stayed closed. He picked up a red wire. "This is the wire for the push coil. I touch it to the current like so—"

There was another "click" and the solenoid pushed the lever in. The gate flickered and the tame side tunnel reappeared.

"Very good, Joey," I said.

He smiled. Marie put her hand on his shoulder and squeezed.

"How many more times do you think we should test it," I asked, "to make sure the linkage won't slip?"

He frowned. "It won't slip." His voice was sharp.

I said gently, "Joey? How do you know it won't slip? We don't know anything about that metal. We don't even know what it is."

He looked away and exhaled sharply then took a deep breath. "Sorry. You're right." He looked down at the floor. "Are you sure you want to open and shut the gate a lot? I mean, we've talked about this before—what if it wasn't meant to be opened this much?"

We did it ten more times.

Joey gave me a look that said, "I told you so" louder than any words could, then wired the solenoid into the wire we'd run, using two wires per pole for redundancy.

When that was done, Clara and I enclosed the plate, solenoid, and switch in wire screening, which we anchored into the wall with ten-inch nails. Then we plastered over this with mud and dirt, in layers, until we had a stretch of wall identical to its surroundings.

Meanwhile, Joey took his radio receivers, batteries, timer, and solar photovoltaic panel, and went to work in the hangar.

Joey and Marie installed things, and then Clara and I hid them.

The radio receiver, timers, and batteries went into a pocket of dirt at the back of the hangar. Joey mounted the photovoltaic panel on the roof of the tower. Since we couldn't hide the solar panel, we ran an overt wire (with a broken conductor) from the panel to the backup battery on the shortwave radio in the tower. A hidden wire, with working conductors, ran down one of the tower legs and under the tarpaper on the roof before it terminated in the hidden pocket at the back of the hangar.

"How much current do the timer and the receiver draw?" I asked Joey.

"Milliamps. Without the solar charger, it would probably run for two years."

I blinked. "I should think that would do the job."

"You bet your ass," Joey said.

"I am, Joey. I am."

Clara rode into the barnyard the next morning. She wasn't on her motorcycle. She was on her horse.

"Wow. Pretty good trail ride. It must be ten miles to the stable," I said.

"Yeah, well—it's not bad if you get up early, before it gets hot." She hung the saddle and tack on the porch rail and tied Impossible in the shade at the side of the house where the grass hadn't been cut for a month.

I'd been up since dawn myself, unable to sleep. I'd asked everyone to be there for a breakfast meeting. Marie and Joey spent the night in Joey's room. Rick didn't come home the previous night, though he'd told me he'd be at the meeting.

The phone rang twenty-five minutes later. Marie and Clara stopped talking and watched as I picked up the phone. Joey, stirring pancake batter at the counter, froze.

It was Rick. "I'm running late." Then, to the side, "Stop it." He was laughing, partially covering the mouthpiece.

"How long do you think you'll be?" I asked. "It's Rick," I said to the guys. Joey started stirring again.

Rick laughed again and I knew he wasn't reacting to me. "Oh, better give me an hour."

I narrowed my eyes. "You said you would be here. I even asked *you* to set the time."

"Well . . . things happened." He sounded less cheerful. "I'll be there in an hour."

I thought about Luis's friend Richard. "We may not have that time. We're going ahead with the meeting. We'll just have to fill you in later, if there's time."

All traces of humor left his voice. "Do what you have to." He sounded indifferent.

"Okay. Call before you come out here, okay? And make it a pay phone?"

"Why a pay phone?" The indifference dropped.

"Think about it."

He was quiet for a moment. "Got it. You haven't gotten the call, have you?"

"Would I have let you talk at all? No call. Not *yet*."

He paused again. "Okay. I'm coming now."

"Really? You're not even breathing hard."

"Oh, very funny. I'll be there in fifteen minutes."

"Good. I appreciate your sacrifice."

He snorted and hung up.

I put the receiver down in the cradle. Joey started pouring batter onto the griddle. Clara and Marie began talking again. The phone rang again. They all stopped.

"Hello."

A woman's voice said, "What number is this, please?"

My heart began pounding. Carefully I said, "This is the number zero." Marie and Clara stood and Joey turned the burner off under the griddle.

"Mr. Cervantes is twelve minutes late for his nine o'clock call."

"Ah." I squeezed my eyes closed. "Have you called Snodgrass, Messenger & Sons?"

"The number in Houston? I was to call you first."

I spoke into the phone. "Well, don't dawdle."

"Of course not, sir."

She hung up.

I dropped the phone back into the cradle and, without a word, walked outside. I heard the others follow.

The sky was clear and it was hot and humid—Texas weather at its worst. There was no sign of trouble, no sign of anything. The alarm at the gate was silent, the fields were empty. I scanned the trees and bushes. My imagination put a federal agent behind each shrub.

I opened the barn and Joey and Marie walked in behind me. "Where's Clara?" I asked, then saw her coming across the yard, leading Impossible, her saddle and tack slung over one shoulder.

"What are you doing?" I asked.

"Can't just leave him out there." She kept walking and I had to duck aside, or get stepped on by the horse. "Besides, with a horse here, there's a reason for all this hay."

I took the padlock off the door to the barn and threw it on the workbench. "What if we have to hide on the other side?"

"We sit it out for a week or two and hope they go away. That's the plan, right?" Clara said, leading Impossible over to the tunnel. "Why'd you take the lock off?"

"No, no—what happens to Impossible?"

"We take him with us, of course. The lock?"

"To the other side? What will he eat?"

"Well, grass is good." She raised her voice. "What's with the lock?" Impossible shied away and whinnied. Clara soothed him with touch and voice.

I blinked. "Oh. Well, if you found a big door with a very heavy padlock on it, wouldn't you want to know what was behind it? We might as well put a sign on the door that says, 'This way to the time machine.' You know?"

Clara led Impossible through the door to the tunnel. I yelled after her, "Something could eat him over there!"

Her voice floated back up the tunnel. "They'll have to eat me first!"

I shook my head. *That's what I'm afraid of.*

When she came back, we opened the main doors, propping them

open, and stacked hay to cover the back wall—the tunnel door.

We were standing around, wondering what to do next, when the gate alarm went off. Joey scurried into the hayloft to look out the window. I took a matchbox-sized black plastic box with two red, recessed buttons out of my pocket. It was the remote control for a car alarm, but its receiver wasn't in any car. For a brief second my finger touched the warm surface of the red plastic. Then I dropped it back into my pocket.

"It's Rick's car," Joey called down. "There doesn't seem to be anybody behind him. He's shutting the gate . . . it's locked . . . he's back in the car."

I went out into the yard to wait for Rick. After a few moments we heard the distant sound of tires on gravel, then his engine.

"Is his muffler going out?" asked Joey. The sound was rougher than usual—deeper. As he got closer, the sound increased, but way out of proportion. I could *feel* it against my skin.

The helicopters popped up, suddenly, like grasshoppers leaping into the air out of the river bottom. They must have come up the Brazos, mere feet above the water, the river bluff shielding the noise from us until they were almost on top of us. Now they roared toward us and the sound beat at us like a storm.

There were three of them. One Apache attack helicopter, wasp-waisted, and two squat Blackhawk personnel carriers. One of the Blackhawks sank onto the grass landing strip and the other passed overhead, blotting out the sun, before putting down in the pasture on the other side of the barnyard. The Apache banked sharply and orbited the yard a hundred feet off the ground in a tight circle a hundred yards across.

I yelled at the others, "Get the door open!" My earlier expectations had been of unsmiling FBI agents in sunglasses and business suits, polite but firm, who might not find the door hidden behind the hay. I didn't think hay would stop this crowd.

Clara, Joe, and Marie tore the hay bales down while I waited in the door, watching as everything came unraveled, the small plastic remote control gripped tightly in my right hand.

Even before the Blackhawks touched the ground, men came pouring out of them—green cammo fire ants boiling out of a nest. I could only see the ones in the field, not those from the airstrip, but they ran toward us spreading into a skirmish line as they came. Rick's car screeched to a halt in the dust storm kicked up by the helicopters. He jumped from the car and ducked into the barn, perhaps fifty feet in front of the charging soldiers. I took him and shoved him on, ahead of me, kicking the interior door shut behind me. The others ran down the tunnel, ahead of us.

"Go, go, go!" I shouted. Things seemed disjointed and remote, like a disturbing dream. Part of me wondered if I was even awake. Somewhere ahead of us I heard Impossible whinny again, then from behind came the sound of the door slamming open as someone rammed into it.

I looked over my shoulder. They weren't running into the tunnel after us, pell-mell. I didn't blame them. They probably thought they'd sewn us up and could collect us at their leisure. We crossed the terminus and I stopped, shouting, "Get the cameras going. You know what to do!"

Then I turned and faced them.

Two soldiers, I didn't know whether they were marines or army, stood at the door. They held rifles, M-16s I thought, pointed in my direction but, thankfully, not directly at me. The muzzles were tilted downward, at the floor between us. They didn't look human—their bodies bulged with armor and they were painted, the jungle cammo pattern of their clothing extended via grease-paint to their faces and arms. They looked like they were waiting for something.

"Something" walked through the door, a minute later, followed by six more soldiers. He was obviously an officer—his face wasn't painted and he carried an unholstered sidearm in one hand and a handheld radio in the other. He advanced down the tunnel without a pause, the six soldiers behind him in two files of three. He closed to thirty feet and I could see him eyeing the two columns of equipment that framed the terminus.

I held up my left hand up, palm out, like a school crossing guard. "That's far enough!" My voice was cracked and strident and I hated the sound of it, but there must've been something in it that sounded desperate for the man in the lead stopped and held up the hand with the radio in it. The soldiers behind him stopped as well, though their rifles went from pointing at the floor to pointing at me.

"You are trespassing, on private property. Vacate these premises immediately!" I didn't think my request had a chance in hell of working, but I wanted it on record. If they'd had time, the guys were at the hangar entrance of the tunnel behind me videotaping this.

"Put your hands on your head and drop to your knees." He was close enough that I could read his insignia, captain, and his name, Moreno. He had the "voice," the voice of someone who ordered people around every day and I felt my arms rise almost involuntarily before I stopped myself.

"I repeat—you are trespassing. You are breaking the law. You are violating my constitutional rights. Do you remember the Constitution? I was under the impression that military personnel still take an oath to defend the Constitution."

That made him mad. He gestured with his radio. "Nichols, Martinez—secure him."

The two lead soldiers said in unison, "Sir!" and strode forward their rifles pointed at me. I took a step back and they broke into a trot. As the muzzles of their rifles neared the terminus, I thumbed the left-hand button on the little plastic box.

There was more of a delay than I remembered, and then there was the flash and I squeezed my eyes shut. I heard something hit the floor and the lights went out as outside power was cut. I heard the generator kick in, and after a couple of seconds the fluorescents flickered back on.

A foot-long section of each soldier's M-16, the flash supressor, sight, some plastic forestock, and length of barrel, lay on the dirt— the tame side of the tunnel was gone. I looked closely at the dirt. I'd been trying for just the tip of the rifle barrels and I was scared that I'd hurt someone, but there weren't any pieces of hand or finger on the ground.

I shuddered, and buried my face in my hands. I heard movement in the tunnel behind me and someone put a hand on my shoulder. "Are you all right?" It was Clara.

I stood and smiled weakly. "Right as rain." I staggered a little and she steadied me. I really was able to walk, but I leaned on her all the way up the tunnel.

Fifteen

"I'm Scared of Things I Don't Understand."

WE WILL ACTIVATE THE GATE TO TALK SOMETIME IN
THE NEXT HOUR. WE WILL DEACTIVATE IT IMMEDIATELY
IF ANYBODY IS WITHIN TEN METERS OF THE TERMINUS.
WE WILL SHUT IT IMMEDIATELY IF THERE ARE ANY
HOSTILE ACTS, EVEN IF THERE ARE PERSONNEL AT THE
TERMINUS.

I wrote it on a sheet of notebook paper. Marie rewrote it, cutting it down to the current version and making it more legible. Clara and Joey came up with the delivery mechanism. Rick delivered it.

"Cameras on," I called.

About two hours had passed since I'd closed the gate down. This time we'd set the video cameras five feet back from the gate, perched on boxes on each side of the tunnel.

Marie and Joey turned them on and double-checked that they were indeed recording, then walked past Rick and me where we stood about thirty feet down the tunnel. They kept going until they were at the hangar door, where they joined Clara, waiting with an air horn in each hand.

"Ready, Rick?"

In Rick's right hand was a water-smoothed rock, not quite a perfect sphere, about the size of a softball but much heavier. The note was secured to it with twine. He hefted the rock then nodded to me. He was the bowler in the group and his delivery had been perfect in the five dry runs.

I wiped my right hand on my pants, then took up the little plastic remote control. "Let's do it."

He brought the ball up under his chin then took two steps forward and bowled the ball—not hard—straight down the center of the tunnel. As it passed the video cameras, I pushed the right hand button and Clara held down the triggers on the air horns, a devastating sound in the enclosed space. The ball rolled slowly on, losing momentum, and for the briefest instant I thought that I'd timed it wrong, that the ball would roll past the terminus before the gate came on, or, as bad, stop dead just short of it.

Then the dark end of the tunnel became the brightly lit tame side and the rock rolled over the terminus. I thumbed the left-hand switch. In the brief instant before the gate shut down I saw open mouths and I saw more men than I could count, not all of them soldiers. The nearer ones flinched away from the blast of sound and light, though one of the soldiers took a step toward the gate and then they were gone again.

Message delivered.

According to the tape, the gate was open for a total of thirty-six video frames—about a second and a half. Those frames showed us twenty-five men. One of them was Captain Moreno. Another fifteen were soldiers dressed and armed like those we'd seen before.

The newcomers wore civilian clothes ranging from business suits to jeans. Most of the civilians were clustered near the gate itself, though they'd flinched back when it activated. The rock with the message tied to it glanced off of one of these guys' ankles. Good thing it didn't bounce back across the line.

Two of the civilians, though, were dressed more formally—dark gray suits and tightly knotted ties. They were standing at the back, talking to Captain Moreno, when the gate opened. One of those two just stared at us, but the other one, a man with short red hair, darted his hand into his jacket. The gun in his hand was just coming out from beneath his lapel when the gate shut down.

Let's stay away from him.

Another interesting thing was that they also had video cameras set up, though their equipment looked a lot better than ours.

"They have us on video?" said Marie. "Shit."

Rick said, "Relax, Madge, your hair looks fine."

Marie frowned. "That's not what I meant. They can ID us now."

"They know who we are, already," I said.

"You mean Luis . . . ?" Clara said.

I shook my head. "No. Luis wouldn't say anything—unless they chemically interrogated him. But they didn't have to. Not when they have accountants.

"They followed the money. They followed it from the zoos to the Austin Bank, to Luis's bank, to the working account, to our individual paychecks. I don't know what they did to get the banks to trace the transactions, but it doesn't matter.

"By the end of the day they will probably have our high school yearbook pictures, our grade point averages, and our dental records."

We opened the gate ten minutes later. I didn't want them to have too much time to think of ways to take the gate. And I certainly didn't want to cut anybody in half.

I was standing alone, six feet back from the terminus, right beside the cameras. The guys were watching from just inside the hangar door.

I was wearing my flight jacket with my hands deep in the pockets. My right hand held the remote control. As usual, it was cold on the wildside, but I was sweating. I flicked the switch.

They'd backed everybody away from the gate, though they'd left the cameras where they were. Captain Moreno and the two men in suits were standing at the thirty foot line. The technical types were a bit behind them and, back at the entrance to the barn, the soldiers stood, alert. They still carried their weapons.

They were talking, but stopped immediately. Captain Moreno started to step toward me, then stopped. He half turned instead to the man beside him.

Now we know who's in charge.

"One of you can come forward," I said. My voice was less nervous. My thumb was on the left-hand button and I was pretty confident that I could close the gate before they crossed it.

"All right." The man in the middle walked forward. He was of medium height and his hairline receded above each temple. Steel-rimmed bifocals perched on a sharp, downward-hooking nose. As he got nearer I could see a scar high over his right eye and lines across his forehead. His hair was shot with gray.

When he was about six feet from the gate, I said, "Far enough. Who are you?"

He ignored the question while he *studied* me, peering at my face with narrowed eyes. I tried to remain motionless, to still a sudden urge to shift my weight from foot to foot. He didn't smile, or frown, or put on any facial expression used in person-to-person communication. He was looking at me like one examines a problem, a puzzle, or an *obstacle*.

I was about to ask the question again when the intensity of his gaze relaxed and he said in a level voice, "I am your best friend . . . or your worst enemy. The choice is yours."

I blinked. "Mr. Your-best-friend-or-your-worst-enemy is a little awkward. Perhaps I could just call you Mr. Bestworst?"

His lips did something like a smile but the rest of his face was still. The scar on his forehead darkened slightly.

"What are you doing on my property, Mr. Bestworst?"

"We can do this hard, Charles, or we can do this easy," he said. "Cooperate and the government will compensate you for your, uh, discovery, and inconvenience. You could come out of this very well off, perhaps with a position further developing this, er, project."

He smiled and this time it looked real, his face crinkling at the corners of the eyes and dimples forming in his cheeks. He spread his hands persuasively, his posture open, relaxed.

Then his hands dropped and the smile dropped. "Get in our way," he said raising his right index finger and tightening his voice, "and you'll think you've been hit by a train."

I couldn't help myself. I took a step back and nearly closed the gate. Mr. Bestworst took a step toward me, matching, and I said, "Get *back!*" The anger I felt at myself for flinching showed in my voice, and he took a slow step back to his original stopping place.

Tersely, I said, "What do you *want*, Mr. . . . dammit, what is your name?"

"Bestworst will do. Just remember what it stands for. What do I want? For starters," he said calmly, "I want to understand what's going on here."

"Well, right now, what's going on is you're trespassing."

He dismissed this with a wave of his hand. "You want a search warrant? Easily done. Backdated, too."

I pointed at our video cameras. "Would you care to repeat the fact that you've invaded my property without a search warrant to the camera."

The scar on Bestworst's forehead darkened again, though Bestworst shrugged. "Let's start with criminal traffic in endangered species."

"Passenger pigeons are not on the list."

"They are now. There are twenty in existence."

This was a tack I hadn't considered. I'd avoided several other species simply because they existed and were endangered on the tame side. "Are you arresting me, Mr. Bestworst? You haven't even shown me your ID. Shouldn't you be reading me my rights?"

"A train, Charles. A train."

I tried another tack. "Perhaps I should be talking to my lawyer instead of you."

"Luis Cervantes by any chance?"

I nodded, stone-faced.

"I don't think he'll be available to represent you." Bestworst smiled briefly. "He wasn't interested in cooperating either."

I didn't like his use of "wasn't." "Just out of curiosity, have you let *him* see a lawyer?"

Bestworst shrugged again. "Cooperate with us."

"You may have control of my ranch—and even jurisdiction. But where I'm standing, you have none. And I'm not particularly concerned," I lied, "about your mythical charges and search warrants."

The geniality dropped from his face like a guillotine falling. "My jurisdiction is wherever this nation's security is threatened."

I felt my face getting stiff. I didn't say anything for a very long time. Finally I said, "You don't even know what we have here, do you? How can you know national security is at risk?"

He shrugged. "How do I know that it's not?"

I stepped to the left side of the wall and picked up the rifle barrels from where they leaned against the wall. I tossed them gently, one at a time, over the line, onto the dirt floor in front of Bestworst.

The perfectly flat surface where the metal of the barrel and the plastic forestock had been sheared by the gate gleamed in the light of the fluorescents. Bestworst eyed the two pieces thoughtfully.

I said, "This conversation is over."

Then I turned off the gate.

"Wow, Charlie. You oughta be in pictures," Rick said. He meant it as a joke, but the humor didn't touch his voice or face. He looked scared.

"You told us it was legal," Clara said. She sounded mad, and I remembered other times she'd gotten angry, and the circumstances. She was scared, too.

Marie held Joey's hand and neither of them spoke.

We'd just finished replaying the video of my encounter with Mr. Bestworst. I got up to shut off the video monitor, then turned to face them.

"It was legal. You can't make something illegal and then prosecute people retroactively, can you?"

"Well, actually," said Marie, "you can."

"You can?" I was horrified.

"My senior honors paper was on the Superfund. There's a concept called strict liability. There are companies who are being charged for the cleanup costs after dumping toxic substances that occurred before it was illegal to dump those things."

I was relieved. "That's because that pollution is still poisoning water tables, though, isn't it? And to cover costs of cleanup? We haven't contaminated playgrounds or anything. We resurrected an extinct species from the dead. No court in the country would convict us." I licked my lips. "But he doesn't want us in court. Courts have public records and publicity is the last thing he wants. He doesn't know what we have, but whatever it is, it's easier to control if nobody else knows about it, right? I mean, we certainly had an easier time of it before they found us."

"But what do we do, then?" asked Rick. "I'm not spending the rest of my life over here. Chris is over there—if this thing isn't settled soon, I'm going back."

I sighed.

Clara said, "What makes you think they'll let you see Chris if you go through that gate? If we don't resolve this, you may spend the rest of your days in a dark hole, locked away from the world, your friends, your family, and, especially, the press."

"It might be worth it," he said, "if they really will lock me away from my mother." He looked at the dirt floor of the hangar, then back up at me. "This plan of yours better work, Charlie. That's all I can say."

I swallowed and tried to look as confident as Captain Moreno. "I think it will work, Rick. But no promises."

Four hours later I opened the gate again. There was a flash of blinding light characteristic of something being sheared by the gate and I said, "Shit!" A man, fell backward, away from me, a pole of some kind held in his hand.

I took a step forward, compulsively. I stopped myself before I stepped across the line to help him. "Are you all right?"

He was one of the technical types, not in uniform, and he seemed to have all his parts. Another two technicians standing behind him moved forward, to help, I guess, but I held up my hand and they stopped.

The man on the ground looked embarrassed. "I'm fine."

I took a closer look at his pole. It was a piece of angle iron with a coaxial cable taped to it. At his end, the cable ran up the tunnel toward the barn. At my end, the cable ended abruptly, cut at the same point as the bar.

"Video camera?" I asked.

"Yeah, and a light." He climbed to his feet, brushing off his butt with his free hand.

They were probably looking at the back of my contraption, trying to figure out the machinery. I smiled. "When I shut the gate again, you can snag it back across with the pole. Don't cross the terminus with any part of your body, though."

He nodded.

"I want to talk to Mr. Bestworst. Could you get him please?"

He started to turn, then paused. "Answer a question, first?"

"Maybe, Mr.—?"

He hesitated, looking over his shoulder toward the door to the barn, then shrugged and said, "Bob Orkand, Sandia Labs. Why is it colder on your side of the tunnel?"

I started to say something about different climates, but stopped when something else occurred to me. "Where do you think the energy to maintain this gateway comes from?" I hadn't the faintest idea what the real answer to his question was, but maybe I was right? It could happen.

The man's eyes widened and he opened his mouth to ask more questions. I was about to remind him about getting Bestworst when Bestworst strode into the far end of the tunnel followed closely by Captain Moreno and the red-haired civilian with the fast gun hand.

"Please stand back from the terminus," I said to Orkand. He backed away, looking past me, trying to see as much as possible of the tunnel behind me.

Bestworst looked annoyed when he had to step around the oblivious Orkand to approach me. He stopped at the six-foot mark, about where he'd stopped before. "It's your nickel," he said.

He was starting to remind me of my father.

"I would like to see Luis Cervantes and Richard Madigan."

"So?" Even more like my father.

I gritted my teeth and resisted the urge to shut the gate in his face. Carefully I said, "I would be very grateful for your consideration in this matter."

His eyes widened slightly. "How grateful?"

I paused. "I would consider answering some questions."

His eyes narrowed. "Would you, now." He thought about it for a moment. "What do you mean by 'see'?"

"See. Standing where you are. You can restrain them, if you like—to keep them from crossing over, but I would like to verify that they're all right—talk to them."

"Hmmm. I don't really see why I should."

I was rapidly passing from distrust to active dislike where Mr. Bestworst was concerned. "If you're not willing to let us see that Luis is unharmed, then the possibility exists that you've harmed him. And if that's the case, then we certainly aren't willing to give you a chance at us. Let us talk to Luis or we shut the gate down." I mentally crossed my fingers. "We won't open it again—not at this location, anyway."

He seized on that like a cat on a rat. "What do you mean, Charlie? Where else could you open the gate? Are you talking some other place or"—his face twisted like he'd bitten into a lemon—"some other time." There, he said it.

I smiled slightly. "That sounds a lot like a question. Remarkably like a question. I've already outlined the circumstances under which I am willing to answer questions."

He sat frozen, thinking about it, while I fidgeted slightly. Finally, he said, "Okay. I can have Cervantes here within thirty minutes. Richard Madigan is in Austin—I can have him here within four hours."

"Why so long? You've got enough helicopters to fly the Houston Boilers to the Super Bowl, which, by the way, is the only way they'd ever get there. Surely you can airlift one innocent lawyer from Austin."

He frowned. "Do you have any idea how much Jet-A a helicopter burns a minute?"

"Single or double turbine? Blackhawk or Kiowa? Unladen European swallow or African? I am a pilot, after all. Throw him in a cop car, then, and have them run the siren all the way. Surely you can do better than four hours."

"What's your hurry, Charlie?"

I felt the palms of my hands get wet. "I'm anxious about their safety. Concerned. Tell you what, I'll open the gate again in two hours. I expect to see both of them, then."

"You're closing the gate now?"

I nodded.

"What if we get them here earlier? Wouldn't you want to know?"

"I'm scared of you, Mr. Bestworst. You seem the kind of guy who breaks down doors. I've got a door you can't break down, and it doesn't do me any good if it's not closed."

He nodded, almost politely, as if what I'd said made perfect sense. I shivered.

"In two hours, then," he said.

I nodded and thumbed the switch.

We spent the two hours outside.

When we'd fled to this side in the morning, the weather was gray and cool with a stiff breeze across the buffalo grass that made it ripple like the sea. By two in the afternoon, though, the overcast had cleared, the breeze had moderated, and the sun shone brightly, making jackets optional.

Clara tethered Impossible on a long rope and halter out in the middle of the airfield, where he spent his time halfheartedly eating grass and starting at every gust of wind. Clara sat nearby, cross-legged on the grass, her shotgun in her lap. Marie and Joey walked, hand in hand, up the length of the north–south runway, a romantic, if heavily armed, sight with their shotguns slung from their shoulders.

Rick sat on the roof of the hangar, his feet hanging off the front edge. I'd tried to talk to him, but he met all my conversational gambits with shrugs. I made sure he was watching his back, then walked across the field to Clara.

Impossible shied away from something new and whinnied. Every few moments he'd trot over to Clara and push his nose down into her hair. She'd pet him for a moment, then he'd go back to chewing grass.

"What's he spooking at?" I asked, sitting down beside her.

"Everything. None of it smells right, though he seems to like this buffalo grass all right. He may even be smelling a predator or two out there. His ancestors probably ran from similar critters." She plucked a handful of buffalo grass from the ground and began weaving strands together. "He'll have to learn what is really dangerous and what isn't if we're stuck here."

"We're not stuck here," I said, though I don't know if I was trying to convince her or me.

"Right." She gave me a look that failed to convey unwavering confidence. "Don't worry, Charlie. If it's a choice between being stuck in some dark hole over there, or freedom here, I know which one I'd choose. I feel guilty, though, about bringing Impossible. It was selfish of me, but I couldn't stand being without him."

I winced. "Even more than your family?"

"More guilt. Not about leaving them behind, but feeling relieved to be free of them, however long. What about you?"

"What are you going to do about Impossible's drinking water?"

"Huh?"

"He's got to drink a lot. There's the stream and the river, but I'd be worried about parasites."

"Charlie! Stop it!" She stood up. "I'm worried enough about Impossible. If you don't want to talk about your parents, don't." She took three stiff steps away. Impossible watched us, ears up.

I dropped my head down, staring at the grass. I was shocked at myself. *Is that where that question came from?* I felt my ears burning as the truth of it hit me. I looked back up, my eyes wet. Clara was standing against Impossible, her arms wrapped around his neck.

She turned her head and looked at me, her arms still around the horse's neck. Her eyes were as wet as my own.

At exactly the same time we each said, "I'm sorry."

She half laughed, half sobbed, and turned back into Impossible. I stood and walked closer. She released Impossible and took two steps toward me. "Impossible will be okay," I said, hoping it was true. "You're right—I didn't want to talk about my da—my parents."

"Why not?"

The corners of my mouth pulled down hard, surprising me. I shook my head, not trusting myself to speak.

Clara blinked and reached out and put a hand on my shoulder. "It's all right. You don't have to."

I took a deep breath and expelled it hard. "I can't. I'll lose it, and now's not the time for me to go to pieces."

She slung the shotgun strap over her shoulder, stepped closer, and hugged me. I stiffened and she started to let go, in response, but I grabbed at her compulsively and hugged back, desperately. I felt her body warm against mine, soft breasts, hard thighs. I smelled her skin and soap overlaid with the strong smell of her horse. I felt her stiffen, then, and I thought I'd gone too far. I let her go. "Sorry," I said again.

She started to step back, then stopped. "No. I'm sorry." She leaned in and kissed me warmly on the lips. "I thought about Rick watching and it threw me. Too bad." She put her arms around my neck and kissed me again. Tentatively at first, then more enthusiastically, I kissed her back. When we parted she was flushed and breathing hard. She looked surprised.

I felt like I could walk on water.

"Like that, is it?" she said.

I nodded.

"It's not just because of Marie?" she asked.

I looked down at my feet. "I don't know. Maybe at first . . . not now though." I looked back up. She was watching me speculatively. "Definitely not now."

She took my arm and walked over to the tether stake. It was one of our screw-in tie-downs that we used on the planes when they weren't in the hangar. She untied Impossible's lead and I bent and began unscrewing the tie-down. I was afraid to ask the same question of her but she answered it anyway.

"I didn't kiss you because Rick was watching, Charlie. I did it because I've wanted to ever since we got back from Cripple Creek. Well, maybe I chose now because he was watching. But not what I did or who I did it to—er, with."

I stood, the stake in my hand. She held Impossible's loosely coiled lead in one hand and her shotgun in the other. I looked at her and down the airfield where Joey and Marie were walking back toward us. I felt the slightest twinge of regret, almost nostalgia, but it was that—nostalgia for something in the past. I looked back at Clara and smiled. "With. It's a nice word, isn't it?"

"Yes, it is."

Sixteen

"Hurt Him and You Die!"

We took a snapshot of the gateway, turning on the video cameras and opening, then shutting the gate immediately after. We played the tapes back frame by frame.

"There's Luis—I guess that other guy is Madigan." Luis and Madigan were standing about ten feet back from the gate. They were both wearing sweat suits and were handcuffed at the wrist to very large soldiers. At the back of the tunnel stood Captain Moreno and Mr. Bestworst.

The rest of the tunnel was empty.

"Huh," said Joey. "Looks like he's doing what he said he would. I must admit, I'm a little surprised. He didn't look like the kind of guy who negotiates."

Rick said, "I don't like it. Why'd they clear the tunnel? Aren't they still trying to figure out your half a machine?"

"Maybe," I said, "they figured out it was a red herring. That guy from Sandia Labs looked pretty bright."

Rick shook his head. "And maybe it's a trap."

I raised my eyebrows. "Like they're going to charge me? From ten feet away? Handcuffed to unwilling participants? We can shut the gate before they even get started."

Rick shook his head. "What makes you think they're going to be ten feet away? What if they're stacked six across at the line now? They've had time to get in position."

I pursed my lips and stared hard at the floor. Finally I said, "You're right. So we'll do it this way." I held out the remote for the gate to Rick. "Both you and Joey will have a gate control. Either of you can shut it down, right? And we'll take another snapshot to make sure they aren't waiting at the terminus."

Rick took the small plastic capsule carefully, using his forefinger and thumb, as if it were hot or might bite him. "What about opening up the gate again—I mean if we have to shut it in an emergency?"

"When we all agree—okay? Don't open it unilaterally. Let's talk first."

"Right," said Rick. Joey nodded.

The snapshot showed us pretty much the same thing—Moreno and Bestworst walked a little closer, but there was no sudden influx of soldiers and Luis, Richard Madigan, and guards were still the closest people to the terminus.

Joey and Rick took up positions at the back of the tunnel, in the open doorway—Clara and Marie watched from the monitor. I hung up my shotgun and harness and took my station five feet in front of the terminus.

I put my right hand in my jacket pocket to open the gate, but of course I'd given the control to Rick and it wasn't there.

"When you're ready, Charlie," Rick called.

"Do it," I said over my shoulder.

The tame side reappeared, the scene unchanged. Luis saw me and looked relieved. Madigan shook his head sharply, surprised, distrusting his eyes, I guess.

I spoke first. "Are you okay, Luis?"

"Well enough—except for having my constitutional rights violated six ways from Sunday."

"Is this Richard?" I pointed with my left hand.

"Yes. He's had a rougher time of it. I've only been in their hands since this morning. With him it's been three days." He looked at

Richard, then back at me. "He's a little pissed at me and a lot pissed at our 'host.'"

Richard nodded at that but didn't say anything.

"Have they let you talk to a lawyer?" I asked.

"Only each other. Don't worry, I'm preparing the civil and criminal charges in my head. When I'm through with them, they'll be unemployed, in prison, and br—look out!"

A man exploded out of the dirt floor of the tunnel immediately before the gate and dove over the terminus. I yelled and stepped back but the man turned his dive into a forward somersault, whipping his legs over and kicking out to catch me hard in the stomach and thigh. As I fell backward I saw the gate flick shut, Rick or Joey doing their job.

I hit the ground hard and lost what little breath was left me after the kick. The man was above me immediately, a handgun jammed hard into my neck, and he began tugging at my right arm, which I was surprised to find was still in my jacket pocket. I let him pull it out, being far more concerned with my breathing.

"Don't fucking move!" he shouted. It took me a minute to realize he was talking to the guys at the gate. I finally succeeded in drawing a large lungful of air and this diverted his attention back to me. "Where is the control!" He was patting my right jacket pocket, then the other. I wasn't able, much less ready, to speak. He pushed the gun harder up under my chin. I could feel the foresight tear skin.

I recognized him now—he was the red-haired man with Bestworst. He'd shed his coat and his tie, and dirt smudged his white button-down.

He rolled me over, facedown, and moved on to pat at my pants pockets. He felt something in my back pocket and ripped the pocket flap to get at it, but it was only my Swiss Army knife. He threw it to the side.

He grabbed the collar of my jacket and hauled me to my feet, his gun held against the back of my head.

I was facing the hangar end of the tunnel. Joey and Rick stood in the doorway. There was no sign of Marie or Clara.

My captor said, "Open the gate! Now!" He was talking loud enough for all of us to hear, probably because he didn't know which one of us could open the gate.

"We can't," I said hoarsely. I could breathe without pain if I took shallow breaths. My thigh throbbed, though.

He ground the pistol harder into my head, forcing my chin to my chest. "Open it *now* or you'll see his brains on the floor!"

I saw Joey start to move his hand to his pocket and I held my palm face out, close to my body where the man with the gun couldn't see it. Joey stopped but his eyes were wide and his mouth parted. Rick was still as stone, watching.

"I told you," I said through gritted teeth. "We can't."

He kicked me in the back of the knee and pulled down hard on my collar. I dropped to my knees. Now I could feel the foresight on his gun grinding into my head, past hair and into skin. "Open. The. Gate." He pulled the gun away for a second and fired a shot past my right ear into the floor of the tunnel.

The muzzle blast burned my cheek and the sound was a palpable blow, like being hit with a baseball bat. I moved to raise my hands to my face, and he shoved the pistol back into my neck. I think he was shouting at me, but all I could hear was a tremendous ringing.

I looked at the guys. Rick was saying something, I could hear his voice dimly through the ringing, from my left ear, I guess.

Rick was saying, "—is the only one who knows how to open the gate, so you better leave him alive if you ever want to get back home."

My captor considered this for a second. Then he said, "Okay, open the gate, Charlie."

I was trembling, my ears were ringing, and the front and back of my left leg hurt from being kicked. My breathing, though, seemed back to normal. The gun came back from my neck, but I could still feel it with my hair. I thought I should be terrified, but I seemed beyond that. "The capacitors have to recharge. We won't have enough juice to open the gate for another thirty minutes."

He pushed the gun back into my head. "Bullshit. You've opened the gate with a gap of eleven minutes and thirty-three seconds."

So they were keeping track. "Yes. But not more than twice. We can get two insertions per charge." I was using my dad's voice—his patronizing I'll-say-this-slowly-because-you're-obviously-a-moron voice. "But not three, not until the capacitors are charged. It takes an hour to charge them to the top, but we can manage one insertion at half charge. That takes thirty minutes after we start the recharge cycle. And we haven't started it yet."

The gun came back away from my head as I spoke. I'd gotten the capacitor line from reading an article on particle weapons research in *Aviation Technology*. He seemed to be buying it. He hauled on my collar, pulling me back to my feet. The world spun around and I wondered what the gunshot had done to my inner ear.

"Get the girls in here," he said.

I started to say something, but Joey beat me to it. "They're not here."

"Don't bullshit me," the man behind me said.

Angrily, Rick said, "It's not bullshit! They ran outside when you started shooting your damn gun. For all they knew, you were killing Charlie, then us. Do you blame them?"

The man pushed me slowly forward. "You two," he said to Rick and Joey, "get down on your knees and put your hands on your heads." Joey and Rick looked at each other and the man added, "If he's the one who knows how to open the gate, I can shoot *you*."

They raised their arms and dropped to their knees.

"Face the wall." He gestured with his gun at the right hand side of the tunnel. Joey and Rick shuffled around on their knees until they were facing the wall. The man pushed me forward at a slow walk. When we passed the guys, he swung me sideways, a shield between them and him. As we neared the door, he swung me about again and edged forward, me in front, slowly. He was trying hard to look in all directions at once.

I cleared the door, looking straight ahead.

From both sides of the door came the harsh mechanical sound of

Mossburg twelve-gauge shotguns chambering rounds. My captor stiffened.

Marie's voice, tight with strain, came from the right and down. "Drop your gun. Drop the gun! Drop the fucking gun!"

From the other side Clara's voice, almost screaming, added, "Do it *now!*"

They were crouched low on each side of the doorway, aiming up, at my captor's head, to keep from shooting each other.

The man did not drop his gun. "This gun goes off very easily. You don't want an extra hole or two in Charlie's head."

Marie stood and stepped closer. "Hurt him and you die! Drop the gun or I'll kill you!" She pushed the shotgun barrel forward until it touched the skin under the man's right ear. "It's loaded with buckshot. Let. Him. Go."

I felt the man flinch, shifting his head, trying to stare Marie down. Marie looked scary, her eyes wide and her teeth bared, and her knuckles white where she gripped the shotgun. I shifted my eyes left, to Clara, in time to see her shift her grip on the shotgun, then lift something else in her right hand.

Shit! I let my knees buckle and dropped suddenly. The man's gun followed me down and I was afraid it would go off at any second. There was a hissing sound and I looked up to see Clara spraying a stream of pepper Mace right into the man's face. He recoiled and gasped, then yelled as the full pain of it hit him. The yell dissolved into a series of wracking, wheezing coughs.

Some of it drifted down and into my eyes, burning painfully, but not, apparently, as painfully as for the man. Marie slashed out with the barrel of her shotgun and his gun spun down to land in the dirt. I scooped it up and scrambled away, rubbing furiously at my eyes with my free hand.

"Don't rub it, Charlie," said Clara. "It'll only make it worse."

She was right. I tried to keep my hands down. My ears were tearing painfully and the edges of my nostrils began burning. I had trouble seeing, but got the sense that Joey and Rick were standing over the man. I knew where he was by the horrid sound of his wheezing breath.

I held up the handgun. "Somebody who can see, take this thing away from me. Somebody else, get an oxygen rig from the plane." I went into a fit of coughing while I tried to remember what the treatment for pepper spray was. Clara, I think, took the handgun from me. "Get some bottles of distilled water from stores. And before you give him any oxygen, search him and tie him up."

They found handcuffs in his back pocket and secured him, sitting, to the left landing gear strut on the Maule. Rick held the oxygen mask for him while Clara used a squirt bottle of distilled water to irrigate his eyes. Marie was standing back with another can of Cap-Stun and her shotgun just in case.

The tears had stopped enough that I could see. Joey and I watched the video of our last encounter. In slow motion, it was clear that they'd used the time to dig the hole, then covered it with a piece of plywood and a very shallow layer of dirt. The board flipped up, sending dirt flying and our visitor had sprung into our lives.

We still didn't know his name, though. I guess he'd left his identification in his jacket, and he wasn't quite up to talking just yet.

He still scared me, though. "Let's get rid of him, before he's fully recovered," I said. My right ear was still ringing and sounds came to me in a muffled, oddly intense way, like those heard underwater.

We gave him back to Bestworst like our first message. We blindfolded him and left his hands handcuffed behind him. Then Rick and Clara held an arm on either side and ran him toward the terminus. Just short of the line, I switched the gate on and they released him. His momentum carried him into the midst of a waiting squad of soldiers. I thumbed the control and the gate shut, just as they started to move.

There was the too-familiar flash of light and two inches of an M-16 barrel landed on the dirt floor of the tunnel.

We stood there, frozen for a second, staring at the dead end of the tunnel. Finally, Rick took a pencil from his pocket and slid it into the hot piece of barrel, police procedural style. He held it up. "Too close."

I nodded. "Maybe we should just give in? I didn't think they'd push so hard."

He looked wistful for a moment, considering it. "No. We're only guilty of having something they want." He flipped the pencil and the piece of barrel flew down the tunnel to land among the debris from my gate device. He looked back at me. "But if we give them any more chances at the gate, somebody is going to die."

None of us ate well.

Clara spread her sleeping bag in the corner, next to Impossible, tethered to the wall. Impossible was eating horse feed from Clara's saddlebags and a bit of hay. Unbeknownst to me she'd moved several bales in from the barn that morning before the army arrived.

Marie and Joey put their bags together on the far side of the hangar, between the Coyote and the wall. My tightly rolled-up bag was still sitting on the plywood table with the video monitors. I was cleaning the dinner dishes with boiled creek water hauled up for that purpose. Rick was listening to his Walkman and staring at nothing.

I was wondering what was happening on the other side, both at the ranch, wherever Luis was, and out in the world, where our countermeasures were in motion. I was also wondering where Rick was going to put his sleeping bag, wondering whether or not I should put my bag near Clara. I had mixed feelings about it. I wasn't sure how welcome I'd be. I wasn't sure how Rick would take it if I was welcome. In a flash of paranoia I also wondered if I should sleep between the others and the gate, lest one of them open it while I slept.

Clara solved the problem by coming over to the table, picking up my bag, and taking it back to her corner.

Rick looked at me and shrugged. He took the earphones off his head and said, "She's like that. Get used to it." He picked up his sleeping bag and unrolled it at the back, beneath the ladder to the control tower. His face was a mask, but there was anger and hurt in his voice.

We spent the night in darkness—the generator made too much noise, even in its insulated cabinet, to make sleeping comfortable with it on.

Clara and I held each other, nestled like spoons, fully clothed. We didn't discuss it—she'd zipped our bags together, but only took off her shoes before slipping inside. Her hair tickled my face and halfway through the night I rolled over, only to feel her arms go around me and her body press warm and soft against my back.

She woke up in the cold light of morning to take Impossible out to graze. Shivering, I followed her forty minutes later with breakfast—a fried egg sandwich and coffee.

"You angel!" She kissed me enthusiastically.

"Is it me or the food?"

"Don't ask. Not before I eat." She bit into the sandwich.

"Whoa—let me get my fingers out of the way."

After she ate, she had me watch Impossible while she dealt with his corner in the hangar, shoveling up the manure and urine-soaked dirt and carting it outside. Then we put Impossible back in the hangar.

The others were up by then—we left the hangar door open for light and I sat on a folding chair in front of the Maule with my shotgun handy while they went about dressing, washing, and feeding themselves.

I could see a small group of buffalo in the distance; snow-white cattle egrets dotted the grass around them and perched on their backs. As the sun rose higher, more and more birds rose from the grass—doves from trees, quail from the grass, cranes moving toward the river, and hawks, high above them all until they stooped, so to speak, to conquer.

Clara joined me, holding two cups, tea for me and coffee for her. She sat on the ground and leaned against my knees. I touched her hair softly, like one might touch a wild thing, trying not to scare it into flight. She pushed her head against my hand and I swallowed convulsively.

"What's that?" she asked, pointing skyward.

I looked. High, even higher than the hawks, a large black bird circled lazily. I squinted my eyes. "It's got the spread pinion feathers like a turkey buzzard, but it's so big." I handed her the shotgun and went to the Maule for binoculars. The bird resolved itself into a large buzzardlike creature, but instead of the red-wrinkled head, the skin was yellow and red and there was a white patch of feathers on each of the wings.

"My god, it's a condor."

Clara took the binoculars from me. "A California condor? Is it lost?"

"No. This was part of the historical range . . . per the fossil record. I just never saw one before—I wonder how many there are? I mean, there are fewer than eight in the wild on the tame side and every one of them was born in captivity."

The condor dipped sharply, spun, and then rose again, one, two, three flaps of impossibly long wings before it resumed gliding. Clara sighed, her eyes locked to the binoculars. "I hope there are millions."

I nodded, then realized she wouldn't see that. "Yes, let there be millions."

We'd waited until midday to take a snapshot of the other side. We'd stayed in the hangar, peeking around the edges of the tunnel entrance. After the last encounter I didn't know what to expect, but I didn't want to take any chances.

A bullet could make it through the gate while it was open.

We narrowed the aperture—the time the gate was open—by splitting the operation. I counted, "One, two, three, four, five." On the count of four, Joey opened the gate with his control and on five I shut it with mine. It practically blinked. Then we went to the video recorders to see what we'd gotten.

Maybe I was still shaky from the attack the night before—maybe not. I felt my knees buckle, though, when I saw the image on the video monitor, and I staggered, catching the table's edge to steady myself.

Clara asked, "Charlie, what's the matter? Oh. . . ."

The video image on screen, flickering from the video-pause, showed a single figure in front of the gate. He was seated on a folding camp stool to one side of the tunnel and reading a newspaper, his back straight and unsupported. Beside him on the bail was a Styrofoam cup. If it wasn't empty, the cup held coffee, black, with artificial sweetener.

I knew, because that was what my father drank.

"Now what the hell does *that* mean?" said Rick.

My father was the only one visible—the rest of the tunnel was empty. The hole in the floor they'd dug for their attack was still there but uncovered and empty, I guess as a demonstration of good faith. The doors to the barn at the end of the tunnel were shut, but the video cameras were still there and the little red LED record lights were on.

"What do we do now, Charlie?" asked Joey.

He was still wearing his flight uniform, something I hadn't noticed from the video, though his hat was someplace else. He'd put the paper down and was looking at the gate when it opened. He *flinched* and I was pleasantly surprised. My unflappable father was surprised.

"They told me what to expect, but I didn't really believe it." He stood slowly. "What have you done, Charlie?"

I was standing there with a handheld VHF radio in my hand. From outside I could hear the distant sound of the Maule's engine. Rick, Joey, and Marie were waiting in it and listening to the radio. Clara, much to my distress, had saddled Impossible and was waiting on the hill at the back of the hangar. She was also listening—at least that was the plan.

Joey had both controls to the gate.

My eyes shifted everywhere, looking for soldiers to drop out of the ceiling, or step out of the walls—even explode out of the bale of hay. My knuckles were white where I held down the transmit button on the radio. If I stopped transmitting, Joey was to shut the gate.

"Please step across the terminus, Dad."

He tilted his head. "I've been sitting here looking at a sign which threatens death and dismemberment. I'm not sure I want to risk it."

My voice became a little more strident. "I'm shutting the gate, Dad. If we're both on the same side, we can talk."

"Why not just leave it open? What's wrong with that?"

"I don't know what they've told you, but they probably didn't mention the part where they held a gun to my head and threatened to kill me."

His eyes narrowed and he looked back over his shoulder. His voice flattened. "No. They didn't say anything about that." He stepped forward.

When he was standing beside me I said, "Close it, Joey." Then, to make doubly sure, I released the transmit button.

Dad turned his head in time to see the dead-end tunnel replace the tame side. He was very slow in turning back to me.

Clara's voice came back over the radio. "Everything okay, Charlie?"

My dad looked at the radio and raised his eyebrows. I lifted the radio to my mouth but waited to thumb the transmit button as I studied Dad's face. He met my gaze, then said, "Don't ask me—I don't have the faintest idea what's going on."

I hit the button. "It's okay. Uh, stand down." "Stand down" was the phrase we'd agreed upon. The one that meant I wasn't transmitting under duress. I certainly didn't say "Things are good." That meant run like hell.

"This way, Dad." I led him out to the hangar, picked up my shotgun from the rack, and asked him to help me open the hangar door.

His head swiveled from side to side, from the Coyote to the gun rack, to the scene revealed by the opening door. His mouth kept opening, as if to ask a question, and then he'd shut it. But I knew he wasn't skipping the questions—he was just making a list, and I knew he wouldn't let go of any of them until he had answers—satisfactory answers—to every question.

Clara arrived first, and for a moment I forgot my father was there.

She rode around the corner of the building at a canter, her hands still, steering Impossible by seat and leg alone. Her survival gear was strapped to the saddle behind her and she'd rigged a saddle holster for her shotgun. I knew her saddlebags were full of feed.

She was wearing jeans, riding sneakers, and her equipment harness. Her hair, short in the middle of summer, now blew around her face. Her breasts rose and fell to the rhythm of the horse's gait.

I took a deep breath of air and exhaled sharply.

Clara sat back in the saddle and Impossible dropped back to a walk and then stopped. I took Clara's shotgun while she dismounted.

"How are you, Captain Newell?" she asked.

Dad shook his head sharply. "Confused." He'd pulled up the collar of his uniform jacket against the chill.

The Maule turned the corner formed by the crossing of the runways and the engine noise became too loud for talk. Impossible started shying from the noise, and Clara took him inside before the Maule got too close. Marie swung the Maule around so it was facing out and shut down by the numbers. Rick and Joey got out and used the screw-in tie-downs to secure the plane.

To stall, I said, "I thought you were on the DFW—Salt Lake-Seattle run until Sunday."

"They delayed our takeoff at Salt Lake and had us put back into the gate. I was met by a man from the Defense Intelligence Agency and a replacement pilot from the airline. They put me on a Learjet into Easterwood and a Blackhawk helicopter out to here. They didn't want me to call your mother and I guess I didn't really want to until I knew what you'd gotten into."

"Um, excuse me a second," I said, and used the tractor to pull the fuel trailer over to the Maule. We topped off the tanks, put the fuel trailer back, and then trooped back inside.

My dad walked with us to the plywood table that held the video monitors, then said, "I take it, there wasn't a summer internship." He leaned forward slightly and crossed his arms. I could tell by the tone of his voice and his body language that his list of questions had gotten long enough.

My shoulders slumped, and I thrust my hands deep into my flight jacket pockets. I didn't say anything for a moment, weighing the possible answers, then settled on saying, "No."

"How long has this been going on?" he asked next.

I winced and looked away. Automatically, I'd translated his question into "How long have you been lying to me?" It took a major effort to turn back. I cleared my throat. "I discovered the gateway last year, in the late fall. I brought the others into it at the end of the school year. When we sold the pigeons."

"The pigeons." He paused. "The passenger pigeons."

I nodded.

He took a deep breath. "That man, uh, Mr. Bestworst?"

I laughed—I couldn't help it. "Is that what he told you his name was?"

Dad stared at me, frowning. "That's what he said, yes."

"I gave him that name. When I first asked him who he was he said he was my best friend or worst enemy. I shortened it to Bestworst. Did he show you any ID?"

"No. I assumed he was DIA, like the guy who met the plane." He digested that for a moment. "So they're doing this completely in the black. That's not good.

"Anyway, Bestworst told me about the pigeons. I'd seen the news coverage, but I thought it had to be a hoax or maybe somebody had been raising them in captivity these last eighty years, in secret. I certainly didn't expect it to be you. Why the pigeons?"

"We needed the money," I said. "For operations. Aircraft, fuel, supplies, salaries, training."

"Operations?" His voice rose and he blinked, then gritted his teeth, visibly pulling himself back. More calmly he said, "What kind

of operations? I guess I mean, what is this place? *When* is this place? Bestworst said things . . ."

"About a time machine?" asked Clara.

"Well, yes. He said one extinct species was bad enough, but four was excessive."

It was my turn to be surprised. "Four?"

"Two species of microscopic insect in the feathers and an intestinal parasite. They have microfossils of the mites but they don't exist today—well, not over there." He tilted his head toward the tunnel. "Ditto for the intestinal worm."

"It's not a time machine," said Clara. "It's an alternate earth, but one without humans."

That took some explaining and I let the guys handle it, sitting back, kind of numb. Dad seemed to take it well, even when Clara talked about mammoths, saber-toothed tigers, and California condors.

"So that's what this place is. Now what kind of operations are you talking about?"

I stirred. "Aerial surveys. Creating landing fields and fuel depots. Gold mining."

"Gold mining." He stared at me with unblinking eyes. "Near here?"

I shook my head. "No. The Colorado Rockies—Cripple Creek."

"Can you open the gate to there?"

I shook my head. "We fly it."

"That's seven hundred miles."

"Six hundred and ninety-four nautical miles," supplied Rick.

"Who flies it? What do you do about the weather? What range does your Maule have? What about your maintenance? Do you know how *dangerous* that is?" His voice rose with each question.

My shoulders hunched farther down with each question. Finally, I held up my hand and began counting off on my fingers. "We all fly it. We're all IFR qualified. We have to do our own meteorology so we're conservative. All our landing fields have AM beacons. The Maule could barely do the distance one way but we don't have to.

We have several fuel stops between here and Cripple Creek. As far as maintenance goes, Marie and I have Airframe & Power tickets, and we're conservative there, too." I took a deep breath. "And yes, we know how dangerous it is. We had a forced landing early on."

He opened his mouth and shut it. Then he dropped into a chair and slumped. "Jesus." He stared blankly ahead, envisioning God-knows-what horrors. Finally he muttered, "I'm too old for this. I have a lot of apologizing to do to your grandfather."

I stared at him, mystified.

He shrugged. "Before you were born I flew two tours in Vietnam. I had had two aircraft go down under me—one weather, one anti-aircraft fire. He said that's when his hair turned white."

"Ohhhhhhh."

"Gold mining." He shook his head. "Get any?"

I kept my face straight. "Four hundred and fifty."

"Dollars? You risked your lives for 450 measly dollars?"

"Pounds. Four hundred and fifty pounds. Actually, 5432 troy ounces."

I guess he didn't have any reaction left to give. "And in dollars?"

Joey said helpfully, "Approximately 2.148 million . . . going by Monday's closing market price."

"Oh." He was silent for a moment—then smiled slightly. "I can see why you wanted to take those risks." The smile dropped off his face and he said, "Now tell me about Mr. Bestworst and his friends from Fort Bragg."

Dad and I waited in the hangar, by the video table.

I'd shown him the videos of our encounters with Captain Moreno's men and the conversations with Bestworst, finishing up with the Bestworst's trigger man—the man from the hole in the tunnel floor. He was not amused. "What do they think this is, Waco?"

Marie's voice came out of the VHF radio in my hand. "We're in position, Charlie." Marie, Joey, and Rick were in the Maule outside, the engine idling, pointed into the wind and ready to rip. Clara waited with Impossible, on the hill. We'd also fueled up the Coyote and left it around the corner, on the north leg of runway 005.

Dad was going to try and talk to Bestworst's superiors. "He's way out of bounds, here. This operation stinks, and I really wonder if he has any authorization from above."

"To be honest," I said, "I expected some suits to show up when they finally tracked us down—FBI or federal marshals. The armed invasion seemed, uh, excessive."

"It is." He blinked, then said, "Charlie, there's the chance that they can't afford to let us talk about it."

I swallowed. "We've discussed the possibility."

Dad shook his head. "The thing to do is to keep things calm, cool them off before they do something stupid. Er, make that before they do something *else* stupid."

I raised the radio and looked down at the monitors. They were showing the real-time feed from the video cameras in the tunnel. "Time for the snapshot," I transmitted.

Joey's voice came back. He and Rick held the gate controls. "You count it off, Charlie."

"Right. I'm in 'deadman' mode. As before. One, two, three, four—"

It did not go right.

On the monitor the gate opened. There was a flash of light from the bottom of the gate typical of something being at the terminus as it opened or shut and an explosion and something nearly as wide as the tunnel moved forward very *fast*. Over the top of it I saw the lights of the tame side tunnel appear and then disappear as the gate shut down and then there were soldiers falling forward hard—some tumbling, some landing on their hands and knees.

And they were on this side of the gate.

"We got trouble!" I shouted into the radio. The soldiers were slow getting to their feet. The large object behind them had fallen forward and I could see mattresses roped to some sort of rigid platform—the back of it was smoking.

One of the soldiers raised a handgun and seemed to point it right at me, out of the screen. He fired, killing the camera, and the screen dissolved in static. Another soldier did the same thing to the other camera.

Dad pulled me by the shoulder and we ran toward the small door set into the left-hand hangar door. He was swearing. "Those *idiots!* They're going to get somebody killed."

I paused in the middle of the hangar and fired two quick shots at the power line going to the generator. The lights went out in the hangar and, consequently, the tunnel.

The light from outside outlined the edges of the door. Dad pulled it open and I went through it right behind him. Behind us, the door to the tunnel slammed open at the same time I shoved the door shut again, plunging the hangar back into darkness. There were several folding chairs between the tunnel and the door we'd just shut. I had hopes.

I shoved Dad toward the Maule, which was waiting, Rick holding the back door open, and I ran for the Coyote. As I reached it, I heard the Maule's engine sound suddenly increase in volume and it pulled away down the runway, throttle to the firewall.

I hit the starter button and the throttle even before I was in the seat. I shoved the gun into the other seat and slammed my foot down on the left rudder. The engine caught with a roar and the plane moved as soon as I released the brake, swinging around. The wind seemed to have shifted to the north—I kept compensating for it as I taxied—and I really should be running up the same runway the Maule had used, but to get to it, I would've had to taxi past the soldier at the hangar. The tail lifted and I flipped the flaps to full and pulled the left half of the seat belt into my lap, then got the other half and tried to connect them one-handed.

I wondered seriously if I had enough runway.

I felt the grass dragging at the wheels, but the controls felt "alive." I reached the end of the runway and pulled back the stick gently. The wheels lifted off the ground and the seat belt clicked shut at exactly the same time. The long buffalo grass beyond the end of the runway hissed across the landing gear and then I was above it, barely above stall speed, but flying.

I looked back at the hangar and saw soldiers running around the corner. The Maule was over the river, running low and fast, straight away from the hangar. I saw a flash of dark horse streak through the grass. Clara was heading due east, keeping the hill between her and the soldiers.

I looked back at my instruments. My air speed was high enough to climb and I eased the stick back, rising sharply at a thousand feet a minute.

Again, I looked back at the hangar, and saw flashing lights, like little camera strobes. *Christ, they're firing at me!*

And they hit me.

The first shot went through the overwing plastic fuel tank. The cabin suddenly reeked of gasoline fumes. Right after that, the engine stopped. Not died—it stopped dead with a horrible cracking sound and enough transferred torque that the plane jerked over, right wing down, so it must've taken a bullet or two. Two more bullets passed through the plastic windshield, but I didn't care. I was too busy killing the master electrical switch and saying, "Please, no sparks, no sparks, no sparks," while I trimmed the plane for minimum sink, maximum glide.

I was about three hundred feet above the ground with the wind off to my left—north. I banked shallow and turned into it, dropping fifty feet in the process. The ground below me was covered with scrub live oaks and mesquite. I could hear the gunshots, now, full-auto, and saw several tear through the aluminum engine cover. A bullet hit a metal strut in the fuselage behind me and I heard a 'Va-whoomp!' as fuel-soaked dacron caught fire.

"Ohmigod. Ohmigod. Ohmigod!" I said, expecting the flames to reach the fuel tank any second and blow me to kingdom come, but the slipstream was keeping the flames to the rear of the aircraft. I shoved the stick forward, sacrificing altitude for speed, then pulled up in time to slam the landing gear into the ground.

The wings tore off, caught by trees, and the landing gear folded and the plane was sliding hard through the brush, a great crackling sound that was part breaking branches and part flames. I unbuckled the seat belt and kicked the door up while the plane was still moving, then dove out. I bounced once and the flaming horizontal stabilizer clipped my shoulder as it slid by overhead, then I was rolling until I fetched up against a tree.

Hard.

The plane stopped in another forty feet and the flames finally reached the tank. The pressure wave rocked me, and a blast of heat forced me to my feet, despite a left knee that wasn't working right, to stumble away from the flames.

After a moment, I heard more gunshots, much closer. Were they after me already? Then I realized it was my shotgun, in the plane, the ammo exploding in the flames.

And I was injured, stumbling through the brush that could hide anything from dire wolves to saber-toothed tigers, with no weapon.

Seventeen

"There Are Bones, Charlie—Human Bones."

The flames were spreading south, fanned by the north wind. I went past the flaming wreckage upwind and limped east, away from the hangar. My knee, which had taken the brunt of my impact with the tree, was swelling. My shoulder, where the flaming horizontal stabilizer had struck it, was slightly burned, a large patch of my shirt charred off, but my rolling over and over had apparently put out the flames.

I had my harness, complete with radio, pepper Mace, airhorn, and survival kit, as well as several rounds of ammo for a gun I no longer had. We were supposed to maintain radio silence unless we needed help. This seemed to qualify. I picked up the radio, set it to the low-power five-watt setting, and transmitted. "Clara?"

"Charlie! You okay?" She was crying.

"Shaken, not stirred," I said. "You?"

"I thought . . ." I heard another sob and she stopped transmitting.

"Can you come get me?"

"I'm already on my way. Five minutes."

"You know where I am?"

"*Everybody* knows where you are."

I looked back at the flames. Dark smoke lifted into the sky. "I'm heading east," I said.

"Understood. Out."

"Out."

I limped on, watching carefully, the can of pepper Mace in my hand. I hoped the soldiers hadn't been listening—we'd left the base radio tuned off of our operational frequency, but, as Clara said, they had eyes and the smoke was visible for miles.

I got a couple of hundred yards away from the wreck and climbed into a low mesquite tree, complete with thorns. My head was barely over the brush line. When I looked back toward the hangar, all I could see was the control tower. Back at the wreck, I saw a flash of green that was *too* green for this landscape. Then a camouflaged soldier walked between two trees, intent on the smoking wreckage.

I scanned north and east, looking for Clara, but I couldn't see her. I looked back at the wreck and saw two soldiers looking my direction. One of them suddenly pointed at me. Swearing, I dropped from the branch, trying to land on my good leg, but I went off-balance and sprawled on the ground.

I got to my feet and limped northeast, hunched over like Quasimodo. I tried to stick to the thickest brush, but it was thinning the farther north I got, opening up into grassland.

There was a shout from behind me, as another of the soldiers spotted me. I kept expecting to hear gunfire, to feel high-velocity bullets enter my back, but they held their fire.

Come to think of it, I might not hear the bullet that got me. It would certainly arrive before mere sound.

The scrub oaks thinned out completely and I was limping painfully through knee-high grass. I glanced over my shoulder and could see five soldiers now, coming toward me at a run, covering three steps for every one of mine.

Clara's head and shoulders rose out of the grass ahead of me. As I got closer, I saw that a ravine cut across the grass, ten feet deep where a shallow stream wet its bottom. Clara was sitting on Impossible, her head eight feet off the ground. I slid down over the edge, dirt crumbling down around me.

Clara took her foot out of her left stirrup and said, "Come on."

The soldiers were less than fifty yards behind. I gritted my teeth and, gripping the back edge of the saddle, got my left foot into the stirrup, then *heaved* myself up.

I yelped with the pain, but managed to swing my right leg over Impossible's rump, straddling a gap between the cantle of her saddle and her bundled survival gear. Impossible danced sideways, eliciting a stream of curses and commands from Clara, coming to a stop in the bottom of the ravine, front feet in the water. The minute I grabbed Clara's waist, she kicked my bad leg out of the stirrup, inserted hers, and jabbed Impossible in the sides. My knee, bent around the curve of Impossible ribs, screamed, and I nearly passed out.

Impossible took off at a gallop, running down the streambed, water spraying out in sheets to either side.

I twisted, to look behind. The first soldier over the edge of the ravine saw us and jerked his gun to his shoulder, and cut loose a burst. He was firing low, perhaps at Impossible, for a line of waterspouts erupted from the stream next to us. Then we were around a bend in the ravine, and out of the line of fire.

I attempted to straighten my leg, to take some of the stress off of it, but it was no good. The up-and-down motion was jarring the knee every time Impossible's rear feet pushed off the streambed.

Clara galloped for several turns—then the rocks in the streambed became large and irregular. She slowed Impossible to a walk.

"We need to get out of this gully," she said. She looked at the sides, but as we'd moved the gully grew deeper, the sides less passable."

"Where'd you enter it?" I asked through gritted teeth.

She gestured over her shoulder with her thumb. "Back where I met you."

"We could climb out, but I doubt Impossible could."

"Why are you talking like that?" she asked, twisting to look at me. "What's wrong? You're white as a sheet! You didn't get hit back there, did you?"

I shook my head. "No. Banged up my knee in the crash. Galloping hasn't helped it any."

She stopped Impossible completely, then pulled her right foot out of the stirrup, passed it over the pommel of the saddle and slid down off Impossible to splash in the shallows. Impossible took a step sideways then dipped his head into the water.

"Oh, no you don't, greedy pig," said Clara and pulled him up on the bank away from the water. "Which knee?"

"The left."

She touched it and I winced. "Puffy. Very hot. Looks like it's about to split your pants, it's so swollen."

"That's no good." I handed her my pocketknife. "Cut the fabric so it doesn't block circulation."

She took it and cut a small hole below the knee, in the loose cloth over my shin, then tore sideways with both hands to split the pants leg up over my knee. The skin was purple.

"I don't think I can walk," I said.

"And you wanted me to leave Impossible on the tame side. Shift up into the saddle, it will strain your knee less."

I struggled over the cantle. She was right—raised higher above Impossible's back, my legs didn't have to stretch as much.

She gave me four ibuprofen out of her personal survival kit. Then she thrust the reins into my hands, "Hold him a second." She scrambled up the side of the gully, pulling herself up using brush and roots. She took a look back and then dropped back down, sliding down the side, dislodging dirt and rocks.

She took the reins from me and started walking down the gully, leading Impossible. "They're following the gully from on top, which lets them cut some of the bends. Fortunately, it's relatively straight in here, but they're moving pretty fast."

"Umm," I said. I was concentrating on keeping my leg still, but even at a walk, it hurt a lot.

The ravine got deeper and wider, but the sides were still too steep to take Impossible out. The brush in the ravine turned to trees—

cottonwoods, cedars, and willows, and the streambed changed back to sand.

Impossible's breathing slowed again and Clara let him drink a bit from the stream then, using a convenient boulder, mounted behind me. She held the reins around me and started Impossible out at a trot, which sent my knee into spasms again.

The wind down in the ravine was a light breeze mostly in our faces, the gully meandering northwest across a north wind. Impossible jolted around a bend and stopped dead. Clara swore and put her heels into his side. He shied sideways, snorting, but balked at going forward. Clara took the flat of her hand and slapped Impossible's rump hard and he jumped forward, going, not to a trot, but a gallop.

"What's got into you, horse?" Clara said, hauling back. She was thrown back and her arms, hands still gripping the reins, squeezed against my side to stay on. I tightened my grip on the pommel to keep us both from going off. Impossible shook his head, refusing to stop, moving down the stream in plunging fits and starts.

Then I smelled it, too, a rank smell, much stronger than dog.

They'd been lying under the trees on the left side of the stream, sleeping I suppose, but Impossible's whinny and splashing hooves got their attention, even though we were approaching from downwind.

They were ridiculously large, taller than my waist at their shoulders and probably each as heavy or heavier than me. They were stout, with massive shoulders and blocky snouts.

Dire wolves.

Impossible plunged past them as they stood or sat erect. One of them, lying relatively near the water, received a spray of water from Impossible's hooves and flinched away, shaking. At first they didn't seem to know what to make of us, more curious than anything, but they trotted after us as we passed them and their interest became more active.

Clara saw them and said, "Oh, shit!" She stopped fighting Impossible and encouraged him in his headlong, plunging flight.

I nearly screamed at the beating my knee was taking. I thought about grabbing the shotgun but there were only five rounds in it. There were at least seven of the wolves. I took the large can of pepper Mace off my harness, held it at arm's length out to the side, aimed backward, and squeezed down the plunger and held it.

The wind was light, but in our teeth, carrying the growing cloud of noxious spray back toward the wolves. I twisted to look back, past Clara, as they ran into it, mouths open, tongues hanging. The first one fell over, kicking up dust and leaves as it rubbed suddenly at its snout and eyes with its front paws.

Three others, right behind, had similar reactions. All of them stopped and backed up, trying to get away from whatever it was that was plaguing them. The other three, who'd been running through the trees, came on, missing the cloud.

I shifted my aim and created a wider bank of pepper Mace in their path. It had the same effect.

It stood to reason, I guess, since their sense of smell was a thousand times better than ours. The whiff I'd gotten was bad enough. I couldn't imagine how bad it was for them. I wondered if they thought we were some giant form of skunk, perhaps, or stink beetle.

It took another quarter mile before Clara could get Impossible to slow to a walk, then finally stop. She jumped down, and led him at a walk, to cool him down.

I took the shotgun out and held it across my lap, head twisted to look back. Impossible's walk felt different to me—halting.

Clara said, "He's favoring his left hind, Charlie. I need you to get off while I look at it."

I looked back, looking for wolves or soldiers, but didn't see any. "Okay." I slid off and stood, one-legged, then hopped and limped over to a boulder in the shade, and sat.

Clara clipped Impossible's lead rope onto his bridle and tied the other end to a tree, then lifted the left hind foot. "Rock in the frog," she said. She popped it loose with her hoof pick, then led Impossible around in a circle, to see how it felt. He still favored that foot, but not as badly.

"It wasn't very deep. I think he'll be okay in a—"

Behind us, in the distance, came the sound of automatic weapons and the screams of wolves.

Impossible shied again and Clara had her hands full, keeping him from bolting. I wished my knee wasn't as banged up—I wanted to climb out of the ravine and see what could be seen. After several seconds, the gunfire stopped. Then there was a heart-wrenching howl of an animal in pain which cut off abruptly with two more closely spaced gunshots.

Clara got Impossible calmed down again, talking to him in a soft, continuous stream of reassurances. "There, there, big boy. It's all right. Those big doggies won't be bothering us anymore. Don't fret. It's okay."

"You wanna take a look?" I asked her, gesturing up.

She looked at Impossible, then led him over to me. "I think he'll be okay, but if he bolts, then let him go. Don't let him drag you—not with that leg. He won't go far—he hates to be away from me, so he'll come back in a moment. If he doesn't trip on the reins and break his fool neck."

"Maybe we should tie him to a tree?"

She shook her head. "He's more likely to stay with you than a tree. He's a herd animal. Just so happens that people are his herd. I know." She opened his saddlebag and took out a double handful of oats.

I cupped my hands and she spilled the feed into my palms. Impossible pushed against her, trying to get at the oats.

"Get back, greedy," she said. "Give him a little at a time. I'll be right back."

She put her can of pepper Mace down beside me and took the shotgun with her.

I heard her walk through the leaves under the oaks, making her way back to gully wall. Impossible pushed at my hands and I dribbled some oats beside me, onto the top of the boulder I was sitting on. He lipped them up, then pushed at my hands again. I checked my surroundings as best I could, then put some more oats on the rock.

This went on for another few minutes, then Clara came back through the trees, holding something in her hand.

"What's the scoop?" I asked, concentrating on dribbling more oats onto the rock.

Clara said slowly, "Can't see much. We're over half a mile away from them, but they're not moving. I bet the wolves scared them pretty bad."

"If that's not all they did to them."

"I guess. Uh, Charlie, I found something."

I looked up. The object in Clara's hand was a forty-five automatic pistol, dirt-caked and rusted. The slide was back like it does when every shot in the magazine has been fired.

"Where did you find *that?*"

She pointed back through the trees. "The gully wall is more like a cliff over there. I had to backtrack a little to climb out, but this was at the base of the cliff. There was more, Charlie. There are bones, Charlie—human bones."

I got back up on Impossible and Clara led him through the trees. I was glad I didn't have to walk, but there were lots of low branches. I became intimately acquainted with Impossible's mane and I had scratches across the burned patch on my shoulder.

It wasn't a large cliff—fourteen feet, perhaps. It was well shaded and there was just a bit of grass and scattered leaves across rocky ground. I slid off of Impossible and stood there, my hand on his saddle, standing on my right leg.

There were, as Clara said, bones. Not just human bones, though, but a mixture, cracked and broken. The long bones had been split for their marrow. One set had to be a sabertooth. A partial skull, upside down and missing its lower jaw, stabbed two amazing curved teeth skyward. Something that looked like a Saint Bernard skull made me remember the dire wolves from the ravine and I shuddered. I limped over and picked it up. There was a small round hole punched in the left cheek and a larger hole, splintered outward, in the back.

I set it down before picking up the last skull. The human one.

The brain case had been cracked open, like a nut, to get at the interior, I guess. I looked back at the jaws of the dire wolf skull and thought, yeah, they're big enough. There were two gold crowns on the upper right side just behind the canine.

He'd grin in the sun and the two gold teeth, like a hidden treasure, would wink in the light.

Uncle Max.

Clara was watching me, carefully. "Is it?"

I closed my eyes. "Yeah." Water leaked down my face.

She put her hand on my shoulder.

"Sorry," I said. "Not knowing—it was worse, somehow." I shook my head and wiped my face with the sleeves of my shirt. Something gleamed in a pocket of dead leaves and I pointed to it.

"What's that?"

She walked over and kicked leaves away. It was an aluminum Boy Scout canteen, the canvas cover was rotted and torn, barely on it. When Clara pulled on the canvas strap, the canteen stayed on the ground and the fragments of canvas fell apart. She picked up the canteen itself and brought it to me.

I shook it, but it was empty. The cap was screwed tightly down. I unscrewed the cap and found a rolled-up piece of paper stuck in the neck.

I pulled it out carefully, trying to avoid poking it down into the body of the canteen. It was an envelope from Brazos Electric Utility and there was writing on the back, small, crabbed, printing in ink.

It started out, *Masha, Sorry, I'm dead. Less than two kilometers from the gate. . . .*

Clara read over my shoulder. "Jesus! Double compound fracture? No wonder he didn't come back. Who is Masha?"

The hair on the back of my head stood on end. "Masha is my mother."

Clara walked around to where she was facing me. "Does that mean what I think it does?"

"That my mom knows about the gate?"

"Yeah."

"I don't know."

She looked back at the skull still in my hands. "Charlie, that could be you."

I looked at her, mouth set grimly in a straight line. "You mean my knee? It's not exactly a double compound fracture, but I take your point. I'm glad I wasn't alone over here."

My radio, set on standby, crackled. "Charlie, Clara, do you read?" It was Marie's voice.

I unholstered the radio. "This is Charlie—Clara's with me."

"She is? Uh, never mind. Listen to the traffic on channel one-two-one-point-four."

"We're switching Clara's radio to one-two-one-point-four now."

Clara pulled her radio out of her holster and twisted the dial. "—ayday. Mayday. Captain Moreno, do you read? Mayday, Mayday we have a casualty and are in need of immediate medevac. Mayday, Mayday, do you read?"

I keyed my radio, transmitting on our operational frequency. "What do you think?"

My dad's voice said, "It could be a trap." There was anguish in his voice.

"We have to find out, though, don't we?" I transmitted.

"Yes, we do. Let me talk to them. Switching to one-two-one-point-four."

"Affirmative, one-two-one-point-four."

At the next pause in the Mayday call, Dad responded. It was his professional pilot's voice, unflappable. "We copy your Mayday. What is the nature of your casualty?"

"Who is this?"

"This is Captain Newell. Who am I speaking to?"

"Lieutenant Malcolm Thayer."

"What seems to be the problem, Lieutenant?"

There was a pause and I thought we'd lost the signal, but then the lieutenant's voice came back. "My men report a compound fracture of the upper arm with arterial bleeding. There's a tourniquet in place, but if he doesn't get to a surgeon, he's going to lose the arm."

"How did he manage to do that?" my father asked.

There was a pause again. "Some sort of wild animal attack. Look, Carlson really needs medical attention."

"Hang on, son. We have to talk about it."

I switched my radio back to our operational frequency. "You there, Dad?"

"I copy. What do you think?"

"They shot me down, Dad. I nearly died. When Clara picked me up, they shot at us again, though they might have been trying for the horse."

"Are you all right?"

"Minor burns and a sprained knee."

"Jesus." He stopped transmitting for a second, then came back. "What do we do about their casualty? Do you think they're lying?"

"I know they're not. Clara and I rode through a pack of dire wolves and used pepper Mace to discourage them when they followed us. I think they ran right into the soldiers following us. Anyway, there was gunfire and wolves screaming." I had a disturbing thought. "At least I think it was wolves who were screaming." I paused. "Maybe we can use this to get rid of them. I'm going to talk to them."

I switched back to nineteen and said, "Lieutenant Thayer?"

"Copy. Who is this?"

"This is Charles Newell. I'm the one your guys nearly killed when they shot down my plane."

I heard him exhale through the mike. "I'm pleased you weren't killed. The man who did that will be disciplined. It wasn't part of our mission."

"If we reopen the gate, what's the chance another load of men will come flying through?"

"Uh, we used up all the mattresses."

"Just what was that thing?"

He hesitated then said, "A bunch of plywood, all of the mattresses from the house, and some C-4. The detonator was rigged to a wire across the gate terminus. When it was cut, it set off the charge." He sounded embarrassed. "We volunteered."

"What *is* your mission, Lieutenant?"

"This has nothing to do with our casualty."

"If you want our help, it has *everything* to do with it."

After a moment he said, "Our mission is to take and hold the gate."

"At what cost? How many Americans were you authorized to kill?"

He didn't answer for a moment. Finally he said, "We were supposed to avoid unnecessary casualties. There's another squad waiting in case we get the gate open. But we didn't build another platform and we really don't have any more padding."

"Unnecessary casualties," I repeated flatly. "On which side? Is this why you became a soldier, Lieutenant? We're Americans, for chrissakes. We haven't broken any laws or threatened the security of this country." I didn't let him respond. "Look, there's a tractor parked outside. Unhook the fuel trailer. There's a drag skid leaning against the side of the hangar. Put a mattress on it and pull it out to your casualty with the tractor. I'll meet the tractor and come back with it."

"And you'll open the gate?"

"That remains to be seen. Out."

"Wait a—"

I switched the radio back to our operational frequency.

"Are you crazy, Charlie?" said Clara. "They shot you down. They've shot at us!" Then she said, as if it were the worst thing of all, "They shot at *Impossible!*"

On Clara's radio, still switched to 121.4 megahertz, Lieutenant Thayer was repeating, "Newell? Come back, Newell?" I reached over and shut it off.

"Marie?" I broadcast on my radio.

"Yeah, Charlie?"

"Wait twenty minutes, then get airborne. Uh, I didn't ask. You guys okay?"

"No problems. We landed on the sandbar at—uh, you know where. I don't see any trouble taking off again." Our rendezvous was supposed to be on a sandbar at the juncture of the Brazos and Little Brazos rivers.

"Okay, I'll contact you when you're over the field. If anybody starts shooting at you, *vamanos.*"

"Yo comprendo, compadre."

"Ciao."

Clara shook her head.

"Look," I said. "How long are we going to last out here, with the dire wolves and the smilodons? Especially me, with this sprained knee?" I pointed at Uncle Max's skull. "See what happened to him?"

She stared down at the skull. "I guess you're right. It's just a little scary out here."

"You're better off without having to ride double. Find a way out of here and head back for the base. I'll talk to you after I've assessed things. Like before, 'things are good' means run like hell."

She sighed. "And 'stand down' means things are under control?"

"Right."

She helped me to climb out of the gully, steadying me from behind, then handing up a gnarled oak branch to use as a cane. I started limping across the grass, walking for a point halfway between the base and the site of the wolf attack. "Be careful, dammit!" she called, then slid back down.

After a moment I heard Impossible's hooves walking across the rocky streambed and diminish in sound as Clara continued downstream. My progress was slow and halting. The pain from my right knee diminished slightly as the ibuprofen took effect.

The control tower was visible in the distance, the hangar a blur beneath it, mostly hidden by the hill. After a moment, the rusty red tractor rounded the corner and drove toward me, dust rising behind it where the sledge was dragging across the ground. I kept limping.

A column of orange smoke lifted over the gully where the soldiers waited, and the tractor shifted course accordingly, moving with fits and starts. Apparently the driver wasn't used to this model.

I eyed the grass, nervously, wondering what it hid. I braced my left side with the branch, but in my right hand I held what remained of the pepper Mace. As the tractor got closer, I could see two figures upon it—one driving, one perched beside him, gun held at the ready.

As the tractor pulled even with me, it started to turn toward me, but I pointed exaggeratedly at the orange smoke. The figure driving waved his hand and turned back on his course. The soldiers at the gully came out of it then, one of them carrying the wounded man over his shoulder in a fireman's carry while two others walked point and tail, scanning their surroundings aggressively, an extra rifle slung over each of their shoulders.

The tractor pulled up beside them and the soldier riding shotgun jumped down to help them lower the wounded man onto the mattress-covered sledge. One of them crouched on the sledge and the other two stood behind the driver, on the tractor.

I limped on.

They pulled the tractor around and, for a moment, it seemed as if they were going to go straight back to the hangar. I felt, for a moment, abandoned and relieved, all at once. Then the tractor swerved and came toward me, and I went back to being worried for other reasons.

They pulled up beside me, eyes wary. They didn't point their rifles at me, but they kept them to hand. I limped over and stood by the big rear wheel. "That clutch takes some getting used to. If you want, I'll drive back. It'll be easier on your friend." I nodded at the pallet.

I heard one of them mutter, "Christ. He's just a kid."

The guy tending the wounded man, said loudly, "Let him, or don't, but let's get *going!*" I saw that he was holding a tourniquet on the patient's upper arm. I didn't want to look any closer at the wound.

The guy driving got out of the driver's seat and jumped down. I limped over, threw my branch-crutch off into the grass, and climbed up. The previous driver crouched on the pallet on the other side of the patient and I took off, smoothly, but driving the tractor on up into fifth gear, moving with speed. It was good thing the tractor used a hand clutch. My knee probably wasn't up to one on the floor.

I swung wide, to take advantage of the flat ground on our east-west runway, pushing the speed. We rounded the bend and I checked my watch. I had approximately ten minutes before the Maule would be overhead.

The hangar door was open and I drove the tractor inside, killing the engine to avoid fouling the air. One last soldier waited inside. His name tag read Thayer and he had embroidered lieutenant bars.

Thayer was taller than me, heavily muscled, like he lifted weights. He was watching me with narrowed eyes. Uncomfortable, I pointed at the storage shelves. "Third shelf from the top, on the right side. There's an IV drip and some lactated Ringer's solution. Anybody here ever start a drip?"

The guy still holding on to the tourniquet said, "I have."

Thayer said, "Johnson, get it." One of the soldiers trotted back to the storeroom.

I climbed down off the tractor and limped over to a folding chair. They'd all been moved, I saw, out of the path between the tunnel and the door. I wondered who'd tripped over what, but I didn't think it would've been wise to ask. I lowered myself into the chair and poked gingerly at the swollen mass of tissue around my knee. It felt hot and puffy.

Thayer came and stood before me. "Open the gate." He tried to make it sound like an order, but it came out more like a question.

"There are conditions."

One of the soldiers, standing by the tractor, raised his M16A and pointed it at my head. "Lieutenant, just say the word."

Thayer looked at him and frowned. "At ease, Sergeant."

I squinted past the gun, though my eyes wanted to fix on the round end of the muzzle flash suppressor. The sergeant's name tag read Costner. And he wasn't lowering his gun.

Thayer stepped between us. "I said, at ease, Sergeant." He didn't raise his voice but he leaned forward, toward Costner.

Costner lowered the rifle, a disgusted look on his face.

Thayer said even more quietly. "Take Johnson. Patrol the perimeter. You may defend yourself from wild animals, but under *no* circumstances are you to fire at people without clearance."

"Sir. Even if they fire first?"

"Sergeant, *even* if they fire first."

I narrowed my eyes. Suddenly I had the feeling I knew who'd shot me down.

Costner collected the other soldier with his eyes and they walked outside. Resentment and anger showed in Costner's every step.

I looked at the patient. The mattress under the man's right arm was soaked with blood. A thin strap, wrapped around his upper arm, had a stick twisted through it that was kept from untwisting by another strap. Farther down, the arm was roughly splinted. The area just above his elbow where the jagged end of the humerus stuck out was not covered. I looked away, swallowing convulsively. "Is he on pain medication?"

"Morphine," said the man rigging the IV drip. The name on his tag was Livingston.

"Good."

"Open the gate," Thayer said again. This time his voice had that ring of command.

"I can't open the gate from here," I said. "In a minute, my friends will be overhead. They can, and will, if I tell them the right words. But you won't get me to say those words by pointing guns at me."

"What are your conditions?" Thayer asked.

"You guys leave with him."

Thayer winced. "That's not possible."

"Why?"

"I have orders."

"Illegal orders. Who is Bestworst, anyway? CIA?"

Thayer's mouth tightened.

"If so, he's operating illegally, too. Their charter doesn't cover domestic operations, does it? Does *his* boss know what he's doing?"

Thayer closed his eyes suddenly and exhaled. When he opened them again, he said, "Let's take a walk."

I touched my knee. "You've got to be kidding."

He looked annoyed. "Just into the tunnel." He held out his hand to help me up.

I got up without taking his hand, wary. He pulled his hand back and put his arms behind him in parade rest. I limped along the wall to the tunnel door and he preceded me, holding the door as I limped through, then closing it behind us.

The generator was still disconnected, but they'd hung chemical light sticks along the wall, lighting the space with a weird, greenish glow. I took a step to the right and sank to the ground, my back against the tunnel wall. I wondered if I should be reaching for the pepper Mace.

Thayer took a step back and sat opposite me.

"I'm going to tell you something, but if you repeat it, I'll call you a liar to your face. Understand?"

I nodded.

"The printed unit orders detached us for a training mission at Fort Hood. I saw them by accident, when Captain Moreno left his briefcase open. This unit does anti-insurgency work in Panama, where our intelligence is supplied by the CIA. And I've seen, uh, Bestworst in that context.

"This whole mission sucks."

He reached into his fatigues at the neck and pulled out his dog tags. A gold ring hung next to them, looped on the chain. "This is my wedding ring. I've got a beautiful wife and two wonderful daughters. I understand dying for my country—for them, but I don't want to do anything that will make them ashamed of me."

"Uh, I see, I guess." I shook my head, confused. "Well, maybe I don't see."

He pushed the dog tags back into his shirt and rubbed his eyes. "You were right. This is an illegal mission. It stinks to high heaven. And if anybody dies—one of you kids or Carlson—and this becomes public . . ." He shook his head. "We'll do it your way. I'll take all my men over to the other side. You call the shots. The captain won't like it, but screw 'em. He has no business in this mess anyway."

He stood and held his hand out to help me up. This time I took it. Before he opened the door he said, "Keep away from Bestworst. Whatever you do."

They carried Carlson, three to a side, on the mattress.

When Thayer said he was going to do it our way, he meant it. "Do you want our weapons?"

"Hell, no. It's dangerous enough over here."

They stopped ten feet back from the gate, next to where the plywood and mattress platform leaned against one side of the tunnel. Seargent Costner was glaring at me, over his shoulder. I spoke into the radio in my left hand. "Ready, guys?"

"Ready," Marie's voice said. They were orbiting the field overhead.

"Remember, the gate will be open for one second only. If you stop in the middle, Carlson won't *need* any medical aid. Start moving, gentlemen!"

They trotted toward the terminus. Just before they reached it, I said, "Now!" into the radio. The gate opened and my right hand squeezed down on the airhorn.

The backup squad was there, standing at ease. They fell back in confusion. The end of the mattress cleared the terminus and the gate flicked back off, counted by Marie.

I slumped to the floor, my knee aching.

The radio crackled. "You okay, Charlie?"

The radio seemed to weigh a ton. "Stand down, guys. Stand down."

* * *

We took the wooden portion of their platform and mounted it on the front of the tractor, widening it with the plywood from our video table so it stretched all the way across the tunnel and bracing the new section with four-by-fours left over from our old cargo sledge. When it was in position just short of the terminus, it stretched from wall to wall with a fourteen-inch gap between the top of the barrier and the ceiling.

Marie, Joey, and Rick were standing at the back of the tunnel and Clara was sitting in the driver's seat of the tractor.

Dad stood on one folding chair on one side of the tractor and I stood on another on the other side. Dad's whole face cleared the barrier. I had to go back and get two flight manuals to stand on before mine did. I've long known I got my height from Mom's side of the family.

I took a deep breath and looked over at Dad.

He was already looking at me—staring, practically.

"What?" I blurted out, flinching.

He held up a hand. "Nothing. Nothing. Just, um trying to figure out who you are."

I flushed. "I'm your son."

He kept looking. "I know the relationship, Charlie," he said steadily. "I just don't know the person." He coughed and looked down. "You ready?"

I swallowed. "Yeah. I guess so."

Click.

Two soldiers, standing before the barricade, unarmed, threw themselves forward and came up hard against the barrier. There was six inches between the plywood and the terminus and they stopped there, not trying to climb, but freezing with their bodies on the terminus. The one on the left stared up at me with wide eyes. The other one had his eyes squeezed shut and his lips were moving.

"Are you going to kill them, Charlie? Are you going to slice them in two?"

It was Bestworst, standing ten feet back with Captain Moreno. He lifted his hand and more soldiers, standing behind him moved forward, led by Sergeant Costner. I saw no sign of Lieutenant Thayer.

I twisted on the chair and looked at Clara. She was staring back at me, eyes wide. I pointed at the tractor and then forward, emphatically. She didn't waste time nodding but reached for the ignition key. Luckily, it was still warm and she shoved it into low gear as the first soldier appeared on the top of the barrier.

Bestworst's confident smile dropped from his face at the sound of the tractor engine. With a groan and shriek of flexing wood, the entire barrier moved forward. There was a crash as the fake machinery on the other side of the terminus toppled.

The soldier in front of Dad was fast, the entire top half of his body was over the barrier and he had a knee on the edge. Dad jumped forward, off the chair, and shoved upward, against the soldier's chest. He teetered but clung to the top desperately. Dad screamed, "Close it, Charlie," and grabbed onto the barricade and pushed the soldier back.

"Get back, Dad!" I shouted, but someone on the other side of the barricade was holding Dad's arm. Dad flattened his body against the barrier and shouted again, "Close it!"

The sergeant's arm, shoulder, and head started over the barrier, and I hit the button. There was a blinding flash and Clara pitched forward against the steering wheel as the front end of the tractor dropped. A cloud of water vapor billowed up around me and I heard liquid pouring onto the tunnel floor—hot coolant by the smell. The undercarriage of the tractor plowed into the dirt and the engine quit with a "clunk."

The front sixteen inches of the tractor, including the steering suspension, radiator, and most of the front wheels were gone, along with all of the barrier.

And Dad, too.

I looked at the floor near where Dad had been standing, dreading that I'd see part of Dad, but there was nothing there. There was something on the floor in front of me, next to a semicircular section of tractor tire. I got painfully down off the chair and looked closer.

There was a slice of nylon helmet cover and a thin piece of Kevlar helmet on the floor.

And a tiny slice of bloody skin and hair.

"Son of a *BITCH!*" I shouted and hit the wall. "Those *stupid* assholes! They're not going to stop until they've succeeded in killing somebody."

Clara was staring at me. "They have your dad."

"Again," I said, trying to diminish the importance of what just happened.

"Do you think he'll be all right?"

"I don't know." I shook my head. "I think they'll hold him, like Luis and Richard. If they let him go, he'll raise too big a stink."

The guys joined us, staring at the front end of the tractor. Rick said, "What are we going to do now?"

I looked at the floor. I felt trapped, frustrated, and angry. "I don't know. Let them sit. We have supplies for six months, longer if we hunt. Maybe they'll finally get somebody a little less ruthless over there. We've disappeared, after all. There should be some hue and cry."

Rick sighed. "I'm not sure I can wait six months, Charlie. Chris doesn't know where I am. Neither does my mother. Think what she'll be going through. What if she investigates and they take her into custody to shut her up? What about *your* mother?"

I clenched my fists and stared at the wall, then shook my head. "Maybe we can figure out a way to get you back without killing somebody." Marie, Joey, and Rick joined us. "Are you okay, Clara?"

She was touching the end of her nose. "A little sunburn. Next time I'll put on sun block."

"Nice driving."

She blinked. "Woman's gotta do what woman's gotta do. I'm glad nobody got hurt." She looked at me. "Those people are crazy. I don't think we should invite them to any more parties."

Rick said, "We've gotta try something."

I squeezed the bridge of my nose with my thumb and forefinger.

My knee was killing me. I stared blindly at the end of the tractor, where antifreeze was soaking into the dirt floor. "Somebody get me some ibuprofen and an Ace bandage, please . . . and a shovel."

Clara brought a canteen of water with the ibuprofen. I took three and washed them down. Rick brought the shovel and Marie grabbed the five-gallon plastic bucket we use to drain engine oil from the Maule.

I scooped the antifreeze-soaked dirt into the barrel, driving the blade of the shovel down into the dirt. I wasn't really paying attention to what I was doing, just step, thrust, scoop until the wet dirt was gone.

"That's strange, Charlie," said Marie. "Aren't you on the term—"

The shovel hit something in the dirt that didn't give, reverberating up the handle with a shock. I blinked. The antifreeze had spilled across the terminus. I pushed more gently with the shovel and was rewarded with a "clank," as if I'd hit a buried pipe.

"It's probably that glassy stuff," I said. I lowered myself to the ground and scooped the dirt aside with my hands, pulling clods of dirt back into the hole excavated for the antifreeze.

I didn't run into the glassy stuff. Instead I ran into a gray metal frame that looked to be the same material as the gate switch. I shook my head, then pulled myself to my feet, the shovel clutched in my hands.

"What's that?" asked Joey.

I took an abrupt step to my left and slammed the blade of the shovel into the wall, a foot above the hidden switch and near the terminus.

"Charlie!" Marie shrieked and jumped back.

The dirt we'd plastered into place showered down and I thrust again, scraping and twisting with the blade. Dirt showered down revealing the wire box we'd built around the switch. I moved closer and closer to the terminus, expecting to run into the glassy material we'd encountered before, but I never reached it.

I ran into the same metal frame I'd uncovered in the floor of the tunnel.

"The last time we did this, the gate was on. That glassy stuff we ran into *was* dirt—it was frozen in place by the gate. And now that the gate's off, it isn't there!"

Rick frowned. "So—how does this help us? Aren't we more likely to screw it up now that we can get to it?"

"Maybe," I said. "Maybe we'll find out something that can help us."

The gateway was a metal rectangle whose inside dimensions were about four inches greater than those of the tunnel. It was thirteen and a half inches deep, front to back. On three sides it was fifteen inches thick from the inside dimension to the outside dimension. The fourth side, the one with the arm that tapered into the switch, was almost twice as thick—twenty-nine and a quarter inches from inside to outside. All corners were rounded.

It was made of the same gray metal as the arm except that, on the center of the inside surface, there was a five-eighths-inch band of a milky white material that appeared to be ceramic. Whereas the metallic surface was slightly rough—uniformly pitted—the ceramic surface was smooth and fluid.

When we'd excavated the majority of the hangar-facing surface, it moved.

"Shit!" Rick and Clara, the two tallest of us, were standing on boxes to scrape the dirt from the upper frame of the gate. It was Rick who'd cursed and leaned forward, both hands pushing against the gate.

"It moved," said Clara.

I studied the excavation. "On its own? Or did it come loose and want to tilt forward?"

Rick suddenly looked like he wanted to let go. "Who knows?"

"Look," I said, "if it tilts forward, it's just going to run into the other side of your cut in the roof. There's not enough clearance for it to fall all the way. Let go."

Rick eased off the gate. It didn't move. I stepped through it, took the handle of my shovel, and pushed against the top. It tilted slightly and the top moved perhaps five inches before it stopped.

Clara said, "It's catching on the sides." She pointed up where the corners of the frame were digging into the side of the tunnel.

It felt massive, the density of stone, if not metal.

"But does it still work?" said Clara.

The pit of my stomach hurt. "Are we sure there aren't any other attachments? Why don't we check again, now that it's tilted?"

We probed the perimeter again, with knife blades and stiff wires, looking for cables or rods or anchor bolts—anything connecting the gate to something else, but again, we didn't find anything.

I closed my eyes and exhaled. When I opened them I said, "I wonder what would happen if we moved it?"

Clara played the pessimist. "It may not matter. We may have already broken it by digging around it. And suppose it is still working? Moving it may not cause it to open in a different place. We may drag it all over the place only to find those same people waiting when we turn it back on."

Marie didn't help. "If there's one parallel earth, there are probably many. Moving the gate may cause it to open on a different world than ours. Maybe one that didn't develop life at all—or one where the K-T impact event broke the earth into pieces and there's nothing but vacuum on the other side of the gate."

Rick and Joey looked grimmer with each sentence.

I swallowed, wondering if I'd already doomed us to the wildside for the rest of our lives. "For better or worse, it's already moved. What do we have to lose by trying?"

The question became *could* we move it.

It was massive—just how massive we couldn't tell without knowing what it was made of or weighing it. Also, it was four feet wider and almost three feet taller than the interior dimensions of the tunnel. And our tractor, the mechanical device that *might* have the muscle necessary to move the device, was missing its front wheels and radiator.

"I think I can make the tractor work," I said. "If I can, how would we get the gate out of here?"

"Pity we can't disassemble it," Joey said. "Give me the measuring tape."

I handed it to him.

"You figure out the tractor, we'll figure out the excavation—okay?"

I remembered the day we built the hangar and smiled. "Okay."

The tractor would run, as is, probably, for about five minutes before it seized up forever. The gate had cut cleanly through the coolant hoses running from the radiator to the engine as well as chopped the fan blade off its pulley. I wondered what they made of the pieces of tractor radiator over on the tame side.

I cut a hole in the side of a five-gallon plastic bucket, flush with the bottom, and ran a piece of garden hose from the hole to the radiator hose that ran to the water pump. The hoses didn't match—the radiator hose was much bigger, but we wrapped rags around the brass end of the garden hose and clamped it down with a hose clamp from the Maule's spare parts bin. We put screws right through the bottom of the bucket and into the sheet metal bonnet of the tractor.

"It'll leak," said Marie.

"Not as bad as the hose."

We filled four empty five-gallon fuel canisters with water from the stream. Clara used Impossible to transport them, two at a time, hanging them off the sides of the saddle. Back at the tunnel, we hung them off the sides of the tractor on improvised wire hooks.

"What are we going to do about the front wheels?" Marie and I crouched beside the grounded front end of the tractor and stared at the place where its undercarriage ground into the dirt floor. The steering linkage and framing pieces ran under the engine and ended, flush with the rest of the missing metal.

"Let's put some plywood under it and just let it slide."

"How will we steer?"

"Steering is for people who know where they're going."

While Marie and I were fiddling with the tractor, the other three were digging out the lower sides of the tunnel, widening it by the gate and also digging a shallow ramp from the lower edge of the gate's frame up to floor level.

"What about the top?" Marie asked.

We had one full-size spade and two folding survival shovels. Joey was scooping dirt with a coffee can and flinging it past the gate, into the dead end of the tunnel. He stopped and wiped sweat off his face with the back of his hand. "We'll pull the bottom until it's flat. That way we just have to widen the bottom part of the tunnel. Well—we have to make more room for *that*." He pointed at the arm of the gate with the switch. "It'll stand up about two feet when it's flat and we'll need to make room for it. Wouldn't want to accidentally turn it on."

"Or break it off," Clara said dryly.

I shivered. "No—that wouldn't do, would it?"

"How about a proof-of-concept demo?" Rick said, leaning on the full-size shovel.

I raised my eyebrows.

He elaborated. "We're wasting our time if you can't get the tractor working."

"Oh—okay."

We had two four-by-fours left over from our old cargo sledge so we used them to lever the front end of the tractor off the ground while Marie slid a two-foot square piece of one-inch plywood under the front frame.

I took our climbing rope and folded it four times to make a tow harness. We looped it once around the bottom frame of the gate and then led it back to two convenient holes in the forward tractor frame.

Marie climbed up on the front end of the tractor, right behind the screwed-down bucket, and lifted one of the five-gallon water cans. I climbed into the driver's seat.

In anticipation, the guys stepped through the gate to get clear.

"Why don't you guys wait *behind* me?" I said.

"Why?" said Joey.

I swallowed. "Well, what if the tunnel caves in?"

Clara moved immediately and the others were not far behind them. "Don't forget your tools," she said.

They filed past me and I hit the ignition key. It fired right up and Marie poured water into the bucket. I eased the tractor into its lowest reverse gear and eased out the clutch. The wheels dug into the dirt floor and dragged the plywood supported front end across the floor slowly.

The rope tightened and the bottom of the frame moved three inches. I eased up. Water was sputtering out the front of the engine. Marie was reaching for her second can of water. The frame moved forward, the top end leaning back and sliding down against the edges of the excavation. It carved dirt off the wall on its way down, then reached horizontal, dropping with a "thump" the last foot onto loose dirt.

I hoped it wasn't fragile. It slid easily enough, but then we ran out of water and tunnel that was wide enough at the same time. When I shut the tractor down, we'd slid it about ten feet. The tractor, without steering, had crept closer to the right-hand side of the tunnel and, without some sort of adjustment, would run into it in another ten feet of travel.

"Well," Rick said, "that seems to answer that question. Now what about the other question?"

"What other question?" asked Joey.

"Is it going to do us any good to move it? Is it going to work now that we've moved it? Is it going to point back at our world or someplace else? Is it going to point right back at Bestworst and his assault force?"

Marie, Joey, and Clara nodded at his words.

I exhaled. "There's only one way to find out."

Clara said, "Turn it on."

I added, "Very briefly."

Joey winced. "We'll have to dig out the upper sides to stand it up, damn it. Why don't we just pull it outside first?"

I shook my head. "There's no reason to stand it up."

Clara frowned. "It may not work horizontal."

"One way to find out," Rick said.

We took the rope off the gate frame since, if it was working, it would cut it in two on activation. We argued about the best way to turn it on.

Joey pointed out, "Remember that glassy stuff that was there when the gate was on? If you're standing by the gate and you turn it on, is that what happens to your legs?"

I stepped back from the gate frame, even though we weren't about to turn it on.

"Let's use a pole," said Marie.

"A long one," I said, agreeing. "Then there's the vacuum cleaner scenario, the one where there's nothing but space on the other side and it starts sucking everything through—we need a way to handle that."

"Well, we could open and shut it *really* fast," said Joey.

"I guess that's one way." I remembered something from a story I'd read, something in a space station—a way to shut doors in the event of meteor punctures. "We can rig it so a lot of air rushing into the gate will shut it off. All we need is a big flat piece—something that will catch the wind. If we mount it on a string and run it to a pulley, then back to the switch on the gate, air rushing that way will throw the switch back to the off position."

We rigged it, using a piece of Styrofoam packing that our spare propeller had been shipped in. While I did that, Marie and Joey went down by the creek and cut a willow sapling about fourteen feet long.

We flipped coins, like we did for our parachute drops. Rick 'won,' though if he were sucked through the hole, I wondered how lucky he would feel.

He stood by the tractor and, just for luck, we roped him to its rear axle. The rest of us waited behind the tractor, except for me, who stood on the tractor seat so I could look through the gate.

Rick reached out with the pole and placed it behind the switch lever. The switch pointed straight up, at the ceiling.

Rick looked back at us and I said, "Ready when you are."

He pushed the pole sideways and the switch moved to the "On" position. I thought there was the slightest flicker, but all I could see through the gate was a stretch of flat dirt. Then Rick had gotten the tip of the pole around the end of the switch and moved it back to the off position. Again, there was some sort of flicker, but I couldn't tell what it was.

"Did it work, Charlie?" Clara asked.

"I don't know. I thought I saw something, but I'm not sure."

"There wasn't any rush of wind," Clara said. "The vacuum cleaner hypothesis, at least, isn't true."

"Rick," I said, "turn it back on and leave it for a moment."

He reached out with the pole and pushed the lever. Again, there was a flicker and this time I saw it. The bottom half of the gate frame was missing, but only on the inside diameter, ending where the milky ceramic line ran around the inside of the frame. If you only looked at the inside, it was as if it were floating about seven inches off the ground.

I climbed slowly down off the tractor.

"Well, Charlie?" Clara asked. I waved my right hand frantically and held my left forefinger up to my lips. She blinked and shut her mouth. I limped up past the tractor and cautiously past Rick, my eyes on the view through the gate.

There was a slight breeze coming from the gate, typical of the pressure differences we'd often had—millibar level differentials caused by different weather systems on each side of the gate.

Four feet from the gate I ran into something that wasn't there.

It was about thigh high and smooth as glass. When I ran my fingers over it, it felt exactly like the glassy dirt we'd encountered when we'd excavated the gate back in July. I leaned against it, and it didn't budge. When I traced its outlines down to the ground, I dug down, with my fingers—the glassy surface continued into the ground. Tracing up, it rounded back toward the gate and seemed to slope down.

I heard Rick gasp when I sat down on the rounded edge and

swung one foot toward the gate. From his point of view it looked as if I were sitting in midair, an impossible position, like I was suspended by wires. I started to slide toward the gate, but the leg I'd left over the edge stopped me and I scrambled back before I slid farther.

Then I heard voices from the gate.

"Does anybody feel a breeze?" It sounded like the man from Sandia Labs—Bob Orkand.

I motioned to Rick and the others to come forward, again holding my hand over my lips. They came and I crouched down, my hand on the invisible barrier. I leaned forward and whispered. "I hear them. Rick, you get ready to turn the gate off. Somebody else grab my legs while I peek through the gate."

I sat on the invisible surface, my back to the gate, and stuck a foot out. Joey grabbed it. I stuck the other out, the one with the bad knee, and Clara took hold of my ankle with both hands. I lay back, flat, facing the ceiling, and motioned them to slide me forward. The surface of the "field" slanted down until it cleared the inside diameter of the gate frame, then dropped down, into the gate, coming at its closest within three inches of the metal surface of the frame. I let my head bend back with the curve of the invisible surface until it was hanging straight down and then held up my hand.

They stopped letting me slide and I held my forefinger and thumb apart. They let me inch forward. My shoulders slid over the edge and I arched my back.

My eyes dropped below the level of the gate and I saw dirt floor stretching away toward light. I arched slightly more and saw the back side of my fake gate machinery and beyond it, feet—mostly feet wearing combat boots with one pair of track shoes incongruously placed among them. There were also the plastic stocks of rifles resting on the dirt floor.

"What's *that*?" somebody shouted, and a figure crouched and put its head low and stared at me.

I jerked my fingers toward my feet and pulled my head up, shouting, "Shut it, Rick!" Joey and Clara hauled me back but before I could sit up, the surface under me disappeared as the gate shut down and my head and shoulders suddenly dropped three feet onto the wet dirt floor.

"Ow, ow, ow!" I said.

"You okay?" Clara asked.

I sat up, brushing mud out of my hair. "Yeah. My knee hurts and I think I pulled something in my neck, but I'm okay."

"What did you see?" asked Clara.

"Our friends in the military."

Her face fell. "Then the gate still points at them . . ."

I laughed. "No. Near as I can tell, the gate on that side has moved exactly as far as it has on this side.

"We just need to move it farther and we're out of here."

Eighteen

"We Don't Want to Cut Anybody in Half."

By late afternoon, the gate was outside the hangar.

We had to move cubic yards of dirt. We had to demolish the fieldstone doorframe where the tunnel opened into the hangar. We had to lever the front end of the tractor around by brute force every time we stopped to 'steer' so the back end of the tractor wouldn't plow into the sides of the tunnel.

We had one cave-in, a partial collapse of the ceiling over the back half of the gate frame, which scared us badly, but after carefully uncovering it, we went on, stopping every so often to peer anxiously overhead.

Once in the hangar proper with the planes parked outside, we moved faster. With the hangar doors wide-open, we didn't have to worry so much about steering. With digging no longer necessary, more people could haul water for the tractor, so the pauses between hauling the gate were fewer.

That's probably what did it.

The tractor died a noble death. With shorter breaks to cool off, some part not adequately reached by our ad hoc cooling system expanded beyond tolerances and there was a harsh clanging sound and the entire tractor shuddered and stopped. When I tried the starter there was a horrible grinding sound as the starter motor tried to engage an unmoving flywheel.

As we stood around the tractor in the late afternoon sunlight, we looked like something out of a German expressionist film, covered in dirt except where rivulets of sweat had carved through the grime.

"Is this far enough?" Joey asked.

I shrugged. "I doubt it. They've almost certainly got sentries out—possibly to the property line. We don't want to walk right back into their hands after all this work to avoid them."

"How do we move it, then?" asked Marie.

I smiled. "How strong do you feel?"

Fortunately our little tank trailer was down to a third empty, perhaps two hundred gallons of fuel—about twelve hundred pounds of dead-weight rather than the thirty-six hundred pounds more it would be full. Still, it took us until late in the evening to get it off the frame of its four-wheeled trailer and gently to the ground.

The swelling in my knee lessened during the night. I wrapped it with two Ace bandages and gritted my teeth.

In the early morning light, we mounted four ten-foot tree trunks, six inches in diameter, lengthwise across the trailer frame and lashed onto the frame with climbing rope.

We raised the gate frame off the ground four inches at a time, using four-by-fours to lever it up, blocking it up with stacks of cut two-by-four blocks ripped from the inner wall of the hangar and chopped up. The gate lifted easily enough with two people each on the long end of two four-by-fours. The other two would block it, then we'd reposition the fulcrums at the other end and do it again, three inches at a time. Repeat as needed until the gate was precariously balanced on piles of block about three feet off the ground, four inches above the modified height of our trailer.

"Careful!" I said, as we eased the trailer underneath. "Don't knock it down again!"

"Relax, Charlie," said Clara. "You sound like your old man." She glanced at me with a sly smile.

I muttered, "Clara, you're a lot of trouble."

Clara laughed.

Rick said darkly, "You haven't seen *anything* yet."

Clara laughed harder.

We eased the gate frame down, a block at a time. When the weight came down on the tree trunk crossbeams they creaked and bent but held. We put the thick side of the frame, the part with the switch arm, closer in to the trailer, to center the mass. It seemed to be balanced.

I lifted the trailer tongue and pulled, pushing with my good leg. The thing didn't budge. Clara, Joey, and Rick joined me and we pulled as best we could, all of us crowded in to get ahold of it. I felt it roll slightly, but when we stopped pulling, it rolled back into the depression formed by the wheels.

"Clara," I said. "Get your horse."

Using cargo-restraining straps from the Maule, Clara rigged a chest strap on Impossible, running it through a loop high on each of her stirrup straps and joining together again eight feet behind the horse.

We went with five ropes tied to the trailer tongue. The center one went to Impossible's chest strap and the other four to simple loops of cargo strap for two-footed beasts of burden.

Clara had to lead Impossible, who was very doubtful about the whole process. "It won't be as efficient as a harness collar. The harder he pulls, the more the strap will interfere with his breathing. But he should still be able to pull harder than four of us."

Marie, Joey, Rick, and I all slung the straps across our chests. "You call it, Clara."

She clucked her tongue and pulled on Impossible's reins. He stepped out, but the moment the slack was out of the rope and he felt the chest strap, he tossed his head and half reared. The rest of us leaned into the straps and I felt the trailer move, rolling easier now that we could just pull and not worry about our grip on the tongue. Impossible felt some of the weight come off his chest and he started moving, too. Clara talked to him constantly, a stream of praise and encouragement.

We stuck to our mowed runway, turning north onto zero-one-five, the runway that cut back past the hill the tunnel was in. We chose that direction because it led to the most open land, sans streams and gullies. There were the inevitable bison wallows, but these could be avoided.

"How far are we going?" Clara asked.

All the way, I hope. I felt my ears turn red and looked down at the ground, pulling steadily against the strap. I looked up after a second and saw that Clara was blushing, too. "We'll just have to see," I said.

Rick started coughing, covering his mouth with his hand. Clara glared at him and he coughed harder. I could see the corners of his mouth turning up behind his hand.

We reached the end of the mowed runway and I called for a break. We dropped where we were, sitting in the grass and gasping for air. Clara loosened Impossible's girth and fed him a horse cookie.

"How far do you think we've come?" Clara asked, looking around.

I limped over to the trailer and retrieved my shotgun before looking back at our control tower, which stuck up over the edge of the hill. "Well, I'd say we're just short of where the house is on the other side—about where I park my pickup."

"That's all?" said Joey. "All this work and we're still in their laps?"

Marie touched his arm and Joey shook her hand off. "If Charlie hadn't cut the damn tractor apart, we could be pulling it with that!"

I ignored him, but Clara snapped back, "If Charlie hadn't shut the gate, we'd *really* be in their laps now."

Rick snorted. "Defending Charlie, Clara? Don't you think he can take care of himself?"

Marie threw her arms up. "Asshole! She's always defending *you*, even after you betrayed her!"

Clara squeezed her eyes shut and tilted her head back. "Stop it, Marie. It's not worth it." A tear squeezed out the corner of her eye and I wanted to reach out to her, but something kept me still, flinching away from all of them.

Rick got angrier. "Give me a break! We *should* have left the gate hidden and toughed it out on the other side! Then we wouldn't be stuck here, would we?"

Marie turned white. "No, we'd be in a cell someplace. You want to be locked up by those guys? I don't go for guys in uniform, but I could see where *you* might! Or maybe Bestworst is the attraction."

Rick eyed Marie. "Better a man in a uniform than a man with a bottle."

Joey said, "You asshole!" and stepped toward Rick, his hand held back to punch.

I squeezed the trigger on my shotgun, discharging a perfectly good round of buckshot into the air. Everybody jumped, flinching toward their weapons. They looked at me, standing there, looking at them, my face frozen, my mind raging.

I turned and limped away.

"Where are you going, Charlie?" Marie asked.

I didn't answer, I didn't stop, and I didn't look back.

I was in the control tower, my foot propped up on the windowsill, a chemical cold pack strapped to my knee.

I felt someone try to open the trapdoor, but I'd moved the bench so its legs sat on the hatch and kept anyone from opening it from below. Then they knocked.

"Go away," I said.

"Charlie?" The muffled voice was Clara's.

"Nobody's home."

"Charlie!"

I groaned, then moved my leg down and slid the bench aside. She pushed the hatch up and I watched the nape of her neck as she climbed into the tower, head down to watch her hands and feet. There were fine blond hairs that continued down her neck and under her jacket and I wanted to follow them, to see where they went.

When she'd closed that hatch again, I shifted the bench back on top of it, then put my leg back up.

Clara straddled the other end of the bench facing me. Her eyes were wide and solemn. "You really scared us, Charlie."

I felt my face get red. "I'm sorry. I shouldn't have fired the shotgun."

She shook her head. "Not that, Charlie. It was when you just left. *That* was scary. I don't think we realized how much we depend on you until you walked away."

"Don't push that on me!" I said, furious, frightened. "You're adults. I'm not your parent!"

She rocked back, shocked at my outburst.

I squeezed my eyes shut and clenched my teeth.

She put her hand on my good knee. "What is it, Charlie?"

"I can't hold it anymore! I've been holding it for so long—the risks, the dangers, the chance I'll get one of you killed. Dad, Luis, Richard—I'm responsible and dammit, I've *been* responsible. I've tried to handle things but they just keep going to pieces—" I clamped my hands over my mouth to stop the sobs that threatened to burst forth.

I took deep breaths, tried to slow them, tried to breathe it all out, to push it out of my body.

Finally, I opened my eyes and said, "I don't think you guys understand how much I depend on *you*."

Clara's shocked look slowly changed to one of understanding. "So when we started fighting . . ."

I nodded, mute.

"If it's worth anything, everybody apologized down there. Rick fell all over himself apologizing to Marie and Joey. Joey sends his apologies. Marie sat down in the grass and started bawling, saying how she didn't like to act that way and didn't know what came over her and could Rick ever forgive her? Now they're all wondering about you."

She slid forward on the bench, moving her leg under my propped-up knee and moving her other leg over my good one. If it weren't for our clothing, it would be like something from the Kama Sutra. She leaned into me, curling her arms in across her breasts. My arms went around her and she sighed deeply.

"You don't have to hold it alone, Charlie. We can help each other." She slid her arms around me, her breasts pressing against me. She rubbed my lower back with her hands. "God, are you tense!" She kneaded harder.

"Ow!"

"Relax," she said.

I pushed my hands down her back and beneath the waistline of her jeans. She tensed suddenly.

"Relax," I said.

She pushed her mouth against mine, suddenly, her tongue slipping between my lips. I worked my hands deeper, brushing my fingertips across her bottom, just tracing the elastic on the top of her bikini briefs. She breathed in deeply.

"Oh, my," she said.

I moved one hand around to her breast and she brought her hands around, fumbling at my belt buckle.

The radio came to life. "Charlie? Clara?"

"Oh, shit!" I said.

Clara sighed, then said, "Turn it off?"

I closed my eyes and held her breathing deeply, concentrating on the weight and the feel of her. "Help me hold it," I finally said.

"I was trying. I was trying!"

We laughed like maniacs, then climbed down the ladder to the others.

Marie burst into tears again, on seeing me, and I said, "Hey, it's okay, Marie."

Rick looked uncomfortable. "I was an asshole, Charlie," he said. "I'm sorry."

Joey hung his head, his hands twisting a clump of buffalo grass he'd carried in from outside. "I *really* need a meeting." He threw the grass over his shoulder and in a much quieter voice said, "Sorry.

This Land-of-the-Pharaohs shtick is getting to me. Wish we had your truck."

Now there was a notion. I unclipped my key chain from my belt loop and held it up.

"Well, why not?" I said.

There was a shallow bison wallow at the corner of the runway, an oblong depression perhaps three feet deep at its lowest spot. The trailer rolled down the gentle incline and into it easily.

"You're sure this is a safe spot?" Clara asked. "We don't want to cut anybody in half when we turn it on."

I turned and peered at the hill again. "I *think* so. The shape of the hill is slightly different on this side and it's hard to tell. If I'm right, though, this should open up where the old garden is—back by the compost heap. It won't hurt if *that* gets chopped into. Besides, by lowering it down like we have, the gate should open up near or below the surface of the ground."

We untied the ropes holding the gate frame to the trailer and then went back to the hangar to eat supper and wait for full dark.

We came back armed for bear, sabertooth, and wolf—our regular gear. We also brought the shovel and the long pole we'd used to turn the gate switch. We used our flashlights freely and made a lot of noise with the horns.

Several birds took to the air and something small scurried away through the underbrush. We didn't see or hear any predators, and the presence of the birds was evidence of their absence.

I took the shovel and crawled under the trailer until I was centered under the gate frame. Clara joined me, muttering to herself. "I could've spent the summer cleaning horse stalls, but nooooooooooooooo, I had to have adventures, see wildlife, travel to alternate universes." She rolled over onto her back beside me with a groan. "God, I need a bath."

"Okay," I said. "Lights off everybody. Remember—no talking after the gate is open." The flashlights flicked off and the cold stars shone above, framed by the trailer cross members and our rough timber support beams. "When you're ready, Rick."

"Close your eyes, guys." Rick's voice came through the dark. I squeezed my eyes shut. "Opening the gate . . . now!"

There was a flash of light visible through my eyelids and a wave of steam-laden air against my face. I opened my eyes. The stars were gone and the darkness above me was absolute. I reached up past the trailer frame and met dirt. Moist dirt, moderately packed, though some promptly fell onto my forehead. I turned the flashlight on.

The gate frame, edge to edge, was filled with dark, root-twined dirt. "Well, we didn't cut anybody in half," I said to Clara.

She turned on her flashlight. "Unless you count invertebrates." She pointed at the truncated end of an earthworm, hanging out of the dirt face and wiggling.

"Gross. How far down do you think we are?"

She pulled a hoof pick from her rear pocket and pushed it into the dirt above. "Deeper than five inches."

I picked the shovel up and moved to the side, where I had a decent amount of space between the trailer and the edge of the gate frame.

I could see the guys peering under the trailer, at the edge of the field. Rick pointed at his mouth and held up his hand in an "OK" sign. I said, "Sure, Rick, go ahead and talk. The gate opened underground."

"I can barely hear you, Charlie," he said. His voice was oddly muffled. I probed around the edge of the gate frame at ground level, but the field went from the gate frame down into the ground, forming a wall all the way around Clara and me. I wondered if it was passing oxygen through and my heart started beating faster.

I knew we could dig under it, a shallow tunnel leading beneath the field, but I didn't know if we should bother. I spoke a little louder, pointing up. "I'm going to try and dig up through the ground." I worked an area right next to the gates edge, lying off to one side and chopping down clods of earth with the shovel. It was much easier than digging down—you didn't have to lift the dirt out of a hole, but I quickly passed two feet without breaking through.

Clara edged over and started moving the dirt that fell to one side. I borrowed her hoof pick and probed every couple of inches. I soon had a hole three feet from gate to top and was kneeling below it to dig. How could we be so far off? Then I hit grass roots, sparse, then thick. I probed and felt the pick break through.

I knelt and held my finger to my lips, then pointed to my flashlight and turned it off. The others followed my example.

I pulled the rest of the dirt down with my hands, carefully widening the hole until it was large enough for my head and the width of the hole below the surface was wide enough for my shoulders.

Though it was probably redundant, I smeared dirt on my face to darken it, then, by standing on tiptoe, I lifted my head above the edge of the hole.

It was overcast but the mercury vapor light in the barnyard shone lots of light on the scene. I was not as near the compost heap as I had thought, being about ten yards off, but I was out in the middle of nowhere, well away from the house and even farther from the barn. The ground stretched away, level with my eyes. I could see the windows of the living room, lit from within, and the back end of my truck, which was parked nose-in beneath the dining room window. There were soldiers standing at the front and back of the house as well as two standing before the barn. I saw lights out in the field and could make out two more soldiers seated in the open doorway of a Blackhawk helicopter. Several shiny unmarked cars were parked beside the barn and there were three panel trucks in front of the house. Rick's car, which had been in the middle of the yard, was parked by the Mooney's hangar.

I looked more closely at the area around my truck, trying to see if there were any guards I was missing when I noticed something different about the house.

There was a sheet of plywood covering the dining room window. *Now why do you suppose . . . ?*

I took bearings on the car, on the front of the house, and on the rear of the house, marking them first on the sides of the hole at chest level, then dropping down and drawing them in the dirt I'd stomped flat below my feet. I checked them several times, then, finally dropped back down and flashed my light back toward Rick.

When I saw that I had his attention, I shined the light on my face and drew my finger across my throat. He nodded and stood. A few seconds later there was another flash from overhead and a thin layer of dirt fell, sagging earth cut from the tame side.

I stood, brushing dirt out of my hair and off my shoulders.

"This is looking more and more like *Attack of the Mole People.*" I shined my light on the ground, making sure my markings were still intact.

"How far are we from the truck?" asked Rick.

I pointed at my middle mark. "The back end is about fifteen yards in that direction. That's the direction it's headed, too. But we're a lot lower than I thought. The ground on the ranch must've been graded up, or something. The gate is about three and a half feet below the surface where it is now. And there's another thing. They've boarded over the window to the dining room."

"Maybe they broke it," said Marie.

I shrugged. "And maybe they're trying to keep someone from getting out of that room."

"Your dad? Luis? And whathistoes—uh, Richard Madigan?" guessed Clara.

I nodded.

"Why didn't they just put them back where they were?" said Rick.

"Maybe they can't," I said. "This Bestworst guy is so far over the line that maybe he can't trust the people who were holding Luis and Richard. He knows they've all seen the gate. Maybe he doesn't want them to tell anybody else about it?"

Joey licked his lips. "What's he going to do? Hold them forever? Kill them?"

I looked at Joey and didn't say anything.

"Luis really saved my ass," Joey said. "I'd be in jail without his help. We can't just leave him there."

"We could get caught," said Rick. "Maybe the way to help them is to get away and get public. Let the power of the press save them."

Joey shook his head violently. "And maybe they'd just disappear. Maybe they'd just say, 'What lawyers?' and make sure that they were never seen again."

Rick looked skeptical and I said, "Maybe they would, maybe they wouldn't. But if they don't have them, it stops becoming an issue, right?"

Rick looked at the sky. "Why do I think I'm going to regret this?"

The hardest part was getting the gate out of that damn bison wallow. We ended up adding another rope with all of us, including Impossible, pulling to get it up out of that depression. Once out, we pulled it twenty yards in the direction of my truck.

While Clara put Impossible back in the hangar, the rest of us dug a trench under the edge of the gate, so that we could pass under it when it was on.

I did *not* lie underneath it this time. If we'd miscalculated and we opened it under the truck, or under a part of the foundation of the house, stuff falling through the gate could kill me. When I thought about it, I was surprised that all the dirt from our previous opening hadn't buried Clara and me.

We turned off our flashlights and Rick turned on the gate with his pole. Nothing flashed and nothing fell through—I wondered if we'd finally broken it—that it wasn't coming on. I dropped down into the trench and squirmed under the field. When I looked up, through the gate, I saw thin lines of light shining between the cracks of floorboards.

Bull's-eye.

I stood and looked around.

My upper body was sticking out of the gate into the crawl space under the house. There was a poured concrete foot around the outside edge of the house and joists and outer walls rested on this. The floor of the crawl space was dirt. Cobwebs brushed my hair and I could see the access door at the side of the house, outlined in orange light from the mercury vapor light in the yard.

I carefully felt the edge of the gateway—a place where I could see the trailer below on one side and dirt floor of the crawl space about eight inches below the other side. The field formed a surface about four inches inward from this edge. When I wrapped my fingers around the outer edge they continued to encounter a similar surface underneath. I traced a little deeper and the surface flowed *up*, toward me, but I didn't see anything. I shivered.

I crawled up over the edge, onto the dirt floor, and out of curiosity I stuck my head back *under* the edge of the gate.

Above me was the upper half of the gate and, above that, stars.

I pulled my head out quickly, shaking.

Clara and Joey's upper half appeared out of the gate. They were peering through the gloom and I realized that my eyes had adjusted somewhat. I leaned close and said, "The scope?"

Clara pushed the stethoscope from our medical supplies into my hand. I crawled over to the dining room and crouched. Already I could hear Luis's voice, but not the words. What I wanted to know is who else was with them and where in the room they were.

"—call it conspiracy to deprive a citizen of his civil rights. Conspiracy is, after all, yet another felony."

Another voice said, "It's very hard to sue the government. You know that. They have all the legal resources in the world and it'll just keep going, appeal after appeal. Frankly, I just want to get out of here, preferably, alive." That was Madigan.

"All that is very nice," said a third voice—Dad. "But it's all contingent on ever getting out of these guys' hands." I would've loved to hear more, but there was work to do.

First, I spot-checked the other rooms. Someone was snoring in my bedroom. There were people talking in low voices in the kitchen, and I heard footsteps on the stairs and the rush of water as someone upstairs was taking a shower.

That made me angry—more angry than the guy sleeping in my bed. I was covered in dirt and sweat and half-afraid that they'd smell me long before they ever saw me. And these assholes were using *my* shower.

I crawled back to the gate and gave the stethoscope back to Clara. Marie handed me the tape measure and turned on her flashlight, holding it in her mouth while she wrote on a pad. I measured the distance from the gate edge to the outside wall and crawled back, my thumb marking the spot on the tape. She'd shine her light on it and jot it down. We took some more measurements and then Clara handed me a coat hanger with a piece of white cloth tied to its end.

At the end of the dining room, next to the wall, was a knothole that had fallen out long ago. It had been plugged with a piece of cork. I located it with my flashlight and, using Clara's hoof pick, pushed it up from beneath, slowly. I listened to see if any of them would notice, but they didn't stop talking. I pushed about two feet of coat hanger wire through the hole and then waved it gently back and forth, careful not to scrape it against the wall.

Luis's voice stopped in mid-sentence and I heard the floorboards creak as he stood up and walked toward the wall. As he got closer, I pulled the coat hanger back through the hole. When I heard his footsteps stop I put my finger through the hole and wiggled it, then put my mouth up to the hole and said quietly, "Luis."

"Charlie?" he sounded incredulous.

Dad's voice said, "Charlie! What are you doing?"

"Quiet!" I hissed. "Put your ear to the hole."

The light from the hole was blocked. "Do they leave you alone, in there?"

I heard Dad shift to turn his head. "We have a bathroom break coming up and then they leave us alone until morning. I can hear the guards outside, though."

"Do you still have your watch?" I asked.

"Yes."

"We're opening the gate into that room in exactly two hours and twenty minutes. You need to stay away from the end of the dining room next to the kitchen. Is that possible, and is anybody likely to come through that door?"

He shifted. "No. That's the door they boarded up. They use the door to the living room. We can move our cots against the outside wall after the bathroom break."

"Okay." I checked my watch again. "That's two hours and nineteen minutes from my mark." I waited for the second hand. "Mark. Got it?"

"Yes."

"See ya." I crawled back to the gate and dropped down to the wild side along with Clara and Marie. Rick shut it down and we stood.

I checked my watch. "Two hours and eighteen minutes, guys. Let's get cracking."

First we measured out all the positions we needed, cutting lines in the sod. Then we relashed the gate to the trailer and moved it into horizontal position for the first part. This, however, also called for lifting one end of the gate another four feet into the air.

We got the first two feet by putting all of us but Marie on the bottom edge of the gate frame, at the back of the trailer. The weight pulled the end slowly to the ground, lifting the front trailer wheels and that end of the gate frame into the air.

While we sat there, holding it in place, Marie piled two-by-four blocks under the front wheels. The next two feet were more tedious, hard inch by hard inch with the four-by-four levers and fulcrums. We had to release the trailer, then the gate propped up by the four-by-fours, then work our way inch by inch until the gate leaned against the timbers from the trailer at a forty-five-degree angle. This barely brought the top inside edge of the gate to the right height. I wanted more clearance, but we were running out of time.

"It'll have to do," I said. "Get the water buckets."

I stood on the "acute" side of the gate, crouching clear of the terminus and clear of the field. Joey stood on the "obtuse" side, which was appropriate, and stood on the trailer frame to clear the field. We each had a bucket of water poised in our hands.

Rick hit the gate switch and there was a flash and a line of flame across the gate opening, two feet from the top. I stood and poured my water down the flickering wood, extinguishing it as quietly as I could. I could hear Joey doing the same thing on the other side.

I was looking at an opening that went from the lower two feet of the dining room, a cross section of floorboard and floor joists (singed), a stretch of crawl space under the house, and a cross section of the dirt below that.

In the dining room, Richard, Luis, and Dad were moving across the floor, toward me. I held my finger to my lips and helped them through. Richard hopped down and tried to walk away from the gate, promptly bumping his head on the field. Marie guided him under it and clear. Luis started to say something, and I put my hand against his lips. Dad looked around, his eyes not adjusted to the dark.

I was listening—listening for something that meant they'd heard us. Or smelled the smoke from the floor. Or heard the water splashing and dripping. But I didn't hear anybody scrape a chair across the floor or walk closer or cry out.

Clara was frowning. She didn't like this next part.

I tapped my watch and she reluctantly held up her thumb and forefinger in an "OK" sign. Marie tapped Dad on the arm and led him away from the gate. As soon as his back was turned, I dropped low and crawled through the bottom half of the gate into the crawl space under the house.

The gate flickered shut behind me.

I had two hours.

I would've preferred to spend the time in my bathtub, perhaps running through three different changes of water and soaking my knee in the hottest water I could stand. Then I would put on fresh pajamas from my bedroom and have a nice sandwich in the kitchen, finished off with cookies and milk, and then sleep in my bed. And not alone.

Instead I huddled in the dirt against the concrete foundation by the crawl space access door and tried to keep my imagination under control.

I knew that any minute they'd check on Luis, Richard, and Dad, find they were gone, and, because of the weird cut in the floor, they'd look under the house and find me. Or they'd spread the alarm and put so many soldiers in the barnyard that my next move would be impossible.

The time crawled.

Ten minutes before the appointed hour, I slipped the latch of the access hatch open with my pocketknife and eased the door inward. The front end of my little Japanese pickup was two yards to my left, parked with its bumper almost to the house. I eased my head out of the door and looked toward the front of the house. Two guards stood there, at the corner. I looked at the back, past the truck, and thought that for a moment there was no one back there. Then a soldier, apparently pacing back and forth, cleared the corner, turned, then walked back out of sight. I withdrew and began debating the way to go about it.

In the end, I decided to just do it. No running, no sneaking. I rehearsed it in my head, timing it again and again.

At one minute I put the pickup key in my hand. At forty seconds I eased the door completely open and blocked it with dirt so it wouldn't catch me. At thirty seconds I crouched in the little doorway. At twenty seconds I moved.

First easing through the door, I stood normally and limped four steps to the driver's door, pulled the door open, and sat inside. The dome light came on and I heard one of the guards say, "What's that?"

I put the key in the ignition and eased the emergency brake off. The clock was down to eight seconds. I pumped the gas pedal twice, then cranked it over. Now the guards were doing more than looking my way. They were running. I shut the door and locked it as the engine caught with a roar. I pumped the gas pedal, revving it up. More soldiers were running from the barn. They stopped, surrounding the vehicle on all three sides, their M16As pointed at me. My watch was down to two seconds. I pushed the clutch in and put it in first gear.

The clock was at zero and I shoved the accelerator down and let the clutch out. The rear tires spun dirt and grass and the truck leapt forward at the side of the house. There was a shot and glass sprinkled over my left shoulder as the windows in both doors shattered. I braced myself for impact, knowing that they hadn't been able to move the gate in time, and then the wall before me burst into flame and the truck plunged through it, scattering flaming embers around me like an explosion. Then the front end of the truck was dropping and the engine raced madly as the rear wheels also came off the ground. I was airborne.

Three vertical feet later, the front wheels hit the ground, buffalo grass whispered against the bottom and sides of the car, and I was thrown forward against the steering wheel. The rear wheels, spinning madly, hit right after, and I was thrown back again. In the rearview mirror I caught a glimpse of a large square image of soldiers running across orange-lit ground like some giant projection TV and then the image winked out—station break. We'll return to *Charlie and the Trans-Dimensional Pirates* after this commercial message.

I took my foot off the accelerator and shoved the clutch in. The bright afterimage of the open gate lingered and I blinked my eyes furiously. The truck rolled to a stop, the engine still running. I turned on the headlights and eased it around in a circle, pulling up beside the cluster of people dancing furiously through the grass, beating at small fires with their jackets and stamping at them with their feet. Behind them, the gate stood, braced by timbers, rising out of the tall grass like some lithic monument on the plain of Salisbury.

With my elbow, I knocked the remnants of the safety glass out of the side mirror and leaned out. I tasted blood and I could feel that the inside of my upper lip was cut and one of my top front teeth was loose. Beside me the mad dance slowed as the last of the embers was stomped out and smothered.

Marie was looking at her sheet of measurements and scratching her head. "Huh. Looks like we were about an inch short. I hope they put out the fire before the house burns down."

Dad was staring at me, an angry look on his face. "You okay, Charlie?" Then, without a pause, "What a stupid, dangerous thing to do! That was *not* a very good landing."

I stared at him a moment, baffled, angry. "And the horse you rode in on," I finally said. "It was no trouble at all to rescue you."

Clara was looking at me, an odd look on her face, like incipient tears, but she took a deep breath and slapped the side of the truck. "What do you expect, Captain Newell? The glide ratio on this thing sucks. Any landing you can walk away from, though—"

I closed my eyes and exhaled, then pointed at the back of the truck with my thumb.

"Anybody need a lift?"

Nineteen

"If I'd Had My Shotgun in My Hands, I Would've Have Fired."

t was almost dawn and none of us had slept. I drove the entire group back to the hangar, then Clara and I used the truck to fetch water from the stream. It was a lot easier than carrying it while walking.

The water was frigid, but we washed anyway, struggling to get the layers of dirt off. Clara and I gave up a sleeping bag, as did Joey and Marie, so that Luis and Richard might have bedding. We had mattresses, though, courtesy of Lieutenant Thayer's crazy launch platform. Dad used a space blanket, a mattress, and a collection of jackets.

When Impossible became restive early in the morning, Clara took him out onto the grass. An hour later she brought him back, then crawled under the sleeping bag and snuggled up against my spine.

"You," I whispered, "have very cold hands."

She worked them under the edge of my shirt and I jumped. "Leave them there and they'll warm up," she whispered in my ear. Then she gently bit my earlobe and slid her hands lower on my stomach.

That's when Dad turned the lights on.

"Tell me why we rescued him," I muttered. Clara giggled and rolled away. I lay on my back and groaned. *Damn, damn, damn.*

There was more groaning, from Rick, Marie, and Joey, and from Luis and Richard, which struck me as funny. After all, they'd been sitting on their duffs while we undertook the seven labors of Hercules, excavating the gate and dragging it all over creation. Still, I suppose they didn't sleep any more than we did.

"We're burning daylight," said Dad, which sounds incredibly rustic, but he got it from John Wayne in *The Cowboys.*

I gritted my teeth and pulled on my clothes.

We moved the gate a mile and a half, towing it slowly with the truck across buffalo grass. At one point we had to clear a way through a thick stand of mesquite and at another point we shifted rocks to make a rocky stream ford passable.

In the twilight, we opened the gate while the frame was still on the trailer to "up periscope." I popped up through the gate to find myself in the middle of a cotton field near Farm-to-Market Road 2818. A half mile down the road there was a thick stand of mesquite, the kind that gets enough water so that it's really trees instead of brush. Above this stand of trees rose a gas sign, marking a country convenience store I knew well, as it was the closest source of groceries to the ranch.

I marked the direction and distance and we shut down the gate and secured it. We checked three more times as we moved it, finally unloading the gate and standing it upright so it opened at the edge of the stand of sagebrush, near a gravel drive a hundred yards behind the store.

I took a quick walk out to the back of the building and looked back. In the dark, it was hard to see the gate against the trees. It was brighter on the tame side, but a mercury vapor light in the front of the store cast a nice dark shadow over the gate and trees. I peeked around the corner—there was only the clerk's car parked out front—no sign of the military. I went back through the gate.

"All clear. No sign of the bad guys." I took off my jacket. "It's warm, too. Humid, maybe in the seventies."

We left the shotguns and our jackets on the wildside, by the gate, protected by a tarp. Dad drove the truck out without headlights and parked it at the pump. Luis and Richard hit the pay phone on the wall outside. The rest of us went inside, surprising the clerk a little and making him look nervously at the cash register. But he didn't bolt for the phone, so it seemed that his reaction was from being alone in the country and not because he was on the lookout for the Trans-Dimensional Pirates.

I wonder what his reaction would have been if we *had* brought the shotguns.

Joey paused before the beer cooler and stared at it. Marie touched his side and he said, "Don't worry. What I'm mostly feeling is disgust." He looked down at his watch. "There's a meeting in downtown Bryan in an hour."

I bought soft drinks for everybody—cold carbonated drinks. The water on the wildside was cold enough, but we didn't have a, refrigeration and we hadn't stocked soft drinks. I mean, just how nutritive is caffeine-free diet cola? It won't even keep you *awake*.

Do without it for over a week and it assumes an unnatural importance.

I paid for the gas that Dad had pumped, then we took the drinks outside to the others. Rick headed for the phone and the rest of us gathered around the truck.

"How'd the phone calls go, Luis?"

Luis smiled. "Fine. I reached Judge Nicoll at home. He doesn't like me much, but he *hates* Miranda violations. He'll see us first thing in the morning. I also reached Marta Rigby from Snodgrass, Messenger & Sons in Houston. She's joining us. Last, I got hold of Bill Kennedy at Channel 11 and told him that the army was illegally occupying your ranch. I suggested he do a flyover in the news helicopter first thing in the morning since the papers were going to 'hear' about it shortly thereafter." Luis did a quick drumroll on the hood of the truck. "Bill feels buried here in our little town— he'd do anything for a scoop. Something that would get the attention of the networks or a metropolitan news agency."

"What'll you do until morning?"

"We'll stay at that sleazy motel near the courthouse—your dad can drop us there."

"That's near where I want to go, too," Joey said. "The downtown AA meeting is three blocks from there."

"I'll stick with Joey," said Marie.

Rick joined us. "I need to be dropped near Northgate," he said.

Dad said, "I can drop you. That leaves Clara, right?"

She blinked. "I'll be coming right back here, but if you'll drop me at the stable on your way into town, I can bring my motorcycle and some horse feed back."

"Don't go near the apartment," I said. "They'll probably be watching it."

She shook her head. "I know, Charlie."

"For that matter, Dad, they'll probably be watching the house."

"Let them," he said. "I'll get one of our friends to take a note to her—they can't be tapping every phone in town. We'll meet away from the house and spend the night at a hotel." He looked directly into my eyes. "Will *you* be okay?"

I laughed. "We call it the wildside, but compared to Agent Bestworst and Captain Moreno, it's tame, tame, tame. *This* is the dangerous side."

He looked away. "Okay."

I looked down at my watch. "After Clara gets back, I'm shutting the gate down. I'll open it precisely at 2300 tomorrow night. If nobody's here, I'll use the pay phone to call Rick's friend, Chris. Everybody has that number, right?"

They all nodded.

"Chris is going to be okay about that?" I asked Rick.

"He said it was cool, just now," Rick said. He glanced up the highway. "Let's get going, before we're spotted."

Dad and Luis climbed in the front—the others climbed in the back. I glanced at the window of the store and saw that the clerk was reading a book, not paying any attention to us. I stepped back to the corner of the building and waved.

The little truck accelerated uncertainly, as if it didn't understand this smooth, hard surface under its tires, then the engine roughness faded and the taillights got progressively smaller.

Headlights appeared down the road in front of the truck, first one set, then two more came over the rise. I tried not to feel nervous. There were a lot of ranches and farms out here. But then the headlights slewed around and pointed off to the side and in the headlights of the truck I saw the other two cars skid sideways, filling the gaps across the road, blocking it.

Maybe they couldn't tap every phone in town, but it seemed like they could tap enough of them.

I turned and limped back to the gate, looking over my shoulder. "Turn around, dammit!" I said, under my breath.

The little truck did just that, the brake lights glowing, and then it bumped off the side of the road and made a U-turn, coming back toward me. I looked up the road in the other direction. Headlights came over the far rise, but that was two miles away. The truck could get back to the gate before they got there.

My heart was pounding and there was a roaring in my ears. I tried to slow my breathing, but then I recognized the sound.

The dark silhouette of a Blackhawk helicopter passed overhead and dropped onto the road before the convenience store, blocking the road completely. As before, soldiers erupted from it, some of them spreading out to block the oncoming truck. The rest ran toward the store.

I ignored my knee and ran for the gate. I heard the thudding of feet on gravel as I passed into it and I skidded to a stop by the switch and turned, nearly falling as my knee shrieked in protest.

Beyond the helicopter, my truck was stopped on the road and surrounded by dark figures with rifles. On this side of the helicopter, two soldiers, fifty feet away, were sprinting at me at an amazing rate.

I shouted, "Stop!" but they just kept running.

If I'd had my shotgun in my hands, I would've have fired.

I threw the switch.

* * *

I don't know how I got back to the hangar. I walked, of course, but I don't remember it. I had two shotguns, mine and Clara's, and my knee was swollen to the size of a small soccer ball. I vaguely remembered passing something with large green eyes that stared at me over a freshly killed deer, but I didn't bother it and it didn't bother me.

Once I was in the hangar, I used the camp lantern instead of firing up the generator. Impossible whinnied in the light and I stumbled over to make sure he had water. There were a few inches left in the bucket that Clara had lashed to the wall so the horse wouldn't kick the bucket over. I refilled it, but he seemed hungry more than thirsty and I knew that Clara had run out of feed that morning.

"Sorry, boy. You can graze in the morning."

I got out another chemical ice pack and took 800 milligrams of ibuprofen. The thought of food made me sick, but I put some soup on anyway and stared blankly at the shadows while it cooked.

What was I going to do?

I hadn't come up with an answer by the time the smell of burning soup pulled my attention back to the stove.

"Dammit all to hell!"

I wasn't mad about the soup, though. I threw it out and, since something about the anger made me realize how hungry I really was, I put more on.

Impossible kept calling to me, hungry, I guess. I thought about going out back and cutting a bunch of buffalo grass, but the thought of going outside, alone, with no one here to come after me—well, it brought up memories of Uncle Max's skull, bleached and broken.

I rummaged through the stores and finally took a package of bran flakes and emptied it into another bucket. Impossible sniffed it tentatively, than stuffed his head deep into the bucket. It apparently met with his heartfelt and enthusiastic approval. I just hoped he wouldn't colic or something.

I got the soup off the stove before it burned this time and ate it sitting on a mattress, a sleeping bag pulled around my shoulders. I thought about the previous night, when I'd shared that same bag with Clara. I wanted to think I could still smell her skin, but all I really smelled was the stink of horse urine from Impossible's corner. Still, since I associated Impossible with Clara, it was something.

The night was very long.

At dawn I tethered Impossible on the grass halfway down the runway, then powered the Maule up and taxied it out of the hangar. At the noise from the engine, Impossible promptly pulled up his tethered stake and went charging down the runway, dragging the tether rope and the stake behind him.

If he got himself eaten or broke his fool neck by stepping on the tether rope, Clara would never forgive me.

I shut the Maule down and climbed out, whistling shrilly. Impossible stopped before the tall grass at the end of the runway and bounced on his front legs, tossing his head and whinnying, not running any farther, but not coming back toward me, either.

I thought about trying to chase him on foot with my bum knee, then limped back into the barn and grabbed another box of bran flakes and a bucket. The knee was throbbing fiercely as I slowly limped back out to the middle of the runway, a good distance from the noisy and smelly airplane. I put the bucket down on the ground and slowly poured bran flakes into it. Then I backed away and sat, my shotgun in my lap.

It took twenty minutes, but Impossible crisscrossed the runway, getting a little closer each time, and finally ate the damn cereal. I'd rescrewed the tether stake back into the ground by the time he'd finished, and this time, I didn't do the half-assed job I'd done at dawn. The two-foot spiral was deep in the sod, the triangular top barely clearing the dirt.

"Move that, you ambulatory pot of glue!"

I loaded the Maule with six half-filled, plastic, five-gallon containers of aviation gas, a case of shotgun ammo, water, food, the gasoline-powered Weedeater, the chain saw, and all the rope I could find. With frequent stops to rest my knee and check for predators in the vicinity of Impossible, this took two hours.

Then I mucked out Impossible's corner and gathered grass, cut from where it grew tall on the runway's edge, and piled it in the hangar where he could get to it. Then I moved him back inside and filled up his water barrel.

He sniffed the grass in the corner disdainfully and looked at me.

"Sorry," I said. "No oats. No alfalfa. No bran flakes." I patted his neck, then turned the generator on and shut the hangar door.

The lights in the tunnel were working, though one fixture had come down in the cave-in when we'd moved the gate. It dangled, supported by the wiring, one of its two tubes shattered. I walked carefully, my eye on the ceiling, especially when I crossed the mounded dirt from the cave-in.

There'd be no one to dig me out if it collapsed again.

I had to dig for the gate solenoid. We'd buried it in our excavations, but I found it and the clamps where I thought it should be, under a foot and a half of dirt. I took it and some of the smaller pieces from my hoax gate machinery, about one armful, and carried them out to the hangar.

When I was back in the hangar I had to wipe the sweat from my face before continuing.

I took the batteries, car alarm radio receiver, and timers out of their hidden pocket at the back of the hangar, and got the solar panel down off the control tower, then loaded it all in the Maule. Finally, I went back into the hangar and shut down the generator.

Before closing the hangar door from the outside, I looked back at Impossible. "Be back this afternoon." I hoped it was true—if I didn't come back, Impossible would die a horrible, slow death. I considered leaving him outside, untethered, but thought his chances of surviving *that* weren't very good, either.

I'd just have to be careful.

With that in mind, I was meticulous in my preflight inspection and checklist. The Maule lifted off the ground, though drag from the growing grass, uncut since the tractor died, added a hundred feet to the takeoff run.

It took less than two minutes to reach the gate. I couldn't help compare it with my multihour, limping journey the night before. My knee ached sharply just thinking about it.

The area around the gate was buffalo grass, perhaps a foot and a half tall, scattered with mesquite. I landed several hundred feet away, in an avenue between bushes. The ground was rough beneath the grass and the plane slowed quickly. Then I taxied between mesquite bushes until I was next to the gate, where I unloaded my supplies and equipment.

It took the entire morning to lower the gate back onto its trailer. I used rope belayed to timbers which were lashed to the heftier mesquite shrubs, and pulled it slowly over, moving its support timbers so it never dropped more than a few inches at a time. When it was back on the trailer and lashed in place, I tried to pull it with the Maule, maximum thrust, taking cylinder head temperatures to dangerous extremes.

It didn't move.

I shut down the Maule and pulled the trailer by hand, using the old trick of tying a long rope to a distant tree and making it as taut as possible, then walking to the midpoint and pulling it ninety degrees. The trailer moved inches. Tighten the rope—repeat as necessary.

By late afternoon, I'd moved it thirty yards. This took 370 repetitions of the tighten/pull sequence. My knee was swollen again, and ached with a constant, fierce pain, and I had blisters on my hands. I'd also run out of ibuprofen in the plane's med kit.

I flew back, barely able to handle the rudder pedals.

Impossible was very glad to see me.

I spent the evening mothballing Wildside Base, including the Maule. I closed the shutters on the tower and moved the radio and computer equipment down into the hangar. I drained the gasoline from the fuel tanks and the oil from the engine, then replaced the oil, overfilling the crankcase. Then I disconnected the batteries and blocked the landing gear so the tires didn't sit on the ground.

Impossible, munching away on a box of Cheerios (hey, they're oats, right?), watched my labors with interest. The work was exhausting but it kept my brain busy. Every time I sat still, the images that filled my mind were Clara, Rick, Marie, and Joey being interrogated by Bestworst.

I worried about my dad, Luis, and Richard, but it was my friends who worried me most. The memory of a gun held against the back of my head added a palpable memory that made the back of my head hurt and my left ear ring.

Finally, after mothballing the generator by the light of the camp lantern, I took four ibuprofen and lay down on a mattress.

Sleep came with bad dreams and sweat.

Saddling Impossible was an ordeal for the both of us. I'd never saddled a horse in my life, much less put a bridle on. I kept mixing up the straps, finally figuring out how the nose band buckled under the jaw. The saddle was easier since there was really only one pad and one strap, with two buckles to do, but I fussed with it since I knew the saddle would roll underneath if it wasn't tight enough.

I closed up the hangar and jammed a stick in the latch, jamming it closed. It would be easy enough to remove it, but impossible to do so by accident.

Impossible took off before I was in the saddle, dancing sideways with me draped ignominiously across the seat and trying not to drop my shotgun. I managed to pull myself upright and steered him back toward the gate. He wanted to trot, but my knee screamed every time he did. I held him, instead, to a walk, trying to sit back with a firm pressure on the reins. This mostly worked, though he seemed confused by the way I held my injured knee away from his side, trying to turn in that direction.

I twisted in the saddle as I drove away from the base and felt like crying. This was my place—my beachhead into this world, and I might never see it again.

I let Impossible drink a bit when we forded the stream, then nudged him on. He wasn't even sweating when we got to the gate.

But I was.

I unsaddled him, replaced his bridle with his nylon halter, and tethered him in the grass.

I dug a trench under the foot of the gate, a little deeper than the thickness of the frame, about two feet. Then I screwed four tether stakes into the soil, two to each side of the trench. When I stood on the end of the gate, the rear wheels of the trailer lifted and my end settled slowly to the ground. Without taking my weight off the frame, I used rope, running from stake to stake, to secure it down.

The rest was rope work, timber props, levers, and sweat. It took until late afternoon to get the gate upright, with pauses to rest, eat, drink, and scare away some red wolves who were interested in Impossible.

The gate was propped up with timbers again, and I'd filled in the trench so the inner frame was barely underground. I studied the layout carefully, running through the next steps in my mind. When no new disasters occurred to me, I went and saddled Impossible but bundled his bridle up and tied it to the back of the saddle. It was getting on toward dusk, a perfect time for predators, but also a perfect time for what I was about to do.

I put Impossible in front of the gate and led his lead rope through the gate, where I tied it to the tongue of the trailer. He started to walk through, but I grabbed his halter and stopped him. "Whoa. Just stand right there, okay?"

I stepped back, to the switch. If I stretched my arm out, I could just reach his rump while leaving my left hand on the switch.

I took a deep breath then simultaneously threw the switch, smacked Impossible's rump with the flat of my hand as hard as I could, and shouted at the top of my lungs.

The gate opened, cutting Impossible's lead rope, and he bolted forward, with a loud whinny. In his path stood a very surprised soldier, who tried to dive aside as the horse plunged at him. Impossible swerved, but his chest struck the soldier's shoulder and the man went flying. Another soldier, farther back, took a step toward the gate, his rifle rising, and I threw the switch.

Impossible's whinny cut off sharply and I was alone again, just me, my pile of equipment, and the predators.

An enormous weight came off my shoulders. As long as they didn't shoot him, Impossible was safe. I could do anything, now, and succeed or fail, I didn't have to worry about him.

I hoped they'd feed him.

I dropped the gate back to the ground.

I didn't *mean* to. Well, that is, I wanted it flat on the ground, but one of the mesquite bushes I was using to tie off a belaying rope tore completely out of the ground as I was lowering it. The gate dropped from forty-five degrees to flat with a thud that I felt from fifty feet away.

Christ, did I break it?

I walked slowly over to it. The sun was still above the horizon, but barely, throwing postcard streamers of light through clouds on the horizon. Dust still hung in the air from the fall, but there were no obvious cracks or dents. There was really only one way to know if it still worked.

I flipped the switch with a length of sapling. There was a flash in the gate and, looking down through it, it seemed to be filled with dark earth.

Perfect.

The gate was opening underground on the tame side. How far remained to be seen, but it was what I was counting on. I shut it down and began working on the gate solenoid.

It took an hour to rig. The more complicated stuff—the timer, radio receiver, charging circuit, and batteries—were still intact in one unit. All I had to do was mount the solar panel on an upright timber facing south, clamp the solenoid to the switch arm and the switch.

The tricky part was mounting the wiring to the solenoid so that it would not be in the field when the gate came on and passing buffalo wouldn't knock it down.

I set it up using the timbers from the trailer, lashing them together to form a solid pillar and burying them three feet deep in the ground. I mounted the box of batteries, receiver, and charging circuit on top, with the solar panel, eight feet above the ground.

I tried the remote control on the gate in the late dusk, standing back from the gate. It opened and shut on cue. I double-checked all the connections several times, then shook my head.

Let it go, Charlie. It'll work or it won't.

I turned on the camp lantern and began dismantling shotgun shells.

There's not that much powder in a shotgun shell. The front half of the thing is filled with lead shot or slugs and then there's a plastic wad, and finally, the charge, in a quarter to a third of the cartridge's length. It took me most of a case to get a pint of grains.

I collected them in the bottom of a coffee can, brought along for that purpose.

There was movement in the grass, something outside the light of the lantern. I sat, for a while, with the shotgun in my lap, looking out into the dark, but nothing came.

After some time, I turned the gate back on and slid things—a shovel, the plastic cans of aviation fuel, the junk parts of my fake gate—across the slippery slope of the gate field. They slid through the air, as if flying, then dropped down onto the black dirt with little thumps.

I *suspected* that the gate was about a foot and a half underground on the tame side. I hoped the vibrations weren't detectable by anybody standing above it on the tame side. I carried the gunpowder in one hand and the lamp in the other, held far apart, and slid down the invisible slope.

Then I realized my shotgun was still leaning against the column of timbers. I put the lamp and the gunpowder as far from each other as possible, and scrambled back up the slope. I had to kick off the ground and *glide* up. I took the shotgun back in with me.

The next part was digging.

I dug a circular pit, about two feet deep and five feet across, and arranged the six plastic gas cans within, like the spokes of a wheel, standing upright, touching each other at their corners and forming, at the center, an open hexagon. The cans barely stuck up above the terminus.

I used some of my displaced dirt to fill the hexagonal center hole. When it was mostly full, I set the coffee can of gunpowder on the dirt, adding a little more dirt to bring its top level with the top of the gas cans, also sticking barely above the terminus. I covered it with a piece of plastic bag and a rubber band to keep the rain and wind out.

The junk from my fake gate I dropped into the hole in the spaces between the cans. I started to throw dirt back into the hole, then stopped myself. It would probably work better with the empty space around it.

The dire wolves showed up, then, but I didn't notice at first. Not until I heard the one in the lead yelp as it bounced off the field behind my back. The one behind him swerved and glanced off the field to the side.

I grabbed the shotgun as the first one recovered and jumped again, higher, but his back legs struck the field again, and he slid back. I almost fired, then, but stopped myself, switching my grip to the pepper Mace spray.

There seemed to be only two of them and as they circled, testing the field, I saw blood on the shoulder of one of them. I realized that these must be the remnants of the pack that ran into me and Clara, and then the soldiers.

When the wind was at my back as I pivoted to watch them, I sprayed, a wide aerosol pattern that the wind carried right into their faces.

They ran, howling.

Stay away from humans, guys. They don't fight fair.

Humans.

I checked everything in the pit again, then threw the shovel out of the frame, picked up the lantern and the shotgun, and scrambled across the field, out of the gate frame.

There was more digging to do.

* * *

I kept expecting to run into the gasoline cans, which was reasonable, but of course it didn't happen.

My knee wasn't working very well and I did a lot of the digging from a seated position, pushing the dirt out as best I could. It took until midnight to get to the bottom edge of the field, then I tunneled in, toward the center of the gate, having to make longer and longer trips out to get rid of the dirt. I switched to my flashlight then and turned off the lamp.

At least I wasn't worried about the tunnel's collapsing on me. The field held the ceiling dirt encased like glass. Still, when I was digging up, once I'd cleared the field on the inside of the frame, I kept expecting to run into the bottom of the gas cans, but they weren't in this universe, were they? I was coming up *under* the gate, through dirt on the wildside. The cans were buried on the tame side, going down through the gate.

The dirt changed color when I hit the tame side and I turned off my flashlight and pulled down the dirt with my hands. My fingers encountered grass roots, then, and I slowed way down. My right index finger poked a hole through grass roots and dirt into empty-ness. I pulled back and heard voices.

Dammit.

I pulled enough grass and dirt down to poke my survival signal-ing mirror partway out of the hole. There were two soldiers standing four feet away and I pulled the mirror back, before it caught the light from the convenience store parking lot and caused somebody to look at my hole.

I eased back into the tunnel and thought about this.

I had to get them out of there before I came through. It didn't have to be for long, but it had to be done. I crawled back through the tunnel and out to my pile of supplies, hoping desperately that one of the soldiers wouldn't step on my hole and fall in. That would cap a perfect week.

I had everything I needed, though to get the plastic bag I had to dump a bundle of freeze-dried meals. Groaning, I took my shotgun, the plastic bag, and a completely full can of pepper Mace back into the tunnel.

I stilled my groans and breathing as I got back into position under the hole. I took the remote control for the gate out of my pocket and held it in my left hand. The can of pepper Mace I pushed up into the hole, wedging it there, half out of the ground. I was hoping that the black plastic cap would be invisible in the dark. Then I took several breaths of air and pulled the plastic bag over my head, tucking it into the neck of my shirt.

I put the shotgun barrel against the bottom of the twelve ounce can of pepper Mace, pointed straight up, and pulled the trigger.

In that enclosed space the sound was deafening. I dropped the shotgun, double-checked my grip on the remote control, and started pulling down dirt and grass, widening the hole. When I wormed my way up out of the hole, there was a cloud of white vapor all around me. I could dimly see figures running away while they rubbed at their faces, but, near at hand, a figure was collapsed on the ground, clawing at his face and choking.

Shit.

I scrambled to my feet and grabbed his collar, then dragged him upwind, as fast as I could limp. I was still holding my breath and the plastic bag over my head was fogging up. A gust of wind carried the mist away, but I didn't think it was safe yet. I staggered on a few more yards, then dropped the soldier's collar and ripped the plastic bag off my face. Soldiers were running toward us, their footsteps crunching through the mesquite leaves, but they were giving the cloud of vapor a wide berth.

I pushed the remote control button.

The gate shut.

At the terminus, the tops of six half-filled of cans of aviation gas were sheared open. Perhaps that would've been enough, the heat generated by the plastic being cut might've set off the fumes, but the spark created when the top half of the coffee can was cut in two certainly set off the pint of gunpowder. Between the two, the underground chamber filled with gas fumes and air became a pressurized combustion chamber.

The ground bulged like a blister and then ruptured. A jet of flame and light shot a hundred feet into the sky, lighting the ground and throwing stark shadows. Most of the blast went straight up, but there was enough lateral force to knock the running soldiers sideways and to slam me back on my side, twisting my bad knee, yet again.

I just lay there.

There was no longer any need to hurry.

Twenty

"Try and Stop Them."

They frisked me, taking the gate control, then hustled me into the helicopter and flew me back to the ranch, getting me out of the way before the county fire and rescue people showed up. I wondered how they were going to explain it?

I made them carry me; I wasn't walking another foot on that leg and especially not for Bestworst. I asked them what they'd done with the horse, but they wouldn't talk to me.

Bestworst took his time coming to see me.

They put me in the barn, my arms handcuffed behind my back, seated on a bale of straw in one of the stalls. I was watched by six soldiers who were supervised by Bestworst's redheaded assistant— the jack-in-the-box man who'd nearly shot me in the back of the head.

"How are your eyes?" I asked him.

He just looked at me for a moment, then exhaled. "Better. How is your ear?" His expression was empty.

"Ringing. Some hearing loss. Don't know if it's permanent."

"We can hope." He didn't look like he cared one way or another.

Bestworst arrived, by car, I guess, and entered the barn with Captain Moreno. His eyes were red and he kept blowing his nose.

For a second I thought he had a bad cold, but then I realized. "Downwind, were you?"

He gave me a baleful look and sneezed. His voice, when he spoke, was hoarse.

"Was the gas really necessary?"

"What happened to the horse?"

He dismissed my question with the wave of a hand.

I persisted. "You want any answers to *your* questions, tell me what happened to the horse."

He looked angry. "The damn horse was turned loose inside the fence on your property. Now why the gas?"

"Did anybody unsaddle him?"

He pointed across the barn. Impossible's saddle and bridle were sitting on the tarp-covered table saw.

I exhaled. If they'd just shot him, I didn't think they'd bother carrying the saddle back here.

"Okay. I used the pepper Mace because I had to be sure," I said.

"Sure of—" He broke into a paroxysm of coughing. He waved his hand at Moreno, unable to stop coughing.

Moreno said, "Sure of what?"

"I had to be sure nobody was on the site when I blew the gate." I waited until until Bestworst's fit of coughing ceased. "You were right. I'm not prepared to kill anybody."

Bestworst went into another fit of coughing. There was a wheezing sound as he inhaled.

"Get him on oxygen," I said. "His bronchi are closing up."

Moreno eyed Bestworst, then turned to one of the soldiers, "Get Livingston. Have him bring the oxygen set from Blackhawk 1."

The soldier came to attention. "Uh, sir? Livingston's under arrest."

Moreno frowned. "Right. All right. Just bring the oxygen set." The soldier left at a run and Moreno turned back to me. "What do you mean—you 'blew the gate'?"

"I used a combination of gunpowder and aviation gasoline and blew it up. Bang. Finito." They looked at me in disbelief. Slowly, with heavy emphasis on each word, I said, "I destroyed it."

I think Bestworst would've laid hands upon me if he'd been able to breathe.

"Ever have asthma?" I asked.

The soldier showed up with the oxygen set and Bestworst took several deep breaths. After a minute, his color came back, and he took the mask away from his face to croak, "Why?"

I thought about the condor, floating high in the sky. And the mastadons, the wild horses, the camels—even the dire wolves. "You wouldn't understand."

He took another hit of oxygen, then leaned forward. "So you'll just have to build another one. Too bad. If you'd given us the other one, you might be free now. Now you're stuck."

I closed my eyes and shook my head. "You don't get it. I blew it up to keep it *away* from you." I opened my eyes. "Why do you think I'll make you another one?"

His eyes narrowed. "What makes you think you have any choice?"

"I was considering the thirteenth amendment of the Constitution. That's the one that deals with involuntary servitude." I gestured at the soldiers standing behind him. "The United States Constitution— the one these guys took an oath to defend."

He glared at me. Out of the corner of my eye I saw one of the soldiers shift his weight, but don't know if he was disturbed by what I said or just changing his posture.

"But besides that, what makes *you* think I *even know how to build another gate?*" I was weary beyond any previous experience and the aches of my body were a loud, dull chorus in the background. This man in front of me, with his single-minded, compulsive, com-passionless drive to control, faded into the background noise.

I knew he was dangerous—I just didn't care anymore.

I closed my eyes and leaned back against the wall. I could hear him breathing, the hiss of the regulator on the oxygen tank, but he didn't say anything. My shoulders, cranked behind me by the hand-cuffs, ached, and I concentrated on relaxing.

After a moment Bestworst said, "Put him with the others."

Fortunately for my knee, we didn't have to go far. They'd put them in the tunnel, figuring, I guess, that it was the last place I'd reopen the gate.

There were eight soldiers on guard at the barn end of the tunnel. My guys were all beyond the terminus. All the remnants of my fake gate and the wooden barrier were gone. I hoped they were wasting lots of time at some lab, somewhere, trying to figure out how the machinery worked.

Dad and Clara said, "Charlie!" at the same time, and started moving toward me. Four guards stepped in front of them, rifles pointed slightly above the prisoners' heads. Dad and Clara stepped back. Dad's fists were clenched and I wondered who he was angrier with—the guards or me?

I saw that they'd been given sleeping bags and bales of hay. The hay was being used intact as chairs, or spread to pad the sleeping bags.

Bestworst's video cameras were still in place and the "Record" lights were on.

Just before I reached the guards, my escort unlocked my handcuffs. I stepped across, past the guards, leaving the escort behind.

Before she could ask, I said, "Impossible's wandering around the ranch—on the tame side. They unsaddled him, but I don't think they fed him."

She nodded, exhaling suddenly. Her eyes ran over my face and clothes. "Are you all right—under all that dirt?"

I smiled. "I've been better. I could sit down."

Dad let me settle on a bale of hay with my back against the wall before he said, "What happened?"

"I destroyed the gate."

He nodded slowly. "The explosion? We felt it. How'd you do it?"

I moved my eyes sideways, at the cameras. "Aviation gas and a case of shotgun shells."

"So the gate is shut," Rick said.

I nodded. "For good." I looked at Luis. "Have any of your phone calls borne fruit?"

He shrugged. "Not so you could tell. They brought us straight here and, except for some individual interrogations out in the barn, we've been right here the whole time."

"Interrogations? What did they ask? What did you guys tell them?"

Luis smiled. "Richard and me, we talked about the criminal penalties they could expect for violating our civil rights. Your father talked about the oath he took when he became an air force officer."

Clara shook her head. "I wouldn't talk to them—period."

Marie nodded. "They tried to threaten me with deportation back to Vietnam, even though I'm a US citizen. I said, fine, let's go."

Rick shrugged. "I didn't have anything to say, so I didn't. They got tired before I did."

Joey hung his head. "They offered me alcohol. I almost got to Bestworst before his assistant pulled me back down. I did get to spit on him, though." He covered his eyes then drew his hands down his face, pulling his cheeks down. "I wanted that drink. I wanted it bad."

Marie put her arm around him. "You didn't take it, though. That's what matters."

Joey shook his head.

"You did good, Joey," I said. "Give yourself a break."

He shrugged, but brightened a bit.

While they told me this, Dad had been staring at the side of the tunnel, his brow furrowed. Now he looked at me and narrowed his eyes. "So you *destroyed* it?"

I blinked. "Right. That's what I said."

He pursed his lips. "Was that really the best thing to do?"

I stared at him, tired, but I could feel all my doubts surfacing, those nagging voices that always sounded like *him*. "What would you have me do?" I asked quietly. Then, almost against my will, my voice rose. *"Give it to them?"*

He blinked. "Maybe. Negotiated, perhaps."

"We *tried* that! They shot at us, they chased us, they threatened us. They *didn't* negotiate." Clara flinched and I realized my voice had risen still more.

Dad frowned. "Well maybe you shouldn't have come back. Just held the gate until cooler heads prevailed."

"And left you guys to rot?"

He looked around at the dirt walls and then at the guards. "Looks like we're still rotting."

"But now they don't have any reason to hold us. Whatever they do to us, they can't get the gate. Dad, it didn't matter if it's these guys with guns, or the attorney general with a check. If the gate still existed, they'd take it, by legal means or other."

"Is that so bad? As long as they let us go and they paid for the property?"

"And then what? Strip mine? Start shoving nuclear waste through the door? What would happen when word of the gate gets out? When other nations find out that there's an entire world over there where there's land without overcrowding, without drought, without polluted soil and water. Are *these* guys going to give them access? I don't think so.

"You ready for that war?"

He looked thoughtful. "Maybe they can keep it classified."

I didn't bother responding to that one.

He just didn't get it. Just like he couldn't see how hard I'd worked, how much I'd accomplished? How much I'd sacrificed? I closed my eyes.

Give it up, Charlie.

It was over. Dad always second-guessed my actions—I doubted he would ever change. It would never matter what or how much I did, it would never be the right thing or enough. I opened my eyes to see him staring at me, half-angry, half-surprised.

My voice was quiet, calm. "It's done, Dad. You want to complain about it, do it someplace else. I'm too tired to listen."

He looked shocked as did Clara, Marie, and Joey. Behind them,

Rick held up his hand in a thumbs-up. Luis gave me a simple nod of approval.

"Where can I lie down?"

Dad started to say something, then stood abruptly and held out his hand. "Here, use my bag." When I looked at his face it was blank, closed, but he helped me over to his sleeping bag and steadied me as I lowered myself down.

"Thanks, Dad."

"You're welcome," he said.

It wasn't an apology, or an acknowledgement, but it wasn't criticism, either, so I took it inside me, and slept.

"Charlie, wake up." It was Clara's voice. I was deep in REM sleep and it took me a moment to surface. Someone was arguing but it wasn't one of us. *The guards?*

I sat up and blinked. The arguing was coming from the barn door. One of the guards—it was Sergeant Costner—was talking through the doorway to someone unseen. "I don't care if you're God himself. You're not coming in here without Captain Moreno's authorization."

A voice from the other side said, "Sergeant, look at my face, then get the hell out of my way."

Costner dropped back suddenly, raising his rifle to present arms and snapping to attention. "General! Sir, I didn't recognize you in mufti!"

A gray-haired man stepped through the door. He was dressed in a business suit, but he walked as if he were marching. The other guards snapped to attention. He glanced at them, then looked at us, at the end of the tunnel.

"Jesus Christ!" He turned and looked back into the barn. "I presume these are your clients."

A woman, wearing a pinstripe suit and carrying a briefcase walked through the door. She was short, below most of the soldiers' chins. She blinked in the fluorescent light.

Luis straightened and exhaled a deep sigh of relief. "That's Marta Rigby from Snodgrass, Messenger & Sons."

The general said, "I'd hoped it wasn't true." He turned back to the guards. "The rest of your unit is assembled outside. Fall in with them."

Sergeant Costner protested. "Sir! What about the prisoners?"

The man in the suit stepped up to Costner and said genially, "Sergeant, do you know what an *order* is?"

Costner turned white. "Sir! Yes, sir!"

"Then carry on, before you make me cranky."

Costner led the other guards out.

I stood and exchanged looks with Clara. She had straw in her hair and she looked wonderful. I took a whiff of myself and wrinkled up my nose.

The woman, Marta Rigby, walked down the tunnel until she stood in front of us. "Luis," she said, nodding. She gestured at the general, still standing by the door. "This is General Alderman. He's the battalion commander in Panama from which these soldiers were 'detatched.' " She paused, then asked, "Which one of you is Captain Newell?"

Dad stepped forward.

"Your wife is outside." She looked around and wrinkled up her nose. "Come on, let's get out of this place."

Dad said, "All of us?"

For a moment, a look of anger came across her face, and she said, "You bet your ass, all of you."

It was midmorning and my eyes took a moment to adjust when we emerged from the barn. I was last, limping, letting Clara help me more for contact than aid.

All the soldiers were standing in formation by the hangar, though Captain Moreno was nowhere to be seen. There were more cars in the yard, so many of them that they lined the dirt road from the gate. Most of them were plain, but two of them said Department of the Army and two others were Brazos County sheriff's.

Standing on the porch was a white-haired man who looked

vaguely familiar and my mother. Mom's posture was stiff until she saw us, but then her shoulders dropped and she exhaled through pursed lips.

General Alderman said, "Here they are, Senator, Mrs. Newell."

Mom came down the steps and touched Dad on the shoulder. "Are you all right?"

He smiled. "I'm all right. Charlie's had a rough time of it."

She turned to me and her face dropped. "What did they *do* to you!"

"It's okay, Mom. Most of it's just dirt."

I heard Clara mutter, "*Most* of it."

The senator on the porch said, "I cannot tell you, ma'am, the extent of my outrage. You can be sure that these violations will be looked into at the highest level."

Mom took her eyes off of me long enough to look at him, then back at us. "This is Senator Loughery of the Senate Intelligence Oversight Committee." She introduced us in turn, though we had to supply Luis's and Richard's names since she hadn't met them.

The door to the house opened and a military policeman came through the door. Behind him came Captain Moreno, another military policeman, and Lieutenant Thayer. Moreno's hands were handcuffed in front of him. Lieutenant Thayer's hands were not secured.

General Alderman addressed the first military policeman. "Put him in your car, Sergeant. I'll be along in a minute."

Moreno gave us one last look, his lips a straight line, then he marched off between the two MPs, his head high and his back straight.

One down, I thought.

General Alderman turned to Lieutenant Thayer and said, "Transport the men and equipment to Fort Hood. I'll meet you there this evening and we'll start the official inquiry." He turned back to Senator Loughery. "I expect your people will have unraveled the CIA end, by then?"

Senator Loughery looked pained. "Frankly, General, I don't know. We'll do our damnedest, though. Keep in touch."

"Yes, sir. Lieutenant, carry on."

Lieutenant Thayer snapped to attention. "Yes, sir." He left the porch, briskly. He winked at me as he went by.

Marta Rigby spoke up. "Senator, I want the names of all those soldiers. They're involved in criminal violation of my clients' civil rights and I intend to prosecute. In addition, they're clearly responsible for extensive damages, both property, physical, and, I don't doubt, mental anguish, which we will bring suit about in civil actions."

General Alderman said, "Councillor, these men currently face military inquiries and possible courts-martial. When the army is done with them, you're welcome to prosecute and sue all you want—but we get 'em first. Believe me, your clients will probably be called as witnesses, though, as I understand it, your main beef is likely to be with the CIA renegade."

Marta arched her eyebrows. "Renegade? They're not wasting any time going for plausible deniability, are they?"

The senator sighed. "Believe me, madam, we'll do our best to find out how high the decision went. *We* don't want illegal covert operations against American citizens any more than you do. Er, make that *any* covert operations against American citizens."

Marta looked at him. "Uh-huh."

The men who brought Bestworst and his assistant out wore mirrored sunglasses and suits. They were respectful to the senator. Bestworst and his assistant were handcuffed behind their backs.

"Senator," said Bestworst, earnestly, "this is a terrible mistake. You've got to get this technology under control. The future of this nation is at stake!"

Senator Loughery looked at him. "Not your way, Madison. In fact, it looks as if *your* way has removed any chance of controlling this . . . thing."

Luis spoke up. "Who are these men, Senator?" He pointed at the men in sunglasses.

Loughery wrinkled his forehead. "Why?"

Luis said, "I want to know what agency they're from. I don't want this man—Madison?—to have disappeared when this case comes to trial."

The senator nodded slowly, then pointed at the first man. "This is Federal Agent Nagle, from the Houston FBI office. I'm afraid I don't know these others, but they're FBI agents under Nagle's supervision. Is that good enough?"

"It depends," said Luis. "Are these two under arrest? Will they be detained?"

Agent Nagle said, "They are under arrest for violations of the National Security Act and Executive Order 12333. Further charges will be considered as this investigation proceeds. That is all I can say right now."

Luis nodded. "Thank you."

Senator Loughery said, "Have you got all of the videotapes?"

Agent Nagle said, "Yes, sir."

For a moment I thought they were talking about *our* videotapes, then I realized they were talking about Bestworst's, that is, Madison's tapes.

Tapes that showed the actual operation of the gate.

I wondered who would see them and if they'd believe them.

"Take them away, then," said the senator.

"You're making a mistake, Senator," Madison/Bestworst said, as they walked him off the porch.

"Perhaps," said Loughery. "But *my* actions, mistaken or not, are within the law."

Under his breath, Luis said, "Save it for the next campaign speech."

Richard muttered, "Cynic."

"Realist," replied Luis.

I turned to watch Madison/Bestworst being taken off to an unmarked car and as I twisted around, my knee gave way. I collapsed against Clara, who barely caught me, slowing, but not preventing my fall.

They took me to the hospital, not, as the senator suggested, in a county sheriff's car, but in my parents' Lincoln, the same car I took the guys to the prom in when this whole mess began. I'd said, "I'd just as soon avoid any more 'official' help." Clara caught Impossible and put him in the barn, and came along. I stretched out in the back, my head in her lap.

Rick followed, with Joey and Marie, in his car.

I let Dad deal with the paperwork, but gave him my Wildside Investments insurance card.

"Is this any good?" he said. "Maybe I should use our insurance."

I nearly blew up at him, but settled for, "Use mine, please. With any luck, we'll make the CIA pay for it, anyway." To my surprise, he did it my way.

The diagnosis was complicated by all the dirt, but came down to a burned shoulder (healing on its own), a torn ligament in my knee (which would require surgery eventually), multiple contusions and bruises, slight hearing loss in my right ear, and exhaustion.

"Can I have a bath?"

Straight-faced, the doctor said, "Please. Really. We would consider it a favor."

They gave me pain meds, a knee brace of nylon, steel, and Velcro, a wooden cane, and then sent me away. "If you haven't gone into shock before this, you aren't going into shock now."

Mom offered me my old bed at home, but I said I wanted to go back to the ranch.

"There are no mattresses!" Dad said.

I shrugged. "There's the couch. I'll make do."

Mom said, "You can hardly walk."

"If there's no one there, who knows what those guys will do? It's my place, and I want to keep an eye on it."

They gave in.

Rick, Marie, and Joey left us there. Rick was going to drop them at Marie and Clara's apartment, then go on to Chris. Clara came with us.

I sat up this time, my leg stretched across the backseat. "Was that car following us on the way *to* the hospital?"

Dad said, "What car?"

Mom said, "Yes, it was."

Clara craned her neck around. "They aren't being very subtle about it."

"They're FBI," Mom said.

Dad's voice raised. "How do you know that?"

"While you were checking Charlie into the emergency room, I went out and asked them. They showed me their ID. They *say* they're doing this for our protection."

I turned back around. "Well, it's hardly covert, is it?"

Clara whispered something in my ear.

"Oh, yeah. Mom? I've got a note for you." It was in my shirt pocket—they'd gone after my weapons and tools when they'd frisked me and missed the thin envelope. I handed it over the front seat and sat back without relaxing.

She stared at it long past the time needed to read it.

Finally she turned her head. Her eyes were wet, but her face was calm. "So that's what happened to him." She stared past Dad's head for a moment, blankly, not focusing on anything, then said forcefully, "The idiot!"

"So you knew about the gate?" I blurted out.

Dad turned to stare at Mom, nearly hitting a car. He swerved back into his lane, swearing.

She looked at me briefly without saying anything, then took a tissue from her purse and blew her nose. "Let's go by the house," she said to Dad.

"I want to go to the ranch," I said.

"It's on the way and it will just take a minute," Mom said. She faced forward, and it was hard to argue with the back of her head.

"Okay, then," I said, and held Clara's hand. I tried to lean back and relax, but it didn't work.

Dad opened the garage with the remote while we were still up the street and drove right in. Mom, Dad, and Clara climbed out quickly but it took me a moment to squirm through the car door in my leg brace.

We ended up in an odd grouping, Clara, Dad, and me by the car and Mom standing facing us, beyond the hood of the Lincoln.

I found myself watching Dad, who was frowning and looking at Mom as if he didn't know her. "You *knew* about the gate?" he said.

Mom nodded, "Of course I knew about the gate. I've always known about the gate." She turned to the storage shelves at the back of garage, bent over, and pushed a dusty ice chest out of the way. Behind it, on the bottom shelf, was an old suitcase, hard-sided, and old-fashioned.

It had been around forever, as long as I had. Every time we moved to a new base, Mom and Dad would have the argument, so alike that by the time we moved here, it had become a ritual.

"When you going to throw this old thing out, honey? Do we have to move it again?"

"It's all I have of my childhood. You wouldn't have me leave my childhood behind?"

We'd always moved it, and I'd never seen it open, though there was a scratch on the top where I'd tried to force it once when I was nine.

Mom dragged the suitcase out onto the cement floor and tipped it over, then reached down and did something to the lock. It went "click" and she opened it flat on the floor. We stepped forward, drawn despite ourselves, and grouped around her.

She pushed aside a camera—an old bellows type, though I've never seen one with three lenses—then set aside a framed diploma and a graduation cap. I *think* it was a graduation cap, but it had five sides and two tassels. The diploma said ΔΙΠΛΟΜΑ across the top in ornate letters and it seemed to be a ΔΟΚΤΟΡ ΟΦΦΙΛΟΣΟΦΙ in ΕΚΟΛΟΓΙ

Below these things was an aluminum case with an ornate combination lock. Mom twisted and turned the dial until it, too, opened. Inside, padded in deteriorating foam rubber, was a block with buttons on it, metallic, like cast silver or tin.

Like the gate.

She pushed a button in the lower right quadrant and a blank area at the top lit up with green letters—Greek again.

"What is it?" I asked.

She turned it off. "A piece of useless junk—now. It's the gate programmer. The thing that reconfigures the destination—the world version that the gate opens to."

"Version? Like which alternate earth?" asked Clara.

Mom nodded.

"Where did you get that?" Dad asked. His voice was hoarse and he was trembling.

"We brought it with us," she said. "Max and I. He kept track of the gate and I kept track of this."

"Brought it?" said Dad. "From *where?*"

Mom looked at him, her head tilted to one side, and sighed. "From our home."

"Ohio?" I said. *I don't think so.*

"Well," Mom said, "one version of Ohio, anyway."

Clara took a step back. "Uh, you're not from this earth."

Mother smiled at her. "No. But I've lived here for over thirty years. This is my home."

"I've gotta sit down," I said.

Dad exhaled sharply. "You and me both." He shook his head. "You tried to tell me, didn't you, that night in New York."

Mom nodded. "You didn't take it very well."

"I asked you to see a psychiatrist." He hung his head for a moment. "Why didn't you just *show* me?"

Mom shrugged. "You were in the military by then. What would you have done? I would've had to reprogram the gate and leave. I was pregnant." She looked down at the control and her next sentence was almost inaudible.

"And I didn't want to lose you."

I winced.

Dad walked over to Mom and hugged her.

I felt uncomfortable, like a voyeur, a witness to something fundamentally private. It was embarrassing. One didn't expect such behavior from one's parents. I looked at Clara, to see if she was as shocked as I, but she was smiling and her eyes were wet.

Better, I guess, than thinking they didn't love each other.

Mom shut the suitcase and sat back on her heels.

"I didn't know about the passageway in the barn," Mom said. "Max must have put the gate there after I moved away with your father. He was angry with me. Aunt Jo was local, like your father, so I was the only one from home, the only one Max could talk to freely about home, about the mission. I was sad, but I thought he'd understand eventually."

"Not that he didn't love Aunt Jo—he even let her take him to that church of hers when she contracted cancer and went strange— but he couldn't talk about our childhood in the preserves, or the vacations at sea, following the whale migrations, or Biome Census Month, or the terraforming of Britannia."

My face felt stiff and the rest of me was numb. "Britannia?" I managed. "Like England?"

"Britannia in our path. It was rendered uninhabitable in the late eighteenth century. Our industrial revolution included crude and very unsafe nuclear reactors. There were thousands of extinctions. It was terrible. Oh, over a hundred thousand humans died, eventually. Serfs, mostly, unable to leave when things got bad."

"Path," said Clara. Her posture was tense, as if she wanted to run, and her eyes were narrowed as she looked at Mom like, well, like she was from another planet.

"Yes. Path. Universe. World. Our version of earth. It got worse, too. The evacuation of Britannia put a huge strain on Europe and the New World. Whole forests were leveled to make the ships that brought them away. The American Natives didn't stand a chance. The railroads crossed North America by 1835. The coal fields were in full production ten years after that. The buffalo lasted another decade after that. The passenger pigeon followed in another three years."

She'd been staring at something we couldn't see as she talked, but at her last sentence she looked back at us. "The passenger pigeons. I should've known this was a cross-path anomaly when I read about them, but the discovery of isolated pockets of a species has happened before. For a moment, I hoped it was some scheme of Max's, that he'd come back, but he took the mission far too seriously to risk the cross contamination. For Max, the mission was everything."

"Contamination?" I said.

"Contamination. The pigeons. What sort of disease might they carry with them? Something they were proof against but could attack avian populations on this side? It's a large enough problem just going from continent to continent. Did you know that over seventy billion dollars of economic damage is done annually by exotic plant and animal life mistakenly or accidentally imported into the United States?"

"But the passenger pigeon is native to the US," I said. My stomach was sinking. I felt angry and scared at the same time.

"It *was*. Not anymore. What bacteria and parasites and viruses came with it?" She sighed. "It's not your fault, Charlie. I would've told you about this long ago if I thought that the gate was still accessible. But when Uncle Max disappeared, and I couldn't find the gate, I thought it was over. No gate, no mission. There wasn't any point."

"So what *was* the mission," asked Dad.

Mom looked at him and took a large breath of air.

"The mission was a simple one. We watched, we waited, and we kept the gate safe."

"Waited for what?" Dad asked.

Mom looked from Dad to me and back again. "There are two different circumstances that would have resulted in making this path, this 'wildside,' accessible to the 'tame side.'

"The favorable one required a massive shift in politics, economics, and attitude. It required an end to nonsustainable development, an end to extinctions, an end to the poisons being dumped into the biosphere. Essentially, it required that this path show it is ready to care for biomes, to use them in ways that don't destroy them. I'm talking about stewardship, and not just by the few, but by the many.

"Then, the diversity of this planet would've been carefully restored. The wild path could've been used as a source for extinct species, as a classroom, as a laboratory. It would have even supported some careful sustainable development."

She looked at Dad. "I'm afraid I didn't see this happening. Extinctions are up. Economic conditions do not favor the careful use of resources. A hungry man thinks only about how he can feed his family today. He doesn't care that how he feeds them today destroys his children's tomorrow."

I shifted my feet, disturbed by the bleak look on Mom's face.

"What were the other circumstances?" asked Clara. "The other set of conditions under which you would have made the wildside accessible."

Mom's face got even bleaker.

"That criterion was very simple. If the human population of your path dropped below twenty million due to environmental degradation, we would have opened the wildside as a lifeboat, a second chance.

"A last chance."

I saw Clara shudder and put my arm around her.

Clara hunched forward and leaned into me. "How many empty earths are there? The ones where humans didn't evolve?"

"An almost-endless number," Mom said.

Clara's voice rose, pitched higher, "Then why is it a 'last' chance?"

Mom shook her head. "How many biospheres should one species be allowed to destroy? There are also an almost-endless number of worlds where humans did evolve. Do you take their second chance as well?"

Clara shook her head slowly. "No. Why twenty million?"

Mom closed her eyes and took a deep breath. For a moment I thought that she was angry, but when she opened her eyes she said, "Because that's all the humans that were left on our path, when the discovery of cross-path gates saved *us*."

I juggled figures in my head. That was less than half of one percent of the current population. Mexico City had a bigger population. Mom would've opened the gate after five billion had died?

I asked a question, "How many worlds have the gate technology?"

"Only one. And fortunately, that's all that ever will."

"Why?"

Mom tilted her head. "It's the nature of the phenomenon. The simple answer is that as long as we're operating cross-path gates, nobody else will be able to. They could discover the technology but it just won't work—they'd think it's a dead end. Not unless we shut down every gate we've ever opened. And we keep several open, just as backups, to prevent this from ever happening. We were lucky to be first."

"If you gave people access to the wildside, what's to keep them from using this gate to go to other paths? I, mean, if they study it long enough, won't they be able to figure it out?"

"Not without the controller, and we wouldn't turn the gate over without first destroying it."

"Couldn't they figure out how to switch it? I mean the principles?" I felt guilty for asking questions with her face still wet with tears, but I couldn't stop myself.

"No, Charlie. Because it's not all *here*. The rest of this gate— the fusion reactor which powers it, and its alignment matrix—are floating in a cloud of interstellar hydrogen in a path where this entire solar system never formed. They can't get at that, no matter what happens. And without that, they'll never figure out the gate.

"Besides, if it becomes necessary to turn the gate over, I'm able to shift the whole mechanism into the reactor path—leaving only the opening which won't close until the reactor fails in a thousand years or so."

"What if they *need* to shut it?" Clara asked.

"They can build a door. They can bury it. They can cork it. They can put an airlock on it. Whatever it takes." She sighed. "If it comes to that, I don't really care." Her shoulders slumped.

"Mom, why not give them the gate now? Before there are any more extinctions? Before billions die?" I knew the answers. I'd given them to Dad when he'd asked the same question back on the wildside.

Mom spread her hands apart. "Think about it. What incentive is there to protect biomes if somebody knows there's a pristine backup available. Whooping cranes? There are millions on the other side—we'll just turn this refuge into condos. Rain forest? Plenty over there—bring in those cement trucks. Waterways? Dump those toxins in—we can always get more fish from the other side.

"Pristine farmland, untouched. Your starving refugees in Africa, Asia, Europe, Mexico—let them homestead. Let them hunt, let them tear up the topsoil, let them mine, let them cut down forests. How long before both sides are ruined?

"You don't use a lifeboat as living quarters, or to store trash, or as a source of building materials. The time will come when you really need it—and it won't be there."

"I knew that, really," I said. "But twenty million people, moving through that little gate?"

Mom said listlessly, "Oh, the gate could be larger. It can stretch to about thirty meters on a side, but you get severe local weather problems if the barometric pressures are too different."

I muttered, "All that effort to fit pieces of an airplane through." Clara and I exchanged glances. She looked as numb as I felt.

Mom exhaled sharply and pulled herself up, metamorphosing into the woman I knew. "I got discouraged, sometimes. I thought that my active role was gone with the gate, but I still watched—habit, I guess. Frankly, it's a relief. With the gate gone, I don't have that burden."

I must've gotten an odd look on my face, because she suddenly frowned. "Give me a hand with this suitcase, will you, Charlie?"

I shuffled forward and helped her put it on the shelf. As we pushed it in she leaned toward me and whispered. "*Is* the gate shut for good?"

I licked my lips. "Well, let's just say you shouldn't get rid of your controller."

She stared at me for a moment, opened her mouth to say something, then shut it again. Finally, she put her hand on my shoulder and said, "We'll talk."

"I'm sure."

Dad and Mom drove me out to the ranch, dropping Clara at the stables.

"You sure you wouldn't like us to take you to your parents' or your apartment?"

"Need to pick up my motorcycle, which is here. Also have to take some feed out to my horse, so I'll be out there pretty quick, Charlie."

My parents didn't talk much the rest of the way out to the ranch, but Mom sat in the center, right next to Dad.

There was a deputy sheriff at the gate and two news vans. The deputy got out of his car when we slowed to turn. Dad rolled down the window and stopped the car.

"Afternoon, Officer."

"Good afternoon. Do y'all have business out here?"

I leaned forward. "I own this property. My parents are driving me home."

"Ah, could I see some ID? I've been told to keep the press off this property."

I dug out my wallet and gave him my driver's license. "Who gave the orders?"

He handed the license back and said, "I believe Senator Loughery talked to the sheriff."

"Ah." I didn't know whether to be pissed or relieved. The last thing I wanted just now was to talk to a bunch of reporters, but did I really want my government keeping the press away from me? "There'll be a young woman on a motorcycle coming out soon. She has a horse on this property that she's coming out to care for."

"I'll pass her right through. May I have her name?"

"Clara Prentice."

He nodded, and we drove on.

There were tire tracks everywhere. I saw cigarette butts in the grass where sentries had paced. The side of the house, where the gate had opened before my truck, was scorched, the outer layer chopped away, but the fire must've been put out quickly, 'cause the plaster within was intact.

When I limped in the front door I saw that an attempt had been made to straighten the place. Though the mattress was missing from my room, the sheets, blankets, and pillows had been stacked neatly on the springs. I thought about checking the rooms upstairs but the thought of limping up the stairs was too much.

"Are you sure you'll be okay?"

I nodded and hugged Mom. There were a million questions to ask, but the possibility existed that they'd bugged the house. The questions would have to wait.

She kissed me on the forehead and held me out at arm's length. "You did right, Charlie, to keep the gate away from them."

I shrugged, embarrassed and pleased. "Time will tell," I said. "You guys go on. I bet you've got a lot to talk about."

"So we do," Dad said, and shook my hand. "See you later, son. It's been . . . educational."

I stood on the porch and watched them drive away.

Clara drove up on her dirt bike five minutes later, an enormous bag of horse feed lashed on the back behind her. She drove the bike right up to the barn and I limped across the yard to join her.

By the time I got there, she'd poured Impossible some feed and was checking his legs for scratches or bumps while he gobbled his food down.

"How is he?"

She looked up at me and smiled. "He seems fine. It can't have been easy, sending him across before you blew the gate. Thanks."

I shrugged. "How could I face you if I left him behind?"

She patted Impossible's neck and said, "You shouldn't be standing on that knee, Charlie." She walked over to me and pulled my arm across her shoulders. "Come on." She helped me across the yard and into the house.

"Wait here," she said, and helped me to sit on the couch, then she went back into the bathroom and I could hear water running in the tub. After a moment, she came back and walked me down the hall, lowered me to sit on the toilet, then turned and pushed the bathroom door closed.

"Charlie, I want to wash." They were the same words she'd used up in the mountains, at Cripple Creek.

"Uh, so I must have the watch?"

"Yes," she said, and began unbuttoning her shirt. "Watch *this* way."

We went through three changes of water before I was clean. Then we put the cushions from the couch on the living room floor and used my sheets and pillows to make a bed.

What we did next belongs to us and I won't share it.

Early the next morning I lay on the grass in front of Dad's hangar, getting dew on my clothes, as Clara played tag with Impossible, chasing him around in circles, then running from him as he chased her. Finally, out of breath, she dropped to the grass beside me. "Damn, it's hot. I'm going to miss the cooler weather on the other side."

I kept my voice down. "We'll have cooler weather here in a month or two. And for next year. . . . We'll have to be careful with our preparations. Don't want the feds to get suspicious."

She pulled back from me. "What on earth are you talking about?"

"The wildside. When we go back."

Her eyes widened. "But you blew up the gate! Or shut it down, which amounts to the same thing. You can't open it from this side."

"Don't be silly. Would I ever do a thing like that?"

"You *said* you did."

I pulled a long stem of grass and stuck it in the corner of my mouth. "Consider the circumstances. And I *did* shut down the gate. But I used Joey's timer, solar panel, and batteries. The gate will open next spring, the fourteenth day of March, five minutes before midnight."

She thumped back onto the grass, staring straight up. "I *knew* you wouldn't give it up. Why then?"

"Had to give the feds some time to give up, or at least lighten their watch. But I didn't want to leave it so long that the timer died.

"There'll be a lot of work to do on the base. We'll need a new tractor. Cutting back the grass on the runway. Getting the Maule in shape. There's a lot of stuff to find out about the wildside."

She propped herself up on one elbow and stared at me.

"You're crazy, you know that?"

I grinned. "Yeah."

"This time they'll bring a battalion."

"This time we'll have a working tractor. We'll move the gate. Hell, if I can get my mom to teach me how that control works, who *knows* what we can do."

Clara rolled completely over, both her elbows on the ground. "Why didn't you tell your parents? When she showed us the control."

"Mom knows. She asked me. As to Dad, well, he has enough adjusting to do right now—better to keep things simple."

"You know? You scare me, Charlie."

"You coming?" I held my breath.

"Why do you think I'm scared? Of course I'm coming."

I exhaled an enormous breath and grinned. "Oh, good. Very, very good." I dragged myself across the ground and kissed her deeply. I started to pull away, but she put her hand behind my head and held me there a moment longer.

When my breathing had slowed again, I said, "You think Joey and Marie will come? Rick?"

"Try and stop them," Clara said. "Try and stop them."

Epilogue

Dear Mom,

Little Masha loved the books. Max thinks his books are okay, but he'd rather be doing fieldwork. He said for his tenth birthday he'd like a tranquilizer gun and some radio collars. He says he wants to use them on the big cats, the S., but I'm afraid he'd use them on his little sister. Sound like his great-uncle?

We had a long visit from Joey, Marie, and their kids. They're still living in Bryan and getting up here to Colorado is really different for them. While they were here, Joey and I went out the Back Door and panned a little gold. Looks like it will be a hard winter over there. The elk and the M. are already moving down to the lower elevations and the coats on the M. are impressively thick.

Rick called from Washington. He says he finally got rid of all the boxes from the move. He thinks he's going to like Georgetown, but doesn't know how long a lecturer's salary will stretch. He doesn't want to touch his share of the Wildside Investments fund, to maximize his earnings.

The FBI came around again, supposedly to see if we'd been having any more problems with the DIA. But of course we haven't—not since the last federal court order. Luis says be polite and say nothing of substance. And turn the videotape on.

They really don't like video cameras.

Hope you and Dad are enjoying the Amazon. Use plenty of insect repellent.

We won't be here when you get back. As soon as winter shuts down the Back Door, we'll be back at the Ethiopian site. We're making real progress with the new arid-tolerant varieties. I think we've reclaimed another thirty square kilometers of desert. It's tiny, I know, but we're getting more people at the training center all the time and several other sub-Saharan countries are sending observers.

We're mutating the mission, I guess, but we're not willing to just watch, to just wait.

I don't want to go the lifeboat route.

Time will tell.